D0056539

WITHDRAWN

Chetco Community Public Library

Brookings, OR 97415

ALSO BY MARY DAHEIM

The Alpine Advocate
The Alpine Betrayal
The Alpine Christmas
The Alpine Decoy
The Alpine Escape
The Alpine Fury
The Alpine Gamble
The Alpine Hero
The Alpine Icon
The Alpine Journey
The Alpine Kindred
The Alpine Legacy
The Alpine Menace
The Alpine Nemesis
The Alpine Obituary
The Alpine Pursuit
The Alpine Quilt
The Alpine Recluse
The Alpine Scandal
The Alpine Traitor

The Alpine Uproar

Ballantine Books
New York

THE
ALPINE
UPROAR

AN EMMA LORD MYSTERY

MARY DAHEIM

Chetco Community Public Library
405 Alder Street
Brookings, OR 97415

The Alpine Uproar is a work of fiction. Names, characters, places, and incidents are the products of the author's imagination or are used fictitiously. Any resemblance to actual events, locales, or persons, living or dead, is entirely coincidental.

Copyright © 2009 by Mary Daheim

All rights reserved.

Published in the United States by Ballantine Books, an imprint of The Random House Publishing Group, a division of Random House, Inc., New York.

BALLANTINE and colophon are registered trademarks of Random House, Inc.

ISBN 978-0-345-50255-1
eBook ISBN 978-0-345-51530-8

Printed in the United States of America on acid-free paper

www.ballantinebooks.com

.   2 4 6 8 9 7 5 3 1

First Edition

The Alpine Uproar

ONE

O N TUESDAY, OCTOBER 5, SKYKOMISH COUNTY SHERIFF Milo Dodge arrested Clive Berentsen, forty-one, in connection with the death of Alvin De Muth, thirty-eight. Dodge and Deputy Sam Heppner took Berentsen into custody at eleven-twenty-five PM. The timing was almost perfect, allowing me to include the story for *The Alpine Advocate*'s weekly deadline.

"I know KSKY has the news," I said to my production manager, Kip MacDuff, the next morning, "but at least we got it in this week's edition."

Kip, who was pouring coffee from the urn behind my new reporter's vacant desk, grinned. "There are some wars you can't win, Emma."

"I know that, too." I paused, contemplating our coverage of the homicide down the road. "I suppose Clive Berentsen will plead self-defense. Do you know Clive or Alvin De Muth?"

Kip shook his head. "Only by sight. Clive's been a long-haul trucker for years. De Muth has done some work on our trucks, but I hardly ever talked to him. I guess he was the strong, silent type." Kip smiled at me. "I don't hang out at the Icicle Creek Tavern. Never was my style. If I want a beer, I go to Mugs Ahoy or our fridge at home. I'm a respectable married man, remember?"

I smiled back at Kip. He'd worked for the *Advocate* since his high school days, starting out as a carrier and eventually taking over the paper's production. He was now in his early thirties; I'd designated him my heir apparent if and when I ever retired.

"You deserve a raise," I said on impulse. "If we crunch some numbers . . ."

"Whoa." Kip held up a hand. "I know the numbers as well as you do. The profit margin is pretty lean. Nobody here expects to get rich."

"True enough." I glanced over at my House & Home editor's empty chair. "Where's Vida? It's ten after eight."

"She's got the bakery run," Kip replied, heading for the door to our back shop. "She traded with Mitch this morning. He had a problem at home and called to say he might not get here until eight-thirty."

Mitch Laskey was my latest hire as the *Advocate*'s sole reporter. "Nothing serious, I hope?"

"Ask Vida." He chuckled. "She's the one who knows everything," he added, then disappeared into his high-tech domain.

Kip was right. Vida Runkel was the source of all knowledge in Alpine and the rest of Skykomish County. No secret was safe, no slip of the tongue went unnoticed, no vow of secrecy was sacred to my redoubtable House & Home editor. She could be annoying, contrary, and even infuriating, but I'd be lost without her. I owned the *Advocate,* but Vida held Alpine in her heart—and the palm of her hand.

I'd retreated to my cubbyhole office when she burst into the newsroom five minutes later. "No maple bars!" she cried. "No sugar doughnuts! What's going on at the Upper Crust?"

I rose from my chair and went to my almost-always-open door. "They can't make everything every day," I pointed out.

Vida, who was wearing a toque plastered with artificial autumn leaves, tromped over to the table where the coffee urn was located. "True, but my mouth was set for a maple bar." She began arranging the pastries on a tray. "Cinnamon doughnuts are good, so are the frosted kind, but I prefer raised sugar. Oh, well." She finished her task and snatched up a blueberry Danish.

"What's going on with Mitch?" I inquired.

"His wife's loom broke," Vida replied en route to her desk. "Brenda has deadlines, too. She's weaving a rug for someone's mid-October birthday in Kalamazoo."

I perused the bakery goods. "So what do you think of Mitch?"

Vida shed her new green raincoat; the hat remained atop her unruly gray curls. "Competent. Pleasant. Good writing, fine pictures. Most of all, he's mature, which was not true of his predecessor."

"You're right," I agreed. "We're lucky to get Mitch. I was afraid we'd get stuck with another recent college grad. The scary part about hiring Curtis Mayne last spring is that he was the best applicant."

"A disaster," Vida murmured. "So irresponsible, a borderline mental case." She sat down in her chair. "I listened to KSKY this morning. Spencer Fleetwood reported that Clive Berentsen will be charged with first-degree manslaughter."

"Standard for a tavern brawl," I said, selecting a cinnamon-sugar doughnut. "How come you don't know everything there is to know about either the victim or the alleged killer?"

Vida's expression was disdainful. "As you're aware, I don't associate with the type of people who spend Saturday nights at the Icicle Creek Tavern. Lowlifes, virtually all of them. I don't understand why Milo didn't arrest Clive on the spot."

"He wanted to be sure," I said as my ad manager, Leo Walsh, came into the newsroom. "You know Milo—he always goes by the book."

Leo made a mocking bow to greet Vida. She made a noise that sounded like a growl. During all the years they'd worked together, the pair had conducted what might seem to casual observers like a simmering feud. I knew better. Beneath the gibes and jeers, they liked and respected each other. When Leo had almost died in July, Vida's concern had been genuine. Indeed, she hadn't criticized him for smoking when he returned to work two weeks later.

Leo turned to me. "You talking about Berentsen whacking Whatshisname?"

I nodded. "It sounds like the good old days—or bad old days, depending on how much you enjoy an old-fashioned tavern brawl."

"Dreadful," Vida remarked. "Yet part of Alpine's history as a logging town. You both arrived too late for the timber industry's heyday." Her glances at Leo and me seemed almost pitying. "Unfortunately, it occasionally brought out the worst in some people."

Leo, who was getting his coffee and a plain doughnut, chuckled. "Oh, yes. Harrowing tales of Saturday nights at both the Icicle Creek Tavern and Mugs Ahoy. Regular knock-down, drag-out affairs, especially at Icicle Creek. Wasn't there another murder at one of those saloons a few years back?"

Vida and I exchanged quick glances. We both remembered the victim, a young man who may or may not have deserved killing. "Yes, ten, twelve years ago," I said. "If you're really interested, you can read all about it in back copies of the *Advocate*."

Leo shook his head. "No thanks. I used to work in the LA area, remember?" He turned back to Vida. "How long did they keep the windows boarded up because they couldn't afford to replace them every month or so?"

Vida heaved a big sigh. "At least a year after one fracas. On the weekends, whichever deputy was on night duty would cower outside in the patrol car, too frightened to restore order. Then there were the bikers who'd roar into town thinking they could win a victory over the loggers. So foolish. The bikers were overmatched."

I caught a hint of pride in Vida's tone. As a native Alpiner, even the worst behavior couldn't dim her high opinion of the town's citizens.

Leo paused on his way to his desk. "I have to ask—did you ever go to the Icicle Creek Tavern on a Saturday night, Duchess?"

Vida scowled at the nickname she claimed to despise. "I most certainly did not, nor at any other time." She paused, pursing her lips. "Well, once or twice, perhaps, but only in the line of duty."

Before Leo could comment, Mitch Laskey arrived. "Sorry I'm late," he said in greeting. "Brenda's loom had a tension headache."

"Did you fix it?" Leo asked.

Mitch settled his long and lanky form behind his desk. "Only time—and the results—will tell. The rug she's making is wool. That's good. If she was using linen or silk, it might be a bigger problem." He leaned back in his chair and yawned. "Coffee. I need coffee." He swiveled around and moved closer to the table. "So what do we have from the sheriff on this tavern murder?"

I strolled over to Mitch's desk. "Nothing official since last night. Check with Dodge when you go through the log to see what crimes and misdemeanors the lesser locals have been nailed for. You should be at the courthouse when Berentsen is officially charged."

"Got it." Mitch had poured his coffee but refrained from taking any of the bakery goods. My new hire rarely seemed to eat much, which, I supposed, accounted for his slim frame.

My phone rang. I hurried into my office to answer it before the call trunked over to our office manager, Ginny Erlandson.

Milo Dodge was on the line. "You sure about this new guy handling the murder?"

"I told you already that he's very experienced," I replied, lowering my voice. "He's not a raw recruit with a brand-new college diploma. Mitch worked twenty-five years for the *Detroit Free Press*. He could probably do this story with his eyes closed. He's covered more homicides than the two of us put together," I added, irritated at the sheriff for questioning my judgment.

"If you say so." Milo didn't sound convinced. "Alpine's not Detroit. You know what happened with that last moron you put on the payroll."

"Guess what?" I snapped. "I don't need reminding. Mitch will be at your office in ten minutes. When are you going to the courthouse?"

"Nine," the sheriff replied. "Got to run. Fleetwood's here."

The click in my ear riled me even further. Of course the voice of Skykomish County, Spencer Fleetwood, had shown up. Gloating, too, and suffused with more self-confidence than ever since he'd gotten approval from the FCC to crank up KSKY's transmission signal.

I got up and went to the doorway. "Mitch, the sheriff's going to be at the courthouse in twenty minutes."

"I'm off," he responded, taking a last gulp of coffee before grabbing the gray windbreaker that matched his full head of wavy hair.

I started back into my office, but Vida, who had been on the phone, called to me. "Emma, that was Maud Dodd at the retirement home. She wanted to know if we caught the mistake in her weekly column about Milo's aunt Thelma. Did you proofread it?"

"I thought you did," I said.

"No, no," Vida replied. "It came in late yesterday just before I left to see the dentist. I put it on your desk."

I grimaced. "I don't remember seeing it. What's wrong?"

Vida was sitting back in her chair, fists on hips, frowning in concentration. "Oh, dear. Maybe I . . ." She reached for her out basket. "Drat! I mistakenly put it there for Kip. Ginny must've picked it up and given it to him." She flipped to page two of her copy of the *Advocate*. "How upsetting! Listen to this, it's about Milo's aunt and uncle—'Thelma Petersen is enjoying her new residence here. Elmer is also enjoying himself, having taken an interest in the handmade holiday crafts Thelma has sold privately for lo these many years. The Petersens' current project is fornicopias, a colorful display on any dining room table.'" Vida tossed the newspaper aside. "I never should have insisted that Maud get someone to type her columns for her!"

I didn't know whether to laugh or sympathize. "You *did* say you couldn't read her spidery handwriting."

Vida had taken off her glasses and was rubbing her eyes in a familiar and ferocious sign of distress. "Ohhh! How embarrassing! And how stupid of me to have mislaid the copy."

I winced, certain I could hear her eyeballs squeaking in protest. "It happens," I said. "You were in a hurry."

"Inexcusable." She'd finally stopped punishing her eyes. "I'll certainly hear about this from Leo," she murmured, glancing at his vacant chair. "Not to mention Milo and half the town."

"You could always use it in next week's 'Scene,' " I said referring to Vida's front-page one-by-three-inch gossip column.

"That's not funny," Vida retorted. "Maud will be humiliated. She's so upset. She's afraid she'll be evicted from the retirement home."

"Maud's overreacting," I pointed out. "Half the people who read her column at the retirement home won't get it." I stopped just short of saying that the other half of the residents were either gaga or almost dead. The callous thought made me realize that I wasn't in a very good mood. I changed the subject. "Fill me in," I said, picking up Vida's copy of the *Advocate* with its lead story under Mitch's byline and a photo he'd taken of the Icicle Creek Tavern exterior. His interior shots included one of De Muth's body lying halfway under the pool table with only his legs and lower torso showing. I'd decided that was too grim for the front page. "I made sure he didn't use any quotes from the other patrons and kept just to the facts that Milo and Sam had given him. Being an old hand at covering homicides, he didn't need reminding. But down the road we'll have to find out what the witnesses had to say about the incident."

"Of course you will," Vida said. "We'd be a poor source of information if we avoided printing what the bystanders saw and how they responded. Human interest, that's so important."

What Vida really meant was that Alpine was agog, its residents waiting impatiently for reactions from their friends and neighbors. "The gossip mill is already grinding," I said. "What have you heard so far?"

"Well now." She rested her elbows on the desk and folded her hands. "I already mentioned Fred Engelman being there. Very unusual, since he never goes to the tavern. Of course it was his ex-wife's birthday, so I suppose he felt an obligation to be with Janie instead of in jail."

"Probably," I allowed. "It's ironic that the first time he shows up in months there's a big brawl and a fatality. He would've been better off spending the weekend in his favorite cell."

"Perhaps." Vida paused. "I rather admire Fred for acknowledging his problem with alcohol, but you'd think he'd join AA rather than checking himself into jail every weekend to avoid carousing and brawling. Admittedly, he never drank during the rest of the week while working for Blackwell Timber, but I don't think Milo likes having one of his cells used on a regular basis. On the other hand, Fred's always very good about keeping the place tidy."

"A real plus," I murmured.

"It is, actually," Vida said. "I understand Fred does some chores at the sheriff's office. He's quite the handyman. I've had him do some repairs at my house and I've always been rather pleased, particularly with electrical problems. Oddly enough, he never wears gloves. He insists that the shocks he gets from live wires are invigorating."

"As fun goes, I suppose that's better than getting blotto on several schooners of beer." I sat down in her visitor's chair. "Fred and his ex, Janie, are on good terms?"

"Apparently," Vida replied. "During their courtship some thirty years ago and even after their marriage, Janie and Fred would go out for a drink or two. But after a while, Fred began losing control and drinking much more heavily. They had three children by then, so Janie stayed home. It got to the point where she couldn't take his awful mood swings and what often turned into violence. Never, of course, directed at her or the children, only at the other tavern drinkers. She finally sued for divorce and married again."

I nodded. "Husband number two being Mickey Borg, who owns the Icicle Creek gas station and minimart. He was with her Saturday."

"Yes," Vida said. "Mickey and Fred *seem* to get along, though it must be awkward. Of the men who were there that night, Fred's had dustups with most of them except the Peabody brothers—two against one, and the Peabodys are built like bulls. Oh," she added as an afterthought, "he never challenged Averill Fairbanks."

Our resident UFO aficionado probably had been spared because he rarely seemed to be attached to Planet Earth. "Averill's annoying," I remarked, "but harmless and nonthreatening. What about Spike Canby, the tavern owner?"

"Yes," Vida said, "I'm sure Fred was tempted to provoke Spike, but perhaps he had enough sense to back down. Fighting with Spike would be killing the goose that laid the golden egg."

"And yet," I said as Ginny Erlandson slogged in with the morning mail, "Fred didn't get involved in the melee that killed Alvin De Muth." I turned to Ginny. "Anything of interest in that stack?"

"No." Ginny handed me my eight-inch-high pile of mostly junk. "Honestly, does Marlowe Whipp think I care about some drunk killing another drunk? The only thing I can think of now is when this baby is going to come. It seems like I've been pregnant for years."

"So it does," Vida said, a beleaguered note in her voice. My House & Home editor, along with the rest of the staff, had suffered almost as much as Ginny had during her third pregnancy. "October 12, correct?"

"A week from yesterday," Ginny said bleakly. "Columbus Day."

"Babies come when they come," Vida said for what must have been the fiftieth time. "You got some lovely presents at your shower Friday night. Cammy Anderson's chocolate cake was delicious. I must get the recipe from her and run it on my page."

"Cammy's a good cook," Ginny said, placing Vida's mail in her in-basket. "I shouldn't have eaten it, though. I was miserable all night."

I didn't dare look at Vida, knowing that her reaction to Ginny's litany of complaints matched my own. "What," I inquired, "did Marlowe have to say about the fatal fight?"

Ginny had delivered Leo's mail and was carrying Mitch's bundle across the newsroom. "That's another thing," she groused. "I've changed the names on most of these mailings to Mitch Laskey, but they're still coming to Curtis Mayne or even Scott Chamoud. I asked Marlowe what was going on at the post office. He said it wasn't their fault, it's the senders' responsibility." She plopped my reporter's mail on his desk, dropping a couple of envelopes on the floor. "Oh, shoot! Emma, can you pick those up for me? I can't bend very well."

"Sure." I retrieved the letters. "I meant," I said, putting them in Mitch's in-basket, "what was Marlowe's reaction to a real live murder?"

Ginny looked blank. "You mean at the tavern?"

"Yes," I said, deadpan, catching Vida's expectant gaze. Even when not totally absorbed with her body and the baby it carried, Ginny had neither a sense of humor nor an imagination.

Ginny shrugged. "The past three days that's all he talks about. I tune him out. One drunk beating up on another drunk isn't that big a deal. At least it wasn't when I was a kid. Three or four guys got killed in brawls, not to mention accidents in the woods or the mills. Lots of lost arms and legs and fingers and toes, too." She shuddered. "Gruesome, but typical of what went on back then. Those things aren't what I want to dwell on when I'm having a baby. I'd rather think positive thoughts about autumn leaves and mountain meadows and big, fat pumpkins."

My eyes strayed to Ginny's bulging stomach. The pumpkin reference was apt, confirming my long-held opinion that Ginny didn't have much imagination.

Vida, however, wasn't giving in to Ginny's indifference to tavern murders. "I might be able to catch Marlowe on his route this afternoon. He comes by my house around two. Usually," she added, grimacing.

"Our mail at home gets later all the time," Ginny grumbled and lumbered out of the newsroom.

Vida sighed. "I refrain from making the all-too-obvious comments."

I agreed. "But should we talk to the people who were at the ICT?" I asked, using the tavern's nickname, which was pronounced *Icked*.

"Yes," Vida responded. "Human interest, as I mentioned."

Not to mention Vida's overwhelming curiosity, I thought. But she had a point. "I suppose," I allowed, "but if these people have to testify at a trial, I'm not sure if we should publish their reactions. It's going to be tough to pick a jury with such a small pool to draw from in this county."

"It often is," Vida pointed out. "Of course, we must be over eight thousand residents since the last census. The influx of commuters and people who can work out of their homes like Brenda Laskey has made Alpine and the rest of Skykomish County extremely desirable. I hate to bring this up, but Ed and Shirley Bronsky's sale of their home to the group that wants to turn it into a retreat center is quite a coup. Naturally, the idea wasn't Ed or Shirley's, but their CPA's."

My former ad manager and his wife's sale of the so-called villa known as Casa de Bronsky, or Bronska, or whatever the hell Ed called it, had been a relief not only to the family but also to everyone else who knew them, including me. When Ed had barged into my office and insisted on replacing Leo during my ad manager's recovery from a gunshot wound, I thought I'd go nuts. The ten working days—or, in Ed's case, nonworking days—had almost driven me to distraction.

"Let's hope the ReHaven bunch finishes at least the exterior improvements on the place before the first big snow," I said. "They'll have to if they plan to open right after the first of the year."

Vida nodded. "Three million dollars to refurbish and repair that monstrosity! It's a wonder Ed and Shirley didn't have to pay *them* to take the place off their hands. No upkeep over the years, so foolish. I'm surprised Ed got two and a half million for it. Of course he started out at what? Eight? I hope he's learned his lesson about squandering money and making his own investments."

"I doubt it," I said. "Ed's not the type who ever learns. Of course he's not likely to inherit another big chunk of cash from a dead relative."

"Reduced to living in a mobile home," Vida said, shaking her head. "And with all those children. So cramped, and no doubt so cluttered."

"It's actually nice for a double-wide," I pointed out. "But Ed's going to have to get a job."

"Not here," Vida declared.

"No, never," I assured her, using the back of my hand to take a swipe at my bangs, which needed a trim. "Shirley's renewing her teaching certificate so she can at least substitute. The older kids are able to work, too. But you're right. Ed's got to get off his fat rear end and bring in some income."

Vida pushed back in her chair. "And I must head out for my ten o'clock interview with Doc Dewey's wife, Nancy. I suppose the Rhine River and those German castles are nice, but when it comes to rivers and autumn scenery, how can you beat driving along Highway 2 through the mountain pass?"

I didn't have to answer Vida's question. Fortunately, Mitch Laskey came in the door. "How did the arraignment go?" I asked.

"What you'd expect," Mitch replied, setting his laptop on his desk. "Not guilty, self-defense, and so on. Berentsen's hired a lawyer from Everett, a woman named Esther Brant. Can he pay for that?"

"Clive's divorced," I said. "His ex lives . . ." I looked at Vida, who had put on her raincoat. "Where?"

"Bremerton," Vida responded, not missing a beat while heading for the door. "They had no children. The wife remarried. The second husband works in the naval shipyard over on the Kitsap Peninsula."

Mitch shook his head in disbelief. "Amazing woman. Is there anything she doesn't know?"

"I don't think so," I said.

Reflecting on Vida's vast stockpile of local lore, it suddenly occurred to me that not only a little, but sometimes a lot, of knowledge was a dangerous thing.

TWO

S HORTLY BEFORE NOON, I DECIDED TO PAY A VISIT TO THE
sheriff. I was still irked over his implied criticism of my hiring acumen, but having known Milo Dodge for so long as ally,
friend, and sometime lover, I could never stay mad at him for
long.

Walking along Front Street, I gazed to my left, beyond the
Bank of Alpine and the Alpine Building. The town's older resi-
dential section, including my own little log house, clung to the
side of Tonga Ridge. The vine maples, cottonwoods, and alders
at the lower elevations were turning color, their slashes of red,
yellow, and orange slowly merging into the dark green stands of
Douglas firs, western hemlocks, and cedars. Vida wasn't wrong
about the local scenery. It was spectacular this time of year with
just a few pockets of snow still tucked into the mountains' re-
cesses and an occasional waterfall trickling over moss-covered
rocks. I stopped at the corner of Front and Third, waiting for a
UPS truck to pass. A few high white clouds moved slowly across
the sky. The temperature was cool but not yet crisp. The smell of
diesel fuel didn't quite manage to spoil the scent of sawdust from

Alpine's only remaining mill. By the time I reached the sheriff's office, the air was also tinged with grease from the Burger Barn across the street. I realized I was hungry.

The sheriff was coming out just as I turned to go in.

"Is this an ambush?" he asked.

"Yes. No." I craned my neck to look up at him. Milo is over a foot taller than I am, and in his regulation Smokey Bear hat he looms like a leviathan. "I thought I should touch base with you on the murder."

"Ah." The expression on Milo's long face was wry. "So you don't trust this Laskey dude after all?"

"Of course I do," I retorted. "But I'm ultimately responsible. It's a homicide, for heaven's sake!"

Milo shrugged. "This one's pretty cut and dried." He gestured at the Burger Barn. "You want to eat or stand here and block foot traffic?"

"Eat," I said.

The sheriff loped ahead of me, jaywalking across Front Street. "No breakfast," he said over his shoulder. "We had a power outage in my neighborhood this morning."

"Did you tell Mitch?" I asked, hurrying to catch up with him.

Milo leaned into the restaurant's door, opening it with his shoulder. "Why? He doesn't live in the Icicle Creek development."

There are times when I honestly don't know if the sheriff doesn't recognize a news item or if he's simply trying to annoy me. "Besides," he added as we went inside, "it came back on about twenty minutes after I got to work." Espying an empty booth near the back, he led the way, giving a couple of nods to some of the other patrons, including Scooter Hutchins and Lloyd Campbell, a couple of our local businessmen.

"To think," I said, sliding into the booth across from him, "I was going to thank you for making such a timely arrest in terms of our deadline. But I realize you probably never gave it a thought."

"I sure as hell didn't," Milo replied, lighting a cigarette. "Good God, don't I have plenty on my plate without worrying about your paper?"

It was pointless to argue. After fifteen years of dealing with the sheriff and trying to make him understand the print media's demands, I knew it was a lost cause.

"Is Clive being a model prisoner?" I asked politely.

"So far." Milo was studying the menu, though I didn't know why. He almost always ordered the same thing. "Clive's pretty upset. He swears he didn't hit De Muth hard enough to kill him."

"He would say that, wouldn't he?"

"I suppose so." Milo slid the menu back behind the napkin holder. "I thought his attorney might ask for bail, but she didn't. I figure she's going for a plea bargain. Anyway, bail might not have been granted since Clive's a trucker."

"That translates as an automatic flight risk?"

"Around here it does." Milo leaned out into the aisle. "What did they do, fire all the waitresses?"

"They're busy," I said. "It's almost noon."

The sheriff exhaled smoke and looked grumpy. "So why's everybody here early?"

"It's five to twelve," I said. "It's Wednesday. They probably want to finish in time to get their copy of the *Advocate*."

"Bullshit." He leaned back in the booth. "Oh, God, here comes Delphine Corson."

"So?"

"She called this morning to ask me not to . . ." He stopped

as Delphine reached our booth. "Hi," he said halfheartedly. "What's up?"

Our local florist was inching toward sixty, but she'd done a good job of keeping her looks. Delphine's short ash-blond hair was cut in a style that accentuated her high cheekbones and azure-blue eyes. "I was hoping to buy you lunch," she said to the sheriff after giving me a quick if not sincere smile. "I see you're already booked."

Milo's gaze was steady. "Oh? You should've called first." He gestured at me. "I picked this one up on the sidewalk."

Delphine's smile became a smirk. "No kidding. Seriously, we have to talk," she said. "Are you free this evening? I'll treat you to dinner."

"The ante's going up," Milo remarked. "I'll have to check my social calendar. It's pretty damned crowded these days."

"Come on, Dodge," Delphine said, leaning a hand on the back of his booth. "Have you tried the Sailfish Grill in Monroe? It's really good."

"I'll call you," Milo said.

Delphine had stopped smiling. "When?"

"This afternoon." His gaze remained steady. "Okay?"

"Sure."

Looking far from convinced, Delphine turned around and headed back toward the front of the restaurant.

"Goddamnit," he muttered, "that new waitress—Lisa or Liza or whoever—was coming our way but gave up when she saw Delphine in the way. Now she's disappeared." He tapped ash onto the Formica tabletop, then swept it into his hand and dumped it on the floor. There was no ashtray because we were sitting in the No Smoking section. The sheriff didn't uphold laws that inconvenienced him.

"Take it easy," I said. "The waitress—whose name is Liz, by

the way—is coming from the other direction. She's lean and mean, recently arrived from Idaho."

For once, the sheriff altered his usual order of a cheeseburger, fries, and a green salad. "Bacon burger, fries, and that new fruit cup."

"We're out of the fruit cup," Liz replied, and added archly, "thanks to you."

"What the hell does that mean?" Milo demanded.

"I heard you arrested the guy who drives the truck that brings the canned fruit here," Liz said, her thin lips barely moving. "So what do you want instead?"

"The salad, blue cheese." Disgruntled, Milo stubbed out his cigarette and tossed the butt into his empty coffee mug. "Did you run out of coffee, too?"

"Not yet." Liz glared at him and snatched up the mug before turning to me. "The beef's rare today."

"Oh." I smiled feebly. "Good. Then I'll have the dip with fries and a salad exactly like the sheriff's."

Without another word, Liz stalked off.

Milo began his customary ritual of rearranging the salt and pepper shakers. "You had a run-in with her already?"

"Last week. I ordered the beef dip rare and it was well done, so I—politely—inquired if any of it was rare. Liz informed me that the only thing rare she'd found around Alpine was real men."

"She'd better watch her mouth," Milo said, craning his neck. "Where the hell is the coffee?"

"Don't have a heart attack," I cautioned. "Your gallbladder episode last winter scared everybody. Anyway," I went on, "when I was here last week I wanted to ask Liz some questions, since she was obviously new in town. I didn't because she wasn't very friendly and I was annoyed. Bad start. I had Vida

interrogate her the next day. Liz moved here from Idaho
Springs in September. Even Vida couldn't find out why, so instead of doing a short newcomer feature, we decided to put it
in the 'Scene Around Town' box on the front page. 'Liz Kirby,
an Idaho transplant, is a new face at the Burger Barn.' Or
something like that. Liz should know that a small town is no
place to remain anonymous."

Milo stopped fiddling with the salt and pepper. "Vida
couldn't get her to open up? Liz must be in the witness protec-
tion program."

"Vida'll find out eventually," I assured him and kicked his
shin, hoping he'd catch on as Liz approached with the coffee
carafe and a clean mug. She poured my coffee first. "Thanks,"
I said cheerfully.

Liz didn't say anything; neither did Milo. I kept expecting
her to remind him he was in the No Smoking area.

"What's with you and the fruit cup?" I asked after Liz had
left us.

"Doc Dewey. He said I should eat more fruit and fewer
spuds."

"You ordered fries."

"So? I was compromising."

I shook my head. "You're hopeless. Tell me why Delphine is
sucking up to you."

Milo's long face looked pained. "I went out with her a few
times," he said, speaking quietly and more rapidly than usual.
"Long time ago."

"I recall your brief and apparently unsatisfactory . . .
courtship. Leo Walsh dated her, too, but that never went anywhere, either."

"That's the trouble," Milo said. "Delphine's always in a
rush to get married again. I don't know why—she and Randy

weren't exactly an ideal couple. That marriage was rocky from the start. But after three dates with a guy, she starts talking long-term commitment. Who needs that kind of pressure?"

I nodded. "She did get engaged to Spike Canby. Then he got hurt in that construction accident on the bridge into town. They broke up not long afterward."

"Right." Milo paused as Liz brought our food, all but dumping it on the table.

The sheriff peered at his burger. "Where's the bacon?"

"We're out of that, too," Liz replied, looking as if she had to force herself from smiling in triumph. "No delivery. We ran out after breakfast."

"You can't find another driver for Berentsen's truck?" Milo snapped. "This town's got plenty of them, with all the ex-loggers."

Liz pressed her thin lips together before responding. "The truck needs new brakes. The guy who got killed was supposed to fix them over the weekend."

"Oh, for . . ." Milo made an angry gesture, narrowly missing knocking over his coffee mug. "Forget it."

"I'd like to," Liz snapped. "This town's a real cesspool." She stomped off toward the serving area.

"I still don't know why Delphine's so anxious to talk to you," I said after a brief pause. "Is she lusting after your body?"

"Don't be a smart-ass." Milo took a vicious bite of his burger. I waited for his response. "Spike couldn't work construction anymore with his bum back," he said at last, "so he had to find a job. I guess he'd managed to save some money and when Virgil Post's family put the Icicle Creek Tavern up for sale, Spike bought it. Right after that, he married Julie Whatever-Her-Name-Was."

"Blair," I said. "She was married before to a guy from Maltby."

"That sounds right." Milo ate two fat french fries. "Anyway, Delphine was at the ICT Saturday night when De Muth got killed. She never goes there, but she's been seeing Gus Swanson since he and his wife split a couple of months ago. Gus worked late because the new models had arrived and he was going over his inventory. He asked Delphine to meet him at the ICT for a drink."

I nodded. Gus owned the local Toyota dealership, which was located off the Icicle Creek Road a couple of blocks from the tavern. "What happened? Did Delphine get into it with Spike and somehow start the brawl that led to the murder?"

Milo shook his head. "Not as far as I know. That is, according to her, they'd just gotten served when all hell broke loose. She and Gus took off. Delphine says nobody was dead when they left. Anyway, she doesn't want me or anybody else mentioning that she was at the tavern. Too embarrassing, I guess, to show up at the place owned by her ex-boyfriend. It's dumb. Who cares?"

"Well . . ." I munched on some lettuce. "Delphine isn't the type who'd usually hang out at the ICT no matter who owned it. I suppose Gus goes there because it's close to the dealership."

"So?"

I shrugged. "I can kind of see her point. She's a businesswoman. She's done quite well for herself since the divorce. That was—what? Fifteen, sixteen years ago? She and Randy had already broken up when I moved to Alpine."

"I still say it's dumb. Everybody in town probably already knows who was at the tavern that night. Hell, you can't keep something like that a secret around here."

"You're right," I agreed. "So are you going to dinner with her?"

"I don't know. It depends on how I feel at the end of the day." He shook more salt onto what was left of his fries. "I don't much like driving all the way into Monroe for dinner. Does Delphine want to get out of town so people don't talk about the two of us?"

"Possibly." I couldn't resist a gibe. "Next week Vida could mention in 'Scene' that the sheriff and the florist enjoyed a scrumptious meal at the Sailfish Grill in Monroe. The restaurant might buy an ad from Leo."

Milo's hazel eyes flickered with what might've been amusement—or mockery. "Fleetwood's not sharing ads from Monroe with you since he got FCC approval for more broadcasting range?"

The query rankled. "He's steered a couple of businesses our way. We've been doing co-op advertising for several years, even before KSKY got the new license." My mood, which had been buoyed by the clear autumn air and quelled hunger pangs, began to darken again. "Let's change the subject. What's Clive Berentsen going to get for whacking Alvin De Muth with a pool cue?"

"Oh . . ." Milo finished his burger and gazed up at the grease-stained ceiling. "Ten to fifteen, probably. Eligible for parole in seven."

"What if the case goes to trial?"

The sheriff looked at me curiously. "Why would it?"

"Well," I said, wishing I hadn't raised the issue, "it was a fight. Berentsen says it was self-defense, right?" I paused as Milo nodded faintly. "If it can be proved that Clive was defending himself, why shouldn't he—or his lawyer—hope to get him off? You don't have a final autopsy report from Snohomish County, do you?"

Milo went on the defensive. "Do I need one? Doc Dewey says De Muth was killed by a blow to the head. End of story."

"So why did you ship the body to Everett for a second opinion?"

The sheriff shot me a stern look. "Doc doesn't have the technology or the time to make a thorough diagnosis. I like to touch all the bases."

I nodded. "I know. Skykomish County doesn't have the money for anything beyond the bare necessities. When will you hear back from the ME in Everett?"

Milo appeared to be ruminating. "Tomorrow, or Friday? They get backed up over there in Everett. Too damned many people in that county and too many autopsies."

"Okay." I put aside the remnants of my beef dip. Only half of it was rare; the rest was dried out around the edges. "So if . . . ?" I left the question unfinished.

Milo sighed. "Let's hope there's no if. I want this one out of the way real quick. Hell, Emma, it's just another drunken brawl. They happen. I'm not looking for trouble."

"Of course not," I said. But I knew the sheriff all too well. A quick glance at him indicated he was uneasy. I guessed Milo realized that not looking for trouble didn't mean he couldn't find it.

THREE

Until almost five o'clock, the rest of Wednesday's workday passed in relative calm. I'd intended to drop by Stella's Styling Salon to get my bangs trimmed, but both she and the other stylist were busy. I considered whacking at them myself, but knew I'd make a hash of it. "Butchering" was what Stella Magruder called any attempt on my part to deal with my thick, unmanageable brown hair.

Vida departed a few minutes early to pick up a dessert at the Grocery Basket for the annual Harvest Home potluck supper at her Presbyterian church. Ginny had left shortly after four-thirty, pleading exhaustion. Kip and his wife were hosting a pizza party for our carriers, a once-a-month get-together to keep up morale and also to figure out if any of the younger set might be slacking, doing drugs, or God-only-knew-what that could impede delivery of the *Advocate*. Mitch's wife was having more problems with her loom. He left just before the calm was broken by an angry Spike Canby, who charged into the newsroom to face off with Leo.

"I want my money back!" Spike demanded, pounding a fist

on my ad manager's desk. "You shouldn't have run that ad in the paper this week! Are you out of your mind?"

"Maybe," Leo replied, his aplomb intact. "What's the problem?"

"This!" Spike jabbed a stubby finger at the current edition on Leo's desk. "Look at page five!"

Leo didn't even blink. "You mean your ad? It's the same one you've been running for over a year. All one column by two inches of it."

"I know that!" Spike paused, hitching his pants up over his paunch. "That's what I mean. 'Where the Sky meets the creek,' 'where the brew meets the ski,' and 'where you and your buddies can take a cue from us and pool your talents.' It sounds as if I'm responsible for that poor bastard De Muth's death!"

"Spike." Leo leaned back in his chair, hands clasped behind his head. "You're off-base. If you felt the ad might be upsetting, you should have told me *before* our deadline. I haven't had a single call complaining about it." Leo's glance strayed in my direction where I stood in the doorway to my office. "What about you, Emma?"

"Nothing," I said.

Leo's expression was ingenuous. "You see? You must be the only one in SkyCo who thinks the ad sounds sinister. Hell, Spike, I tried a half-dozen times to get you to change it, but you kept saying that Julie thought it sounded terrific."

Spike scowled. "It was her idea."

"I know."

I also knew. Julie Canby had been publicity chairman for a garden club when she lived in Maltby and fancied herself a PR pro. When Spike bought the tavern, he wanted to change the lingering image of the ICT to that of a classier watering hole. Leo had some good ideas, but Spike insisted on letting his bride write the copy. Given that the small weekly ad didn't bring in much revenue, we'd let the Canbys have their way.

Spike had literally backed off, but stood with his arms folded across his chest. Though not very tall, he was quite broad through the shoulders and chest. What had been muscle while he worked construction was turning into fat. The combination of lack of exercise and maybe sampling too many of the liquid products he peddled was making him look more like a fat cat than a sturdy bulldog.

"Are you saying it's Julie's fault?" he demanded.

"It's nobody's fault," Leo said. "If you'd asked me to pull the ad, I'd have done it. We can put together something different for next week."

Spike scratched his forehead where his black curly hair had begun to recede. "No extra cost?"

"Not if the ad stays the same size," Leo said. "It'd be smart to take out a larger space and change the visuals. That way, you'd show that you intend to stay the course, despite what happened over the weekend."

"I'll see what Julie thinks," Spike mumbled. "Hey," he added, moving closer and holding out his hand. "No hard feelings, Leo. This thing really rocked our world."

Leo stood up and shook the other man's hand. "It happens."

"That De Muth was kind of an ornery cuss," Spike said, and winced. "Sorry. Shouldn't talk like that about the guy now that he's dead. He was a good customer. Kind of a loner. Julie always felt sorry for him. I guess that's why she . . ." Spike stopped speaking and shook his head. "Life's a crock, isn't it?"

"It's got a downside," Leo allowed.

Spike nodded at me, apparently as an afterthought. "Hey," he said, reaching the newsroom door, "don't be a stranger, Leo. Haven't seen you for a while at the tav."

Leo grinned. "I don't get out much. I've been thinking about entering a monastery."

"Right." Spike attempted an obligatory chuckle and left.

"Dumbshit," Leo muttered. "What does he expect when he owns a tavern? People actually go there to get drunk and stupid." He smiled ruefully. "I did it myself for too many years."

"But not anymore," I said, coming over to stand by his desk. "You do have a way with our advertisers, Leo."

"It's my job," he said, turning off his computer monitor. "Making nice. Every so often, I feel like a fraud."

"I know," I agreed. "I have to do the same. I wonder why Julie Canby feels so bad? Or should I say *guilty*?"

"Turn of phrase?" Leo suggested. "Or reality? Among the drawbacks of being a tavern or bar owner, not to mention a bartender or a waitress, is that whenever somebody leaves in no condition to drive and gets into an accident—especially a fatal one—there's got to be a sense of guilt. I know from my pathetic past that people in the booze business try to judge when somebody's over the limit, but it's not easy. I remember one night in . . ." He paused, staring off into space. "Van Nuys or someplace." Leo's smile was crooked. "You see? I can't even remember where I was. I probably didn't know at the time. Anyway, it was a busy evening. A guy came in and sat on the bar stool next to mine, ordered one drink, didn't try to make conversation, paid up, and left. The next day I found out he'd gone the wrong way on 170, crashed into a station wagon, and killed a family of four, not to mention himself. He'd been way over the legal limit for alcohol. Obviously, he'd had plenty to drink before he came into wherever the hell I was that night. But nobody noticed. The guy acted perfectly normal." Leo shook his head. "*I* felt guilty. You can imagine how the bartender felt."

"Oh, yes." I shook my head. "You're right. This is the first time Spike and Julie have had any serious problems since they bought the ICT a year or two ago. I don't know either of them very well. I'm not even sure what Julie looks like."

"Kind of a pretty brunette," Leo said, standing up. "A little hard around the edges, and the cheerful attitude seems forced. They live east of the tavern across from the golf course."

I still couldn't put a face on Julie Canby. "Frankly," I admitted, "I don't know some of the ICT crowd."

"Not your sort," Leo said as he picked up his laptop. "Do you want to get a feel for the place? When was the last time you were there?"

"Ah . . ." I tried to remember. "Six, seven years ago? I can't remember why. It was after the Post family bought it from the Skylstads who, I think, were the original owners. The Posts tried to clean the place up and they had some success, but in the end they surrendered. They couldn't afford to turn away the loyal rowdy set."

"How about the two of us going there tomorrow night?" Leo suggested. "I've got that chamber of commerce dinner this evening. You know—where I try to convince our local merchants that advertising can actually help them make money."

I cringed at Leo's idea about going to the ICT, but maybe I should check out the crime scene site even though Mitch had already given it the once-over. "They serve some kind of food, right? Who cooks?"

"It's described as food," Leo replied. "I've never eaten there. Julie's in charge of the kitchen where she cooks what some might call food." He started for the door. "If you're in a risk-taking mood, let me know."

I said I'd think about it. Less than five minutes later, I was ready to leave, remembering that tonight it was my job to lock up. I'd reached the front door when it was opened by a pale blond woman wearing a brightly striped full-length cape over a black turtleneck sweater and matching slacks. The turquoise necklace and earrings were an unusual lime-green shade, but the stones in her two rings were the more familiar aqua color.

"Yes?" I said, trying not to exhibit as much curiosity as she was in her slow head-to-toe appraisal of me.

She closed the door behind her. "I'd like to put something in the paper," she said, her voice low and husky. "How do I do that?"

"Do you mean an ad?" I asked.

She shook her head. The long blond hair was as pale as her skin. Her age could've been anywhere between forty and sixty. "It's . . . news."

I hesitated before forcing a smile. "I'm Emma Lord, the editor and publisher. Are you talking about the guest columns we run on the editorial page, or is this a news item?"

She scratched her upper lip. "I'm not sure."

"What's it about?" I asked.

"Clive." She averted her slate-gray eyes.

"Clive Berentsen?"

"Yes." She kept looking at the floor instead of me.

"What about him?"

"He's innocent."

"You're referring to what happened at the Icicle Creek Tavern?"

She nodded but still didn't meet my gaze.

"You should be talking to the sheriff, not to me," I said, growing impatient. "We're officially closed for the day."

The words didn't seem to make a dent on my visitor, but she finally looked me in the eye. "Someone has to speak out."

"I'm sorry," I said. "Even if I interviewed you about the

Berentsen tragedy, it wouldn't be published in the paper until next Wednesday."

"Oh." She seemed surprised, and nibbled on her thumb. "I didn't realize . . . What about the radio station? Where is it?"

She couldn't have changed my mind more effectively if she'd offered me a million-dollar bribe. "Look," I said, "come into the newsroom. Let's talk about what you think needs to be made public." I started out of the front office, turning once to make sure my caller was following me. "I'm afraid I don't know your name," I told her as I flicked on the lights.

"It's Heeka," she replied. At least that's what I thought she said.

I sat down at Mitch's desk and offered his visitor's chair. "I'm sorry," I apologized, "but I didn't quite catch that. How do you spell it?"

With a graceful motion of the cape, "Heeka" seemed to float into the chair. "J-i-c-a-r-i-l-l-a. But I go by Jica." She pronounced the shortened version the way I'd first heard it. "The name is from a Southwest Native American tribe."

"Really." I felt a bit embarrassed. "My brother, Ben, served as a priest in Tuba City, Arizona, for many years. I ought to know the name."

Jica smiled benevolently. "The tribe goes back hundreds of years. It's part of the Apache Nation now. The members live mostly in New Mexico."

"Ah." I nodded. "Maybe that's why I don't recall hearing it from Ben. Um . . . your last name?"

"Weaver," she said, still smiling. "*Jicarilla* is Spanish for 'little basket maker.' "

I nodded again. "You're a tribal member?"

"Legally, yes." She grew somber. "I'm one-quarter Jicarilla Apache. I've never lived on the reservation."

"You live here now?" I inquired.

"No. I live in Snohomish."

"But you know Clive Berentsen?"

"Yes." Her slim hands drifted into her lap. "I met him a year ago when his truck was parked by my antiques store. I had a vintage Coca-Cola clock in the window and he came in to say it looked exactly like the one his grandfather had at his gas station in Arlington."

Jica stopped speaking, her gaze roaming around the newsroom's low ceiling. "And?" I prodded after almost a full minute.

She still hesitated before looking at me again. "We became friends. Clive likes antiques, not acquiring them, but simply studying them and thinking about their history. He's a very sensitive person. He's what I would term a good soul."

"I'm afraid I don't really know him," I said after another pause on her part.

Jica regarded me with something akin to pity. "Then you couldn't understand why his arrest is so unjust."

"Probably not."

"Being a truck driver, Clive sees a great deal of roadkill," Jica went on. "It upsets him so when those innocent forest dwellers are run down on the highway. Often he has to stop his truck because he feels ill. His connection to nature is awe-inspiring. To even *think* he could kill another human being . . ." She shook her head. "It's impossible."

I considered my own words carefully. Blurting out that Jica sounded as if her brain's shelf date had expired was a bad idea. "So," I began, "the only way that Clive might get into a fight with someone else would be in self-defense?"

"Not even then." The pitying look was more apparent. "It had to be an accident."

"Were you there?"

"Yes."

I had trouble picturing this ethereal creature at the often rowdy ICT. "You saw what happened?"

"No."

I tried to sound empathetic. "You were . . . what? Not where you could see what was going on?"

"I'd left the tavern." She touched her left ear. "I have very sensitive cochlea. It had gotten quite noisy. I went outside and strolled along the river. It was pleasant at that time of night. I began to feel restored, physically, mentally, and spiritually."

"How did you find out what happened?"

"The sirens. I heard them coming closer and then saw the flashing lights. When they stopped at the tavern, I knew there must have been a mishap."

A *mishap*. I clamped my lips shut and took a deep breath. "What did you do then?" I finally asked.

"I waited." Jica frowned. "There were more sirens and flashing lights. I thought about asking someone what was going on, but nobody was coming out of the tavern, not through the front entrance, that is. I couldn't see the rear."

"And?" I felt as if I should be holding up cue cards.

"All the commotion was bothering me. My ears, you know." She waved a hand at her right ear this time. "I'd brought my car. Clive's truck was in for repair. His other car was at home. *His* home, I mean. I'd picked him up. I was feeling some very serious negative energy, so I left. I knew someone else would give him a ride. A few weeks ago, I had to leave early. That young couple—Hanson?—took him home. They live next door to Clive's apartment."

I recalled that Walt and Amanda Hanson lived in a condo at Parc Pines, not far from my house. "When did you learn about the tragedy inside the tavern?"

"Not until the next day. Sunday." Jica's expression was remorseful. "I called Clive and he told me about the accident involving Mr. De Muth. He said perhaps the poor man had fallen and struck his head on the pool table. I haven't spoken to Clive since. I had the car radio on this morning when I drove to my shop and heard a brief story about his arrest on one of the Everett stations. I was stunned."

"Of course." I tried to sound sympathetic. "Did it occur to you at the time—that is, when the emergency vehicles arrived at the tavern—that Clive might be the one who was hurt?"

She smiled. "No, no. Clive's not accident-prone. He's in excellent health. I assumed it was one of the other customers, perhaps the man who sees flying saucers. He doesn't seem to have a firm grasp on reality."

No kidding. "Are you going to visit Clive in jail?" I asked.

"I don't know." She frowned, fingering her sharp chin. "Jails are unpleasant. I left a note for him at the sheriff's office on my way here. Now," she continued, suddenly very businesslike, "how can you get this message across?"

"I can't," I admitted. "Not until our next issue."

"I see." Jica paused yet again. "Then I should go to the radio station."

Given her strange testimonial, I decided it might be interesting to see how Spencer Fleetwood would handle the situation. Certainly there was nothing I could do to stop her. Nor was I sure how to handle Jica's assessment of Clive Berentsen. Her description was too personal, going beyond the often quoted comments of people who had known a murder suspect and insisted that he or she was pleasant, normal, and friendly—if a bit standoffish. I did, however, wonder how much of what Jica had told me was true as opposed to a fantasy she had woven around her current boyfriend.

I stood up. "To get to KSKY, go back down Front Street, turn right onto Alpine Way, and make a left to the Burl Creek Road. Just follow it until you see the transmission tower and a small cinder-block building. I don't know if Mr. Fleetwood will be there or not. In the evenings he often turns the programming over to students from the community college or lets his engineer run tapes."

Jica glided along beside me as we left the newsroom. "Thank you. Do you really think I should talk to the sheriff?"

I didn't say that I wondered why Jica Weaver hadn't been interviewed already. Maybe it was because she hadn't been inside the tavern at the time of the brawl. "If you think it'd do any good," I said, opening the front door, "you might call him tomorrow. I take it he wasn't in when you dropped by with your note for Clive."

We'd reached the sidewalk. "The sheriff had left for the day," Jica said.

I checked to make sure I'd locked the door. "You're going back to Snohomish tonight?"

"I think so," she replied. "It's a long drive, though." Without another word, she wandered along Front Street in the direction opposite the sheriff's headquarters. I watched her for a few moments to see if she was going to her car, but she crossed Fifth and waited for traffic at the corner. After a half-dozen vehicles had gone by, Jica went across Front Street and stopped to study the window displays at Harvey's Hardware. Wherever my ethereal visitor was going, she wasn't in any hurry to get there.

When I arrived home, the only item of interest in my mailbox was the PUD bill, which, as usual, had gone up. There were two calls on my answering machine. One was a wrong number, but I recognized the apologetic voice at the other end. It was Grace Grundle, a slightly addled old lady who doted on her many cats. Apparently, she'd intended to call the pet store, but had misdialed. It wasn't the first time I'd had calls for Tye-Tonga Pet Shop. Our numbers were different by only a single digit.

The other message was from Edna Mae Dalrymple, our local librarian, asking if I could substitute tonight at bridge club. "Charlene Vickers has come down with a nasty cold," Edna Mae said in her twittering voice. "As soon as school starts, so does the cold and flu season. Not that I'm blaming the children, of course," she rattled on. "Still, I do think that when the weather changes, their parents should dress them more warmly. I saw one of the Wilson boys at the library this afternoon in shorts! I don't know what people are thinking of." Edna Mae stopped to catch her breath. "Anyway, could you fill in for . . . oh! It's Wednesday, isn't it? Bridge club isn't until tomorrow at Janet Driggers's house. I'll call you back."

It was a typical episode. Edna Mae is extremely competent at her job, but outside the library she tends to be a bit dizzy. With the phone still in hand, I dialed Milo's number at home. It was going on six o'clock. After four rings I got his recording: "Not available. Leave a message, name and number." The sheriff didn't go in for elaboration—unlike Vida, whose messages always demanded every scrap of information except for the caller's blood type. I hung up. Milo disliked messages that weren't informative.

As I sautéed a chicken breast and boiled rice, I wondered if he'd accepted Delphine Corson's offer of a free dinner. The sheriff's social life was about as dull as mine. He dated even less frequently than I did. As far as I knew, there had been no woman in his life in recent years except me, and that was a casual relationship based on friendship, trust, and propinquity.

Not such a bad basis for sex, I thought as I gazed out through the front window while my dinner was cooking, but not even close to the kind of love and passion I'd experienced with Tom Cavanaugh, the father of my son. After Tom died, I'd had a rocky liaison with Rolf Fisher, who lived and worked in Seattle. I'd unintentionally stood him up in early July and hadn't heard from him since. At first, I missed him. He was smart, attractive, and amusing. But Rolf was a game player, and I'd never figured out the rules. Maybe I was better off without him.

Then again, I reflected, seeing my long-married next-door neighbors walk hand in hand from their car to their house, maybe not. Val and Viv Marsden had celebrated their twenty-fifth wedding anniversary in August. They'd hosted a barbecue in their backyard for relatives, friends, and neighbors. Although we'd never been close friends—my fault, not theirs—I'd known them well enough to see the comfortable intimacy they shared. On many occasions, including that warm August evening, I'd noticed the gamut of emotions they could express without ever saying a word or even a glance. Never having been married, I envied the Marsdens. Watching them now, I recalled a day in June five years ago when Val had helped Tom clear away some of the overgrowth in my yard and haul it off in the Marsdens' truck. Tom was staying with me to plan our wedding. I remembered thinking how wonderful it would be when we got married, how good it was to have congenial neighbors, how well Tom seemed to fit into the role of my home's caretaker.

Before the weekend was over, Tom was dead. So were my dreams. I still wondered what it might have been like if he'd lived. Maybe it wouldn't have been as blissful as I'd imagined. Tom was a city person, born and raised in Seattle, then living

in San Francisco for almost thirty years. Still, the fantasy of our
life together occasionally came back to haunt me.

Love plays strange tricks on our brains. I couldn't help but
wonder if Jica Weaver's description of Clive Berentsen was accurate—or if she, too, was prone to spin fairy tales with happy
endings.

FOUR

VIDA WAS AGOG THE NEXT MORNING WHEN I TOLD HER and Mitch Laskey about Jica Weaver's after-hours visit. "Clive has a lady friend?" my House & Home editor cried, batting at the little black balls that hung from the brim of her Spanish hat. "And she's not a tart as I might expect? I didn't know she existed. How can that be?"

"Because she's from Snohomish?" I suggested, not daring to look at Mitch—who was intrigued as well as amused by his colleague's encyclopedic knowledge of Alpine. "Or maybe *you* should visit the ICT."

Vida shuddered. "*Please!* I wouldn't dream of it!"

Leo, who had been on the phone, rang off and chuckled. "Come on, Duchess. Tag along with Emma and me tonight. We've decided to have a romantic rendezvous there if we can find two bar stools next to each other that still have all their padding."

Vida gaped at Leo. "You're not!"

Leo glanced at me; I gave him a thumbs-up. "Yes, we are," he insisted. "Crime scene stuff." He looked across the room at

Mitch. "Tell us what to look for. Maybe small claw prints on the burger patties?"

"It's combat duty," Mitch said. "Though to be honest, it's upscale compared with some of the watering holes I was forced to visit in Detroit. There was one place that served gopher . . ."

"Stop!" Vida put her hands over her ears, knocking the Spanish hat askew. "Don't tell me any more disgusting tales of your past life. I haven't had my morning pastry."

"Try the elephant ear," Mitch said. "They were still warm from the oven when I bought them."

"I believe I shall," Vida said, going to the coffee table and cutting off a generous slice of the big, almost round cinnamon-and-sugar-covered pastry. "Is your wife's loom working properly?"

"I hope so," Mitch replied. "I'm wondering if maybe the thing got damaged in transit from our home in Royal Oak." He stood up after Vida took a large chunk of elephant ear to her desk. "I'm off on my rounds," Mitch announced. "Anything else I should know before calling on Sheriff Dodge's crew?"

"Not really," I said. "Do you have that list of people who were at the tavern Saturday night? I only took a quick look at it Tuesday before the arrest was made."

"Sure," Mitch replied, bony fingers on his keyboard. "I'll zap it into your computer."

He'd barely left the newsroom when Vida followed me into my office. "Well? I'd like to see that list again, too."

I printed two copies and handed Vida the first one. "It's quite a mix," I pointed out. "Not the same rough-and-tumble types they had at the ICT in the old days."

"Of course not," Vida agreed, sitting in one of my two visitors' chairs and frowning as she went over the names. "Somewhat more . . . refined these days. Not that I'm denigrating the character of those who frequented the tavern in bygone years. Being loggers, they had to be very hardy, rugged, and willing to take risks. The work was—it still is—dangerous, both in the woods and in the mills."

"Yes," I agreed, finding some irony in Vida's exclusion of the riffraff that had often patronized the ICT in a different era.

"Mugs Ahoy," she went on, "has always drawn a somewhat higher class of clientele. That's because it's located in the heart of the commercial district, rather than on the fringe. Before World War Two, that section of Alpine was virtually out of town. It wasn't until the fifties that the Icicle Creek development was built and the golf course was laid out." She tapped a name on the list. "Marlowe Whipp strikes me as an unlikely customer. So does Delphine Corson."

"As a matter of fact, Delphine isn't a regular," I explained, telling Vida about the local florist's attempt to keep her presence a secret.

"How silly," Vida scoffed. "I heard she was there the next day. Billy mentioned it," she said, referring to her nephew, Bill Blatt, who was a sheriff's deputy. "I thought it unlike her, but she's seeing Gus Swanson, and his car dealership is right by the tavern. Delphine is basically a sensible woman with a good head for business, but when it comes to men, she can be quite foolish. Gus and Beverly Swanson are merely separated at this point. He shouldn't be dating until one of them files for divorce."

"Maybe she'll fall for Marlowe Whipp," I said. "He's not married."

"He was, years ago. His wife, Cathie, died young. That's why the elder Whipps have helped raise Marlowe's son, Frankie. Goodness, I meant to talk to Marlowe yesterday, but I never saw him on his mail route." She glanced at her watch. "It's going on nine. He should be coming by with our delivery soon. I'll go look for him in a few minutes. Let's review these other people quickly."

"Clive Berentsen, the accused, and Alvin De Muth, the deceased. Regulars?"

"Probably. Both worked with trucks, Clive as a driver, Al as a mechanic." Vida studied her copy of the list. "Fred Engelman, who should have been spending the weekend in jail, but wanted to attend his ex-wife's birthday party. I think that's rather nice."

"The ex-wife, Janie, now married to Mickey Borg, who owns Icicle Creek Gas 'n Go next to the tavern, a natural hangout for them."

"Yes. I never go there for gas," Vida said. "I much prefer Cal Vickers's Texaco station. Nor would I go to the Borgs' minimart. Prices are higher than in grocery stores, and I've heard that he sometimes sells beer and cigarettes to minors. If so, Milo ought to look into it. The practice is despicable." She moved on swiftly to the next name. "Holly Gross. Do I need to say more?"

"She *is* gross," I said, "in many ways. Did she ever marry any of her children's fathers?"

Vida shook her head. "There was a teenage marriage years ago. No children and the union lasted less than a year. Holly prefers living on welfare and off men who . . . well, accept her favors."

"I wonder if she went to the tavern alone."

"Maybe. She was probably trolling." Vida wrinkled her nose in disapproval. "She's definitely a regular, and not just on Saturdays. Occasionally, she goes to Mugs Ahoy, though Abe Loomis wishes she wouldn't. Abe can be fussy about standards for his clientele."

The owner of the rival tavern could also be depressing. Over the years, his employees had tactfully tried to tell him that he shouldn't chat with customers because his expertise was managing the business. The truth was that patrons who unloaded their troubles came away feeling much worse after listening to Abe's doleful responses. Known around town as Abe Gloomis, he survived as a barkeep by serving good beer and edible food at reasonable prices. He also ran a fairly tight ship and kept the tavern relatively tidy.

Vida pushed the Spanish hat farther back on her head. I gathered that those dangling black balls were bothering her. "What caused the fight? Billy told me it was over money, but he didn't sound sure."

"I honestly don't know," I admitted. "Money is always a good way to make people mad. Who pays for what, who doesn't pay their tab, who borrowed money from somebody else and didn't pay it back or got turned down when they asked for a loan . . ." I shrugged. "Mitch said Sam Heppner thought it started at the pool table. Maybe they were betting on the games."

"Perhaps." Vida glanced again at the list. "Norene and Bert Anderson. Norene works at the tavern and Bert owns the local body shop. Obviously, they belong with this crowd. As for the Peabody boys, I assume they're regulars. They almost fit the old mold—big, strong, and not particularly bright."

I nodded. "Purvis and Myron, our local jacks-of-all-trades, especially heavy lifting. Good-natured, though."

"True. As for Averill Fairbanks, I don't know what to say." Vida frowned. "I've never considered him a tavern type of person. He can't spot space ships and aliens in a bar."

"No, but he might see more of them when he leaves."

Vida gave me the courtesy of a small smile. "Perhaps. He

must bore the other customers with his far-fetched tales of aliens landing on Flapjack Peak or little green men paddling down Troublesome Creek." She paused. "Walt and Amanda Hanson strike me as a bit odd for this group. He works at the state fish hatchery. But what does she do? Did she ever get on full-time at the post office?"

"I don't know," I said. "I think she works there only during the holiday rush. They have no kids. Amanda filled in last spring at Barton's Bootery for someone who was ill or out of town."

"Yes, I remember now. I used it in 'Scene.' Clancy and Debra Barton went to the UK for three weeks." She paused, re-settling her hat. "That leaves the owners, Spike and Julie. Have we left out anyone?"

"Not unless the sheriff's head count isn't complete," I said. "He didn't have Jica Weaver's name on the list, but I suppose that's because she wasn't inside the ICT at the time of the incident."

Vida carefully folded her list and stood up. "I must see if I can catch Marlowe Whipp. If I do, shall I bring him in here?"

"Do you think we should interrupt him on his route? He's not the fastest mailman at best."

"It won't take long," Vida insisted, and went off to meet the postman on his appointed rounds.

Five minutes later, Ginny buzzed me to say that Vida wanted me to come into the front office. Sure enough, when I arrived she had Marlowe Whipp backed up against the counter in front of Ginny's desk. Ginny, however, was nowhere in sight. She seemed to spend a great deal of time these days in the rest-room.

"Marlowe has an interesting tale to tell about the Han-sons," Vida declared.

Marlowe, who is well into his forties, looked as if his third-grade teacher had called on him and he didn't know the answer. "I wouldn't say it was really . . . interesting," he said, looking warily at me. "Is this going to go in the paper?"

"I doubt it," I said and smiled encouragement. "What about Walt and Amanda?"

Marlowe had set his mailbag down on the floor. He kept looking at it as if he expected a bunch of outlaws to rush through the door and steal his precious load of circulars, brochures, and catalogs. "I know Amanda. Kind of. From when she works part-time at the post office," he explained, speaking the way he walked, which was slow and meandering. "She's . . . oh . . . a . . . a nice young woman, but . . . well . . . she likes to . . . flirt."

Vida was eying Marlowe as if she were a ravenous cat and he, a plump chickadee. "A tease or something more flagrant?"

Marlowe looked puzzled. "Flagrant?"

"Yes, yes. Is she having fun when she flirts or is her behavior an actual invitation to seduction?"

"Oh." Marlowe frowned. "To be honest, she's . . . um . . . never flirted with me. As I recall."

"Really." Vida kept a straight face. "You would, I assume, hear rumors if Amanda was seeing another man?"

"I would?"

Vida tapped a foot, which was, as always, shod in a black sensible mid-heel pump. "Are US postal workers immune to gossip?"

"Gosh," Marlowe said, "I don't think Amanda's worked at the post office since . . . January?" He darted an apprehensive glance at his mail pouch. "I should be—"

Vida interrupted. "What set off the fight between Clive and Alvin?"

"Well . . ." Marlowe removed his USPS hat and scratched his bald spot. "Amanda and Walt had been playing pool. With . . . who was it? Oh. Mickey Borg and his wife . . . what's her name?"

"Janie," Vida put in.

Marlowe nodded. "That's right. But she used to be married to—"

"Fred Engelman," Vida snapped. "Go on."

I sensed that Marlowe wasn't ready to continue, so I spoke up, lest he forget that I was a real person and not a wax dummy. "Where were you when this happened?"

"At the bar," he replied. "Well . . . no. I'd been at the bar, but Spike got grumpy, so I moved. To the pull-tabs on the wall."

"Grumpy?" I remarked. "About what?"

"I don't know." Marlowe rubbed his shoulder, maybe to ease chronic pain from toting heavy mailbags. "Spike can be . . . touchy."

"I'm not familiar with the layout of the place," I admitted. "Are the pull-tabs within view of the pool table?"

Marlowe nodded. "They're by the restrooms," he said. "The pool table's between the end of the bar and . . . I'm not sure where the door goes. Maybe it's . . . no, the office is by the rear exit. The door by the pull-tabs is probably . . . a storeroom? Oh! There's some pull-tabs by the front door, too. I never win on them. A couple of weeks ago . . . or was it right after Labor Day?" He paused, seemingly deep in recollection.

"Marlowe!" Vida barked. "Get on with it! What did Amanda do with regard to Mickey Borg?"

Marlowe actually recoiled. He reached down and grabbed the strap of his mail pouch, as if it might be a weapon—or a talisman. "Give me some time, Vida. I already told Sam Heppner all this stuff."

"I hope," Vida said through clenched teeth, "Sam stayed awake during the interview."

Marlowe looked baffled. "Because it was so late at night?"

I thought Vida might explode. Instead, she took a deep breath before speaking again. "Please. Just tell us about the commotion."

Still clutching his mail pouch, Marlowe gulped. "Well . . . there was a lot going on. Mickey Borg said he didn't feel good. Janie didn't want to leave yet. Fred offered to take her home." Marlowe stopped for a moment, maybe exhausted from speaking much faster than usual. "Fred and Janie were kind of chummy, if you want to know the truth. But they used to be married, so . . ." He shrugged. "Amanda Hanson told Janie she'd take Mickey home. Walt Hanson said their Miata only had room for two. Walt sounded ticked off. Holly Gross . . . gosh, she's on the make most of the time. She'd been cozying up to Clive Berentsen, but he gave her the brush-off. Al De Muth got kind of mad at Clive then, said he shouldn't be so rude to Holly. Amanda was giving her husband, Walt, some dirty looks while she talked to Mickey. Then Holly butted in on Al and Clive. I think she wanted Al to go home with her, but he said he had a headache." Once again, Marlowe stopped for breath.

Vida scowled. "*Al* had a headache?"

Marlowe nodded. "That's what he said. He was nice about it, though. The next thing I knew, Walt went over to Amanda and grabbed her arm and said they were leaving. Amanda told him to . . . leave her alone. All of a sudden Al and Clive went at it, and the next thing I knew, Clive swung a pool cue at Al, who went down and never got up."

"Where," I asked, "were you during the actual fight?"

"I'd moved away from the pool table toward the front door," Marlowe replied. "I wanted to leave, but my jacket was by the bar. I couldn't get past Spike Canby and Bert Anderson. Spike was coming from behind the bar to break up the fight. Bert was in his way. I thought maybe he—Bert—was protecting his wife, Norene. She was taking another pitcher of beer to the Peabody brothers."

"Who else was fighting besides Clive and Al?" Vida asked.

"Mainly them," Marlowe said, licking lips that had gone dry from his lengthy recital. "But I think Amanda threw something at Walt, and Janie Borg was screaming at Mickey, who was on the floor."

"Why," Vida inquired, looking almost as dazed as I felt, "was Mickey on the floor?"

"His stomach," Marlowe replied. "He had bad cramps. After the police and everybody came, one of the medics, Del Amundson, told Mickey to get his stomach checked. It could be appendicitis." Marlowe was holding the mail pouch in both hands. "Please. I've got to run."

"Run?" Vida said under her breath. "Yes, of course. Thank you."

He left, displaying some fancy footwork I'd never seen before.

"Honestly," Vida gasped, "I am quite confused."

"That makes two of us," I said.

"Perhaps I should've taken notes," she murmured. "Generally, I don't need them."

As far as I was concerned, Vida's flawless and prodigious memory was the Eighth Wonder of the World. "I hope Sam Heppner followed Marlowe's rambling story better than we did."

"Sam's detail-oriented," Vida said. "He's been a deputy for years, and Milo will want to be factual even . . ." She stopped, a curious expression on her face. "I hear a cat. Did one creep into the office?"

"It's been known to happen," I said, and listened for a few moments. "It's not a cat. But it's close by."

Vida and I both jumped as Ginny's head suddenly bobbed above the reception counter where we were standing. "Help me," she said in a breathless voice. "I'm in labor."

"What in the . . ." I stared as she hauled herself to her feet. "Where . . . Here, let me help you." I hurried around to the other side of the counter. In the space under her desk was a blanket, two pillows, and a couple of plastic Evian water bottles. "Ginny!" I exclaimed as I tried to get her into the chair. "Have you been napping under your desk?"

"Only since . . ." She winced with pain, uttered a gasp, and pressed a hand to her back. " . . . last week." Clumsily, she sat down, short breaths coming rapidly. "I get *so* tired."

"Of course." I wasn't without sympathy. "But you should've told me. We could've figured out a better setup." I looked around, suddenly realizing Vida had disappeared. "How many minutes apart are the pains?" I asked, glancing into the newsroom. It was empty. It occurred to me that Vida had probably gone to the Bank of Alpine to let Rick, Ginny's husband and the manager, know that their baby was on its way.

"Eleven minutes and eighteen seconds," Ginny replied after a pause, presumably to calculate exact timing. She checked her watch. "The next one should be at nine-thirty-four."

"I'll let Kip know what's going on," I said, heading for the back shop.

I couldn't catch what Ginny said in response, but as long as she hadn't announced that she could see the baby's head, we had plenty of time. The hospital was only three blocks away.

Kip, whose wife had had their first baby in the early spring, grinned at my news. "Great! Maybe Ginny will get a girl this time." He suddenly sobered. "Who's replacing her?"

I grimaced. "I'm not sure. I've put it off because whenever I mention finding a temp, Ginny starts to cry and says whoever we get will be better than she is and she'll never be able to come back to work."

"That's crap," Kip said as we both headed for the front office. "Ginny's good at what she does. You'd never hire anyone else full-time."

"Of course not."

We entered the front office just as Vida came through the door. "Rick's getting your car, Ginny. Come, I'll guide you out to the curb. He should be there very shortly."

"Okay." Ginny's voice was feeble. "Help me up."

Kip gave her a hand. "I've had practice this time, Gin," he said with a big smile. "You need a coat?"

"No. Yes." She leaned on Kip. "My heavy brown cardigan. It's under the pillow under the desk. Oh—and my purse. It's under the desk, too. And my other shoes and . . ."

"We'll make sure everything gets to you," I said. "If there's anything else, I'll come by the hospital with it later, okay?"

Kip turned Ginny over to Vida. By the time the two women had reached the door, Kip had found the cardigan and the purse. I spotted Rick pulling up in the Erlandsons' Saturn SUV. Unfortunately, he had to back up on the diagonal to get into the empty space next to Vida's Buick. He ran up over the curb, denting the back bumper on one of Mayor Fuzzy Baugh's concrete planters.

"Our car!" Ginny cried, and promptly doubled over, yelping in pain.

"A simple job to get rid of the dent," Vida soothed, holding on to Ginny and half dragging her to the SUV's passenger side while Rick got out to check the damage before coming to his wife's aid.

"I can fix that!" Kip shouted. "Don't worry. Just go, man!"

Rick went—back behind the wheel, leaving Vida to struggle with a moaning, groaning Ginny. I was about to offer my help but, as usual, my House & Home editor was up to the task. The last I heard from either Erlandson was Ginny wailing that she couldn't fasten her seat belt. Rick stepped on the gas—and hit the planter again. Obviously, he'd forgotten to take the car out of reverse. A moment later he pulled out into traffic, narrowly missing a school bus, which, luckily, was empty at this time of day.

"Good Lord," I muttered. "Can they go three blocks without killing themselves?"

"I hope so," Vida replied. "I called ahead to let the hospital know they were coming." She walked over to the planter, which was undamaged. "Fuzzy's winter pansies are rather nice," she remarked. "I wonder if I dare use this incident for 'Scene' next week? I don't usually put staff members in the column, but this is rather exceptional."

"It sure is," Kip said, shaking his head. "You'd think Rick would be calmer. Heck, it's the third time around for him."

"Maybe's he's forgotten. There's been a bit of a gap since the two boys were born." My eyes strayed in the opposite direction down Front Street. "Are you both going to stick around the office?"

"Yes," Vida replied. "I'm not going anywhere until I meet Maud Dodd for lunch. I must apologize for the cornucopia disaster, though I've only gotten two calls about it."

"I'm not going anywhere, either," Kip put in. "I'm trying to figure out a new program for . . ."

I held up a hand. "Don't. I won't understand whatever it is. I'm going to Stella's to get my bangs trimmed. She just opened and shouldn't be too busy yet." I didn't bother getting my jacket. The morning was cool, but I was wearing a long-sleeved sweater.

As my two staff members went back inside, I crossed Front Street at the corner of Fourth and headed for Stella's Styling Salon two blocks away in the Clemans Building. Although one of the other stylists and the new girl she'd hired to do nails both had clients, Stella was free at the moment, waiting for her ten o'clock.

"Oh, God, Emma!" she cried. "You *are* Emma, aren't you? I can't see your eyes. Where's your guide dog?"

"Okay, okay," I snapped, accustomed to Stella's not unwarranted criticism of what I did—or didn't do—to my hair. "Just let me see my eyebrows again and I'll be out of your hair. So to speak."

"You will never be out of your own hair with that mop," she declared, beckoning me to her station. "Sit. I'll get you a smock. This won't take long. I'm going to use a meat cleaver."

Less than a minute later, Stella returned with the requisite blue smock. "So," she said, surveying me in the mirror, "what's new? Besides death by pool cue at the ICT?"

"Ginny just left to have her baby," I replied. "She wasn't due until Tuesday, but you know how that goes."

"I sure do, with three of my own." Stella cocked her head to one side. "Frankly, you need it all cut. You look like you put your head in a blender. I'll do the bangs, but make an appointment before you leave."

"Okay," I said meekly. "By any chance, do you know of anyone who's looking for some temporary office work? I have to replace Ginny for six weeks. She wants to come back sooner than I think she should, but our maternity benefits aren't exactly lavish."

"Actually," Stella said, beginning to snip away, "I do know someone who's interested in a short-term job. She's my ten o'clock."

"Who?" I asked, blinking as cut hair fluttered onto my cheeks.

"Amanda Hanson," Stella responded. "She plans to work for the post office again when the holiday rush starts, so the timing's right. Shall I mention it to her?"

I hesitated. "Is she reliable?"

"As far as I know. She's done some other part-time work and I don't recall any complaints. You know I'd hear if there were any in this town. Shoot, you'd hear, too."

I nodded. It was a mistake. Stella's scissors slipped, cutting off an extra half-inch. "Sorry," I apologized, reverting to meek Emma, Hair Care Dunce.

"Never mind," Stella said. "I might as well even it up. Knowing you, it'll be another three weeks before you get a real cut. Say, wasn't Amanda at the tavern the other night?"

"Yes," I said. "She and Walt were among the bystanders."

Stella's mirror image grinned. "Aha! My appointment with her should be interesting. An eyewitness report."

I grimaced. "I hope it's better than the one we got from Marlowe Whipp this morning."

"Marlowe!" Stella chuckled. "He's an odd duck, always bragging about women flirting with him, including Amanda when she worked at the post office. When he brought our mail Friday," she continued, surveying her handiwork, "he insisted Janie Engelman was always giving him the eye."

"Janie Engelman?" I said. "You mean Janie Borg?"

Stella mussed up my bangs to get a better perspective. "Oh,

right. I keep forgetting that she remarried after the divorce from Fred. In any event, it seemed unlikely that Janie made a play for Marlowe." She snipped off a few stray strands. "So Monday I asked him if the tavern disaster put a damper on Janie's ardor. He acted as if he didn't know what I was talking about."

I watched myself frown. "Why? What did the brawl have to do with Marlowe and Janie?"

Stella shrugged. "As I said, Marlowe's an odd duck. I figure his fantasies were dashed by grim reality. Sometimes people actually believe their own make-believe. And then the real world wakes them up." She undid the smock and whisked me off with a soft brush. "There. You can now see, though the rest of it still looks pretty scary."

As I rose from the chair, I saw Amanda Hanson coming through the door. "Maybe," I said, lowering my voice, "you could ask Ms. Hanson if she'd be interested in working for us. I'm kind of desperate."

Stella tossed the smock into a bin. "Do you want to ask her?"

I hesitated. "I suppose I should. She'd think it odd if I left without saying anything and then you asked if she wanted to work for me."

"Go for it," Stella said. She turned around to greet Amanda.

Even though the bangs trim was free, I took a ten-dollar bill out of my purse and joined Stella by the front desk. "Say," she said to Amanda, as if the idea was spontaneous, "do you know Emma Lord?"

Amanda's brown eyes studied me briefly as I put the ten in the tip jar. "The newspaper, right?" Amanda said.

Stella nodded. "Emma has a question for you. I'll go get a smock."

Amanda suddenly looked on her guard. "What?" she asked.

"Our office manager, Ginny Erlandson, is having a baby," I said. "She wasn't due until next week, and I've put off hiring a temp. I understand you plan on going back to the post office for the holiday rush. Would you be interested in helping us during the interim?"

"Maybe." Amanda seemed relieved. Maybe she thought I intended to grill her about the ICT tragedy. "How long is Ginny going to be gone?"

"Six weeks," I replied. "I hope the timing would work for you."

"What's the salary?"

"Sixteen fifty an hour."

"Benefits?"

"SkyCo medical and Washington State dental, half paid by the paper, half by the employee. A 401(k) plan that I also match. However," I went on quickly, "I wouldn't be able to do any of that on a temporary basis. I assume you have coverage through your husband's job with the department of fisheries."

"True." Amanda's gaze moved away from me and toward Stella who, I assumed, was tactfully taking extra time to set up. "I'll think about it. Today's Thursday. I'll try to get back to you tomorrow."

"Good. Thanks." I waved at Stella and left. Sensing a lack of interest on Amanda's part, I wondered if she'd even bother to call to turn down my offer.

I was wrong. Less than twenty minutes after I got back to the office, Amanda phoned to say she was ready to go to work immediately. I was surprised, but told her I'd see her at eight the following morning. I assumed she needed the money.

I was wrong about that, too. What Amanda wanted was something I could never give her.

FIVE

K IP FOUND GINNY'S SPARE SHOES BEHIND THE WASTEBAS-
ket by the file cabinet. He volunteered to drop them off
on his lunch hour. "Looking for her sneakers reminded me I
was supposed to take Chili's shoes to Amer Wasco for new
soles," he explained. His wife's name wasn't actually Chili, but
she'd been called that since childhood. Kip was reluctant to say
why, but I gathered it was a reference to some kind of embarrassing mishap involving an overdose of chili peppers. "I keep
forgetting and have to put her off. The hospital's only a block
away so I might as well stop by the cobbler shop. Any news on
Gin?"

"No." It was a little after eleven. "We should hear soon,
though."

Kip returned to the back shop just as Mitch Laskey entered
the newsroom. Vida looked up from her keyboard.

"Well?" she demanded.

"Well what?" Mitch asked in his typical affable manner.

"What did you find out from the sheriff this morning?"

I was standing just outside my office. Mitch glanced at me.

"I believe Sheriff Dodge is hung over this morning. He wouldn't come out of his office. Jack Mullins did some wink-wink stuff about his boss being under the weather."

Vida, who had removed the bothersome hat with its dangling black balls, arched both eyebrows. "Really. That isn't typical, Mitch, in case you were wondering."

"As a matter of fact," he said, going to his desk, "I *was* wondering. Dodge strikes me as a guy who keeps a pretty tight rein on himself."

"He is," I said, feeling a need to defend Milo despite my surprise. I'd never seen the sheriff drunk. "Jack Mullins better keep his big mouth shut. We don't need rumors about Milo getting blotto in the middle of a murder case or at any other time."

Mitch looked sheepish. "Sorry. Don't worry, I won't tell any tales. I still have to adjust to small-town mentality."

"You will," Vida said, making it sound like a command. "Milo has his faults, but drinking to excess isn't one of them. Emma knows that better than anyone."

I wasn't sure how to take that remark, but let it pass. Still, I wondered why the sheriff had apparently ended up with a hangover. Was he having such a wonderful time with Delphine? Or did he overindulge to put up with her company? Surely I wasn't jealous. For years I'd hoped he'd find the right woman so I could stop feeling guilty when I rejected his sexual overtures.

Vida turned in my direction. "You did say that Delphine Corson wanted to speak privately with Milo, didn't you?" She saw me nod. "It's foolish for him to socialize with a witness in a murder investigation. If, in fact, that's what he did."

"Delphine was trying to bribe him with a free dinner," I said as Leo Walsh entered the newsroom.

"Him who?" Leo asked, stopping in front of Vida's desk.

"The sheriff," Vida replied.

"Hunh." Leo shook his head and chuckled. "She never tried to bribe me with much of anything during our brief whatever-you-want-to-call-it. I always had to pick up the tab." He went over to his desk and sat down. "Hey, Emma, we're going Dutch tonight. Understood?"

I smiled and nodded. "It's a business expense."

"Hold it!" Mitch said as he finished pouring himself more coffee. "Delphine Corson, local florist, romantically involved with . . . the Toyota guy?" He saw Vida nod confirmation. "What's her problem?"

For once, I beat Vida to the answer. "She doesn't want the public to know she set foot inside the ICT. That's despite the fact that everybody already knows because that's how it is in a small town."

Mitch nodded. "So there's another reason for cozying up to Dodge."

I hadn't thought of that, having ascribed her motive to personal embarrassment that might temporarily harm her business. "Such as?"

"I don't know," Mitch admitted, sitting down at his desk. "Shall I talk to her? I can play the dim-witted-new-man-in-town card."

"Yes," I said. "How many witnesses have you talked to so far?"

"Among the customers, only the hulking Peabody brothers," Mitch replied. "Neither of them had much to say."

"What about the Canbys and Norene Anderson, the waitress?"

"Julie Canby heard the rumpus, but she was closing the kitchen," Mitch said, checking the text he'd entered into his computer. "She figured the noise was the usual Saturday-night rough stuff. Hannibal could've driven his elephants through the tavern, and she wouldn't care unless they interfered with her bagging the evening's glass breakage."

I'd walked over to Mitch's desk. "So she saw nothing?"

"Not until the place suddenly went quiet after De Muth hit the deck. That," Mitch added with a wry little smile, "made her think something was wrong. Then there were some screams and shouts. She arrived on the scene just as everybody was wondering why De Muth wasn't getting up. Julie realized he was dead."

Vida was listening intently. Maybe Leo was, too, though he seemed engrossed in his computer screen. "What about Spike?" I asked.

"Spike's upset, as you know from his tirade about the ad." Mitch glanced at Leo. "You talked to Spike since?"

"Huh?" My ad manager looked up from his monitor. "No. Julie's dreaming up some user-friendly words for the ad. Taking out more space won't cost much, but maybe she's figuring out how many people can read agate-size type and save the Canbys twenty bucks a week."

Mitch nodded. "That sounds like Spike. Anyway, he insists he tried to break up the fight, but Bert and Norene Anderson were in his way and suddenly De Muth hit the deck. Apparently Norene had just served Delphine and Mr. Toyota—Gus, right?—and was talking to somebody before she went back to the bar." Mitch grimaced. "I've covered plenty of brawl-related stories. They're hard to sort out, especially when liquor's involved, because it fogs up both the brain and the memory."

I nodded. "Oh, yes. That's why we have to be so careful about what we put in the paper." I looked at Leo. "What was it Spike told you about Julie feeling sorry for De Muth?"

Leo frowned. "She has sympathy for loners like him, even though Spike thought De Muth was an ornery cuss."

Vida turned back to Mitch. "Anyone else?"

"The Andersons." He glanced at his screen. "Bert owns the body and chop shop, so he probably knew both Berentsen and De Muth pretty well since all of their own jobs are truck-related."

"And?" Vida urged.

Mitch sighed. "Norene didn't say much. Somebody said she'd been stung by a wasp or a bee. I figured her for the gabby type. What little she added was vague. She didn't see the blow that struck De Muth." He glanced from Vida to Leo to me. "Well?"

I shrugged. Leo nodded. Vida, naturally, spoke up: "I haven't seen much of her recently, but she was a talkative child. My Meg was in school with her. Norene was a mediocre student, but very outgoing."

Mitch smiled. "Waitresses and barmaids often are. People-oriented, if they're any good at what they do."

I thought of the surly Liz at the Burger Barn. Given Mitch's criterion, she was in the wrong job. "What about Bert?" I asked.

"He seemed upset, too," Mitch said. "He liked De Muth, though he allowed that he was moody and would provoke arguments sometimes just for the sake of arguing. Still, they were both regulars at the ICT and usually got along. They had business dealings, too. De Muth sometimes worked on trucks and other vehicles that needed bodywork or were beyond repair. He'd turn the wrecks over to Bert for demolition."

Vida shuddered. "I'm so glad Bert finally put up that big fence around the wrecking yard on the other side of the railroad tracks. Until then, the property was a terrible eyesore."

"Vida," Mitch said in his droll manner, "do yourself a favor and don't visit Detroit. If you want to ogle vehicle wreckage, including on the city streets, that's your destination. I haven't seen Bert's pile of junk, but it has to look like the Garden of Eden by comparison."

Vida sat up straight. "I'd never dream of going to Detroit. I'm not much of a traveler. If you've lived your entire life in Alpine as I have, there's very little in the rest of the world to match its scenic beauty."

"This is beautiful country, all right," Mitch agreed. "My wife and I are anxious to see more of it."

Leo couldn't resist needling my House & Home editor. "Wait until the low-hanging gray rain clouds lift," he said to Mitch. "It usually happens at least one more time in October before the long wait till May. Oh, and by the way, if you get homesick for Detroit, take a drive out on the Burl Creek Road. A lot of the folks who live there decorate their gardens with rusted-out DeSotos, F-Series Ford pickups circa 1958, and the much rarer remnants of a Model A chassis."

Vida glared at Leo. "That is so unfair! Granted, some people don't enjoy gardening and tend to be slothful by nature. But I would hardly compare Alpine to Detroit. Parts of your old stomping ground in Los Angeles might be a more apt analogy."

"True enough, Duchess," Leo admitted with his off-center grin. "On the other hand, Alpine doesn't have Beverly Hills or Bel Air."

Before Vida could respond, her phone rang. She picked it up on the first ring. "Vida Runkel here," she said in her usual brisk manner. "Slow down, please," she urged after a pause. "I can't understand you."

Leo, Mitch, and I remained silent, watching Vida, who was now holding up one finger to signal she was receiving news of interest to the rest of us. "That's wonderful, Rick," she said at last. "Tell Ginny the main thing is that the baby is healthy. Besides, he'll have hand-me-downs from his two brothers."

"Another boy," I murmured. "Let's hope Ginny stops griping about that by the time she comes back to work."

"Don't count on it," Leo said under his breath.

Vida congratulated Rick one last time and hung up. "A boy, eight pounds, four ounces, twenty inches long, born at eleven-eighteen, delivered by Dr. Sung." She glanced at her watch. "Twenty minutes ago. It was good of Rick to call me first, though he sounded rather muddled."

"Have they named him?" I inquired.

Vida shook her head. "Ginny refused to consider a boy's name this time, being so sure that she was having a girl. Personally, I think it's just as well. I had three girls, which made raising them much simpler. The same should be true of bringing up boys. If anything, I believe boys must be comparatively easy. Girls tend to be moody and unpredictable. If Ginny had a girl, the poor child might become unbearably spoiled."

The word *spoiled* automatically conjured up a vision of Vida's grandson, Roger. When it came to him, Vida had a maddening blind spot. He was twenty-three, taking—and quitting—an occasional class at the community college. His attitude toward work followed the same pattern. Get hired, get fired—or simply not show up. Vida, of course, always blamed the teachers, the employers, or a world that didn't appreciate Roger's fine qualities. I changed the subject.

"Mitch," I said, "I'm puzzled by something in these witness accounts. Have you talked to Fred Engelman?"

"No," Mitch replied. "He lives in a camper somewhere along the Icicle Creek Road. I called him twice, but he doesn't have an answering device. I'll try to catch him at Blackwell

Timber. He's the one who used to get into fights all the time, right?"

I nodded. "That's why it seems odd that he apparently wasn't involved in this one. Maybe he was on his best behavior because it was his ex-wife's birthday."

"What about Berentsen's girlfriend with the goofy name?" Mitch asked. "Should I talk to her or is it worth a trip to . . . Snohomish? And what's with this *mish* at the end of so many local place names?"

"The *mish*," I explained, "is a Native American name around here for 'river,' as in Snohomish, Skykomish, Stillaguamish, Duwamish, and so forth. Hold off interviewing Jica Weaver. The sheriff should talk to her first. In fact, I'm going to stop by his office on my way to lunch and see if he's recovered from whatever he was doing last night."

I tried to keep my tone neutral. Obviously, I failed. Vida gave me a sharp look. "With Delphine?"

To save face, I shrugged. "Whoever."

Vida didn't quite manage to conceal a smirk, but turned to her keyboard. "It's never too soon to suggest items for 'Scene,' " she reminded us. "I *will* use Rick's minor car mishap, but without names. Nervous fathers-to-be have a certain charm. As usual, I'll put the baby's birth on my page. I trust that the child will have a name by press time."

"Say," I said, having a sudden thought, "getting back to Jica Weaver, did any of you listen to KSKY this morning?"

"I did," Leo replied. "I wanted to check on a co-op ad we did with them for the Columbus Day sale at Stuart's Sight and Sound. Why?"

"Jica Weaver was going to the station last night to proclaim Berentsen's innocence. Maybe Fleetwood wasn't there or he felt like I did about going public with something as flimsy as a girlfriend's opinion."

"I'll ask him," Leo said. "I'm going to KSKY later." He glanced at Vida. "A cooking store in Monroe wants to be one of your sponsors. You don't want your *real* employer to lose out on that, Duchess."

"Certainly not," Vida asserted. "A cooking store." Her tone turned musing. "My, my, that's good news." In an instant, she whipped off her glasses to glare at Leo. "Why didn't you tell me this before?"

"I didn't know it until a few minutes ago," Leo said. "Spence sent me an FYI e-mail. You got one, too."

"Oh." Taken aback, Vida blinked rapidly. Having held out for a long time on using a computer, she often forgot that it had uses beyond typing up news copy.

"That's some kind of bright spot," I said. "I don't see how Fleetwood could turn us down." I looked at Vida, who had put her glasses back on. "If he did, you could threaten to quit and KSKY's ratings would plummet."

"Perhaps," Vida said with an inclination of her head. "I try to bring a certain amount of local lore and neighborliness to my program."

Vida's Cupboard had been an instant hit when she began her fifteen-minute weekly broadcast three years earlier. It usually aired live on Wednesdays, but this week she'd insisted that Spence move the show to Tuesday because of the conflict with the Presbyterian Harvest Home supper. It was a testimonial to her popularity that Mr. Radio had complied. It also gave her the opportunity to remind her brethren about the potluck. When I first learned of the original offer for Vida to do the program, I'd had qualms, but my House & Home editor had vowed never to use material better suited to the *Advocate*. Naturally, she'd kept her word. The show featured interviews with local residents, helpful hints on gardening, and reminders of upcoming events in Alpine. The irony of the cooking store advertisement didn't elude me. Although Vida ran recipes and other food-related advice on her page, she never applied any of the information to herself, relying instead on her family's time-honored concoctions and methods. Unfortunately, her ancestors were reputed to have been the worst cooks in Skykomish County's history. If the Detroit bar actually served gopher as Mitch claimed, it probably wouldn't taste worse than most of Vida's culinary efforts.

Glancing at the clock, I noticed it was going on twelve. "I'm heading out to check in with the sheriff," I said, ignoring what I figured was Vida's intrigued expression. "I'm running out of ways to write another editorial begging the state to do something about the horrendous accidents on Highway 2. Maybe the fresh air will inspire me."

I thought I heard Vida snicker.

THAT FRESH AIR HAD TURNED CHILLY WHEN I STARTED DOWN Front Street. Maybe we were due for an early frost. Approaching Parker's Pharmacy, I suddenly remembered that I had to replenish my stock of Band-Aids, Kleenex, and mouthwash. Trying to recall if I needed anything else, I didn't pay attention as I crossed the well-worn blue and white hexagonal tiles leading inside the store. The door flew open and almost hit me.

"Watch it!" Patti Marsh shouted. "Oh," she said, "it's you."

Her greeting lacked warmth, but that was no surprise. We had a history. "Hello, Patti," I said.

"Hello." She shot me a hostile look. "I hear the sheriff's seeing Delphine Corson."

"I heard that, too," I said, forcing a smile. "I guess she figures Gus Swanson and his wife are only temporarily estranged. Or maybe Delphine's playing the field after Spike Canby dumped her."

"That was a while ago," Patti pointed out, both of us stepping aside for a young woman pushing a baby in an elaborate stroller that Averill Fairbanks might have mistaken for an alien space ship. "Delphine has kept her looks," she added.

"Where does she keep them?" I retorted, and immediately wished I'd kept my big mouth shut.

Patti, however, seemed to find my remark amusing. I figured it wasn't because of my flippant response, but that she felt she'd succeeded in her attempt to rile me. "Delphine has a way with men," Patti said. "Gus and his wife may not be divorcing, but he certainly acts like he's crazy about her. Last Saturday, she was showing off a very pretty Judith Ripka bracelet he'd given her."

"Nice," I said, trying to lighten my tone. "A man dating a florist can't send flowers." I refrained from saying that he shouldn't give his girlfriend candy when she was carrying an extra twenty-five pounds.

"I suppose," Patti said. "Got to run. Jack and I are going to dinner at Le Gourmand tonight and I have an appointment with Stella for a foil job." She touched her short hair, which was a different shade—or shades—of blond every time I saw her. Luckily, our meetings were infrequent.

Inside the drugstore, I grabbed a forest-green basket and headed down the aisle that featured Band-Aids and a raft of other wound care products. I was trying to find the Quick Stop variety when something Patti had said came to mind. She'd mentioned seeing Delphine on Saturday. Where and when? I wondered. To my knowledge, Patti Marsh and Delphine Corson weren't close. I had no idea what Delphine's bracelet looked like, but I knew that Judith Ripka items weren't cheap. Few women—at least in Alpine—would wear anything that expensive and elegant during the day. If Delphine was showing off her new bauble, what better way to do it than in a social setting? Pricey designer jewelry seemed out of place at the Icicle Creek Tavern. But that didn't mean Delphine hadn't worn it anyway.

I now had a question for Milo that had nothing to do with asking him if he'd jumped in the sack with the local florist. That was none of my business. Nor did I want to know.

Strange how even in middle age we mortals can still fool ourselves.

SIX

"WHY," I DEMANDED EVEN BEFORE I SAT DOWN IN MILO'S visitor's chair, "didn't you mention that Jack Blackwell and Patti Marsh were at the Icicle Creek Tavern Saturday night?"

Milo, looking a bit sleepy, scowled. "Because they weren't. What's with you?"

I sat down. "You're sure about that?"

"Christ!" Milo snatched up his pack of cigarettes. "Yes, I'm sure. You saw the witness list. Hell, if I thought I could add that bastard Blackwell to it, I'd have done it. In fact, I'd put him at the top."

If there was no love lost between Patti and me, there was plenty of hostility between the sheriff and the owner of Blackwell Timber. Years ago, when the sheriff's job was still an elected position, Jack had run against Milo. The two had never gotten along, and when a murder investigation involved Patti's former son-in-law, Jack hadn't liked the way Milo handled the case. The two men had almost come to blows at Mugs Ahoy. The voters had reelected Milo by a wide margin, but Jack and his ego had neither forgiven nor forgotten.

"I ran into Patti Marsh at Parker's," I explained while Milo lighted his cigarette. "She got . . ." I hesitated, not wanting to admit that Patti's original intention in bringing up Delphine's name had involved annoying me. "She told me that Delphine had an expensive designer bracelet that Gus Swanson had given her. Patti saw it on Saturday."

Milo shrugged. "So?"

"So where did Patti run into Delphine?"

"How the hell do I know? The beauty parlor? The grocery store? At the corner of Sixth and Front?" He took a second puff on his cigarette and regarded me with skeptical hazel eyes. "Don't go trolling where you know damned well there aren't any trout. You know I hate guesswork."

I did know, and felt a little foolish for dumping speculations in the sheriff's lap. "Okay. Have you talked to Jica Weaver?"

"Heeka?" Milo's long face looked puzzled. "You mean Berentsen's girlfriend? Dwight Gould went to Snohomish to interview her this morning. He's not back yet." He stopped to sip coffee from his NRA mug. "How'd you hear about her?"

"I'm a reporter, in case you've forgotten. She came to me. And Jica's name is pronounced the way I said it, like José or Juan. She stopped by the office to insist that Clive Berentsen's innocent. When I told her I couldn't print that—at least not now—she went off to see Spencer Fleetwood at KSKY."

"Dwight won't swallow that." Milo looked dour. "He'd like to put Blackwell's name on the suspect list, too. Dwight's never gotten over his ex-wife Kay dumping him for Jack Blackwell."

"Kay and Jack were married for only about ten minutes, as I recall," I said. "That was before my time, but didn't she leave him for another guy and move to Everett?"

"Yeah, and after a couple of years she divorced him and

married somebody else. Dwight doesn't know where she is, and what's more he doesn't give a damn. It's no wonder he's stayed single all these years. It's a good thing he and Kay never had kids. That's the tough part when marriages break up, with the wife getting the better custody deal."

The sheriff spoke from experience. His own wife had left him for another man while their children were still in their teens. Old Mulehide, as he called Tricia, had remarried and moved to Bellevue across the lake from Seattle. Milo had seen less and less of his kids as the years went by. Though he sometimes expressed regret, I wondered if, in fact, he was relieved. The sheriff had enough mayhem, mischief, and even murder on his plate without adding a big serving of typical parental woes.

I tipped my head to one side. "Are you feeling okay? You look a little peaked."

Milo shot me a sour glance. "I'm fine. I don't give a damn about fancy labels and sniffing corks and all that ritzy crap. I don't like wine and it gives me heartburn. Did you forget I don't have a gallbladder?"

"Hardly. Though sometimes I think *you* forget," I said. "I won't lecture you, though. I'm not fond of wine, either. I assume Delphine was paying."

"If she wasn't, why would I drink that sour stuff?"

"So it was a bribe," I said, making an attempt at nonchalance.

"I guess." Milo puffed, exhaled and sipped. "Dumb idea. She knows you can't keep secrets in this town."

I tried to phrase my question in a detached, professional manner. "Then why did she ask you to dinner? Did Delphine want to talk about what happened Saturday at the ICT?"

"She's already given a statement. Delphine and Gus were at a table where they couldn't see much." Milo flipped through a yellow legal-size tablet. "Sam sketched the layout of the tavern. Delphine and Gus were here," he said, shoving the floor plan at me and pointing his finger. "The pool table is over there beyond the bar," he went on. "They probably couldn't see much from their table, unless the fight spilled out into the customer section. Delphine said she could hear yelling and cussing and a big commotion, but not what actually happened. Gus backed her up with basically the same kind of statement except for one thing. He added that there was a brief lull—his word—just before everybody started yelling again."

"Did anyone else mention that?"

"Not so far. Frankly, the eyewitness statements are a mishmash." Milo leaned back in his chair. "What else would you expect from a bunch of people who were at least semi-drunk?"

I nodded. "Leo and I are going there tonight to take a look at the place. I haven't been there in years, not since . . ." I clamped my lips shut.

"Don't remind me," Milo said, turning the tablet around so he could see it. Suddenly, he frowned. "You and Leo? I thought the new guy was covering this case."

"He is," I said, starting to get up. "But I want to refresh my memory."

"With Leo?"

It dawned on me that without intending to, I'd turned the tables on Milo. Or, given the off-and-on nature of our relationship, maybe *small snack trays* would be more apt than *tables*.

"I've got to make sure there aren't any glitches this time around," I said. "I trust Mitch because he's experienced, but he's still not used to small towns. Leo offered to take me there because Spike Canby is an advertiser. He got mad at us for suggesting in his ad that customers went there to get killed."

"Bullshit," Milo declared. "Spike's ad is the size of a postage stamp."

"That's the other thing." I winced slightly as I picked up my heavy handbag from the floor. "Leo's coaxing Spike into buying more space."

"He's a tight bastard. Good luck with that." He gestured at my handbag. "What do you women carry around in those satchels? Shoes? Or barbells?"

"The older we get, the more stuff we need to keep from looking like hags. I've got surgical instruments in here so I can do my own face-lift."

Milo regarded me with a faint frown. "Your face looks fine to me."

"Thanks. Your eyes must be going."

"Hey," he said as I turned toward the door, "where are you heading?"

I turned around. "To Pie-In-The-Sky for a sandwich. Why?"

"They've got soup there. Want to pick up a bowl of chicken noodle for me? With those good crackers? Oh, and a piece of blackberry pie."

"Sure," I said. "See you in a bit."

Emma Lord, Nursemaid to the Sheriff, I thought, trudging past the post office and the highway department to the Alpine Mall. *Emma the Sap.* At the corner of Front and Alpine Way, I stopped for one of the town's two traffic lights. Across the street, I could see Old Mill Park with its statue of the town founder, Carl Clemans, and the original mill that had been turned into a museum. The maple, mountain ash, and cottonwood trees had turned from gold to bronze. I gazed to my right, looking up at Mount Baldy. Hardly any snow remained, unusual for the fifty-two-hundred-foot peak. Summer had been too dry and too hot. There had been several forest fires, though thankfully not near Alpine. The ski industry would be in peril if we didn't get heavy snow this coming winter. *Drought* was almost a foreign word to the residents of western Washington, but now it was becoming part of our daily vocabulary. I couldn't write editorials begging Mother Nature to send us rain, but I'd done a couple in August and September about conserving water and electricity. Averill Fairbanks had written me a letter insisting that Alien Forces from Venus had built a shield around the earth and had figured out a way to make our planet dry up so that the Venusians—whom he described as looking like grasshoppers—could use all the water for themselves. The concept of grasshoppers in a bathtub eluded me, but I'd printed the letter on the editorial page because it was signed and not libelous. Except, of course, to the Venusians, who weren't subscribers.

As usual, the line at the pie and sandwich shop was long. I stepped behind Marje Blatt, Vida's niece and the receptionist at Alpine's medical clinic. Marje wore a starched white uniform, which she and Doc Dewey preferred to the casual attire that often made medical practitioners indistinguishable from the window-washing crew. She was a few inches shorter than Vida, but stood straight as a phone pole.

I tapped her shoulder. "Hi, Marje."

She turned slowly, bright blue eyes studying me as if she were trying to remember if she'd seen me on a WANTED poster. "Hello, Emma," she said. "Aren't you overdue for your annual checkup?"

Brisk and business-like as usual, I thought. "I'll call in the next few days," I said. We both knew that I'd forget.

"I'll send a reminder."

"Thanks." We each moved up a space. "I'll get a flu shot, too."

"Wait until November," Marje advised.

I realized I hadn't seen her for several weeks. Her piquant face was pale, and her short auburn hair looked dull. As we stepped closer to the counter, I wondered if the Icicle Creek Tavern tragedy had brought back some heartbreaking memories. Marje had been engaged to a young man who'd spent his final hours at the same site. But standing in line at Pie-In-The-Sky wasn't the right place for intimate conversation.

Ten minutes later, I was back in the sheriff's office. "You owe me eight dollars and sixty-five cents," I said, setting Milo's soup, crackers, and pie on his desk. "Unlike Delphine, I refuse to bribe you."

"Where's my coffee?"

"You didn't ask. What's wrong with your coffee here?"

"The coffeemaker broke," Milo replied. "Lori's over at Harvey's Hardware buying a new one."

"Wait until she makes it," I said testily. "Unlike her predecessors, Lori can brew liquid that tastes more like coffee than sink sludge."

Milo dug into his pocket. "Here," he said, tossing a ten-dollar bill at me. "Keep the change."

"Gee, thanks." I picked up the money and put it in my wallet. "I'll see you later."

"You aren't eating here?"

"I wasn't going to. I thought you wanted to enjoy the misery of your own company. Why do you ask?"

"Got a call from the Everett ME a few minutes ago," Milo explained, removing the lid from his bowl of chicken noodle soup. An enticing plume of steam rose up, briefly overcoming the usual stale smell of cigarettes. The sheriff picked up the plastic soup spoon and scowled. "Why can't they give you a *real* spoon? These damned things are too flimsy."

"Use a straw," I said, deciding I might as well eat my turkey sandwich and chips while I heard what Milo had to say. "Is the final autopsy in?"

"No. It probably won't be until Monday or Tuesday." He paused to break up some crackers and drop them in the bowl. "Too many people in SnoCo these days. Why don't they all move to the other side of the mountains and croak over there?"

"Good question," I remarked. "So why did the ME call?"

Milo waited until he finished his first taste of soup. "Good stuff." He downed another mouthful. "It's the pool cue. According to forensics, the one we sent to Everett isn't the one that killed Alvin De Muth."

I used a napkin to wipe off some mayo that I'd gotten on my hand. "Are you sure you sent the right one? You've got eyewitnesses, and Clive Berentsen doesn't deny he whacked De Muth."

The sheriff was still downing his soup and crackers, but ogling the slice of blackberry pie. "When I left the tavern, I made sure we took all of the pool cues, a total of nine. The Hansons and the Borgs were using their cues in the game. After Clive and De Muth started going at it, Clive grabbed one of the other cues from the rack. None of them test out as the weapon."

"I don't know much about pool cues," I admitted, "but could their surface be so smooth that any kind of trace wouldn't show up?"

"SnoCo's high tech gizmos should've found something," Milo said. "We're not talking top of the line or even matching cues, but Spike's are all made of maple. Most of them are fairly worn and nicked up."

I had no suggestions. I sat quietly for a moment, watching the sheriff pick up the soup bowl and drain it. "Gee," I said, "did you do that with your vichyssoise at dinner in Monroe last night?"

"My what?" Milo asked, wiping his chin. "Back off. What should I do? Pour the broth into my empty coffee mug?"

I smiled. "Your table manners are fine. Do you have a theory?"

"You know I hate theories." Milo took a bite of pie. "Mmm. Damned good." He took another bite, chewed slowly, and regarded me with eyes that could intimidate a suspect and, at the same time, exude integrity. "You ever play pool?"

"Way back when," I said. "High school, maybe college. I was terrible at it. Why?"

"Those cues weigh anywhere from sixteen to twenty-one ounces. Oh, some of the expensive ones weigh more, but Spike Canby buys on the cheap. About half of his cues were passed on from the Post family. The cues are long and slender. I don't have a so-called 'theory,' but I wonder how you could kill somebody with a pool cue, especially in a confined area. Depending on how you swung it, the damned thing might break."

"Doc Dewey's initial cause of death was a blow to the head," I reminded Milo. "Did you ask the ME about it?"

The sheriff's expression was wry. "Most MEs, including this one—Colin Knapp, fairly new guy over in Everett—can be damned cagey until all the final results are in. Knapp's competent from what I hear, but he's kind of a wiseass. He told me you could kill somebody with a head of cabbage if you smacked him a certain way."

"Maybe you should've designated the kitchen as a crime scene."

"I've thought about doing that at Vida's the few times I've eaten there." Milo looked beyond me as someone tapped at the door. "Yeah?"

Lori Cobb, the sheriff's receptionist, poked her head in. "Coffee's on," she said. "Hi, Emma. You want some, too? It'll be about ten, twelve minutes, according to the directions."

"No thanks," I replied. "I'm heading back to the *Advocate*."

Lori closed the door. It was going on one o'clock and I decided to save the other half of the large turkey sandwich for dinner. Or maybe a midafternoon snack. "How's the prisoner?"

"Berentsen?" Milo shook his head. "Depressed. Upset. Mad at himself and the rest of the world."

I put my lunch leftovers into the large paper bag provided by the sandwich and pie shop. "No plea bargain request from Clive's lawyer?"

"Not yet. I haven't heard anything from her since the arraignment. Say," Milo said suddenly as I picked up my handbag, "does Marisa Foxx know her? You and Marisa are kind of chummy these days, right?"

"Yes. It took us long enough, though. We have a lot in common. I played my first poker game with her group a couple of weeks ago. I lost twenty-eight dollars."

"Maybe you can't afford to hang out with those rich lawyers." Milo's tone was droll.

"They're not all lawyers," I explained. "There's a couple of college teachers, an engineer, an architect, and a dot-com retiree from Sultan. The mix changes because of everybody's busy schedule. Tonight I'm playing bridge. I'm not so rusty at that game."

Milo got up from his chair and stretched. "God, I feel better. Must have been the pie." He shook himself like a dog coming out of a bath. "If you see Marisa, ask her if she knows this Esther Brant from Everett."

"I will," I promised, "but we don't play poker again until next week." I opened the door and was face-to-face with Jack Mullins. He looked faintly startled. "I'm just leaving," I told him.

Jack, who's usually the most outgoing of Milo's deputies, ignored me. "Bad wreck on Highway 2," he announced from the threshold. "A panel truck took out a car and went into the Skykomish River. Probable fatalities. Sam's on his way and I'm going, too."

"I'll come," Milo said, grabbing his hat and jacket. "We'll take the Grand Cherokee."

Both men rushed off. I walked into the reception area where Lori was on one phone and Dustin Fong on the other. I could hear the sirens and, after long practice, recognized the ambulance, the medic van, and the fire engine, all heading for Alpine Way and the green truss bridge over the Sky. I decided to wait for Lori and Dustin to hang up so I could find out where the accident had occurred and send Mitch Laskey to take pictures.

Dustin was the first to disconnect. "Did you hear Jack?" he asked, maintaining his usual calm and good manners under duress. "It sounds bad. That's four accidents involving trucks since Labor Day between Index and Alpine, two of them with eighteen-wheelers. I don't know why big rigs go over Stevens Pass. They're better off taking I-90 Snoqualmie, even if it's out of their way."

Lori had also finished her phone conversation. "At least it's not raining or snowing. I wonder what happened?"

"Where did it happen?" I asked.

"Just past the ranger station," Dustin replied. "In fact, one of the forest service people called it in. The truck was heading west, just beyond the Skykomish deli."

"Got it," I said. "Thanks."

As soon as I reached the sidewalk, I called Mitch on my cell.

"I'm all over it," he said. "I was just coming back from lunch when I heard the sirens. I'm crossing the bridge right now. Later."

I hurried back to the office. It seemed strange to find the reception desk vacant. Only Leo was in the newsroom, and he was about to leave. "Bad accident, I hear," he said, shrugging into his brown tweed sport coat. "I'm off to see the Wizard of the Airwaves. Assuming Fleetwood hasn't raced to the wreckage to do a remote broadcast."

"Don't forget to ask him about Jica Weaver," I said.

"Can't forget that name," Leo responded as he went out the door.

Before I could reach my office, Kip breezed in from the back shop. "Ta-da!" he exclaimed in an unusual show of exuberance. "We're online!"

"We're what?"

"You know the last couple of computer expenses I asked for?"

"Sort of." Despite the goatee he'd grown in the past year, Kip's face was still boyishly excited. "And?"

"*The Alpine Advocate* is up and running on the Internet." He beamed at me. "Want a look?"

"Yes, sure." I let him lead the way into my cubbyhole. After a couple of seconds he'd brought up our brand-new website. I was flabbergasted. "This is what you were talking about when you asked me to pay for all the high-tech stuff?"

Kip nodded enthusiastically. "You'd never let me explain what it was for, so I went ahead and did it." He suddenly looked uneasy. "Are you mad at me?"

"No!" I laughed and hugged him. "I should've let you do this a long time ago. I'm almost as bad as Vida about dragging my feet into the twenty-first century. I know that other dailies and weeklies have sites, including *The Monroe Monitor* and *The Snohomish Tribune*. We can get extra advertising, right?"

"Sure," Kip said. "I showed it to Leo a few minutes ago. He thinks it's great. But the best part—well, just as big a deal—is that we can print news when it happens on the site."

"We can?" I said, reverting to my usual low-tech, no-tech self.

"That's right." He moved the cursor to a heading that read BREAKING NEWS. "We go to this and write up what's just happened. Granted, it probably won't beat KSKY most of the time, but you'll be able to stop beating yourself up when there's big news before pub day."

I wanted to make sure I knew what Kip meant. "So if this accident is really bad, we can put it on the site now?"

Kip looked blank. "What accident?"

"A truck and another vehicle near the ranger station," I replied. "You didn't hear the sirens?"

Kip shook his head. "No. It's hard to hear stuff in the back shop. That part of the building seems more insulated. Plus I was pretty focused on finishing this by the time you got back from lunch."

I understood. When Kip was doing his computer thing, he retreated into a world where other humans could not follow, especially a cyberphobe like me.

I got back to concepts I understood, namely news reporting. "But can we put the accident on this site?"

"We could," Kip replied. "We *can*, I mean, but until everybody knows we have a website, nobody's going to check it out. We'll run the announcement in the next edition, then we can start with the other functions. Besides, there are a couple of bugs I want to work out between now and then."

"Okay. That sounds fine. I assume Leo will be telling our advertisers about this in the meantime."

Kip nodded. "You bet. He's going to e-mail them this afternoon."

"Good." I felt stupid. "What would I do without you? Why didn't you make me listen?"

"Well . . ." Kip lowered his eyes. "You've been through a lot lately." He paused. "Those people who wanted to buy the paper and your . . . fiancé's kids showing up. Leo getting shot. And that weirdo dude who took Scott Chamoud's place as a reporter. All that was really rough on you."

"Yes," I agreed. "It was rough on all of us."

"You had the worst of it, though," Kip said in one of his rare moments of candor. "Anyway," he went on, apparently embarrassed by being so open, "I've been thinking about the website for the last year or two, but I'm not good with the design part. I had to talk to some of the other people who'd set up newspapers online and pick their brains. That helped, but it was Chili who actually pulled it all together. My wife's got some artistic talent. In fact, since we had our baby, she's thinking of writing and illustrating a children's book. I think she did a pretty good job on the *Advocate,* don't you?"

"Oh, yes! I especially like the photo of the trees and Mount Baldy at the top above our logo. Who took that?"

"Buddy Bayard," Kip replied. "I paid him out of the production budget. That's okay, isn't it?"

"Definitely." Buddy and his wife, Roseanna, owned a photography studio. Until we were able to update our equipment, we'd had Buddy do all of the *Advocate*'s photo work. He and Roseanna hadn't been happy when we pulled our business, but in recent months we'd used some of his stock photos and also asked him to provide pictures for a couple of special sections. He'd even done some news photography during the interim after I fired our previous reporter and before I hired Mitch.

"We can use more of his scenic stuff online," Kip suggested. "If you look at some of the other newspaper sites, many of them are cluttered and not just with advertising." He stopped and looked out into the newsroom. "Hey, Mrs. Runkel, want to see our new gig?"

Our House & Home editor had just returned from lunch and was looking vexed. "New gig?" she inquired, coming into my office. "What on earth do you mean?"

Kip stepped aside. "Take a look."

Vida leaned down to study the screen. "Well now. That's quite nice. We can change this all the time?"

"Yep," Kip said. "Post news, change ads, art, whatever. We've gone modern, Mrs. Runkel." Having known Vida since childhood, somehow Kip could never call her by her first name, a habit that she never discouraged.

"My, yes." Vida's voice was musing. "I wonder now . . . is this where I should start my advice column?"

"You're going to do an advice column?" Kip asked in surprise.

Vida glanced at me. "We've discussed it, haven't we, Emma? Is the timing right?"

I had to think about it. "Maybe," I hedged. "If you do, it might be better to run it in the paper."

"If I have room," Vida countered. "That's often a problem. I wouldn't want to shortchange my responses to . . ." She stopped and her ears seemed to prick up like a cat's. "The sirens again. Dear me, that sounds like something very bad." Turning swiftly, she headed into the newsroom and out to the front office.

I thanked Kip again and followed Vida, who was standing in the open doorway looking out onto Front Street. "A big wreck," I explained, giving her a quick rundown of what I knew.

"I heard the sirens as I was finishing lunch with Maud Dodd," Vida said. "That was the ambulance, wasn't it? It didn't turn at the main intersection so it must be headed for the hospital on Pine Street."

We waited a few seconds. The siren stopped, indicating that

Vida was probably right. I was about to speak when I heard a second siren. "The medic van," I murmured. "More than one injury, and maybe a fatality."

Vida shook her head in dismay. "That short stretch between Index and Alpine has so many narrow shoulders and sharp curves. Something must be done by the state highway department."

"You know I've written several editorials urging the state to widen the road," I said. "It's not just speeding or drivers trying to pass other vehicles when the visibility is poor, but they crash into trees and rocks and whatever else is too close to the highway."

"So treacherous," Vida murmured. "Not to mention 522 on the other side of Monroe. There's a reason it's called 'the Highway of Death.'" She shuddered. "The medic van sounds as if it's going to the hospital, too. Goodness, I hope no one we know is involved."

Once again, the siren stopped nearby. Several pedestrians had gathered along Front Street and a few others had come out of the various businesses, including the Venison Inn. One of them was Bunky Smythe, a recent addition to the USDA Forest Service. He was neither gawking nor speculating, but rushing to his official van.

I ran after him. By the time I'd covered the half-block between our office and the Venison Inn, Bunky was behind the wheel.

"What's happening?" I yelled at him.

He swiveled to look at me and hesitated. We'd only met twice since he'd been assigned to the area in the early summer. "Ms. Lord?" he called and saw me nod. "A couple of people got killed right by the ranger station. Got to go." He pulled out into traffic as I stepped back.

Vida had followed me. Her expression was grim. "Two dead?"

"That's what Bunky said."

"They don't take dead people to hospitals." She hurried to her Buick, which was parked next to my Honda. "I'm going to find out who's being admitted."

I started to say that Mitch would know, but stopped. There was no way short of physical force to keep Vida from her quest. Mitch—like the rest of us—would have to get used to our House & Home editor occasionally treading on toes.

I finished my turkey sandwich and tried to figure out the topic of my next editorial. Another Highway 2 improvement piece was timely, but none of the other rational arguments I'd used so far had done much to wring money out of the state's budget. I culled through my file of possible subjects, but remained uninspired. After over a half-hour of futility, Mitch finally returned. He came straight into my cubbyhole, somber, but in control. "That was ugly," he said, slumping into one of my visitors' chairs. "The panel truck lost control when the driver tried to pass a motorcyclist, crossed into the other lane and wiped out a sedan with four passengers. The truck went over the bank and into the river. Two dead, four injured."

"Damn," I said softly. "Anybody local involved?"

Mitch was holding his cell phone, a high-tech device that he could use as a computer, a DVD player, a camera, and possibly a uranium detector for all I knew. "Passengers in the sedan were four older people from Wenatchee apparently heading home. Driver Eugene Ferguson and passenger Helena Ferguson, husband and wife. Helena died immediately on impact, Eugene was pronounced dead before they could get him into the ambulance. The other couple, James and Erna Willis, have been taken to the hospital here. Their condition is critical. The motorcyclist, Nathan Barfield, twenty-six, from Monroe, was treated and released."

I held up a hand. "How did he get off so easily?"

A faint smile played on Mitch's lips. "He wasn't directly involved, but when he heard the crash, he turned around and went off the road. He was wearing a helmet and landed in the dirt."

"What about the truck driver?"

Mitch grew solemn again. "This one you might know. Michael O'Toole of Alpine, twenty-four, multiple injuries, also critical condition, taken to the hospital in Monroe. He was driving an older panel truck. It was empty, so apparently he was going someplace to pick up an order."

It took a few seconds for the name to register. "Mike O'Toole!" I finally exclaimed. "He's one of Buzzy and Laura O'Toole's sons. You may know Buzzy—he's the produce manager at Jake and Betsy O'Toole's Grocery Basket. Buzzy and Jake are brothers."

Mitch shook his head. "Don't think so. Brenda usually does our grocery shopping. You must know the whole family."

"Yes." The news was unsettling. Buzzy and Laura had gone through some rough patches before Jake finally brought his brother into the business. I didn't remember much about their children but vaguely recalled that Mike had failed his first driver's test. "Has the sheriff informed Mike's parents?"

Mitch shook his head. "I don't know. I did what I needed to do and got the hell out of there. Traffic backed up in both directions. I wasn't sure I *could* get back to town, but I finally made it."

"Good." I said. "Vida's at the hospital. She may not hear about Mike O'Toole if he was taken to Monroe."

Mitch's smile was more genuine this time. "Wild horses couldn't keep her away, I suppose."

I didn't argue. Standing by Leo's vacant desk, I reflected on the conflict between professional obligations and personal relationships. Jake and Betsy O'Toole were fellow parishioners and longtime acquaintances, if not close friends. I didn't know Buzzy and Laura nearly as well. In any event, they were Mike's parents and would probably rush to their son's side at Valley General Hospital in Monroe. Jake and Betsy might remain in Alpine, holding down the fort at the store. I didn't want to intrude, but it occurred to me that with the *Advocate* going online, I had to change my way of thinking about news gathering. I was about to operate in a new mode, without the luxury or the burden of waiting until deadline approached.

Mitch had poured himself a mug of coffee and sat down at his desk. "You look worried." He paused. "Sorry, none of my business."

I smiled faintly. "This isn't Detroit, it's Alpine. I may be the editor and publisher, but there's not much difference in rank on this staff."

Mitch nodded, tugging at one of his long earlobes, a habit I'd begun to notice when he appeared to be pondering something. "Then I'll ask the obvious. This Mike must be in a bad way or they wouldn't have taken him to a bigger hospital, right?"

"That's probably true," I agreed. "Or, because of the other two injured parties, the decision might've been made because Doc Dewey and Dr. Sung couldn't handle more than two emergency cases."

"Maybe." He gazed at the screen of his cell phone, poked something on it and turned to his computer monitor. "I asked one of the medics—Amundson?" He saw me nod. "I asked him if this O'Toole kid was an experienced driver. Amundson didn't know."

"Frankly, I don't know what the O'Toole boys do for a living other than working as courtesy clerks at the Grocery Basket. Maybe he was making a produce run for his dad at the store."

"Want me to check it out?" Mitch asked.

I paused. "Yes." My reporter's inquiry would be strictly business, more discreet than if I pried into the O'Tooles' private life.

"I'll go in person," Mitch said, getting up and grabbing his jacket.

Before he could reach the door, Vida tromped into the newsroom. "Well now!" she exclaimed, fists on hips and black patent-leather handbag dangling from one wrist. "I ran into my nephew Billy at the hospital. He'd gone there to check on the Wenatchee couple who were involved in the accident." She took a deep breath. "It seems that Mike O'Toole was driving that produce truck because any pre-weekend run was usually made by Clive Berentsen. Doesn't that beat all?"

SEVEN

"MIKE O'TOOLE'S A TRUCK DRIVER?" I EXCLAIMED AFTER taking in Vida's announcement. "What do you mean by 'pre-weekend run'? I thought most of the Grocery Basket's deliveries were made by truckers outside the area."

"They are," Vida said, taking off her coat and sitting down at her desk. "But surely you know that the O'Tooles have a truck they use when they run out of certain items and have to restock, especially in the winter when Stevens Pass is closed to drivers from the eastern side of the mountains. In this case, the store had run out of pumpkins and other gourds. Apparently, half the town is getting ready early for Halloween."

In my mind's eye, I pictured a white truck with an overflowing wicker grocery basket painted on the cab's doors. "Of course," I said. "I've seen it parked behind the store a zillion times. It's old. I suppose I thought it was a bit of nostalgia, or maybe for local customer deliveries."

"It *is* old," Vida replied. "It belonged to Jake and Buzzy's father, Millard, who started the store years ago. But the truck's still used and well maintained. I believe it's some kind of Dodge."

Mitch nodded. "It was a 1968 Dodge Fargo A100. As a guy from the Motor City, I can tell you that if the truck's been kept up, it's worth at least five grand. Or was, until it went in the river."

Vida leaned forward, her gray eyes suddenly cold as she stared at Mitch. "Trucks can be replaced. Children cannot. Consider how the O'Tooles must feel right now."

Mitch's own gaze didn't waver. "I'd rather not." He turned away and studied his computer monitor.

Vida shot me a questioning look. I shrugged and went into my cubbyhole. Five minutes later, Leo returned.

"Fleetwood had taken off for the accident site before I could get to the station," Leo said, standing in the doorway to my office. "I waited around for him and when he didn't show after fifteen minutes, his engineer-of-the-month from the college told me his boss was trying to do a remote, but was having problems. I left, but not before I asked the kid if a Ms. Weaver had visited KSKY in the last couple of days. He—his name is Cole Something—said she'd come by last night but Fleetwood was gone so she 'floated,' as the kid described it, out the door."

"Not a bad description of Jica Weaver," I remarked. "Maybe Cole has a future in journalism. If there *is* a future these days."

"Sad but true," Leo said, coming closer and leaning on the back of one of my visitors' chairs. "By chance, I decided to stop by the Grocery Basket to check on their plans for the autumn harvest ads." His leathery face turned grim. "I was there when Buzzy got the news about Mike."

"Poor Buzzy!" I exclaimed. "How did he take it?"

Leo shook his head. "You can imagine. Buzzy's not the strongest blade of grass in the lawn. He went to pieces, and

Betsy had to take over. She was upset, of course, but you know her—she's strong, probably stronger than Jake."

"The family anchor," I murmured. "Laura's no tower of strength, either." With Leo blocking my view, I couldn't see into the newsroom. "Is Mitch here? He was heading for the Grocery Basket."

"No. I met him going out as I was coming in. Think he can handle this? I don't mean the news coverage," Leo added quickly, "but the personal stuff."

"I hope so." Fleetingly, I recalled my own career as a reporter for *The Oregonian*. I knew that in a big city, media types could usually afford the luxury of distance from their human subjects. I'd learned in a hurry that there was a huge difference in a small town where everybody knew everybody else. "He's savvy," I added. "He'll catch on."

"He'll have to." Leo was silent for a moment. "I know I did."

"Yes. Did you turn on the radio to see if Spence ever got on the air with the news?"

"I didn't check," Leo said. "If the remote setup flopped, he probably did the broadcast from the station. I'll check in with him tomorrow about those co-op ads."

Vida had suddenly appeared, hovering behind Leo. "I forgot to tell you," she said, "that I saw the baby at the hospital. Quite homely, but so often newborns are. I tried to call on Ginny, but she was asleep. No stamina, really. The third birth is comparatively easy. Or so I found with my three girls." She started back into the newsroom, but stopped and turned around. "Speaking of my daughters, I'm having dinner tonight with Amy and Ted. I must ask Roger about Mike O'Toole. They've been chums—not close, Mike being a year older. His younger brother, Kenny, is a year or two younger than Roger."

As Vida continued on to her desk, Leo's expression was droll. "That should be . . . interesting," he murmured, sharing the same negative opinions I had of Vida's grandson. "Okay," he went on more loudly, "do we leave for the ICT from work or later?"

"Later," I said. "I'd like to go home first and eat food that doesn't have paw prints on it."

"We could have dinner at the Venison Inn," Leo suggested. "Only deer-shaped hoof prints, and they're kind of cute."

I smiled. "Okay. How about six-thirty? I'd like to stay around in case there's any news about Mike."

Leo agreed and left. Kip had come out of the back shop and gone into the front office, where he'd promised to fill in for Ginny when he finished his other duties. He'd told me that our classified ads, which were usually taken by Ginny, might increase after we went online. I assumed he was setting out some guidelines for Ginny and her temporary replacement, Amanda Hanson. Mitch, meanwhile, was busy on the phone. His visit to the Grocery Basket hadn't added anything new because all of the O'Tooles were gone and the rest of the employees were either upset or ignorant about why Mike had taken over the produce run. Shortly after four o'clock, Mitch came into my cubbyhole.

"I just talked to Dustin Fong," he said, leaning against the door frame. "The older couple at the local hospital are in critical condition, but might make it. The O'Toole kid's another matter." He paused, frowning. "Two leg fractures, a broken arm, ruptured spleen, punctured lung, and severe concussion. Apparently he wasn't wearing a seat belt, though that may have kept him from drowning. He was able to get out of the cab before it was completely submerged."

"Mike may've broken one law with his driving, but ignoring the seat-belt requirement saved his life. *If* he lives." I sighed. "I should call Father Kelly in case nobody else has notified him."

"Your pastor, right?" Mitch grinned. "How'd he manage when he first got here? It couldn't have been easy in what you described as a white-bread town ten years ago."

"It wasn't," I replied. "There was very little diversity until the community college was built. Still, it didn't take Father Den too long to be accepted, at least by his parishioners."

Mitch nodded once. "That's good. Brenda and I wondered what being Jewish in a small town would be like." His lean face looked sheepish. "Not that we practice our religion much, but . . ." He shrugged.

"My first reporter, Carla Steinmetz, was Jewish," I said, "but she didn't practice hers, either. Not," I added, "that there's a synagogue around here. Leo's Catholic, but his appearances at Mass are few and far between. I don't think you'll find much anti-Semitism in this part of the world, even in Alpine, where it's basically the Lutherans against the rest of the world."

Mitch chuckled. "Is that good or bad?"

"I'm not criticizing. This town was founded by an Episcopalian, but the majority of the timber workers were Scandinavian. German, too, which accounts for the Lutheran dominance. It's changing, though. The college brought in people of various races and religions. Alpine's content to rely on family feuds for hostility and excitement."

"Old-fashioned hatred," Mitch noted. "Easier to understand, I suppose."

Mitch ambled back to his desk. I called the rectory at St. Mildred's, but the secretary, Mimi Barton, said Father Den had already gone to Monroe with Jake and Betsy. After hanging up,

I succumbed to the moment and reread my file on Highway 2. Maybe I'd take a new angle, urging the state patrol to add more troopers to the stretch from Snohomish to Stevens Pass. Cedar trees didn't march onto the road and unless there was an avalanche, boulders didn't roll in front of cars. Drivers had to use better judgment, and if paying hefty fines was one way to save lives, we needed more law enforcement. Milo and his gang were responsible only for SkyCo's relatively short stretch of Highway 2. The rest of the dangerous roadway was up to King and Snohomish counties—and the state. I finished my first draft just before five. It needed work. I'd tiptoed a bit around driver responsibility. With Mike O'Toole fighting for his life in a Monroe hospital, I didn't want to rub any salt into already deep wounds.

Vida had left a few minutes early. Kip showed me some detailed directions for the online classifieds before leaving for the night. Mitch made a last-minute call to Monroe, but Mike's condition was unchanged.

"I didn't reach Fred Engelman today," he added. "Jack Blackwell told me Fred was tied up for most of the afternoon. Did you know there's money to be made in sawdust?"

"Ah . . . how do you mean?"

Mitch grinned. "I may be new to small-town living, but we do have a timber industry in Michigan. More to the point, an old college pal of mine teaches at Bowdoin in Maine. He told me a couple of weeks ago that the mills back there are starting to sell sawdust to dairy farmers and particleboard makers. The big market is wood pellet manufacturers. With the rising cost of energy, tons of people have stopped buying oil and are heating their homes with wood pellets instead. You say Blackwell's a pain in the ass, but he's shrewd. He couldn't stay in business if he wasn't. Even though the big demand is mainly in the Northeast now, Jack's looking down the road to increase his own profits."

"I never said Blackwell was stupid. You'll do a story on it?"

"Sure." Mitch straightened up. "I'll get back to him tomorrow and have another go at Fred Engelman."

"Great," I said as my phone rang.

Mitch snapped a salute before going back to his desk. Edna Mae Dalrymple's twittering voice was on the line. "Oh, I'm so glad I caught you! I thought you might've left for home. Seven-thirty, at Janet Driggers's house. This is a reminder, Emma. Charlene's still ailing."

I'd forgotten about the bridge date. "I thought Char might be able to play tonight," I said, stalling for time. "I have something to do this evening. Business," I added.

"Oh, dear! Oh, dear, dear!" Edna Mae sounded flustered. "I've no idea who to ask now. What shall I do?"

I glanced at my watch. It was five after five. "I might be able to make it," I said, "though I could be a bit late. Is that okay?"

"I . . ." Edna Mae faltered, probably considering which of the other six players would be most pissed off. "It *should* be a congenial group. Darlene Adcock, Dixie Ridley, Mary Jane Bourgette and her daughter, Rosemary, Molly Freeman, Janet, of course, and . . . oh, my, who else?"

"You," I said. "And me. That makes eight."

"Oh! So it does!" Edna Mae's giggle was more like a bird's trill. "Yes, yes, then we'll see you . . . when?"

"Before eight," I promised and rang off.

I hurried out to Leo's desk. "Let's eat," I said. "I forgot I had a bridge date. I'll have to leave the ICT by seven-thirty."

"Reeking of cheap beer?" Leo's crooked smile was ironic. "Don't you ladies pull the drapes so the high school faculty wives aren't seen glugging down wine like a bunch of homeless derelicts in a dark alley?"

The reference was to Molly Freeman, the principal's wife, and Dixie Ridley, the football and basketball coach's other half. "At least Linda Carlson won't be there," I said, mentioning the PE teacher's name. She was one of the members who'd blackballed me a few years ago when the rumor mill was feasting on my so-called affair with Milo. Dixie and Molly had gone along with Linda at first—faculty families sticking together—but they'd apologized later. Even such social occasions as playing cards could become not only judgmental, but downright nasty. "The Dithers sisters aren't playing tonight, either," I went on. "They're probably watching TV with their horses."

"In their living room?"

"Of course." ·

Leo turned off his computer and stood up. "Let's go. We have plenty of time. The Venison Inn shouldn't be busy yet. Kip left five minutes ago."

"I'll turn off the lights and lock up," I said, returning to my cubbyhole to get my purse and the brown leather jacket I'd splurged on at a Nordstrom end-of-winter clearance.

Five minutes later, we were ensconced in a booth toward the back of the restaurant. Sunny Rhodes, the sometime hostess and full-time wife of bartender Oren Rhodes, had seated us. "I can take your drink orders," she said, flashing the bright smile that had earned her nickname. "One of our waitresses is running a little late."

I looked at Leo. "Drink?" I said in a doubtful voice.

Leo shrugged. "I'll have a Coors Light."

I wasn't fond of beer, but told Sunny I'd have the same.

She looked surprised. "I thought you always ordered bourbon or Canadian, Emma."

"I do," I said. "But not tonight."

Sunny didn't bother to write down our requests. "It's going to be slow," she said, gazing around the dining room. "There's a candlelight vigil for Mike O'Toole."

I was surprised. "Who told you that?"

"Clancy Barton," Sunny replied. "He's in the bar, having a drink with a shoe wholesaler. His sister, Mimi, called from St. Mildred's just before you got here. It'll be held in Old Mill Park."

"That must have been a last-minute decision," I said. "I talked to Mimi not quite an hour ago."

"Could be," Sunny said. "I don't know much about Catholics." She took in a short breath and looked embarrassed. "Sorry. I mean, I know you people have a lot of rituals and all that, but I'm glad Father Kelly is holding the vigil in the park so everyone can come. If you know what I mean."

I wasn't sure, unless Sunny thought Catholics practiced some sort of secret ceremonies. Leo, however, intervened. "You mean like the Masons?"

Sunny blushed. "Oren says the Masons just do those things to keep the traditions. I've been in Eastern Star for years and it's not very mysterious. It's just . . . nice. A pleasant way for women to get together."

"So's bingo," Leo responded, his green eyes twinkling. "That's about as secret as we Catholics get. Nobody knows what numbers will pop out of the big glass ball. Very suspenseful."

"Really?" Sunny sounded skeptical. "I'd better put in your drink orders. Dr. Starr and his wife just came in, but they have a favorite table so I don't need to seat them."

I could see the tall figure of Alpine's dentist and his petite wife, Carrie, heading for the second window booth. As usual, Dr. Bob was wearing one of his colorful ikat sweaters that I recalled came from Peru. Mrs. Starr was more conservatively dressed in forest-green slacks and an ecru suede jacket I'd ogled in the window display at Francine's Fine Apparel.

"If we drink beer now," Leo said, "we won't have to mix our grains at the ICT. One beer ought to do it after we get there. You should be able to take in the layout pretty fast so you can get to your bridge club." He cocked his head to one side. "You aren't worrying about me staying and getting hammered, are you?"

I shook my head. "I stopped fussing about that a long time ago. Your record's unblemished. In fact, I was thinking about Sunny. She seems kind of odd."

Leo, who had a partial view of the area leading into the bar, motioned for me to be quiet. A moment later, Sunny appeared with our beers, which she placed very carefully in front of us.

"Mandy Gustavson will be waiting on you," Sunny informed us, "unless you know what you'd like to order now."

"Not quite," I said. "By the way, did your son Davin know Mike O'Toole very well?"

Sunny grimaced. "Not exactly. Mike's a bit older."

I knew that. Davin and Roger were the same age and had always been pals—for better or for worse. Davin had been one of our carriers for several years, and was about to finish getting his AA degree from the community college. Roger was still trying to decide on a major, but the curriculum didn't offer any classes in "Loafing" or "Sloth."

I smiled at Sunny. "Kenny's the younger one, right?"

"Yes," she replied. "He was in the same high school class with Davin. I don't know Mike very well. I think he liked to tinker with cars, but I didn't realize he was a truck driver."

"I'm not sure that was his regular job," I admitted. "It sounds as if he was doing his dad a favor for the produce section."

Sunny's face tightened. "I'm not sure Mike had a regular job. I mean . . . I don't know." She ducked her head and looked down the aisle between the booths. "I should check on Dr. and Mrs. Starr. Excuse me."

"You're right," Leo said. "Sunny's not so sunny. I wonder why."

I shook my head. "The only thing I can think of is that Mike O'Toole may have more problems than bad driving. Vida intended to ask Roger about him this evening. I don't think her grandson's reliable."

Leo laughed. "That kid's a train wreck. I can't believe he's kept out of serious trouble over the years."

"Lucky," I murmured. "Too lazy to get into real trouble."

"Maybe." Leo picked up the menu. "London broil. And you?"

"The same," I said. "We're going Dutch. We can split the bill."

"Let me treat you," he offered. "I still feel guilty about taking off so much time this summer to recover from getting shot. I don't know how you got through it without killing Ed Bronsky."

"You were gone only a couple of weeks," I said. "I know that when you came back, you were still hurting."

Leo looked rueful. "True. But work is all I have."

I started to contradict him, but realized I'd be uttering clichés. Instead, I was candid. "Me, too. Maybe it's enough."

Leo's expression didn't change. "Maybe."

IT WAS ALMOST DARK BY THE TIME WE LEFT FOR THE ICICLE Creek Tavern a little after six-thirty. Fog was settling in over the mountains, creeping its way through the evergreens on the slopes of Baldy and Tonga Ridge. We'd taken our own cars. I followed Leo across the railroad tracks and turned left by Icicle Creek Gas 'n Go. An older man was pumping gas into his Volkswagen Bug. Glancing inside, I could see Mickey Borg in the minimart, waiting on a couple of teenagers.

There were a half-dozen vehicles parked in the tavern's gravel lot—one van, one pickup, a couple of beaters, an old Lincoln Continental, a dented SUV, and a Jeep. None of them looked as if they'd fetch a decent price on a used-car lot. I recognized only two—Bert Anderson's rusty van and the Canbys' aging Hyundai.

"Feeling out of place?" Leo asked as I met him by the front door.

"Well . . . I'm not a snob. I hope not, anyway," I said, "but I do feel like I'm slumming. I haven't been here in ages."

"Unfortunately," Leo said, opening the door for me, "I have. Once in a while I need to chat up Spike and Mickey, not to mention an occasional patron who might or might not buy an ad in the paper."

The interior was dim, dreary, and relatively quiet. Two couples I didn't recognize sat at tables. Four men, including Bert Anderson from the chop shop, were seated at the bar. So was Holly Gross, attempting to make conversation with a chunky bald man whose name I couldn't recall but who I knew worked for Blue Sky Dairy. Spike Canby was behind the bar, pouring a mug of beer from a tap.

"Look who's here!" he called. "It's the press!"

Everybody at the bar except the bald man turned to stare. The two couples at the tables glanced up but quickly turned away, apparently unimpressed. Norene Anderson came into view, carrying two plates of burgers and fries. "Hi," she said without enthusiasm before delivering the food to the nearest of the two couples.

"I figure the only way Bert can get a meal is to have his wife serve him here at the tavern," Leo murmured with a sidelong glance at Norene's husband.

My eyes wandered to the bar. Bert's burly body was dressed

in grimy overalls. He was staring up at the ceiling, where faded banners from various beer companies dangled from the rafters. We sat close to the bar where we could see part of the pool table area and one of the pull-tab machines on the wall by the restrooms. Each of the ten tables could seat four comfortably, or maybe not so comfortably, considering that some of the chairs looked rickety. None of the furniture matched. I suspected that it had been acquired on the cheap from thrift stores and garage sales. Whatever the source, the chairs were an improvement. A previous owner had provided wooden crates after he got tired of replacing chairs that had been demolished in the wake of earlier brawls. Spike had also put new glass in the mirror behind the bar. The last time I'd seen the original, it was cracked in several places, giving a spidery effect that was, in a bizarre way, an interesting focal point. The dozen bar stools needed reupholstering, the bare wood floor was badly marred, but the place looked relatively clean.

I was sitting fairly close to Holly Gross, the scrawny blonde who lived on welfare to support her three children in their mobile home at the trailer park. The bald guy didn't seem interested in spending his money on Holly. He put a ten-dollar bill on the counter and left.

Norene approached us, sticking a pencil into the wild mass of auburn ringlets that hung to her shoulders and hid her eyebrows. "Mr. Walsh," she said in a voice that might have been deferential. "Ms. Lord?"

I nodded. "I haven't been here for a long time. Leo and I thought we should show our support for the tavern after what you all went through last Saturday."

Norene's doughy face puckered. "Awful. Who could've expected such a thing to happen here?"

I refrained from reminding Norene that De Muth's death

hadn't been a first for the ICT. In fairness, the previous fatality had occurred under different ownership. "It sounds as if it was one of those arguments that get out of hand," I said.

Norene nodded. "Silly, really." She leaned closer. "Holly's not worth fighting over."

I registered surprise. "That's what it was about?"

"As far as I can tell." Norene shot a quick look at Holly, who had just been served another beer. "It's bad for business. Look how quiet it is now." Apparently, she caught Spike's eye and straightened up. "What'll you have?"

We both ordered a local microbrew. "You should try the onion rings," Norene urged. "Julie's got a real knack for making them."

"Sure," Leo said. "Sounds good."

Norene smiled. Her shiny crimson lip gloss had been applied with a haphazard hand. "You'll love them. Be right back."

Holly picked up her beer and came over to our table. "Is Norene bad-mouthing me again?"

Leo chuckled. "Don't you girls like to bad-mouth each other? It's a good thing we guys don't pay attention."

Without being asked, Holly pulled out a chair and sat down. "You're one of the good guys, Leo. Don't let Norene tell you that the tavern has gone downhill since the fight. The place was practically full right after work. It always is between five and six-thirty. This is just a . . . a lull." She edged closer to Leo. "How come you don't hang out here much? You're always fun."

Leo nodded at me. "The slave driver here keeps my nose to the grindstone. I have to hustle twenty-four seven."

Holly studied him with pewter-gray eyes and laughed. "I do some hustling, too. Keeps me on my toes. Sort of." She actually simpered.

"Did you see the fight?" Leo asked.

Holly took a big swallow of beer. "You mean Fred and Mickey?"

"They fought?" I said.

Holly shook her head. "They argued, but I thought they were going to go at it. Don't get me wrong—Fred didn't drink that night, except for some club soda. Mickey—Janie's new husband—didn't feel good. He wanted to go home, but Janie said it was her birthday and she was going to stay. Fred would take care of her. Mickey got mad. I don't think he liked Fred showing up for his ex's party."

Leo frowned. "That's what started the fight? How did Clive and Alvin De Muth get involved?"

Holly waved a hand in a careless gesture. "That was something else. Al and I were . . . well, making some plans for later on. Then all hell broke loose by the pool table. Maybe Clive was pissed off because his girlfriend walked out on him. Miss Hoity-Toity, I call her. Not Clive's type at all." Holly fiddled with one of her false eyelashes. "Clive's real people. His girlfriend's from another planet. Maybe she went off with Averill Fairbanks to look for space aliens."

"Does Averill come here often?" I asked.

"He's kind of a regular, but he can nurse a schooner forever." Holly paused as Norene brought our beers. "Hey, Norene, watch your mouth. I'm a good customer, remember?"

"How can I forget?" Norene snapped. "Who's watching your kids? Or did you leave them in British Columbia? What do you do up there besides knock down Canadian brews with their higher alcohol count?"

"What I do is none of your beeswax. I like Canada. I like Canadians. So what?" Holly deliberately turned her back on Norene. "Old hag," she muttered. "Always on my case. She's just jealous."

I feigned innocence. "Of . . . ?"

Holly looked at me with those cold gray eyes. "What do you think? Norene's a drag. Bert likes to cut loose and party. It's nice doing business with him—in more than one way." Holly simpered and winked. "When I got here, Norene was telling Spike she might have the flu. Last weekend it was a migraine on Friday and bee stings on Saturday. Before that, it was her sinuses." Seeing Leo light a cigarette, Holly reached out a skinny hand. "Mind if I bum one off you?"

"Go ahead." Leo slid the pack across the table. "Take two."

"Thanks." She put a cigarette between her fuchsia lips and leaned forward, exposing a lot of pale skin but not much cleavage. "Light?"

Leo obliged with a match. "You owe me, babe," he said. "Tell us what happened with Clive and Alvin."

Holly took a deep drag and exhaled. "Oh, God, do I have to? I already talked to that pain-in-the-ass Sam Heppner. Dodge, too." She shot me a hostile glance. "What's wrong with you? The sheriff needs to get laid. Or did Delphine Corson sub for you this week?"

I stared back at her before turning to Leo. "I'll have one of those cigarettes, Leo. It's getting chilly in here."

With his eyes fixed on Holly, Leo shoved the pack and the matches in my direction. "Stay focused, Holly. What started the fight?"

To my surprise, Holly giggled. "Me." She giggled again, puffed on her cigarette, and drank more beer. "Men!" She shook her head, the limp blond strands of hair slithering over her narrow shoulders like lazy snakes. "Isn't that what you guys usually fight about?"

"I'm not a fighter," Leo said calmly.

Holly nodded. "I know. I can tell you're a lover. That's why you're okay with me." She turned around to face the bar. "Hey, Spike, put on some music. I want to dance."

Spike, who'd been talking to a couple of new arrivals, made a helpless gesture. "Can't. The sound system's still busted. It'll be fixed tomorrow for the weekend customers. Sorry."

Norene reappeared, carrying a plate of onion rings. "Here you go," she said. "Nice and hot. Julie's specialty. Enjoy." Without looking at Holly, she stomped away to greet Jack Blackwell and Patti Marsh, who'd just come through the door.

"Oh, shit!" Holly exclaimed. "Here comes Patti-Cakes, the biggest two-faced bitch in the county! I'm outta here!" Cigarette clamped between her lips, she yanked a couple of onion rings off the top, snatched up her beer, spilled a few drops on the table, and hurried away past the pool table, where she disappeared from view.

"Competition?" I murmured, taking a Kleenex out of my purse and wiping up the spilled beer.

"Sour grapes," Leo said, retrieving the spare cigarette Holly had left on the table. "Patti has a regular sugar daddy in Jack Blackwell. Besides, she still gets some money from her daughter, doesn't she?"

Norene was all smiles as she seated Jack and Patti not far from the entrance. "Maybe," I replied, "though Dani's Hollywood career never really took off. I think she's been in a couple of TV movies and at least one series that got canceled a few years ago."

Leo looked thoughtful. "The Dani Marsh drama was before my time. Did Dani ever come back to Alpine after her ex was murdered?"

"Not that I know of," I said, glancing at my watch. It was a quarter after seven. "Patti's visited her a few times in LA. Dani had too many gruesome memories of Alpine, especially," I added, gazing at the bar, "this place."

"It doesn't seem to bother her mother," Leo noted, watching Patti laugh heartily at something Jack had said to Norene.

"Nothing bothers Patti," I said. "She has a very thick skin and a very thin conscience. Patti doesn't live in the past, only for the moment."

"We aren't getting very far grilling witnesses," Leo pointed out before tasting an onion ring. "Hmm. Not bad. Have one."

I was pleasantly surprised. "Maybe Julie's got a knack for deep-fried food. Maybe we should have eaten here after all. And maybe the onions will kill my beer breath before I get to Janet Driggers's house."

Leo nodded discreetly in the direction of the bar. "Want to talk to Bert Anderson? He's coming this way."

"Hey, Leo," Bert said in a deep, rough voice. "How're you doing?"

"Got a minute?" Leo asked.

Bert grinned, revealing crooked teeth. "Not much more than that. I'm headed for the can. What is it?" He glanced at me. "You're the newspaper lady, right?"

"Right." I smiled and tried to look amiable.

Leo went straight to the point. "What was your take on the fight the other night?"

Bert shrugged. "Not much. I got here just before it started. I thought I'd have a couple of beers and take Norene home. Her car was in the shop. *My* shop. It should've gone in to Al's, but . . ." He shook his head. "Anyway, I can handle a brake job."

"But you saw what happened Saturday night," Leo said.

"Yeah, more or less." Bert shook his head. "I don't know what set those guys off. Somebody told me Al got mad at Clive and told him he wouldn't work on his truck. I guess that's when they got into it. It was a mismatch, far as I could see. Clive's bigger and stronger. Al's skinny, but not the wiry type whose looks can fool you. One swing of the pool cue and blam! Al goes down." Bert grimaced. "Damned shame. Al was one hell of a mechanic. Hey," he said, putting a beefy hand on Leo's shoulder, "got to go. Literally."

As Bert lumbered off, I sat back in my rickety chair. "Okay. Al and Clive fought over a woman, a truck, a game of pool, or . . . what?"

Leo's eyes twinkled. "Or who was buying? God only knows, Emma. When you've had six or ten beers, you can fight over just about anything. Years ago, I punched somebody in Torrance for blowing his nose in my cocktail napkin."

"Did he punch back?"

"Oh, yeah. He knocked me out cold. I spent the night in the storage room. I never went home, but straight to work the next morning." Ruefully, he shook his head. "That was the first time Liza threatened to divorce me. She got up to seven before she actually did it."

I patted Leo's hand. "You're lucky she didn't kill you."

"Am I?" His expression was ironic. Picking up his glass, he downed the rest of his beer. "Let's get out of here. We're not learning much and I'm getting a bad case of déjà vu."

"Okay." After I put a ten-dollar bill on the table, Leo did the same. I stood up and walked over to the pool table. I could see the entrance to the kitchen on the left, and the rear exit.

"There's an office across from the kitchen," Leo said, coming up behind me. "Restrooms by the pool table, two other rooms toward the front for storage and utilities. It's pretty basic, very simple."

"Except for the murder," I said.

"How do you mean?"

"I'm not sure." I frowned. "I'm wondering if this really is just an ordinary bar brawl that got out of hand." Turning around, I gave myself a good shake. "That sounds crazy. Maybe it's the memory of that other murder here. I feel as if the tavern could be haunted."

Heading toward the front door, Leo gave the occupants one last over-the-shoulder look. "If the place isn't haunted, maybe the people are. Is there a difference?"

I hesitated. "No. We all have ghosts following us around."

Opening the door, Leo sighed. "Yes. And they never go away."

EIGHT

W E MET MICKEY BORG IN THE PARKING LOT. HE SEEMED
surprised to see us. "What's up with you two?" he
asked in a wary voice.

"Just a little on-site crime scene visit," Leo said, smiling.
"How're you feeling? I heard you were under the weather the
other night."

Mickey, whose bushy eyebrows, tufts of black hair, and
small pointed nose reminded me of a gremlin, rubbed his stomach. "I think it was flu," he said. "It's going around. Spike and
Julie Canby had it a week or so ago, I think Al was coming
down with it Saturday, maybe Walt, too. Sometimes I wonder
if I've got an ulcer." He turned his head in the direction of the
gas station and minimart. "I've been damned lucky—haven't
been held up for almost two years. You see those news stories
all the time about convenience store owners getting gunned
down. It's enough to make a guy afraid to go to work."

"Say," Leo said as if he'd just thought of it, "did you see the
fight at the ICT Saturday night?"

"Not really." Mickey rubbed his stomach again. "I felt like

crap and wanted to go home, but Janie was having a good time. It was her birthday, and she was feeling *good*. But it was getting late and I'd worked all day. I was beat and spent half the night in the john. I didn't pay much attention to the shenanigans at the pool table."

"But," Leo persisted, "you were in the bar when Clive hit Al with the pool cue, right?"

Mickey shrugged. "I guess so. Frankly, I thought Walt Hanson hit Al. Maybe I was running a fever. It's all sort of fuzzy, which is what I told Dodge." He started for his car, which was parked next to the minimart and across from the ICT. "I'm still not a hundred percent. Take it easy, folks. 'Night."

Mickey limped a bit as he walked away. "Not a very good witness," I murmured.

"None of them are," Leo said, taking out his car keys. "Even in more sane and sober settings, people get confused about what they saw, or thought they saw, or wished they'd seen." He shook his head. "Mitch went over the official statements and couldn't get an accurate account. I don't suppose Dodge could, either." Leo patted my arm. "Good luck with that bridge game."

I smiled. "Thanks, Leo."

"Sure." He looked up at the dark, starless sky. "No rain for now. I think I'll swing by Old Mill Park for Mike O'Toole's vigil."

"I should be there, but I'm already a sub. It's too late to back out now. Can you take some pictures if Mitch isn't there? He may not know about the vigil since it was set on such short notice."

"I'll handle it," Leo replied, "though I'm not as handy with a camera as Mitch is. Maybe Vida will stop by."

We got into our cars and went our separate ways after Leo

turned onto Front Street to head for Old Mill Park. I continued along the Icicle Creek Road until I reached Fir, where I slowed down by my little log cabin. It was dark, of course, since I hadn't been home all day. I checked the dashboard clock, which registered 7:32 PM. The other players knew I'd be late. I pulled into the driveway, collected the usual batch of boring mail, and went inside to switch on a couple of lights. There were no phone messages. I brushed my teeth, gargled with Listerine to kill the liquor smell, and made a haphazard attempt to rearrange my hair.

Five minutes later, I was in the Pines, an upscale development by Alpine standards. Originally called Stump Hill after the last clear-cut, the property had been subdivided fifteen years ago. With their children grown and living elsewhere, Al and Janet Driggers had sold the family home recently and bought a smaller but much newer house among the young evergreens that had replaced the unsightly stumps. I'd driven by the house several times but hadn't yet been inside.

Janet greeted me at the front door. "Hi, Emma! Come see what a lot of dead people paid for. Or should I say their relatives?" She shrugged. "It works for us either way. People just won't stop dying around here."

I was used to Janet's blunt and sometimes bawdy manner, assuming it was her way of dealing with Al's undertaking business. She worked part-time for the local travel agency, but in recent years had taken on more duties at the funeral home. I couldn't resist asking an obvious question. "Are you handling the De Muth departure?"

Janet was already leading me down the hallway where she'd hung a half-dozen autumnal Japanese tapestries. "I don't know," she said as we went into her state-of-the-art kitchen complete with granite counters and cherrywood cabinets. "Al

Chetco Community Public Library

De Muth doesn't have any relatives around here. He was a lone wolf."

"So I've heard," I said, admiring my surroundings. "Nice. Lots of space, too. Was the kitchen like this when you bought it?"

"No. In fact the original owners had a breakfast nook, but we didn't need it," Janet explained. "Our old house was bigger except for that tiny kitchen. We'd thought about taking out the pantry, but while the kids were still at home, we used it for storage. Finally, Al and I said to hell with it and bought this house instead." She leered at me. "Want to see our bedroom? I got some silver-plated handcuffs for Al as a housewarming present."

"I think I'll skip that this time around," I said, unable to keep a straight face. "Our fellow cardsharps must be getting impatient."

"They're getting tanked," Janet retorted. "They started early on the Chardonnay and moved on to the Riesling. In a half-hour I can serve them furniture polish and they won't know the difference."

We left the kitchen via the dining area that adjoined the living room, where the rest of the women were seated at four card tables—except for Edna Mae, who was hopping around and admiring the Driggerses' collection of Eskimo soapstone carvings.

"Take a seat, Edna Mae," Janet shouted. "Some of that stuff's erotica. You won't understand it."

"But," Edna Mae said, wide-eyed and holding an object in her hand, "what about this darling walrus?"

"That's no walrus, sweetie," Janet said with her usual puckish expression, "it's—never mind. Put the damned thing back on the mantel and draw a card to see who deals."

My ace of hearts was high. I started out with Rosemary Bourgette as my partner. She was a relative newcomer to the group, the daughter of fellow parishioners Mary Jane and Dick Bourgette. Rosemary was also SkyCo's prosecuting attorney.

"Okay, Emma," she said, revealing her dimples with a friendly smile, "don't try to grill me about the ICT disaster. My lips are sealed."

"Of course they are," I said, feigning innocence. "We're here to play cards. I dealt and I pass."

Darlene Adcock, the wife of Harvey, our local hardware store owner, stared at me. "Maybe we should grill *you*, Emma."

"I'm not the one covering the story," I said. "Grill Mitch Laskey."

"But," Darlene persevered, "you must know *something*."

"Nothing you won't read in the paper or hear over KSKY," I replied.

Janet, who was Darlene's partner, waved the hand that wasn't holding her cards. "Skip the stiff. Are you going to bid or what?"

"Oh!" Darlene ran a nervous hand through her graying blond hair. "Yes, yes, I am. One diamond."

"One spade," Rosemary said.

Janet smirked. "Two hearts."

I grimaced at my meager six points. "Pass. Sorry, Rosemary."

My partner nodded once, her expression as inscrutable as if she'd been studying the accused in the witness chair.

"Oh, dear!" Flustered, Darlene sipped more wine. "Pass."

Janet made a face but didn't chide Darlene for not bidding again. I led a low spade into dummy, and Rosemary took the trick with a king. Janet trumped Rosemary's ace of spades and went on to three hearts.

"Good thing you didn't go to game," Janet remarked to Darlene.

"What?" Darlene seemed lost in reverie. Or Chardonnay. "Yes, yes, it was. We'd have gone set." She turned to me. "I thought Al De Muth had a son. Doesn't he live around here?"

"A son?" I was surprised. "Nobody's mentioned any family."

Janet had all but pounced onto the table, staring at Darlene. "Where'd you hear De Muth had a kid? We need to know in case the burial is from our funeral home."

Darlene looked defensive. "My husband told me a young man came into the hardware store a couple of times with Alvin De Muth. Harvey assumed they were father and son."

I watched Rosemary's reaction. There wasn't any, just the same impenetrable expression she'd worn during the bidding. "Well?" I finally said to her. "That's not privileged information."

"I don't know anything about it," Rosemary replied. "Honest."

I believed her. "Then De Muth doesn't have any ties to Alpine?"

Rosemary shrugged. "Not that I know of. He's lived here for several years. His address is on the Burl Creek Road not far from the fish hatchery."

Janet nodded. "I know where he lives. *Lived*, I mean. It's an A-frame somebody put up years ago as a summer home but never used."

"Could be," Rosemary allowed. "All I know is the address."

"Maybe his son lives there, too," Darlene said.

Janet nodded. "Al and I will check it out. They won't keep De Muth on ice forever in Everett. If there's an heir, he can pay for the funeral."

I cut the cards for Darlene. My mind wasn't on the hand I

was dealt. Instead, I was wondering if Milo had searched the dead man's home and if he'd found any sign of kinfolk. De Muth was described as a loner, but I hoped someone, somewhere was sorry he was gone.

WE PASSED THE REST OF THE EVENING WITHOUT FURTHER REFerence to the ICT tragedy. The others had contagious giggle fits and misplayed their cards, and by ten o'clock Edna Mae couldn't tell a heart from a diamond or a club from a spade. Never a wine lover, I sipped slowly on a single glass of Riesling. When we parted company a little after ten-thirty, I seemed to be the only one who was sober. "It's a good thing I don't have to drive," Janet called out as I left. "I'm too drunk to walk."

When I got home, I called Milo. "What's this about De Muth's son?" I asked after a grumpy hello from his end of the line.

"Son? What son?" he retorted.

"Darlene Adcock says De Muth had a son. Harvey's seen them together at the store."

"That's the first I've heard of it," the sheriff replied testily. "How did Harvey figure that? Did they wear matching outfits and name tags?"

"Harvey gathered it was De Muth's son," I said.

"Harvey's woolgathering. It sounds like something from one of your wine-guzzling bridge gang. Why don't I post a deputy outside of whichever member's holding the event and arrest them all for DUI?"

"Go ahead," I said. "Maybe that'll teach Dixie Ridley not to trump my trick when she's my partner."

"I should arrest Rip," Milo said, referring to Dixie's husband, the high school football coach. "Last week he couldn't count past eleven and got penalized in the last thirty seconds for having too many players on the field. That's why the Buckers lost to Arlington."

"Speaking of arrests, how's the prisoner?"

"Still feeling sorry for himself for being an asshole." Milo's sigh was audible. "Jeez, what a waste! Clive's as much a victim as De Muth."

"That's an odd thing for you to say."

"You're right. Forget I said it."

"Could Clive claim it was self-defense?"

"He probably will," Milo replied. "That could get him off the hook. I'm going to have to send him to Everett. With only a half-dozen cells and not enough staff, I can't keep him here if his court date is set more than a month from now. I've already released the other three drunks we picked up over the weekend, and Fred Engelman will be checking in tomorrow night for his usual weekend stay."

Given that the sheriff's tone had mellowed, I ventured to ask him about De Muth's A-frame. "Did he live there alone?"

"Far as I can tell. Not much of a place—just some old furniture, a new TV, and a lot of junk food. No sign of a woman. Nothing to suggest alcohol abuse, only some beer in the fridge. No sign of drugs, either. No criminal record. He slept, he ate, he went to work. He was a good mechanic. From what we've learned, no son, no family ties. De Muth moved here four, five years ago. We're doing a title search for ownership of the A-frame. Nobody I know of has lived there in recent years except him. The place may've been abandoned. It happens."

"And I hear the witness statements are all over the map."

"You expected something else from a bunch of boozers and losers?"

"They weren't all losers, really," I pointed out. "Have you heard from Jica Weaver?"

"Who? Oh—Clive's girlfriend. Yeah, she came by to see Clive this evening, but I'd left for the day. She's a space case, according to Sam Heppner, but he did say she was fairly easy on the eyes and what he described as 'refined,' which to Sam means she didn't cuss him out or take a whiz in the reception area."

"Sam has a way with words." Suddenly I realized how tired I was. It had been a long day. I slumped back onto the sofa. "I suppose Harvey made a mistake. Or Darlene misunderstood. Sometimes she's a bit scatterbrained."

"If there is somebody out there," Milo said, "they'd claim the body if they knew De Muth is dead. The leeches always crawl out of the woodwork if they think they can get a couple of bucks off a dead relative."

"True." I hesitated. "Do you want to come over for dinner tomorrow night? The Grocery Basket has a special on Dungeness crab. Which reminds me, anything new on Mike O'Toole?"

"He's still alive," Milo said. "That's a start. Sure, buy a crab for each of us. I haven't had any in a long time."

Had any what? went through my mind. "Good. Six o'clock. Hey, did Mike drive that grocery truck very often?"

"No," Milo replied. "If they needed to make a special run, Buzzy usually did it. I imagine he's kicking himself six ways to Sunday now. Poor bastard. See you tomorrow."

ON THE DAY AFTER A BRIDGE CLUB GET-TOGETHER, VIDA always marches straight into my office before she even takes off her coat, let alone her hat. On this foggy Friday morning, the hat was an amber satin toque with an artificial topaz clasp and three pheasant feathers. I'd never seen it before and thought it would have looked perfect on Queen Mary of Teck.

"My daughter Amy found it for me on eBay," Vida explained, stroking the feathers. "You'd be amazed at the bargains you can find on that site. Amy says she seldom leaves home to shop anymore. I don't condone not buying from local merchants, but these days it's difficult making ends meet. She paid just six dollars for this hat. It does have a certain drama to it, don't you think?"

"Definitely," I agreed. "It's too bad Buck Bardeen doesn't look like King George the Fifth."

"Buck is much too tall and broad," Vida conceded, speaking of her longtime companion. "Still, Buck is a retired military man and King George was in the Royal Navy. Then again, Buck is alive and George isn't. How was the visit to the tavern?"

I recounted what I could remember. "More muddle," I concluded. "At least I refreshed my mind about the crime scene."

"Disappointing." Vida shook her head; the feathers swayed. "Was bridge club any better?"

"Not really," I admitted. "Rosemary Bourgette was there, which meant we couldn't really get into the case since she'll be prosecuting it. Darlene Adcock mentioned that Harvey thought De Muth had a son, but Milo hasn't found any relatives."

"Curious." Vida fingered her chin. "Well now. What next?"

"That's up to Mitch," I said. "Was Roger helpful with regard to Mike O'Toole?"

Vida sighed. "Roger and Mike weren't chums. It was very difficult to get anything out of Roger. He can be terribly discreet."

Glum, sullen, ornery, and *uncooperative* were some of the words I'd have used. "So you didn't learn anything?"

"I can't learn what Roger doesn't know," Vida retorted a bit

Amanda nodded. "Milwaukee."

"And Walt?"

"Walt what?"

"Is he from Milwaukee?"

"No."

I paused. This wasn't the Amanda Hanson I knew, if only in a somewhat distant way. She'd always struck me as vivacious, if vapid. Maybe Vida's interrogation wasn't going to be as easy as I'd thought. "Have you ever worked for a newspaper?"

"No."

"You have an hour for lunch plus a morning and afternoon break if you need it."

Amanda didn't respond.

I broke the awkward silence. "Anything else you need to know?"

"Not really." She stood up.

"Okay." My smile was forced. "Good luck."

"Thanks." Amanda swiveled around on her platform shoes and strode out of my cubbyhole. I watched Vida, who seemed focused on her monitor, but I knew her eagle eyes were following Amanda's every step. After a brief wait, Vida rose from her chair, heading for the front office. A middle-aged man entered the newsroom a couple of minutes later. He looked around as if he were lost, and spotted Mitch.

"I'm Fred Engelman," he announced, just loud enough that I could hear him. "You're Mr. Lashley?"

"*Laskey*," Mitch corrected the newcomer. "Have a seat. Coffee? Bear claw? Cinnamon twist?"

I hadn't seen Fred Engelman in some time. He'd grown a short beard since then, and his hairline had begun to recede. He'd also lost some weight, maybe because he'd quit drinking beer. I had an overwhelming urge to eavesdrop. Vida and Leo

indignantly. "Roger referred to Mike as . . . undependable. That's not the right word, but I think that's what he meant."

Pot, meet kettle, I thought. "He didn't say in what way?"

"No. Though he did mention going to Mike's vigil. I offered to go with him but he was meeting some of his chums." Vida scrunched up her fist and pressed it against her chin. "I intended to go anyway, but Amy seemed a bit down so I stayed to cheer her."

I feigned interest. "Oh? What's wrong?"

"I'm not sure. Perhaps menopause. And Roger, who has so much on his mind lately. This is a hard time for young people. He'd still like to become an actor. Or a musician. If only Amy and Ted could afford to send him to a school specializing in the arts. I've offered to help pay his way, but it would mean Roger leaving Alpine. That upsets me."

I refrained from saying that I'd help pack his bags and even drive the kid at least as far as the state line. But although Vida is quick to criticize just about anyone else including God, she wears blinders when it comes to her grandson. I've often wondered if she'd be more realistic if her other two daughters and their families lived closer.

After she went into the newsroom, my phone rang.

"I overslept," the female voice on the other end said. "I'll be there in twenty minutes. Sorry."

"Is this . . . ?" I stopped as the phone clicked off and I realized the caller was Amanda Hanson. Our new hire was off to a bad start. It was ten past eight. I'd expected her to show up much sooner, if only to let me show her how to make the coffee.

Instead, I did it myself. Kip, Leo, and Mitch all watched me with caffeine-deprived faces. "What happened to Ginny's sub?" Mitch asked.

"She overslept," I replied, moving out of the way as Kip set the Upper Crust's pastries onto the tray. "Or so she claims."

"Dock her," Leo said. "Make sure she understands this isn't the post office. We can't have slackers around here."

I glanced at Leo, who was looking unusually grim. He sounded that way, too. "Are you feeling okay?" I asked.

"Yes," he replied, his tone softening. "Why wouldn't I?"

I shrugged. "So much flu and colds going around lately. I thought maybe you'd caught a bug, too."

Leo offered me an imitation of his off-center grin. "I'm too ornery to get sick."

"Good," I said, keeping my voice light.

Kip tossed the lavender bakery bag into a wastebasket. "Want me to break in Amanda? I know Ginny's routine pretty well."

"Thanks," I said, "but send her in to see me before you start, okay?"

Kip saluted. "Will do."

Vida had been on the phone. When she hung up, she looked exasperated. "I just called the hospital to see how Ginny and the baby are doing. They plan to send her home this afternoon. Doesn't that beat all? What's wrong with doctors these days? I was in the hospital for over a week after I had each of my daughters. Dr. Sung must've made that decision. Doc Dewey wouldn't have time for such silly notions."

"It's standard," I said. "And it's stupid. My money's on Ginny. If she carries on the way she did before she had the baby, she can probably coax Dr. Sung into another twenty-four hours if only to spare Rick having to deal with her complaints."

"I hope so." Vida stood up. "I'll help you show Amanda the ropes, Kip. You shouldn't take on the entire responsibility."

"Sure," Kip agreed. He knew as well as I did that Vida's curiosity was greater than her desire to assist him. By the time she

finished grilling Amanda, our House & Home editor would know everything about the newcomer including when she'd started teething as a baby. She'd also retain every detail, a talent that served her well in the newspaper business, allowing her the luxury of never having to take notes.

A half-hour later, Amanda Hanson entered my cubbyhole. She was pretty, despite the pug nose, short neck, and overly plucked eyebrows. In her three-inch brown platform shoes, she gave the impression of being tall, although she probably carried an extra ten pounds. Stella had highlighted Amanda's short dark hair. She looked professional in a long-sleeved brown sweater and camel-colored slacks. Her only jewelry was a small gold leaf-shaped pendant, a plain gold wedding band, and what might have been diamond studs in her pierced ears. She stood between my visitors' chairs and gave me what I perceived was a challenging look.

"I'll be on time Monday," she said.

"Good." I smiled. "Have a seat. Kip and Vida will be helping you get started, but I wanted to get acquainted first. I know you've been in Alpine for a few years, so you know something about the *Advocate*'s schedule and content."

"Yes." She sat. "It's the only paper we get. Walt and I watch the rest of the news on TV."

I nodded. "Many locals do that. How do you like living here?"

"I don't." She didn't change her expression. "Walt has to go where the state sends him."

I was beginning to feel defensive. "I'd never lived in a small town until I moved here," I said. "Where had you been before Alpine?"

"Outside of Spokane," Amanda replied. "Not that I'd call Spokane a big city. It's more like the Midwest."

"Were you raised in the Midwest?"

were both absent from the newsroom. I couldn't resist going out to Leo's desk and pretending that I was looking for something.

Mitch seemed to have guessed what I was doing. "Emma, do you know Fred?"

"By sight." I walked to Mitch's desk and shook Fred's hairy hand.

"Mrs. Lord," Fred said with a gap-toothed smile. "I've seen you at the Venison Inn and around town. Glad to meet you. I like the way you keep telling those dumb bastards in Congress to okay the Alpine wilderness bill. They're dragging their feet."

"Call me Emma," I said, not bothering to correct his misuse of the "Mrs." title. "It's good of you to come in."

"I told Blackwell I'd be late this morning," Fred responded, offering me the extra chair by Mitch's desk. "It's the least I can do. Besides, I'll work late tonight before I check into the jail."

I indicated that I preferred to stand. Fred hesitated, but sat down. "That's very smart of you to understand your own weakness," I said. "Most people don't."

Fred shrugged. "It's better than killing somebody when the booze has taken over." He scowled. "Like poor Clive did. I feel sorry for him."

"For De Muth, too," I remarked.

Fred grimaced. "De Muth was an oddball. One of those moody guys. You never knew which way he'd swing. I kept away from him as much as I could, even in my drinking days."

Mitch nodded. "De Muth comes across as someone who didn't make friends. He doesn't seem to have any family around here, either."

"I guess not." Fred took an inhaler from the pocket of his plaid flannel shirt. "Allergies," he said after a couple of puffs. "Sawdust. Good thing I quit smoking."

I sat on the edge of Mitch's desk. "I understand De Muth was a good mechanic."

"He was," Fred agreed. "He trained some of the younger guys, too. He must've had a lot of patience to do that."

I thought about Harvey Adcock's mention of a son. Maybe Harvey had seen one of the trainees with De Muth. "Did he hire any of them?"

Fred shook his head. "Not that I know of. He'd teach them the tricks of the trade, but I guess he liked to work alone."

"So," Mitch put in, "what did you see happen last Saturday?"

"Let me think . . ." Fred scratched his chin. I wondered if the beard itched. "I was sitting with Janie—my ex—and her new husband, Mickey Borg. It was Janie's birthday. That's why I came. We get along pretty good." He made a face. "Damn. If only I'd stopped . . . never mind, water over the dam. Or beer, I ought to say." He offered Mitch and me a rueful smile. "Mickey didn't feel good. Janie thought he was coming down with the flu. In fact, Mickey spent half the night in the can. Nobody else could get in there, being a one-holer, and a couple of the guys had to go outside to . . ." Fred looked at me. "You know—to take a whiz."

I nodded. "We girls also have to take a whiz sometimes."

Fred chuckled. "Sure. In fact, earlier on, Clive used the ladies' can because Mickey was in the men's. De Muth and one of the Peabody brothers just went outside. Not many people around that time of night after the gas station closes at eleven. When you gotta go . . . well, you do what you gotta do."

"True," Mitch said, rearranging some of the items on his desk, a habit I was beginning to recognize as evidence of impatience. "I've seen the statements that all of you gave the sheriff. The real trouble started just before eleven-thirty, right?"

"Well . . ." Fred scratched his chin again. His dark eyes roamed to the pastry tray behind Mitch. "Maybe I will have a bear claw."

Mitch turned around and put the pastry on a paper napkin. "Here. How about coffee?"

"No, thanks. I'm already over the limit for caffeine this morning." Fred took a small bite of pastry before resuming his account. "Bert Anderson showed up about then to wait for his wife, Norene. Al De Muth came back from taking a whiz and Mickey finally came out of the can. Al and Clive were arguing about something, I don't know what, because Mickey was telling Janie he wanted to leave. He was feeling really crappy. Janie was having a good time, and it *was* her birthday, so I told Mickey I'd bring her home if he wanted to go. Mickey got mad. He thought I was trying to pull something with Janie, but I'd just given her a big birthday hug. Like I said, we're on good terms. The next thing I knew, Clive and De Muth were at each other by the pool table. Somebody—maybe it was Norene—thought they were fighting over Holly Gross. I don't know about that, I wasn't paying attention. Oh, and just before, Averill Fairbanks said he heard a space ship outside and he left. But not for good, I guess, because he didn't take his jacket or what he calls his special UFO glasses. Then De Muth fell down—I couldn't see why—and everybody suddenly shut up. Julie Canby had come out of the kitchen to say it was closing. I think she was the one who realized De Muth was dead. It all happened so fast that it's hard to sort out." Fred's expression was apologetic. "To think I was sober, but I'm still kind of mixed up about everything. You can imagine the rest of the crowd."

"We can," Mitch said with an ironic smile. "You didn't actually see Clive hit Al with the pool cue?"

"No." Fred winced. "Janie was singing to me. One of our old songs from when . . . the good old days." He took another bite of bear claw. "I didn't know Amanda worked here."

"She just started," I said. "She's filling in for Ginny Erlandson, who had a baby yesterday."

"I see." Fred nodded. "Anything else you need from me?"

Mitch shot me a quick glance. "Your statement's pretty consistent with what you told the sheriff. I can't think of any other questions."

"I've got a couple of minor items," I said. "Are Amanda and Walt Hanson regulars at the ICT?"

Fred frowned. "I don't know. Back in my drinking days, I don't remember seeing them there." Again, he looked rueful. "I don't remember much from back then, to tell the truth. Maybe the Hansons are friends with Marlowe Whipp. Amanda's worked at the post office off and on."

"Were they sitting together?" I asked.

"Um . . . no, Marlowe was at the bar. The Hansons were at one of the tables." Fred paused. "I mean, they were, until they got up and went to play pool with Janie and Mickey."

I was getting confused, too. "When was that?"

"Oh . . . maybe around eleven? I wasn't keeping track of time."

"Mickey played pool even though he didn't feel good?"

"Shoot!" Fred said softly. "I'm not sure . . . no, that was when Mickey went to the men's can. The can's by the pool table. I guess that's why I thought he and Janie were going to play pool. Janie came back and sat down with me again. She told me Mickey wasn't feeling good. Stomachache, headache, the whole flu thing."

"A headache?" I felt as if I were sinking in wet cement. "Mickey complained about his stomach, not his head. But someone mentioned that De Muth had a headache."

"That's right," Mitch chimed in. "Marlowe Whipp, right?" I gave Mitch a dazed look. "I think so."

Fred slapped his hand on the desk. "Yes! It *was* De Muth. But that was later. We thought it was a joke because Holly was coming on to him. She'd already propositioned Clive, but Norene told Janie and me he told Holly to buzz off. Clive didn't want a case of The Clap."

"That's . . . sensible." I was still confused, but had a final question. "Did Jack Blackwell and Patti Marsh come to the ICT that night?"

Fred looked sheepish. "They did. They stopped in around ten-thirty and had a drink and left. Maybe Jack wanted to make sure I wasn't boozing. I never drank during the work-week, though. A mill is a bad place to have a nasty accident."

Vida returned to the newsroom just as Fred finished speaking. She looked as sour as if she'd been sucking on chokecherries. With the barest of nods for the three of us, she tromped over to her desk and snatched up the receiver before she sat down.

"I better get to work," Fred murmured, glancing at the clock above the coffee urn. "It's after nine. I told Jack I'd be at the mill about now."

I slid off Mitch's desk. "Thanks for stopping by." I joined Fred as he started for the door. "I gather Jack and Patti left before the brawl."

Fred nodded. "I think they took off a little after eleven. If they go out drinking, it's usually at Mugs Ahoy or the Venison Inn."

I stopped short of the newsroom door. As Fred made his exit I saw Amanda at the front desk. She was alone, working at Ginny's computer. She didn't look up. I assumed the tutorial session had concluded.

"What's wrong?" I asked Vida, who had just hung up the phone.

"Wrong?" She glared at me. "Ms. Hanson, that's what's wrong. She's extremely pigheaded. Why did I ever complain about Ginny?"

"Pigheaded?" I forced myself not to smile. "How?"

"I've always thought Amanda was featherbrained," Vida replied, "though she's not like that now. Indeed, she's quite condescending, as if I didn't know a thing about running this office. Even Kip seems put off, and he's usually very patient. Amanda is going to cause problems."

I shrugged. "We'll cope. If serious problems arise, let me know."

Vida nodded once. "Don't say you haven't been warned."

NINE

VIDA HAD CALLED THE HOSPITAL IN MONROE TO CHECK
on Mike O'Toole, but she couldn't get through to the
nurses' station. Apparently they were changing shifts. She'd
call later. I told her I was going to the Grocery Basket on my
lunch hour to pick up a couple of Dungeness crabs.

"I'll try to talk to Jake or Betsy if they're at the store," I
said. "I want to take the crab home and put it in the fridge."

"Two crabs?" Vida scowled. "For Milo? Have you lost
your mind? Those crabs will cost at least fifty dollars. What's
the occasion?"

"There isn't one," I said. "Though it never hurts to give the
sheriff a couple of stiff drinks to see if he loosens up about a
murder case."

Vida looked over my shoulder to see if Mitch was listening. He'd stood up to put on his jacket, preparing for his
morning rounds, which included studying the sheriff's log. As
soon as he went out the door, Vida spoke up. "Don't be foolish, Emma. I simply don't understand what goes on between
you and Milo. It's none of my business, but sometimes I feel

you're both looking for something neither of you will ever find in each other."

The lecture took me aback. Vida, who'd genuinely liked Tom, had never discouraged me from continuing the relationship even though "Tommy," as she always called him, was still a married man when we resumed our love affair. I knew she was also fond of the sheriff—as she was of me.

"We're adults," I said, feeling defensive. "I don't intend to do anything but cook, eat, and drink."

"Oh, piffle!" Vida yanked off her glasses and began rubbing her eyes. Squeak, squeak, squeak. I gritted my teeth. "Ohhh . . ." Vida wailed, "to think you're both old enough to know better!"

"Hey—have I ever once asked you about Buck Bardeen?"

Vida stopped grinding her eyeballs and stiffened. "About what?"

I leaned on her desk. "You and Buck have been seeing each other for years. Have I ever so much as hinted that I'd like to know what goes on with the two of you?"

Vida sniffed and put her glasses back on. "That's different," she said and pursed her lips.

"How?"

"Never mind." She sat up very straight and tucked her flowered blouse into the waistband of her brown skirt. "You're quite right. I shouldn't interfere. Excuse me. I must ring the hospital again."

It was useless trying to get anything further out of Vida. I went back into my office and reworked the Highway 2 editorial. At noon, I drove to the Grocery Basket. The reader board, which usually displayed the weekly specials, had GET WELL, MIKE! in big, black letters. I barely knew Mike O'Toole. In fact, I couldn't quite picture him except as a preteen a dozen or so years earlier in mid-January when his sled skidded into the indignantly. "Roger referred to Mike as . . . undependable. That's not the right word, but I think that's what he meant."

Pot, meet kettle, I thought. "He didn't say in what way?"

"No. Though he did mention going to Mike's vigil. I offered to go with him but he was meeting some of his chums." Vida scrunched up her fist and pressed it against her chin. "I intended to go anyway, but Amy seemed a bit down so I stayed to cheer her."

I feigned interest. "Oh? What's wrong?"

"I'm not sure. Perhaps menopause. And Roger, who has so much on his mind lately. This is a hard time for young people. He'd still like to become an actor. Or a musician. If only Amy and Ted could afford to send him to a school specializing in the arts. I've offered to help pay his way, but it would mean Roger leaving Alpine. That upsets me."

I refrained from saying that I'd help pack his bags and even drive the kid at least as far as the state line. But although Vida is quick to criticize just about anyone else including God, she wears blinders when it comes to her grandson. I've often wondered if she'd be more realistic if her other two daughters and their families lived closer.

After she went into the newsroom, my phone rang.

"I overslept," the female voice on the other end said. "I'll be there in twenty minutes. Sorry."

"Is this . . . ?" I stopped as the phone clicked off and I realized the caller was Amanda Hanson. Our new hire was off to a bad start. It was ten past eight. I'd expected her to show up much sooner, if only to let me show her how to make the coffee.

Instead, I did it myself. Kip, Leo, and Mitch all watched me with caffeine-deprived faces. "What happened to Ginny's sub?" Mitch asked.

"She overslept," I replied, moving out of the way as Kip set the Upper Crust's pastries onto the tray. "Or so she claims."

"Dock her," Leo said. "Make sure she understands this isn't the post office. We can't have slackers around here."

I glanced at Leo, who was looking unusually grim. He sounded that way, too. "Are you feeling okay?" I asked.

"Yes," he replied, his tone softening. "Why wouldn't I?"

I shrugged. "So much flu and colds going around lately. I thought maybe you'd caught a bug, too."

Leo offered me an imitation of his off-center grin. "I'm too ornery to get sick."

"Good," I said, keeping my voice light.

Kip tossed the lavender bakery bag into a wastebasket. "Want me to break in Amanda? I know Ginny's routine pretty well."

"Thanks," I said, "but send her in to see me before you start, okay?"

Kip saluted. "Will do."

Vida had been on the phone. When she hung up, she looked exasperated. "I just called the hospital to see how Ginny and the baby are doing. They plan to send her home this afternoon. Doesn't that beat all? What's wrong with doctors these days? I was in the hospital for over a week after I had each of my daughters. Dr. Sung must've made that decision. Doc Dewey wouldn't have time for such silly notions."

"It's standard," I said. "And it's stupid. My money's on Ginny. If she carries on the way she did before she had the baby, she can probably coax Dr. Sung into another twenty-four hours if only to spare Rick having to deal with her complaints."

"I hope so." Vida stood up. "I'll help you show Amanda the ropes, Kip. You shouldn't take on the entire responsibility."

"Sure," Kip agreed. He knew as well as I did that Vida's curiosity was greater than her desire to assist him. By the time she finished grilling Amanda, our House & Home editor would know everything about the newcomer including when she'd started teething as a baby. She'd also retain every detail, a talent that served her well in the newspaper business, allowing her the luxury of never having to take notes.

A half-hour later, Amanda Hanson entered my cubbyhole. She was pretty, despite the pug nose, short neck, and overly plucked eyebrows. In her three-inch brown platform shoes, she gave the impression of being tall, although she probably carried an extra ten pounds. Stella had highlighted Amanda's short dark hair. She looked professional in a long-sleeved brown sweater and camel-colored slacks. Her only jewelry was a small gold leaf-shaped pendant, a plain gold wedding band, and what might have been diamond studs in her pierced ears. She stood between my visitors' chairs and gave me what I perceived was a challenging look.

"I'll be on time Monday," she said.

"Good." I smiled. "Have a seat. Kip and Vida will be helping you get started, but I wanted to get acquainted first. I know you've been in Alpine for a few years, so you know something about the *Advocate*'s schedule and content."

"Yes." She sat. "It's the only paper we get. Walt and I watch the rest of the news on TV."

I nodded. "Many locals do that. How do you like living here?"

"I don't." She didn't change her expression. "Walt has to go where the state sends him."

I was beginning to feel defensive. "I'd never lived in a small town until I moved here," I said. "Where had you been before Alpine?"

"Outside of Spokane," Amanda replied. "Not that I'd call Spokane a big city. It's more like the Midwest."

"Were you raised in the Midwest?"

Amanda nodded. "Milwaukee."

"And Walt?"

"Walt what?"

"Is he from Milwaukee?"

"No."

I paused. This wasn't the Amanda Hanson I knew, if only in a somewhat distant way. She'd always struck me as vivacious, if vapid. Maybe Vida's interrogation wasn't going to be as easy as I'd thought. "Have you ever worked for a newspaper?"

"No."

"You have an hour for lunch plus a morning and afternoon break if you need it."

Amanda didn't respond.

I broke the awkward silence. "Anything else you need to know?"

"Not really." She stood up.

"Okay." My smile was forced. "Good luck."

"Thanks." Amanda swiveled around on her platform shoes and strode out of my cubbyhole. I watched Vida, who seemed focused on her monitor, but I knew her eagle eyes were following Amanda's every step. After a brief wait, Vida rose from her chair, heading for the front office. A middle-aged man entered the newsroom a couple of minutes later. He looked around as if he were lost, and spotted Mitch.

"I'm Fred Engelman," he announced, just loud enough that I could hear him. "You're Mr. Lashley?"

"*Laskey*," Mitch corrected the newcomer. "Have a seat. Coffee? Bear claw? Cinnamon twist?"

I hadn't seen Fred Engelman in some time. He'd grown a short beard since then, and his hairline had begun to recede. He'd also lost some weight, maybe because he'd quit drinking beer. I had an overwhelming urge to eavesdrop. Vida and Leo were both absent from the newsroom. I couldn't resist going out to Leo's desk and pretending that I was looking for something.

Mitch seemed to have guessed what I was doing. "Emma, do you know Fred?"

"By sight." I walked to Mitch's desk and shook Fred's hairy hand.

"Mrs. Lord," Fred said with a gap-toothed smile. "I've seen you at the Venison Inn and around town. Glad to meet you. I like the way you keep telling those dumb bastards in Congress to okay the Alpine wilderness bill. They're dragging their feet."

"Call me Emma," I said, not bothering to correct his misuse of the "Mrs." title. "It's good of you to come in."

"I told Blackwell I'd be late this morning," Fred responded, offering me the extra chair by Mitch's desk. "It's the least I can do. Besides, I'll work late tonight before I check into the jail."

I indicated that I preferred to stand. Fred hesitated, but sat down. "That's very smart of you to understand your own weakness," I said. "Most people don't."

Fred shrugged. "It's better than killing somebody when the booze has taken over." He scowled. "Like poor Clive did. I feel sorry for him."

"For De Muth, too," I remarked.

Fred grimaced. "De Muth was an oddball. One of those moody guys. You never knew which way he'd swing. I kept away from him as much as I could, even in my drinking days."

Mitch nodded. "De Muth comes across as someone who didn't make friends. He doesn't seem to have any family around here, either."

"I guess not." Fred took an inhaler from the pocket of his plaid flannel shirt. "Allergies," he said after a couple of puffs. "Sawdust. Good thing I quit smoking."

I sat on the edge of Mitch's desk. "I understand De Muth was a good mechanic."

"He was," Fred agreed. "He trained some of the younger guys, too. He must've had a lot of patience to do that."

I thought about Harvey Adcock's mention of a son. Maybe Harvey had seen one of the trainees with De Muth. "Did he hire any of them?"

Fred shook his head. "Not that I know of. He'd teach them the tricks of the trade, but I guess he liked to work alone."

"So," Mitch put in, "what did you see happen last Saturday?"

"Let me think . . ." Fred scratched his chin. I wondered if the beard itched. "I was sitting with Janie—my ex—and her new husband, Mickey Borg. It was Janie's birthday. That's why I came. We get along pretty good." He made a face. "Damn. If only I'd stopped . . . never mind, water over the dam. Or beer, I ought to say." He offered Mitch and me a rueful smile. "Mickey didn't feel good. Janie thought he was coming down with the flu. In fact, Mickey spent half the night in the can. Nobody else could get in there, being a one-holer, and a couple of the guys had to go outside to . . ." Fred looked at me. "You know—to take a whiz."

I nodded. "We girls also have to take a whiz sometimes."

Fred chuckled. "Sure. In fact, earlier on, Clive used the ladies' can because Mickey was in the men's. De Muth and one of the Peabody brothers just went outside. Not many people around that time of night after the gas station closes at eleven. When you gotta go . . . well, you do what you gotta do."

"True," Mitch said, rearranging some of the items on his desk, a habit I was beginning to recognize as evidence of impatience. "I've seen the statements that all of you gave the sheriff. The real trouble started just before eleven-thirty, right?"

"Well . . ." Fred scratched his chin again. His dark eyes roamed to the pastry tray behind Mitch. "Maybe I will have a bear claw."

Mitch turned around and put the pastry on a paper napkin. "Here. How about coffee?"

"No, thanks. I'm already over the limit for caffeine this morning." Fred took a small bite of pastry before resuming his account. "Bert Anderson showed up about then to wait for his wife, Norene. Al De Muth came back from taking a whiz and Mickey finally came out of the can. Al and Clive were arguing about something, I don't know what, because Mickey was telling Janie he wanted to leave. He was feeling really crappy. Janie was having a good time, and it *was* her birthday, so I told Mickey I'd bring her home if he wanted to go. Mickey got mad. He thought I was trying to pull something with Janie, but I'd just given her a big birthday hug. Like I said, we're on good terms. The next thing I knew, Clive and De Muth were at each other by the pool table. Somebody—maybe it was Norene—thought they were fighting over Holly Gross. I don't know about that, I wasn't paying attention. Oh, and just before, Averill Fairbanks said he heard a space ship outside and he left. But not for good, I guess, because he didn't take his jacket or what he calls his special UFO glasses. Then De Muth fell down—I couldn't see why—and everybody suddenly shut up. Julie Canby had come out of the kitchen to say it was closing. I think she was the one who realized De Muth was dead. It all happened so fast that it's hard to sort out." Fred's expression was apologetic. "To think I was sober, but I'm still kind of mixed up about everything. You can imagine the rest of the crowd."

"We can," Mitch said with an ironic smile. "You didn't actually see Clive hit Al with the pool cue?"

"No." Fred winced. "Janie was singing to me. One of our old songs from when . . . the good old days." He took another bite of bear claw. "I didn't know Amanda worked here."

"She just started," I said. "She's filling in for Ginny Erlandson, who had a baby yesterday."

"I see." Fred nodded. "Anything else you need from me?"

Mitch shot me a quick glance. "Your statement's pretty consistent with what you told the sheriff. I can't think of any other questions."

"I've got a couple of minor items," I said. "Are Amanda and Walt Hanson regulars at the ICT?"

Fred frowned. "I don't know. Back in my drinking days, I don't remember seeing them there." Again, he looked rueful. "I don't remember much from back then, to tell the truth. Maybe the Hansons are friends with Marlowe Whipp. Amanda's worked at the post office off and on."

"Were they sitting together?" I asked.

"Um . . . no, Marlowe was at the bar. The Hansons were at one of the tables." Fred paused. "I mean, they were, until they got up and went to play pool with Janie and Mickey."

I was getting confused, too. "When was that?"

"Oh . . . maybe around eleven? I wasn't keeping track of time."

"Mickey played pool even though he didn't feel good?"

"Shoot!" Fred said softly. "I'm not sure . . . no, that was when Mickey went to the men's can. The can's by the pool table. I guess that's why I thought he and Janie were going to play pool. Janie came back and sat down with me again. She told me Mickey wasn't feeling good. Stomachache, headache, the whole flu thing."

"A headache?" I felt as if I were sinking in wet cement. "Mickey complained about his stomach, not his head. But someone mentioned that De Muth had a headache."

"That's right," Mitch chimed in. "Marlowe Whipp, right?" I gave Mitch a dazed look. "I think so."

Fred slapped his hand on the desk. "Yes! It *was* De Muth. But that was later. We thought it was a joke because Holly was coming on to him. She'd already propositioned Clive, but Norene told Janie and me he told Holly to buzz off. Clive didn't want a case of The Clap."

"That's . . . sensible." I was still confused, but had a final question. "Did Jack Blackwell and Patti Marsh come to the ICT that night?"

Fred looked sheepish. "They did. They stopped in around ten-thirty and had a drink and left. Maybe Jack wanted to make sure I wasn't boozing. I never drank during the work-week, though. A mill is a bad place to have a nasty accident."

Vida returned to the newsroom just as Fred finished speaking. She looked as sour as if she'd been sucking on chokecherries. With the barest of nods for the three of us, she tromped over to her desk and snatched up the receiver before she sat down.

"I better get to work," Fred murmured, glancing at the clock above the coffee urn. "It's after nine. I told Jack I'd be at the mill about now."

I slid off Mitch's desk. "Thanks for stopping by." I joined Fred as he started for the door. "I gather Jack and Patti left before the brawl."

Fred nodded. "I think they took off a little after eleven. If they go out drinking, it's usually at Mugs Ahoy or the Venison Inn."

I stopped short of the newsroom door. As Fred made his exit I saw Amanda at the front desk. She was alone, working at Ginny's computer. She didn't look up. I assumed the tutorial session had concluded.

"What's wrong?" I asked Vida, who had just hung up the phone.

"Wrong?" She glared at me. "Ms. Hanson, that's what's wrong. She's extremely pigheaded. Why did I ever complain about Ginny?"

"Pigheaded?" I forced myself not to smile. "How?"

"I've always thought Amanda was featherbrained," Vida replied, "though she's not like that now. Indeed, she's quite condescending, as if I didn't know a thing about running this office. Even Kip seems put off, and he's usually very patient. Amanda is going to cause problems."

I shrugged. "We'll cope. If serious problems arise, let me know."

Vida nodded once. "Don't say you haven't been warned."

you're both looking for something neither of you will ever find in each other."

The lecture took me aback. Vida, who'd genuinely liked Tom, had never discouraged me from continuing the relationship even though "Tommy," as she always called him, was still a married man when we resumed our love affair. I knew she was also fond of the sheriff—as she was of me.

"We're adults," I said, feeling defensive. "I don't intend to do anything but cook, eat, and drink."

"Oh, piffle!" Vida yanked off her glasses and began rubbing her eyes. Squeak, squeak, squeak. I gritted my teeth. "Ohhh . . ." Vida wailed, "to think you're both old enough to know better!"

"Hey—have I ever once asked you about Buck Bardeen?"

Vida stopped grinding her eyeballs and stiffened. "About what?"

I leaned on her desk. "You and Buck have been seeing each other for years. Have I ever so much as hinted that I'd like to know what goes on with the two of you?"

Vida sniffed and put her glasses back on. "That's different," she said and pursed her lips.

"How?"

"Never mind." She sat up very straight and tucked her flowered blouse into the waistband of her brown skirt. "You're quite right. I shouldn't interfere. Excuse me. I must ring the hospital again."

It was useless trying to get anything further out of Vida. I went back into my office and reworked the Highway 2 editorial. At noon, I drove to the Grocery Basket. The reader board, which usually displayed the weekly specials, had GET WELL, MIKE! in big, black letters. I barely knew Mike O'Toole. In fact, I couldn't quite picture him except as a preteen a dozen or so years earlier in mid-January when his sled skidded into the

NINE

VIDA HAD CALLED THE HOSPITAL IN MONROE TO CHECK
on Mike O'Toole, but she couldn't get through to the
nurses' station. Apparently they were changing shifts. She'd
call later. I told her I was going to the Grocery Basket on my
lunch hour to pick up a couple of Dungeness crabs.

"I'll try to talk to Jake or Betsy if they're at the store," I
said. "I want to take the crab home and put it in the fridge."

"Two crabs?" Vida scowled. "For Milo? Have you lost
your mind? Those crabs will cost at least fifty dollars. What's
the occasion?"

"There isn't one," I said. "Though it never hurts to give the
sheriff a couple of stiff drinks to see if he loosens up about a
murder case."

Vida looked over my shoulder to see if Mitch was listening. He'd stood up to put on his jacket, preparing for his
morning rounds, which included studying the sheriff's log. As
soon as he went out the door, Vida spoke up. "Don't be foolish, Emma. I simply don't understand what goes on between
you and Milo. It's none of my business, but sometimes I feel

snowy intersection of Fifth and Front Street. He broke his arm when he hit a fire hydrant. We'd run his school picture along with the three-inch accident story. He'd been a pleasant-looking boy with light brown hair and a toothy smile. I'd probably seen him many times, either at the Grocery Basket or around town, but I wouldn't be able to pick him out of a crowd. I made a mental note to get a more recent photo of Mike for our next edition.

The store seemed ordinary, with high school kids and adults buying lunch from the deli, older folks strolling unhurriedly along the aisles, and mothers shopping with their toddlers securely strapped into the green grocery carts. I headed directly for the seafood section. A bald, middle-aged man whose first name was Darryl and whose last name eluded me offered his usual friendly smile.

"We've got some really nice crabs," he said. "Oysters, too, the extra small Hama Hamas."

Darryl knew I loved oysters. But Milo didn't care for them, somehow believing that only the idle rich indulged themselves with such delicacies. I'd once asked him where he got such a peculiar notion, and he'd mumbled something about his mom or his dad telling him that oysters Rockefeller were only for the ultrawealthy or else they'd go by another name. I argued with him—in vain.

"Just the crabs today, Darryl. Can you clean them for me while I get a couple of other things?"

"Sure can." He reached inside the display case where the orange-shelled crabs nestled in beds of ice. "I'll give you the two biggest ones."

"Good." The bigger the crab, the less I was paying for the shell. "What's new with Mike?"

Darryl's usual cheerful expression disappeared. "Poor kid,"

he murmured. "I haven't heard anything since I got to work. Still critical. But at least he's alive."

"Is either Jake or Betsy around?"

Darryl began wrapping up the crabs. "Jake's with one of the turkey wholesalers. We're starting to take Thanksgiving orders next week." He grimaced. "Life goes on. I think Betsy's in dairy, facing out the shelves."

My eyes widening, I watched Darryl weigh the crabs—and come up with a digital readout of fifty-one dollars and thirty-three cents. He smiled. "I know—it's pricey. But it's worth it, especially when you figure how dangerous it is for those crabbers to bring them out of the water. Seems like almost every year, a ship goes down."

I nodded. "I know. Years ago, I remember showing my brother, Ben, the monument at Fishermen's Terminal in Seattle. I'm glad that there's a tribute to those who risk their lives to satisfy our yen for seafood." I didn't say so, but I recognized the irony that driving a truck to procure pumpkins could also be hazardous work.

Betsy was rearranging the Western Family butter that was on sale this weekend. "I'll take two," I said.

Betsy jumped. "Oh! Emma! You startled me." She stood up and handed me the packages of butter. "I'm a nervous wreck. But that's nothing compared with Buzzy and Laura."

"Any news?" I asked.

Betsy sighed, her face so pale that I could barely see her freckles. "No. But deep down, I think Mike will make it. He'll have a lot of rehab, maybe even some soul-searching about what he wants to do with the rest of his life. At least that's how I'm looking at it." She shook her head. "It was a stupid stunt, trying to pass that guy on the motorcycle. Why do kids think they're immortal?"

"I guess it's their nature. Had Mike done a lot of truck driving before this?"

"Some." Betsy bent down to even up the rest of the butter. "He's always been nuts about cars and trucks. Buzzy told us he was thinking about becoming a mechanic. That might not be possible if Mike ends up with any physical limitations. Mechanics have to be in tip-top shape."

"Are Buzzy and Laura still in Monroe with Mike?"

"Yes. Kenny is staying with us." Betsy moved a few steps to the cheese section. "Kenny's so different from Mike. He's quiet, a good student, easygoing. Oh, he's a grown man now—almost twenty-two—but I didn't want him staying alone. He got his AA degree from the college here and started at the University of Washington this fall. Of course he came back last night. I suppose he'll return to the UDUB the first of the week, unless . . ." She faltered.

"I understand." I patted her arm. "Mike is young and must be in good physical condition. That should help him pull through."

Betsy nodded. "I hope so. Father Den was at the hospital last night. He's been a pillar."

I nodded. "I should e-mail Adam and Ben to add Mike to their lists of special Mass intentions. It's good to have a couple of priests in the family, though I wish I saw them more often."

Betsy didn't respond at once, staring off into the distance toward the milk and cream shelves. "I often think of Adam as a sign of hope for our kids—and Laura and Buzzy's. Your son took a long time to figure out what he wanted to do with his life, but when he finally decided, he chose something worthwhile. So many young people drift these days."

"Oh, Adam drifted all right." I smiled. "I was beginning to think he'd end up attending every college and university west of the Rockies—and still not get a degree. But I can thank Ben for getting Adam focused. My brother was a terrific example, especially since Tom wasn't . . . well, let's face it, he was an almost absent father."

"Life's hard." With her fists on her hips, Betsy looked at me. "Honestly, Emma, I wonder how any of us can raise kids these days. You get to the point where you feel you're a successful parent if your children haven't been arrested by the time they're eighteen."

"Your four seem to have turned out well," I said.

Betsy sighed. "At least they all got through high school. Ryan's doing okay at Seattle U, but Erica keeps changing majors at WSU, Melissa isn't interested in going to college, and Tim is . . . well, sometimes I think Tim's just hanging around the house waiting for Jake and me to croak so he can take over the store."

"Tim's working, isn't he?"

Betsy shrugged and waved a hand. "He's supposed to be learning how to run this place. But he spends most of his time playing computer games in the office. I have to boot his butt out just about every time I go in there to work. And you know how small and cramped that office is—about the size of yours."

I stepped aside for an elderly woman to pass. "Are your kids close to Mike and Kenny?"

"Fairly. You can't force cousins to be buddies. Let's face it, Jake and Buzzy are brothers, but they couldn't be more different. It's the same way with the younger generation." She looked sad. "Our four brats think they're better than Buzzy and Laura's two, if only because Buzzy's never had a head for business and has ended up relying on Jake and me. It's not right, but there's nothing we can do about it at this late date.

Jake and I should've kept our mouths shut around our kids when we griped about having to bail out Buzzy and Laura over the years."

"But you say Kenny is a good student?"

"He is," Betsy said, her tone ironic. "Maybe the best of the whole O'Toole bunch. He's kept out of trouble. Kenny isn't a risk-taker like Mike or even a couple of ours."

"But Mike's never really been in trouble, has he?"

Betsy's gaze wandered back to the cheese display. "Nothing serious." She pointed to the yogurt shelves. "I'd better hustle. Obviously, we're shorthanded. I'm thinking of putting Tim in charge of the produce until Buzzy gets back to work. It'll be good for Tim to walk in the real world instead of zapping aliens on the computer."

I finished my purchases and headed home. Milo's dinner was costing me almost ninety bucks. Along with the crabs and the butter, I bought potato and Caesar salads in the deli, a loaf of garlic bread, and a chocolate torte. By the time I wrote a check for the total, I decided that if the sheriff thought he was going to get a second dessert, he was wrong. The torte, made by a Seattle pastry company, cost twelve dollars. I'd also spent another seven bucks on a pastrami and Swiss cheese sandwich for my lunch.

When I got back to the office, Mitch was sitting at his desk, shaking his head. "I've had some weird interviews in my time," he said, "but even in Detroit, I never met anybody quite like Averill Fairbanks. Anybody, I should say, who wasn't high on heavy-duty drugs."

"Averill's an original." I sat down in Mitch's spare chair and took out my sandwich. "How'd you happen to run into him?"

Mitch swung around in his chair and stretched out his long legs. "I stopped at that teriyaki joint in the mall and decided to eat in Old Mill Park. It's not bad outside, after the fog lifted. Anyway, Averill was sitting at the base of that statue, talking to himself."

"He does that," I said. "Sometimes he talks to the statue. It's of Carl Clemans, who founded Alpine and owned the first mill."

Mitch nodded. "So I duly noted. I'd gone over Averill's statement, and it was totally incoherent. 'Worthless' is how Dodge put it. But what the hell, I decided to talk to the old coot just to cover all the bases." He shook his head. "Bad idea. He kept talking about seeing Venus at the tavern. 'Luminous,' he said, 'a sister,' a 'goddess.' I got that part, having a basic knowledge of the universe from taking astronomy at Michigan State, but when Averill mentioned that Venus was 'amoral yet enchanting,' I started to wonder. I asked how he could see Venus if he didn't take his special UFO glasses outside with him. Of course I know that anybody without special gear can see Venus on a clear night, but Saturday was overcast. Averill said he didn't need glasses because Venus was standing by the river, her tears mingling with the flow of mountain waters."

"Hmm." I finished a bite of sandwich and put the remainder back into the white paper sack. Eating pastrami and its trimmings in front of my reporter wasn't exactly image-enhancing. "Could he be referring to Clive's girlfriend, Jica Weaver?"

"Maybe." Mitch raised his arms and yawned. "I don't think he meant Holly Gross, though she was at the tavern, too."

I gestured toward the front office. "So was Amanda Hanson, along with Norene Anderson, Julie Canby, and Janie Borg."

"But none of them was outside."

"That we know of. When did Averill come back into the tavern?"

"I don't know that he did," Mitch answered. "Heppner told

me they had to take his jacket and glasses and whatever else he left behind to him the next day."

"Maybe you should talk to Jica in person. I'd like to get your impression. Sam Heppner interviewed her, but he's not very perceptive."

Mitch nodded. "Heppner strikes me as a real blue-collar type of cop. Steady, reliable, but no imagination. Not shrewd enough to finesse meaningful answers. Maybe I'll leave early this afternoon and take Brenda with me. She loves browsing in antiques stores. Having her tag along would make my visit less formal. Jica might open up a bit."

"Oh, she'll open up," I assured Mitch. "But what she says won't contribute much unless you're able to zero in on something solid."

Mitch laughed. "Emma, do you know how many kinds of wackos I've interviewed over the years? I've got my trade secrets. Trust me."

"I do," I said, and meant it.

MITCH LEFT THE OFFICE AROUND THREE-THIRTY. SINCE IT WAS Friday, I warned him about heavy traffic between Alpine and Snohomish. He reminded me that the admonition was unnecessary. He'd already seen the carnage that Highway 2 could cause.

"You shouldn't have sent him to interview Jica," Vida declared after he was gone. "I sense from what you've told me that a woman would have a better chance figuring out if Jica has any real information. Either you should have talked to her again or I should."

"It's too late now," I said. "Besides, you weren't here when I spoke to Mitch about it."

"I certainly wasn't," Vida retorted. "I didn't realize he was going to Snohomish until just now."

Her reproachful tone irked me. "A woman *is* going to talk to Jica. Mitch is taking his wife with him."

"His wife?" Vida looked exasperated. "What does she know about reporting? She's a *weaver,* for heaven's sakes!"

Vida made the word weaver sound as if it were synonymous with *hooker.*

"Brenda probably knows how to talk to other women," I said. "You met her. She's smart and sociable."

Vida's severe expression remained in place. "I met her for about five minutes. You couldn't have spoken with her much longer than that. Mrs. Laskey seemed anxious to leave the office. I found that rather insulting."

"Brenda had to meet with the real estate agent and wait for the moving van and solve about ten other problems that day." My patience was growing paper-thin. First Leo and now Vida seemed to be off their feed. With Ginny out of action and Amanda an unknown quantity, I was beginning to feel like a skipper on a fishing boat. The *Good Ship Advocate* might be sailing into troubled waters.

"Brenda Laskey should've come out with her husband when he interviewed for the job," Vida said. "She stayed back there in Royal Whatever—Royal indeed! What could possibly be 'royal' about Detroit? Then she suddenly showed up the day before Mitch started his job and he didn't have time to tie up the loose ends of the move. The only thing she seemed concerned about was her loom."

"She probably had things back in Royal Oak that required her attention," I pointed out, trying not to sound annoyed. "They'd lived there for almost thirty years. They have family. It couldn't have been easy for them to pull up stakes."

"Family?" Vida gave me her most owlish stare. "What do they have in the way of family? I've never heard Mitch mention children."

"He told me they had three, but they're scattered with one in graduate school, and . . . I forget where the other two are."

"Not very close-knit, if you ask me," Vida snapped. "Oh, I don't blame them for choosing Alpine, of course. That was very smart of them. But it still seems . . . odd."

"Mitch said they were in a rut, especially him," I explained, and not for the first time. "He'd gotten stale on the job, he was tired of the pressure to meet constant deadlines on a daily, and the paper itself was downsizing, so he knew it was just a matter of time before he'd be forced into retirement. Mitch wasn't ready for that, and he and Brenda agreed that a change of scenery might give them a whole new slant on life."

"Well now." Vida seemed appeased. "They couldn't have chosen more beautiful scenery or a finer town to escape big-city horrors."

I could've mentioned that even now Mitch was covering one of our own horrors, but having defused Vida's ill temper, I kept quiet. A moment later Amanda poked her head into the newsroom.

"The sheriff's on the line," she announced. "He wants to speak to you *pronto*. His word, not mine." She retreated into the front office.

Vida harrumphed. "Cheeky, don't you think?"

I shrugged and went into my cubbyhole.

"What's the rush?" I said into the phone.

"I have to take a rain check," Milo said. "Mulehide's in town."

I thought I'd misheard. "What?"

"Mulehide. My ex-wife. Are you deaf?"

"No." I paused, flabbergasted. "Why?"

"Tanya's finally getting married," Milo replied. "Not to that last loser I told you about—hell, all of her boyfriends were losers. Anyway, this is some new guy. He's employed."

"As what?"

"Damned if I know. Mulehide said he works for the City of Bellevue. He could be the mayor or the guy who stands in the middle of street construction with the STOP and SLOW sign."

"I already bought the crab."

"It'll keep for a couple of days, won't it?"

"Yes," I admitted. "But I may eat most of it myself. Why is Tricia coming all the way to Alpine? She hasn't been up here in years."

"She wanted me to come to Bellevue tonight," Milo replied. "I told her I couldn't—I was working a homicide. It's a bitch driving in bumper-to-bumper Friday traffic on Seattle's frigging Eastside. Mulehide wants to go over the wedding plans with me. I'm supposed to pay for half of it. She'll be lucky if she doesn't become the next victim around here."

I sympathized with Milo, but I was still irked. "Tanya *is* your daughter. She probably wants you to walk her down the aisle."

"What aisle? The wedding's going to be held in Marymoor Park by some damned windmill. August. I forget which day."

"Okay. Good luck." I rang off first.

I sat quietly for a moment or two, wondering if I should freeze one of the crabs when I got home. They were fresh, but never tasted quite as good after being frozen. I was still mulling when my phone rang again.

"*Bonsoir,*" said the male voice. "Or should it be *bonjour*? It's late afternoon on the Skykomish, but it's midnight on the Seine."

With a start, I recognized Rolf Fisher's voice. I almost snapped that he could say *adieu* instead, but naturally I was curious. "Rolf?"

"It is I," he replied, "sitting on a balcony overlooking the glittering lights of Paris. Would you care to join me for dinner tomorrow evening?"

"Are you nuts?" I exclaimed. "I haven't heard from you in months!"

"True. It seems my absence hasn't made your heart grow fonder."

"Quite the opposite," I retorted, aware that my previous loud remark had caught Vida's attention. She had shot me a quick glance and now was pretending to be absorbed in an orange flyer she'd taken out of her in-basket. "I think I'll hang up."

"Don't you want to know if I'm really in Paris?"

"Actually, I don't."

"Untrue. I don't hear the sound of a disconnect."

I lowered my voice even further. "Okay. If you're in Paris, tell me why and make it short. An inch at most, in column count."

"I quit my job at AP. I figured they were going to retire or can me eventually so why not beat them to it? I wanted to enjoy my sudden leisure, so I flew to London two weeks ago. An old buddy of mine from the UK bureau told me he knew a chap who wanted to rent his cottage in the Loire Valley. Was I interested? I said yes. I move in Sunday."

"That's an inch and a half, maybe two. I'm hanging up now."

"You don't like France? Or do you hate me?"

"I think France is great. I don't hate you, but you can be a jerk."

"Fair enough." A sound like a wry chuckle reached my ear. "I *am* a jerk. But you're not much better. Women usually give notice when they stand a guy up. Being a no-show puts you at the top of the would-be jerk class. Or should it be 'jerkette'?"

"You never bothered to find out why I couldn't come into Seattle that weekend," I countered. "You simply went to ground. Yes, I was upset, not just with you, but with myself. And then I was mad and then . . . I decided you weren't worth the emotional drain."

"God, but you're a rational woman. Not always an attractive feminine quality, but I'm perverse enough to like it. By the way, I did call about the homicide case that made you reject me that weekend."

"You called the sheriff, not me," I said.

"I called your office, too, but you weren't in. Whoever answered sounded flaky."

"True," I murmured.

"So what have you got against France?"

I hesitated. "Honestly? My late fiancé and I were going there for our honeymoon. End of explanation."

"Fair enough." It was Rolf's turn to pause. "But Tom's been dead for quite a while."

"You think I need reminding?" I snapped.

Rolf ignored the comment. "You have a valid passport from your trip to Rome with your priestly brother a few years ago. I hate to tell you this, but Paris and France have survived about a trillion tragic love stories. Yours would fit right in. And you might actually like it here."

"No, thanks." I noticed that Vida still seemed caught up in the orange flyer. "You may not believe this, but it's true. I'm breaking in a new reporter and covering yet another homicide."

Rolf sighed heavily. "That's what you were doing three, four months ago. You're in a rut. Get out of it."

"Please. Don't badger me."

"Okay. But promise you'll think about it."

"I . . . Oh, damn, I won't be able not to. But that doesn't mean I'll change my mind. What," I began hurriedly to prevent Rolf's ongoing argument, "are you going to do while you're in France?"

"I'm going to write a book."

"What about?"

"Does it matter?"

"No. But what am I supposed to do while your literary juices are flowing freely?"

"Pose for the nude illustrations I'm considering?"

"Stop being a jackass."

"Start thinking about Paris. *Au revoir.*"

Rolf ended the call.

I didn't know whether to laugh or cry. There was too much on my plate already—a homicide case, a sense of unease hovering over my staff, the conversion to an online edition, and two expensive Dungeness crabs in the fridge. I didn't need or want any further distractions.

So of course I thought about Paris.

TEN

VIDA, OF COURSE, GAVE ME NO OPPORTUNITY TO TRY TO forget about Paris—or Rolf. "What," she asked entering my office some five minutes later, "was that all about? I couldn't help overhearing, but you seemed upset. Surely it's not connected to the Icicle Creek Tavern disaster? Or was it Milo who disturbed you?"

"Milo's the one who's disturbed," I replied. Vida was all ears when I related Tricia's imminent arrival in Alpine and Tanya's wedding plans.

"I hope Milo's daughter has made a good choice," Vida said skeptically. She'd sat down in one of the visitors' chairs and was frowning. "Goodness, I haven't seen his children in ages! I might not even recognize them. Do you suppose we'll be invited to the wedding?"

"You might be," I said. "I won't. I never met those kids or Tricia."

"That's so. They left Alpine before you arrived." Vida looked at me with her owlish expression. "Then you're not upset?"

I figured I might as well give in, since Vida never backed off in her quest for knowledge. "It was Rolf Fisher, calling from

Paris." I made short work of that recital. "I'm not going. I think I've gotten Rolf out of my system."

Vida nodded. "That's probably wise. I'm told that France has its charm," she continued, picking up steam, "but so many people from Alpine who've visited there complain that the French are snobbish and refuse to speak English even when it's obvious that they know the language. Jean and Lloyd Campbell enjoyed their tour of the château country last year, but they certainly wouldn't want to live there. And such gruesome stories they heard about some of those places! Jean could barely talk about the poisonings and murders and other kinds of violence. It's very expensive, too, especially in Paris. I remember how Darla Puckett was utterly put off when she spent two weeks in France a few years ago. Everything was so *old,* and much of it needed repair."

I kept a straight face. "I think the French do a pretty good job of maintaining their historical sites. The country *is* much older than ours."

Vida bristled slightly. "We've kept the original mill in excellent condition as our history museum. Oh, I'll admit, most of the houses built for the workers and their families had to be replaced or renovated, but you can't say we've let things go around here."

It was unwise to make further comparisons between Alpine and Paris. "Do you want to eat crab for dinner?"

"Crab? But isn't . . . oh, Milo can't come. No, but thank you." Her gaze darted around my cubbyhole. "Buck and I have plans."

As she spoke, Leo had come into the newsroom and was tiptoeing toward us, a finger of warning at his lips. He was about to pounce on Vida when she whirled around in the chair. "Leo! What are you doing?"

"My God," he exclaimed, grinning. "You really do have eyes in the back of your head!"

"Certainly not. What a ridiculous idea. However, I *do* have very keen hearing," she continued as Leo leaned against the empty chair. "I could hear you breathing. All those filthy cigarettes make you wheeze."

Leo feigned indignation. "They do not. I have allergies. Ms. Hanson is wearing a very heady perfume."

"Yes," Vida agreed. "It's not cheap, either. Jasmine-based, perhaps."

"I should have a chat with her before we close up," I said. "I've been neglectful."

Leo shrugged. "According to Kip, Amanda seems to be doing okay. She doesn't need a lot of direction."

Vida twirled one of her plump gray curls. "Hmm. Initiative. I wouldn't have thought that. I really can't believe I misjudged her. I pictured her as flighty. Still, I resent her rather officious attitude." She glanced at her watch. "Oh, my! It's almost four-thirty! I'm leaving a bit early. It might be wise to talk to Billy at the sheriff's office."

Leo and I watched Vida hurry out of my office. "Something's up," he murmured.

"Why do you say that?"

Leo waited while Vida turned off her computer, gathered up her belongings, and made her exit. "Don't get me wrong," he said. "Vida can't help horning in on a juicy story, but she's usually coy about it. An accidental meeting with Bill Blatt or one of her 'I-just-happened-to-run-into' tales. I don't play detective, but why do I think she was blatant about talking to her nephew? It's got to be a cover-up for something else that's going on under those goofy hats of hers."

"You may be right," I said. "Would she be paying a visit to Clive? She hardly knows him."

Leo chuckled. "I wouldn't put it past her. If he isn't one of her bosom bodies, this is her big chance to get to know him better. He can't escape from jail."

"Let's hope she hasn't baked him a cake. The file inside would be easier to eat than the rest of it."

Leo obligingly chuckled again before heading back to his desk. Five minutes later, I went out to the front office, wearing my empathetic boss's face. It never fooled any of my regulars, but Amanda Hanson didn't know me very well.

"How was your first day?" I asked, quickly adding, "I thought it best to let you ease into the job without me looking over your shoulder."

Amanda put aside the classified ad form she'd been studying. "Thanks. It's been fine. Much less pressure than the post office during the holiday rush."

I caught a whiff of her perfume. It probably was a jasmine scent. "Did Kip tell you about the morning bakery run?"

"Yes." Amanda smiled, a facile expression that matched my own ersatz empathy. "My first morning is Tuesday."

I leaned on the counter. "Any problems or questions?"

She looked thoughtful. "Not offhand. I assume Monday will be busier than today was."

"True. The closer we get to deadline, the more action. No crank calls, I take it?"

"No."

"They usually come in Wednesdays after the paper hits the street and the boxes. Say," I said, as though I'd just thought of it, "I meant to ask if you'd recovered from the incident at the ICT Saturday."

Amanda wrinkled her pug nose. "Recovered?"

"Yes. It must've been traumatic."

"It was stupid. Walt and I hardly ever go there. The tavern's a dump."

"It's better now than it was before the Canbys bought it."

"I never saw it back then. I'm glad I missed it."

"How come you were there Saturday?"

Amanda yawned. Maybe I was putting her to sleep. "We'd gone to see *Closer* at the Whistling Marmot," she said after twisting this way and that in her chair. "I guess it was okay, but we got out before nine-thirty and didn't feel like going home. On a whim we decided to check out the Icicle Creek Tavern. That was a big mistake."

"Because of the brawl?"

I saw a fleeting, almost mischievous expression on Amanda's face before she shrugged. "The brawl, the other customers, the food, the whole sleazy mess." She made a face. "Walt and I couldn't wait to get out of there."

I hesitated, recalling Marlowe Whipp's different account of the Hansons' behavior. He'd told us that not only had the couple played pool, but Amanda had been flirtatious and Walt had used strong-arm tactics to get her to leave. "How come you didn't take off sooner? You might've avoided the rough stuff."

"We were hungry." Amanda's face was impassive. "We'd skipped dinner and got some popcorn and Cokes before the movie started. As long as we were at the tavern, we figured we might as well eat. It took forever to get served. I think both the waitress and the cook spent half their time outside smoking."

"Norene and Julie?"

Amanda frowned. "I guess that's who they are. The cook's married to Spike, right?"

I nodded. "Yes. The waitress, Norene, is Bert Anderson's wife."

"Slow as mold. And Julie's not much of a cook."

"She does a nice job with onion rings," I remarked. "I'm sorry you had such a miserable time. Was the fight as bad as it sounded?"

"If somebody ends up dead, I suppose it was." Amanda seemed unmoved. "I didn't see much of what was going on. Norene had finally brought our food. We ate as much of it as we could and were about to take off when that De Muth guy fell down."

"So you didn't see the fight?"

"Not really."

"But you stayed on afterward."

"Like we had a choice? Spike told everybody to stay put." Amanda's eyes narrowed. "Are you working for the sheriff? Walt and I already told him or one of the deputies what we saw—or didn't see."

I tried to look sympathetic. "One of the things that we're responsible for at the *Advocate* is making sure we check the facts of any articles we run. This particular story is complicated. I'm having a hard time getting everything straight. And no, I don't work for the sheriff—I work for our readers, who want to find out exactly what happened. That takes checking and rechecking." I'd managed to keep my voice pleasant. "I'm confused because I understood you and Walt were playing pool when the fight occurred."

Amanda's gaze shifted to the front door. "Not really. We were just standing by the pool table. Here comes a visitor." She put on her frozen smile.

To my chagrin, our former ad manager, Ed Bronsky, waddled in. "Aha!" he cried, beaming at me. "Caught you before closing time!" His grin faded as he saw Amanda. "Whoa! Where's Ginny?"

"She had her baby yesterday," I replied. "Do you know Amanda Hanson?"

Frowning, Ed approached the counter. "Yes." He nodded, his triple chins jiggling as he held up a hand. "Let me think—

I never forget a face. You're . . . something to do with Santa Claus . . ."

Amanda didn't bother to hide her impatience. "Last December at the post office. You were sending back a too-small Santa suit the day after Christmas. You wanted a return receipt to make sure the item had been delivered so that you could get a refund because there was a big rip in the pants."

Ed looked indignant. "There was. The suit was damaged goods."

Amanda shrugged. "Maybe. But you refused to pay the first-class postage that's required to get the return receipt. You got very angry with me. I had to ask my supervisor, Roy Everson, to take over."

"Roy got it sorted out," Ed murmured. "I didn't understand all those rules and regulations. They're pretty darned confusing."

During this exchange, I tried to figure out how to escape from Ed, but his bulk blocked the exit to the front door. I knew he'd follow me if I went into my office to collect my belongings. I was stuck, so I bit the bullet, asking if he needed help.

"No," Ed replied, turning away from Amanda's obvious hostility. "In fact, I'm the one who can help you."

I was skeptical. "How?"

"Let's talk." He grunted slightly as he made a little bow. "After you, Madam Editor and Publisher."

I trudged back to my cubbyhole but didn't sit down. Leo wasn't at his desk so I assumed he was in the back shop with Kip. "It's ten to five. What are we going to talk about?" I asked, turning off my computer.

Ed looked somewhat longingly at my visitors' chairs, but remained standing. "I hear the paper's going online. I can help you with that. It's not as easy as Kip thinks."

"Kip is very sharp," I said. "He's been one step ahead of everybody around here when it comes to computers. I have implicit faith in him."

Ed chuckled. "Oh, sure, all the techno stuff is his ticket. I'm not talking about that. I mean input."

"What kind of input?"

"Look." Ed grabbed a yellow legal pad on my desk and turned it sideways so we both could see whatever he was about to put down. "You're not talking once a week any more, this new deal is twenty-four seven, with updates almost every hour. Sure, it won't attract a lot of local folks in the middle of the night, but what about subscribers living in other parts of the country or Europe, Asia, or Africa?"

"We don't have any subscribers in Asia or Africa," I pointed out. "We have two or three in Europe, but they spend only part of the year there. Even when they're abroad they don't seem to mind waiting to get the paper by mail."

"Doesn't matter," Ed murmured, writing some numbers on the pad. "Let's say every two hours for updating. Breaking news, weather, sports scores from the college on down to Little League, even some of Vida's gossipy stuff," he jabbered on, drawing a circle—a *big* circle—that I assumed indicated himself. "I'd be the point man, tracking every possible angle and lead." Ed added an arrow and a square—presumably the *Advocate* office. "All I'd have to do is sit at my computer and post every new development almost as it happens."

Yes, I thought, *Ed sitting.* He'd never have to move his double-wide butt from his double-wide mobile home. Why hadn't I seen this coming?

"Look," I said, pointing to the fat blue circle on the yellow page, "I am, as you know, utterly ignorant of how this whole thing is going to turn out." That was at least partly true. "The decision is ultimately mine, of course, but Kip's in charge of the project." Wiggle, wiggle, getting off the hook. "I take it you haven't talked to him?"

Ed shook his head. "You're still the boss as far as I'm concerned."

"The boss is at a loss," I asserted. "Going online is Kip's idea and it's a good one. But how we implement it is still undecided. Why don't you talk to him about it in another week or so?" Or month, or year, or never. "Has Shirley got her teaching certificate?"

"Any day now," Ed replied. "Shirl hopes she can start subbing before the holidays. She's waiting for me out front." He grimaced. "We only have one car now."

I was well aware that the Bronskys had been forced to sell one of their two Mercedes-Benz sedans. It was a miracle that they hadn't been reduced to a bicycle built for two. "Good for Shirley," I said, picking up my handbag and hoping Ed would take the hint. "Have a good weekend."

"Uh . . ." He hesitated. "Sure. Thought we'd drive by the old place and see how the ReHaven renovations are going. That's big news, and I have the inside track on the project. You know those East Coast types—they play it close to their chests, but they know all about me."

I took a couple of steps and tried to smile. "Right. Got to go."

Ed glanced out into the newsroom. "Where's Leo? Think I should mention my project to him?"

"Not now. He's officially off the clock."

"Hey—was I *ever* off the clock?" Ed retorted. "Advertising's not a nine-to-five job."

"It wasn't for you," I said, wanting to add that his job had been more like nine-to-ten, eleven-to-noon, two-to-four, and out the door. Trying to circumvent Ed's bulk, I bumped into the filing cabinet and dropped my big handbag.

"I'll get it," Ed volunteered, bending down to grab the

shoulder strap. He picked up the handbag, let out a howl of pain, and doubled over. "My hernia!"

The handbag fell back onto the floor. "Are you okay?" I asked, fumbling around him to retrieve my purse.

"No!" He remained bent over, clutching his groin. "You got bricks in there?"

"I do carry a lot of stuff," I admitted. "Can you stand up?"

"Not sure." He moved a bit, moaning and groaning, but didn't seem able to upright himself. "Get Shirl."

Leo, who apparently had come out of the back shop, appeared in the doorway. "Hey, Ed," he called, "you need a hand?"

Huffing and puffing even more than usual, Ed managed to get a grip on the edge of my desk. "Yeah . . . yeah. I . . . do. Ooof!"

Somehow, Leo got an adequate grip on his predecessor's girth and eased him into a semi-standing position. Red-faced and panting, Ed took several deep breaths while still holding his side.

"Hernia," I informed Leo. "Shirley is waiting for him outside."

Leo nodded. "Okay, Ed. Let's see if I can get you out to your car. Shirley's driving, right?"

Ed nodded weakly. Leo tried to position Ed so he could lean and walk, but my ex-ad-manager's extremities seemed to have turned into Jell-O. He flipped and flopped like a flailing fish.

"I'll get Kip to help," I said, and squeezed past the pair to exit my cubbyhole.

Kip was putting on his all-weather jacket when I reached the back shop. "First Ginny," he said when I told him what was happening, "and now Ed? Jeez, what's going on around here?"

"Don't ask," I urged him, "and don't you dare ask why Ed came in the first place. Just get him the hell out of here and into his car."

I watched from the newsroom as Kip and Leo finally managed to haul Ed out of my office. I followed them out to the front door, where I spotted the Mercedes parked a couple of spaces down from Kip's red pickup. Despite much moaning and groaning from Ed, Leo and Kip dragged their burden outside and down the street. I stood in the doorway until they stuffed Ed into the passenger seat. Shirley, who was behind the wheel, let out several squeals and squawks that I translated as dismay. His task accomplished, Kip headed directly for his pickup, but Leo joined me. "What's up with the man who almost put the *Advocate* out of business single-handedly?" Leo inquired as Shirley started the Mercedes and pulled onto Front Street.

"I don't think he's given up trying," I said as we went back inside so Leo could get his briefcase. "Somebody ratted us out about the online project."

"News travels too damned fast in Alpine," Leo said. "I'll pass on asking what Ed was doing here. I'd like to face the weekend without hearing his latest harebrained scheme."

"I'm going to try to forget all about Ed." I had a sudden idea. "Could you endure another dinner with me? The sheriff stood me up in favor of his ex-wife."

Leo laughed out loud. "God, I didn't know she was still on the planet. How come?"

I explained about their daughter's upcoming nuptials. "So I'm stuck with two fresh crabs," I concluded.

"And I'm stuck with one old crab," Leo said ruefully. "I'm driving down to Monroe to meet a longtime pal who's visiting his wayward son at the state reformatory. I hope we'll go to a restaurant instead of the prison dining hall."

"I take it your buddy doesn't live around here?"

Leo shook his head. "Jim's from San Mateo. He's a retired radio-TV ad rep. Our paths used to cross fairly often. It was a friendly rivalry, right down to seeing who could drink the most double martinis. He blames himself for his son's life of crime. Between work and booze, Jim was't home much. Unfortunately, I understand too well how that goes."

"Your kids stayed out of jail," I pointed out. "What did Jim's son do to end up in Monroe?"

"Drugs," Leo replied, putting on his snap-brim cap. "The kid . . . no kid by now, Pete must be at least thirty. Most of the trouble he's gotten into was pretty small-time, but the stretch at Monroe is for dealing. This is the first time Pete's been in jail."

"That's too bad. Is his mother still around?"

Leo nodded. "She didn't give up on Jim. Tough lady. They had three daughters who turned out just fine. But Angie refuses to see her son in a prison setting, so she stayed home."

"That can't be easy," I murmured, wondering how I'd feel if Adam were behind bars instead of serving his parishioners in an isolated Alaskan community. Ironically, there were times during the dead of winter when I felt as if my son actually was in a prison. Although Adam had chosen his life, I had nightmares when he talked about such harrowing adventures as confronting angry bears or clinging to a rope in blinding snow to avoid a fatal misstep.

"I'm off to dodge Friday-night Highway 2 traffic," Leo said, interrupting my reverie. "I wish those folks in Olympia would read your editorials and do something about that road to the next life."

"Me, too," I murmured, leaving the newsroom with him. Amanda had returned to her desk, having been absent during Ed's traumatic departure. She was talking on the phone. "See you Monday," I called to her as Leo and I went out the front door. We parted company to reach our respective cars.

I was behind the wheel of my Honda when I saw Vida walking briskly to her Buick two parking spaces away. I rolled down the window and shouted at her. "Any news?"

She gave a start, searching for the source of my voice. "Oh. There you are." She tromped over to the Honda's driver's side. "Not really," she said. "Fred Engelman checked in for his weekend at the jail just before I left. He seemed quite chipper."

"Maybe Milo has some chores for him," I said.

"Milo left just before Fred arrived." Vida's gray eyes flickered up and down Front Street, taking in the vehicle and foot traffic. "Tricia came to meet him at the office."

The light dawned in my brain. "Oh? How is she?"

"Gone to fat," Vida replied. "She's gained at least twenty pounds since she lived in Alpine. Those dreadful Eastside suburbs—how can you get any exercise when everybody lives right on top of everybody else and you spend most of your time driving those horrid freeways?"

"Were you able to visit with her for very long?"

"Long enough," Vida replied, waving at Harvey Adcock as he crossed the street at the corner of Fifth and Front by his hardware store. "Tricia's become a stranger. This wedding is an extravaganza, just showing off. I don't blame Milo for being upset. The flowers will cost over two thousand dollars and the cake is half of that. It's being made in the shape of Seahawk Stadium because that's where Tanya and her fiancé met. Honestly!"

"Maybe they should get married on the fifty-yard line instead of at Marymoor Park," I said.

Vida sniffed. "Tricia actually told me that the park isn't that far from Seahawk headquarters. Tanya works for the team, you know."

"I didn't. Milo never mentioned it."

"She handles season ticket applications," Vida replied. "I must dash. Enjoy your crab."

I'd intended to tell her about Ed's visit, but she was obviously in a hurry. I smiled a bit weakly. "Enjoy your . . . evening with Buck."

Waiting to pull out into traffic, I figured that Vida's excuse for going to the sheriff's office was to see Tricia, not her nephew Bill Blatt. *Sly boots,* I thought. She must've guessed that Milo wouldn't want his ex to meet him at what used to be their home. Tricia probably wouldn't approve of his random housekeeping habits. And of course Vida would want to see how Tricia looked and acted after so many years away from Alpine.

Just as I was about to put my foot on the gas pedal, I had another brainstorm. I got the cell phone out of my handbag and dialed Marisa Foxx's work number. As I expected, she was still at work. Marisa was diligent, and her law practice forced her to keep long hours.

"Do you like crab?" I asked without preamble. Marisa also didn't like to waste time on chitchat.

"Of course," she replied. "Why do you ask?"

I explained. She accepted.

I suddenly remembered I'd forgotten the rest of the sandwich I hadn't gotten around to finishing. I turned off the engine, jumped out of the car, and went into the office. Amanda was staring intently at her computer monitor. For a split second, she looked startled to see me. "I was looking at the classifieds and legal notices," she said, speaking faster than usual. "Kip told me to make sure they were entered properly."

"Good," I said, noticing that Amanda had turned in her chair so that I couldn't see the monitor. "Do you want me to check, too?"

"No." She gave me a thin smile. For a brief moment, I caught the heading at the top of the screen. I saw what looked like "Journeys of the Heart." My initial reaction was that Amanda was trolling on an online dating site. "Thanks anyway," she said, and turned away.

"Okay." I continued on to my office where I retrieved my half-sandwich from the small cooler I kept by the filing cabinet. As I went back through the newsroom and into the front office, Amanda had turned off the computer.

"I'm going home now," she said. "See you Monday."

"Have a nice weekend," I responded.

Driving along Front Street, I wondered if Amanda was seeking a romantic partner in cyberspace—or a real-life potential lover. It was none of my business, as long as she didn't let her explorations interfere with the job.

When I arrived at my little log house, once again there was only junk mail. But I had a call on my answering machine: "You should be home by now," Rolf Fisher's voice said. "Imagine a russet-and-golden autumn along the Loire. Imagine enjoying it with me." I heard him heave a sigh that I assumed was of feigned longing. *"Vive la France! Au revoir, ma cherie."*

"Damn!" I said aloud as I hit the Delete button. The message had come in just a few minutes after I'd talked to Rolf at the office. It was now almost five-thirty, the middle of the night in Paris. I was sorely tempted to call him back and wake him up. But I wasn't a vengeful teenager. Or was I? With my hand on the receiver, I grappled with an adolescent urge. After a full minute, I left the phone in place and went into the kitchen. Marisa would arrive a little after six. She was always an interesting, intelligent companion. We would talk about many things, but Rolf Fisher wouldn't be one of them.

Marisa showed up at six-ten. As ever, she was well groomed

in her simple, tailored manner. Every short blond hair was in place, there were no wrinkles in her gray Max Mara suit, and the maroon satin blouse added a perfect accent of color. There was no indication that she'd probably put in a grueling day at the office. I hadn't changed from my usual sweater and slacks. My brown hair didn't look at all like Stella's professional version, and I hadn't bothered to add a dash of lipstick.

"I brought beverages," she said, holding a plastic bag from the state liquor store. "Canadian for you, a Pinot Blanc for me."

"Great!" I took the bag from her and started for the kitchen. "You sit, I'll pour," I said.

"Sounds good to me. I had a horrendous brief to put together this afternoon. I'm beat." Marisa removed her suit jacket and sat down in one of my armchairs.

"I'll let you decompress," I said, heading for the kitchen.

A few minutes later, I returned to the living room, handed Marisa a glass of wine, and sat down on the sofa. I raised my highball glass. "Here's to the working girls."

"Amen," Marisa said. "I'll be working part of tomorrow. When I first arrived in Alpine, I made sure my weekends were sacred. But as the population increases slowly but surely, so does litigation. Not to mention," she added with a rueful smile, "the crazy kind of cases you find only in small towns. I turned down the last one. Maybe you heard about it." She inclined her head toward the west side of my lot.

"The Nelsons?" I laughed. "Is this about Luke and his wife's new baby?"

"Yes. I'm not breaking client confidentiality because I'm not representing them and I don't know what lawyer in his or her right mind would take them on. Anyway, the family wants to sue Cindy and Richie MacAvoy for allegedly stealing their baby's name."

"I heard something about that," I said. "The Nelsons have never been my favorite neighbors. The kids were always out of control growing up, and the parents never bothered to discipline them. What sort of grounds did they have for even thinking a lawsuit was possible?"

"Luke's mother, Laverne, is a cousin of Richie MacAvoy's mother," Marisa explained. "The cousins' grandmother was named Chloe. When Richie and Cindy got married and had a baby last winter, they named her Chloe. But the Nelsons insisted they had dibs on the name because they'd made a deathbed promise to name their first girl Chloe after Grandma. Luke and his fiancée, Sofia, had a girl at the end of July and got married in August. Instead of simply calling her Chloe, too, they wanted to sue the MacAvoys for usurping the name. The Nelsons insisted they had it in writing, but couldn't find the paper they'd supposedly signed. I told them they had no case." Marisa shook her head. "I was almost afraid to come here tonight for fear the Nelsons might be hiding in the bushes next door, lying in wait to attack me."

"Those bushes are mine," I said. "I planted rhododendrons, azaleas, viburnums, camellias, weigelas—whatever will grow and block me off from the Nelson brood. Their property is a mess and the house is falling down. Thank goodness the neighbors on the other side are so nice."

Marisa's expression was mischievous. "Do you want to file a lawsuit? I've had several involving feuding neighbors."

I sipped at my drink and relaxed. "I can't afford you. Which reminds me—do you know an Everett attorney named Esther Brant?"

Marisa nodded. "She's very sharp. I've gone up against her twice. I won the first case, she took the second one. Why do you ask?"

"Clive Berentsen has hired her to defend him," I said. "I was curious, of course, assuming he'd have to get a public defender."

Marisa grew thoughtful. "Esther didn't handle criminal cases until a couple of years ago. But a close friend of hers—or her family, I forget which—was charged with involuntary manslaughter. Esther felt there had been extreme provocation and agreed to represent the accused. She got him off and in the process, discovered she liked criminal practice, at least every once in a while if the case had merit."

"I assume she's not cheap."

"You assume correctly." Marisa frowned. "Who's paying?"

"I don't know," I admitted. "I wouldn't think Clive could afford big bucks, though I could be wrong. He's divorced, but never had any kids according to Vida, who also mentioned that she thought his ex moved away and remarried. I suppose Clive could have stashed away some money. Truckers make a decent wage, and somehow I wouldn't think of him as somebody with expensive tastes."

"Not if he frequents the Icicle Creek Tavern," Marisa said. "A simple-pleasures sort of man."

I nodded. "He has a girlfriend, Jica Weaver, who owns an antiques shop in Snohomish. I met her the other day. She assured me Clive wasn't the violent type. Jica's not the kind of woman I would've thought he might attract. A bit otherworldly, possibly a dilettante."

"Ah." Marisa took another sip of wine. "Maybe she's paying for Esther. How well do you know Clive?"

I grimaced. "I'm not sure I'd recognize him. It's wrong to make assumptions about people. For all I know, he writes haiku."

Marisa looked thoughtful. In fact, I wondered if she'd heard what I just said. I started to remark that it was hard to read other human beings, but the words never got out of my mouth.

"I know Jica," Marisa said suddenly. "A couple of years ago, I bought an oval vegetable bowl for the Lenox china my mother gave me after I got my law degree." She paused, smiled, and shook her head. "The pattern is 'Marissa' and Mom insisted it was *me*. It's not, it's too fancy, it's not even spelled the same way. But I couldn't hurt her feelings. Anyway, Jica had the bowl in her shop and it cost a hundred and fifty dollars, which was probably fair enough. I told her the story behind my purchase and she seemed amused. I say 'seemed' because she sort of drifted during my recital. Maybe I bored her." Marisa shrugged. "Jica may be attracted to uncomplicated men. Some very bright, educated women are. Clive might be ordinary and therefore refreshing." Her gaze wandered around the room, as if she thought she might find such a catch tucked away in a corner. Or maybe she was looking for the one who got away.

"It sounds like a simple crime," I said after a brief silence. "Two beer-drinking men get into an argument and fists fly. One of them ends up dead, which was never the other man's intention."

Marisa nodded. "Under state law, intoxication isn't a factor. Drunk, sober, or in between, the charge is still—in this case—involuntary manslaughter. Unless, of course, Clive claims self-defense."

"I suppose he could," I said. "I don't know if I've heard who threw the first punch."

"It needn't be a punch," Marisa said, frowning slightly. "It could be a threat, and not necessarily to the defendant. Provocation could come in the form of menacing a loved one. Do you know what started the fracas?"

"The versions so far vary," I replied, trying to piece together witness statements, firsthand accounts, and what other people had heard about how the fight had started. "A couple of witnesses thought it had something to do with Holly Gross. Holly agreed. Do you know her?"

Marisa shook her head. "I know *of* her. A few years ago, she tried to make an appointment concerning child support for one or all of her kids. My secretary, Judi Hinshaw, told Holly that I didn't usually do pro bono work. Holly apparently thought I'd be delighted to take her on for free. Judi suggested that she get someone from Legal Aid."

"I don't suppose Holly mentioned the names of the deadbeat dads. I understand she's had children by more than one man."

"If Holly mentioned names, I don't think Judi passed them on to me." Marisa smiled wryly. "The only way you can get some of those guys to pay up is to let them sit in jail on the weekends and dock their wages."

"If that happens, Milo's going to run out of cells." I stood up. "How about a refill while I get dinner on the table?"

"Fine," Marisa replied. "I'll help."

"You don't need to. This is an easy dinner." I led the way into the kitchen. "I bought the crab for the sheriff, but he had to cancel. His ex is in town to discuss their daughter's upcoming wedding."

"Milo's certainly not a deadbeat dad," Marisa remarked.

"No. He paid his dues until the kids were eighteen." I poured more wine into Marisa's almost empty glass. "Now he's supposed to dole out some big bucks for his half of the nuptials."

"That's fair, I suppose." Marisa gazed around the kitchen. "Let's hope the wedding is a onetime-only event. I could practically live on divorce money. Marriage is an endangered species." She watched me while I took one of the crabs out of the fridge. "Maybe it's just as well I've stayed single. My, but that's a big crab! I see the Grocery Basket has oysters on sale this weekend. I think I'll get some."

"It's tempting," I allowed, removing the potato and Caesar salads before closing the fridge. As usual, Marisa had steered the conversation away from her private life. And mine. Our friendship had grown in recent months, but we never discussed our love lives—or lack thereof.

Shellfish seemed to be a much safer topic—for both of us.

ELEVEN

I T HAD BEEN A PLEASANT, LOW-KEY EVENING. MARISA WENT
home shortly after nine-thirty. I slept until almost ten the
next morning, not realizing that the week's events had tired me
out. There was no further word from Rolf, but Adam had
e-mailed me. He'd hoped to come to Alpine for Thanksgiving,
but a young couple at one of his mission churches wanted to
get married on the Saturday after the holiday.

"I know you'll be pissed," he wrote, "but the couple chose
the twenty-seventh because it's the groom's parents' anniversary. I'm not allowed to be pissed, given my priestly vocation,
but if it were possible, I would be, too. Maybe I can make it for
Christmas, but I'm not promising anything this year. Meanwhile, feel free to send presents and money."

Some things about my son never changed. I e-mailed him
back that I was indeed pissed and if he couldn't come for
Christmas maybe I should go to St. Mary's Igloo and celebrate
it with him. I'd never been to Alaska, but I'd toyed with the
idea of making the journey. Apparently Adam was still online
because he responded almost immediately.

"Don't. If you ever do come up here, make sure it's during the summer before the mosquitoes get to be the size of pterodactyls. I don't want to spend my time trying to keep you attached to a frozen rope or having a nervous breakdown when you see my modes of land, water, and air transportation during the winter. Meanwhile, send thermal underwear and heavy boots with serious traction. I could use a new pair of snowshoes, too. Check out the MSR Denali Evo model. When you see the price, note that they're not as expensive as a car. Thanks, MOM."

The capital letters were deliberate. I'd told Adam long ago that they were short for "Made Of Money," which apparently was how he regarded his mother. I thought that once he was ordained, he might stop seeking my financial aid. That had never happened. Sometimes I felt as if *I* had taken the vow of poverty. Even though he had finally received a decent sum from his late father's estate, he'd insisted on putting the money into a fund to be used only for his parishioners. It was a noble concept, but my tenuous dream of my son's financial independence had disappeared into the long Alaskan nights.

A half-hour later, I went outside. The autumn weather had changed overnight, with almost clear skies, sunshine, and that brisk, crisp feeling that comes with nature's decay and yet is invigorating. I decided I'd do some more garden cleanup before the first snowfall.

My nice neighbors, Val and Viv Marsden, were already busy raking leaves and filling a composter. I greeted them from across the fence.

"If," Viv said, using the back of her hand to brush a bit of dirt from her forehead, "you want anything hauled away, the Peabody brothers are coming by around one. We're taking out that old holly bush. It's gotten out of control."

THE ALPINE UPROAR 171

I gazed across the yard at the massive holly. "It's never pro-
duced berries, has it?"

Viv shook her head. "No. We kept hoping, but maybe it
needs a mate. Now it's getting so big that it obscures our view
of the street."

Val had wandered over to join us. "Hey, what's going on
around this town?" he asked, leaning what looked like a
brand-new shovel against the split-rail fence. "Is another tavern brawl—excuse the expression—on tap for tonight?"

I laughed. "I hope not. We don't need any more bad news."

Viv nudged Val with her elbow and winked at me. "You
see, Emma? Now you know why I've nagged Val about hanging out in taverns after work. We couldn't have raised our kids
if he'd kept spending his paycheck from the state fisheries on
beer."

We all chuckled. Val was allergic to alcohol and hadn't
taken a drink since his freshman year at the University of
Washington. "I could get in trouble at work just talking about
taverns," he said, turning serious. "Like a moron, I asked Walt
Hanson about what happened at the ICT. He gave me a dirty
look and turned away so fast that he almost fell into one of the
hatchery ponds."

"Touchy subject," I said. "His wife, Amanda, is filling in for
Ginny Erlandson, who had her baby this week."

Viv smiled. "We heard. Another boy. Is Ginny disap-
pointed?"

"She'll be fine," I said. "That reminds me, I should buy a
gift."

"Ginny and Rick have a nice little family," Viv said. "I always wonder about couples who don't have children. Maybe
Walt and Amanda would've been better off if they'd had kids."

Val shook his head. "Some people shouldn't be parents.

Look at the Nelson bunch next to Emma. They weren't cut out to raise kids. The Hansons would have problems with or without adding children into the mix. I don't know how they've stayed together this long."

I asked the obvious. "They're in trouble?"

Val grimaced. "I don't think Amanda's been happy since they moved here. And that makes Walt grouchy. It's no picnic working with him. You never know what's going to set Walt off."

"I suppose," I said, "she blamed him for being transferred here."

Viv's expression was ironic. "Amanda blames Walt for everything, including the weather. Which," she went on, looking skyward, "is good today so we'd better get back to work." She punched Val in the upper arm. "Let's hit the dirt, darlin'. The Peabodys will be along in a while."

I returned to my own patch. It was almost noon. Clipping, clearing, and cleanup filled the next hour. By the time the Peabodys pulled up in their battered truck, I had enough yard waste to fill a small dumpster. I decided to take the offer of adding my pile to the Marsdens'.

I'd never been able to tell Myron from Purvis. They weren't twins, but only about a year apart, and both were well over six feet tall and must have each weighed 250. They seemed to be balding at the same rate, their agate-blue eyes were identical, and neither spoke much. For a long time, I'd considered the brothers to be slow-witted, but Vida informed me that wasn't so. Their mother, Alva, had been a nonstop talker. Neither her husband nor her sons had ever been able to get a word in edgewise. "Alva Peabody," Vida insisted, "would talk to me until I withered. Imagine!"

I'd admitted being stupefied by such a garrulous woman.

Now, as the Peabodys headed into my yard after they'd finished hacking down the holly and put the remains in their
truck, I marveled that they were able to talk at all. "I appreciate your help," I told them. "Are you sure you have room for
my stuff?"

One of them—I decided he was Myron—nodded. "It'll fit
in."

Purvis—I was still guessing, of course—nodded, and began
gathering up the leaves, branches, and other debris. It took two
trips to the truck for the Peabodys to dispose of what would've
taken me a half-hour of work if I'd done it myself.

I handed each of the brothers a twenty-dollar bill. "Thanks."

"Right," Myron said, showing a gap-toothed smile.

"Hey, you two must have had a weird adventure the other
night at ICT," I said.

The brothers glanced at each other. Purvis spoke first. "You
mean Clive and Al?"

"Yes."

"Real bad," Myron murmured.

"Fights happen," Purvis said, frowning at some fresh
scratches on the back of his hand that had probably been
caused by the holly.

Myron nodded. "Al should've backed off."

Purvis also nodded. "He was under the weather."

I felt confused. "I thought it was Mickey Borg who was ill."

"Him, too," Purvis said.

"Flu." Myron grimaced. "It's going around."

"Yes," I agreed. "It's that time of year. Did Al say he was
sick?"

"He had a headache," Purvis replied. "He looked bad."

"Who started the fight?"

Again, the brothers looked at each other. Was the younger

deferring to the elder? Or the other way around? Which one was the elder or the younger? Which one was Myron and which one was Purvis? Did it matter? They seemed to be one person in two bodies.

"Clive," Myron finally stated.

"Why?" I asked.

"That lady," Purvis said. "Clive's lady."

Myron nodded. "Al was rude to her."

Purvis also nodded. "She left."

I tried to digest this new bit of information. "Jica Weaver," I said under my breath. "I thought the fight was about Holly."

Both Peabodys shook their heads. "No," Myron said.

"Holly was going with us," Purvis added, his ruddy face darkening.

Taking a pocket watch out of his overalls, Myron squinted at the face. "Getting on to two. Got to go."

"Right," Purvis agreed.

They both nodded at me before going to their truck. I stood at the edge of my driveway, trying not to visualize the ménage à trois of the Peabody brothers and Holly Gross. It was a difficult image to dismiss. So was their take on the ICT tragedy. Myron and Purvis had given statements. I wondered if they jibed with the account I'd just heard.

There was only one way to find out. I went inside and called the sheriff. He didn't answer his home phone, so I dialed the number for his cell. He didn't answer that, either. In fact, I got a message saying that the party I was trying to reach was out of range.

The sheriff was seldom incommunicado—unless he was fishing. There are many dead zones around Alpine where rivers, streams, and lakes nestled in the rugged terrain. A riot could break out at the Alpine Mall, a gun-toting psycho might be on top of the old water tower, an arsonist could set fire to city hall, but if the fish were biting, Milo didn't much care. To make sure he was still alive, I rang his office.

Doe Jamison was on duty. "You're right," she said. "The boss went fishing at Goblin Creek. After last night, he had to get away."

"It was that bad with the former Mrs. Dodge?"

Doe was admirably if annoyingly reticent about the sheriff and his personnel. "Let's say that he needed a break," she replied.

"I understand. Maybe you can help me. Have you got the Peabody brothers' statement handy?"

She paused. "I can find it. Why? Has something come up?"

"I'm on a fishing expedition of my own."

"Okay. Hold on."

Five minutes passed before I heard Doe's phlegmatic voice again. "Do you know which Peabody is which?" she asked.

"No. I'm not sure anybody does unless it'd be Vida."

"Their statements were taken by Sam Heppner," Doe said. "The brothers arrived a little after nine, sat at a table, and ordered beer and food. They're regulars, especially on weekends. An hour or so passed. By the way, Sam has a notation that the Peabodys seem vague about time. They ordered a couple more beers and then one of them—Sam's got a question mark after Purvis's name—tried to use the men's room but Mickey Borg was in there and wouldn't come out. Purvis—assuming it *was* Purvis, not Myron—went out the back way to take a leak. As he was going out, Al De Muth was coming in, cussing out somebody under his breath. Purvis thought he was bitching about Mickey's long session in the can. The brothers then joined the Hansons and the Borgs at the pool table. Al and Clive were arguing, but the boys didn't pay much attention until the fight broke out. The Peabodys wanted to break it up but before they could act, Al suddenly went down."

"That's it?"

"That's what Sam put down," Doe said. "You know Hepp-ner—he hates taking statements. The Peabodys don't like giv-ing them."

"They're not talkers," I said, and explained that I'd spoken to them earlier. "I got an even more abbreviated version. The brothers didn't mention Holly going home with them?"

"No. I can check her statement. Just a sec."

I waited, standing by the front window as a red motor scooter rolled along on Fir Street. Mike Corson—Delphine's son and the Saturday mailman—pulled up in his US Postal Ser-vice Jeep to stuff what looked like another bunch of junk into my box. A chipmunk raced across the front yard. Idly, I won-dered if chipmunks, like dogs, bit mailmen.

"More of Sam's notes," Doe finally said. "No, there's noth-ing in them about the Peabody brothers. Holly went home on her own."

"That doesn't mean she couldn't have had them join her at the mobile home park," I pointed out. "How did she say the fight started?"

"She claims it was over her," Doe replied. "She also says she was pretty drunk. Let me check something . . ."

Again, I waited. A forest service truck drove by. A couple of kids on bikes pedaled in the other direction. One of Mrs. Holmgren's cats wandered into my yard, sniffed around, and meandered off again.

"I'm looking at Janie Borg's statement," Doe said. "She mentions that Holly came on to Clive and he called her a tramp. Al came to Holly's defense. Before the fists started fly-ing Al told Clive he wouldn't fix his truck because he was, and

I quote, 'one bigmouthed bastard.' That, Janie stated, is when they started to go at it. Have you talked to Clive?"

"No," I admitted. "This story belongs to Mitch. He's a veteran reporter so I didn't want to interfere. Anyway, I hardly know Clive."

"You might want to stop by," Doe said. "Clive's getting bored with Fred's stories about his drinking days."

"Oh—that's right," I said. "Clive has Fred for company over the weekend. Is that cruel and unusual punishment?"

"I can tune him out," Doe replied, "but Clive's a fresh audience for Fred. He gets preachy, insisting Al would still be alive if not for Demon Rum. At least Fred didn't call liquor 'firewater.' I might've decked him."

I smiled to myself. Doe was part Native American, a stocky, stolid young woman whose dander wasn't easily raised. I had to assume Fred and Clive were probably driving her nuts on what should've been a fairly quiet Saturday holding down the fort at the sheriff's office.

I hesitated, not wanting to trump Mitch. "I suppose I ought to know what Clive looks like. I don't recall meeting him." My watch told me it was almost two-thirty. "I have an errand to run and then I'll stop by. See you." I hung up and changed clothes before driving to kIds cOrNEr at the mall. The capital letters spelled the owner's first name, Ione. Her last name was Erdahl.

"Another Erlandson shopper?" Ione asked when I entered the store. "We've had several of them already."

"Okay. Don't let me duplicate what the others bought."

"Get onesies," Ione said. "You can't go wrong. Babies use up about three a day." She pointed to a display next to the counter. "This bunch just came in Friday. They've got matching pants and jackets."

"I'll go for a set in the brown shade." I tried not to flinch at the price tags. "I'll take a set in that raspberry color and a dark green one. I need a gift card. You'll do the wrap—"

My cell phone rang. "Sorry," I said to Ione. After fumbling around in my handbag, I found the cell on the third ring.

"We've got a bit of a mystery," Doe Jamison said.

"What is it?"

"Yesterday some college kids were horsing around where Burl Creek joins the Sky," Doe explained. "Guess what they found?"

I had no idea. "What?"

"A pool cue caught up in the underbrush. Dodge is on his way."

TWELVE

AFTER SHELLING OUT FIFTY-SIX BUCKS FOR THE NEWEST Erlandson, I drove to the sheriff's office. Doe was behind the counter, talking to Dwight Gould. The two deputies were looking at a plastic-encased pool cue propped up against Lori Cobb's desk. "We bagged and tagged it," Doe informed me. "Dodge should be here any minute."

"It looks like a pool cue to me," I said. "But is it from the ICT?"

Dwight looked sour, a not-uncommon expression for the longtime deputy. "Maybe."

"Spike Canby's going to take a look," Doe said. "He's not sure that any of his cues are missing." She made a face, indicating her disgust.

"When did the college students bring the cue in?" I asked.

Doe glanced at Dwight. "It was just before you stopped by to take your break. A half-hour ago?"

"Not that long," Dwight retorted. "I should be back out on patrol. Let me see if Dodge is here yet." He picked up his regulation hat and went out the door.

180

MARY DAHEIM

"Dwight's an asshole sometimes," Doe said, and immediately apologized. "Sorry. I don't usually bad-mouth my co-workers."

I glanced again at the pool cue. "The kids found it yesterday but waited until now to bring it in?"

"They're kids," Doe said. "Eighteen, nineteen. There were four of them, two girls, two boys, and at least one of them knows how to read. They remembered something about a pool cue from the *Advocate* story."

"Gosh," I said in mock surprise, "I didn't think anybody under thirty read the newspaper anymore."

Milo loped through the door with Dwight bringing up the rear. "Don't ask," the sheriff said. "I'm never going back to Goblin Creek. I didn't even get a bump and I lost two leaders." He barged past me and went through the counter's swing door. "Let's see the damned thing."

"It's definitely a pool cue," Doe said dryly.

"Right." Milo studied the object for almost a full minute. "It looks beat up enough to belong to Canby. But then it would, if it had been traveling downstream in the river." He moved a few steps to look at a detailed county map on the wall. "It's what—a mile and a half from the ICT?" He paused, frowning. "No, closer to two."

Dwight gestured at the cue. "No prints, I'll bet. Probably no forensics hocus-pocus to help us out."

The sheriff glared at his deputy. "For chrissakes, we've got the guy locked up and a signed confession. Clive Berentsen, in the tavern, with the pool cue. You want to bring in Colonel Mustard?"

Dwight, who was actually a year older than his boss, wasn't backing down. "You haven't got the weapon. Didn't the ME in SnoCo say the pool cues he checked out weren't used to kill De Muth?"

Milo scowled at Dwight, creating an awkward moment—at least for me. Doe seemed unmoved. She was probably used to the men's bickering.

"Okay, smart-ass," the sheriff finally said, "let's ask Berentsen if he recognizes this thing."

"You can ask Fred, too," I said.

Milo stared at me as if he hadn't noticed my presence earlier. "What are you doing here? Did somebody steal that Dungeness crab?"

I held up the elegantly wrapped baby gift. "Yes, but I got it back and I'm giving it to you."

"Bullshit. Come on, Dwight, let's talk to Clive."

"And Fred," I called after the two men as they disappeared down the corridor to the cell area.

"Talk about crabs," Doe muttered.

"Do Milo and Dwight bicker a lot?" I asked.

Doe sighed. "No, not really. But Dwight's been in a bad mood lately. So has the sheriff." She made a sharp gesture. "There I go again, bad-mouthing my colleagues. Please tell me to shut up."

"Forget it," I said, moving to the end of the counter. "I've got my own staff problems these days. Not," I added quickly, "that it can't happen anywhere. If one person gets in a bad mood, it rubs off on others." I took a few steps toward the hallway. "I haven't heard anything out of Clive or Fred since I got here. Did Clive pass out from listening to Fred's sad stories?"

Doe shook her head. "Fred's in the men's restroom, installing new faucets. The old ones wore out. He's really handy."

"You should put him on the payroll," I said.

"We can't afford . . ." Doe put a hand to the earpiece she'd been wearing. "Got it," she said, scribbling some notes before hurrying to the far end of the counter. "Dwight!" she cried, "two-car collision at Grotto where the campground road joins Highway 2, no injuries, but traffic's backing up."

Dwight, who always moved slowly, ambled out from the hallway. "Damned idiots. It'd serve 'em right if they ended up in the river." He was still muttering as he made his exit.

The sheriff emerged, headed behind the counter, and propped up the plastic-encased cue against the wall. "Clive hasn't a clue. Too wasted that night. Fred says they all look alike to him, and he never plays pool anyway. Where the hell is Canby?" He scowled at Doe. "You said he'd be here by three. It's almost three-fifteen."

"He was busy," Doe replied. "He's also shorthanded. Norene's sick, so Julie has to cook and wait tables."

Milo reached into the pocket of his plaid flannel shirt and took out a pack of cigarettes. "You're still here," he said, glancing in my direction.

"I'd like to meet Clive."

He lighted a cigarette before responding. "Why?"

I shrugged. "I should know what the guy looks like."

"Go ahead," Milo said, waving a hand in the direction of the cells.

I started for the hallway. "Why don't you get a real visitors' room?"

The sheriff tapped ash onto the bare floor. "You know I don't usually keep perps in here for more than a few days. Berentsen's lawyer is supposed to post bail for him Monday."

I stopped in my tracks. "She is? How much?"

"Ask the judge." Milo turned around and went into his office.

I assumed Fred was still in the men's room. Only one of the four cells was occupied. The man sitting on his bed had his head down and looked as if he was about to fall asleep.

"Clive?" I said.

He gave a start. "Wh . . . ?" Shaking himself, he rubbed his head and got to his feet.

I introduced myself, shaking hands with Clive through the bars. He was around forty, average height and weight, thinning brown hair, and looking so pale that he might have been a lifer at the midway point of his prison stretch.

"I don't think we've met," I said, "but I'm sure I've seen you around town."

Clive nodded. "I recognize you. I like your editorials. Usually." He smiled slightly. "Sorry I can't offer anything to drink. Any news on the O'Toole kid?"

"Not since yesterday," I said. "This may sound odd for a journalist, but I'm almost afraid to ask."

Clive hung his head. "I should've made that run to Monroe. I could've driven the O'Tooles' truck."

"Yours is . . ." I paused, trying to remember what someone had said about Clive's vehicle.

"It needs new brakes." Clive's face hardened. "It's still at De Muth's shop. Not that it matters now."

"Do you know Mike O'Toole?"

Clive nodded. "He's a good kid, basically. It's just that . . . well, he's a kid. He wanted to be a mechanic."

"Cal Vickers at the Texaco station can't handle everything in town. Mickey Borg never works on cars and I'm told he even resents customers who don't want to pump their own gas. And the dealerships are always more expensive. We could use a good mechanic around here," I said without thinking.

Clive looked stricken. "Don't remind me."

I winced. "I didn't . . . damn, I put my foot in it."

Clive shrugged. "It's true, though. Al De Muth was tops, at least when it came to trucks."

"Look," I said, wanting to make amends, "I'm sure you didn't mean to . . ." I stopped. When I was with *The Oregonian* in Portland, there had been several occasions when I'd interviewed people who had been responsible or blamed themselves for someone else's death. I hadn't known any of those guilt-ridden subjects, nor did I ever see them again. But Portland was a big city and Alpine was a small town. Even if I hadn't met Clive Berentsen, the situation felt personal. Maybe I'd grown softer or maybe I'd forgotten how to feel neutral. Whatever the reason, I had a need to comfort the dejected man on the other side of the bars.

To my surprise, Clive seemed to understand. "Hey—it happened. I'd had a few beers, I was drunk, Al was being an asshole, he took a swing at me, and I swung my pool cue at him. It's that simple." His face crumpled. "Then he died."

A second or two, I thought, and one life ended as another was forever changed. I summoned up my nerve. "He swung first?"

Clive nodded. "He missed. I should've kept my mouth shut in the first place. I was out of line."

"What did you say to Al?"

Taking a deep breath, Clive rubbed at his temples. "Oh—it was about Holly Gross. After Jica went outside, I went up to the bar and sat down next to Al. I wanted to ask him when my truck would be fixed because I needed it Monday. Before he could answer, Holly tapped me on the shoulder and said if I needed company, she could give it to me. I told her to . . . to go away. She did, but Al didn't like the way I talked to her and he acted all pissed off. I don't know why, they aren't a couple, but then she offered to go with him. He told her some other time, maybe. I guess he didn't feel so good and he went over to the pool table."

Clive's pale blue eyes wandered around the confines of his cell. Realizing that he was getting to the hard part of his story, I merely nodded. "What happened next?"

"I still wanted to know about my truck," Clive went on. "I got off the bar stool to talk to Al. I guess he was still mad at me because he told me I could drive my truck over a cliff for all he cared. Then we got into it and that was . . . that." He sank down on his bunk, holding his head.

"I suppose your attorney has talked to you about self-defense."

He nodded once. "What difference does it make?"

"To you—or to Al?"

"To either of us. Al's still dead and I killed him. End of story."

"I met Jica," I said. "She insists you'd never kill anyone, even in self-defense."

"Accidents happen." Clive looked up, his expression still disconsolate. "And Jica never bad-mouths other people."

"That may be, but she's convinced you're not a violent person. Jica must be very fond of you."

"I don't know why." Clive shook his head. "She's something, isn't she? Awesome lady."

A sound behind me caught my attention. I turned to see Fred Engelman rolling his sleeves down over his hairy arms. "Sorry, I've got to get in my cell."

I smiled at Fred. "The faucets work, I assume."

"Oh, sure." He shrugged. "It's not that hard a job. The water pressure isn't so good, though. Dodge should get that checked out. I'll remind him." He wagged a finger at Clive who was still sitting on his bunk, looking glum. "Say, buddy, that's no way to entertain a lady. I ought to know, having lost the best wife in the world because I drank too much. Turn your back on booze and turn your front to the folks."

Clive glanced in our direction. "Right, Fred." His tone was weary.

Fred gave a thumbs-up sign. "I mean it. You've got to stop beating on yourself and change your ways. Take it from one who knows." He nodded at both of us, ambled a few paces to the next cell, and closed the iron bars behind him.

"I should be going," I said rather vaguely. Fred might not mind spending the weekend in jail, but I was feeling claustrophobic.

Clive looked at me again. "Thanks for stopping by."

"Sure." I tried to smile. The usual clichés of parting company didn't fit, so I simply walked away.

When I got to the front, Doe was on the phone and Milo was talking to Spike Canby. "They all look alike to me," the tavern owner said, waving at the pool cue.

"You don't count the damned things?" the sheriff demanded.

"No. Why should I? They're not some fancy matched set. If one disappears, Julie picks up a replacement at a garage sale." Spike glanced at me but didn't say anything.

Milo set the cue against the wall. "This is going to Everett. You're done here." He turned his back on Spike.

"What the hell difference does it make?" Spike shouted. "You got your man. That pool cue could've come from anywhere. It's not like we take inventory. You want me to count the balls, too?"

"Count 'em if you got 'em," Milo muttered.

Spike opened his mouth to speak, but thought better of it. He stomped away, pushing one of the swinging front doors so hard that it slammed against the inside wall. Doe put down the phone and turned to her boss. The usually stolid deputy looked stunned for a moment before she spoke. "Mike O'Toole died this afternoon at two-fifty-six."

Milo leaned his head against the wall. "Jesus!"

I closed my eyes and crossed myself. We all seemed at a loss for words. The terrible silence was finally broken by the sheriff. "That really tears it," he said in a hoarse voice before he slumped down into a chair at the counter.

I steeled myself and went to comfort Doe, who seemed frozen in place. "Who did you talk to?" I asked.

She didn't seem to hear me. I put a hand on her arm. "Doe?"

At last she responded. "Jake O'Toole." She cleared her throat. "He could hardly talk. All I know is . . . what I said." She shuddered. "I didn't even know Mike."

I nodded. "I didn't, either, but it's a terrible shock when somebody so young dies."

Milo crushed his cigarette in an empty coffee mug and sat up straight. "I've seen him around. God, the poor family. The O'Tooles are good folks. Life's such a bunch of crap."

"It can be," I said quietly. "Was Jake calling from the hospital?"

Doe shook her head. "I don't know."

"I'm going to stop by the store." Ordinary routine seemed to help me deal with tragedies. "If you hear anything more, let me know." I stared at Milo. "Okay?"

"Yeah. Right." He was gazing off into space.

Five minutes later, I pulled into the Grocery Basket's parking lot. A young man was on a ladder, taking down the GET WELL, MIKE! message on the reader board. I watched him from the car. He looked vaguely familiar. I wondered if he was Mike's brother.

Getting out of the car, I went over to the reader board. "Kenny?" I ventured.

The young man looked down at me. "Yes?"

"I'm so sorry for all of you. Is there anything I can do?"

With his soft features and beardless face, Kenny looked younger than twenty-two. He also seemed puzzled. "No. Thanks, though."

I realized he didn't know who I was. "If you can think of anything—anything at all—call me at home or at work. I'm Emma Lord from the *Advocate*."

Kenny didn't move for a few moments before he replied. "I know. I've seen you at church." He looked at the letters in his hand. "You're a writer. You can tell me what to put up here. I don't know how to say . . . what should be said."

"Your parents and your aunt and uncle will know," I told him.

He shook his head. "I have to do it now." He glanced at the reader board where only the last few letters of the original message remained in place. "I can't leave this blank."

"No," I agreed, "you can't." The sky had started to cloud over. Only tired phrases staggered through my mind. "Have you got plenty of letters in that box?" I asked, stalling for time.

Kenny O'Toole glanced at the cardboard carton in front of him. "I think so. I've got a bunch of numbers, too. For when they put up sale prices."

"Okay." I tried to think of something that didn't sound like utter pap. "How about this—'Too young, too soon.' Then the year of his birth and . . . this year." Somehow, I couldn't say *the year he died*. "Then just 'Mike—RIP.' "

Kenny stared into the carton. "That's good. Thanks."

"Are you the only family member here?"

Kenny shook his head. "Aunt Betsy's inside."

I went into the store, which seemed eerily quiet. Small groups of shoppers—no more than three or four—stood together in the aisles or near the front end. Only two checkers

were at the stands. For the first time, I noticed that the lighting seemed to make every face I saw look pallid.

I scanned each aisle, but didn't see Betsy anywhere, so I headed for the office. Just before I reached it, a slim middle-aged woman I recognized but whose name eluded me called out. "Ms. Lord?"

"Yes?"

She came toward me, her dark hair pulled back in a pony-tail. "I just heard about Mike," she said. "It's such a waste. He came into the tavern a few times. This has been a terrible week around here."

I realized I was talking to Julie Canby, Spike's wife and maker of onion rings. "It's tragic. How are you holding up, Julie?"

"Ohh . . ." She frowned. Up close I noticed that her olive skin was virtually unlined. "I'm all right. I've weathered a few storms in my life. Spike's still trying to get himself together. Nothing's easy, is it?"

"No," I responded. "I just saw Spike. Some college kids found a pool cue in the Sky by Burl Creek. He didn't recognize it, though."

Julie shook her head. "He wouldn't. Spike's not one for de-tails. He's all about being a good barkeep and treating the cus-tomers right."

"Of course. Is it true you realized De Muth was dead?"

"By the time I came out of the kitchen, everybody acted as if they were in shock. Poor Al. He never seemed happy. A bro-ken heart, maybe." She sighed. "But he never talked about it to Spike. Most customers unload after a few beers. Not Al. He kept himself to himself, as they say. He didn't seem to have any family around here. Being lonely is tough. Looking down at him, I couldn't help but feel that he'd led a hard life. And yet I think he was basically a good man."

"It's a good thing you kept your wits about you," I said. "It sounds like nobody else did."

"I'm a nurse. I worked for a doctor in Snohomish for over twenty years until he retired. I changed careers when I married Spike. Frankly, I'm a better nurse than a cook."

"You did fine by me with your onion rings," I said.

Julie smiled. "Thanks. I heard you came in with Leo. Being in the kitchen means I almost never get to mingle with the customers."

"No girlfriend for De Muth, I assume?"

Julie shook her head. "He never brought a woman with him. Not," she added with a touch of bitterness, "that living with somebody can't mean you're still lonely."

I assumed Julie referred to her first marriage to the man in Maltby. "Take care of yourself," I said, inching toward the office door.

"You, too." She moved on, her step brisk.

I knocked twice. Betsy called out, telling me to come in.

"Emma!" she said in surprise, getting up from her chair. "I thought it was Kenny."

"He's finishing the reader board," I said. "Oh, Betsy, I'm so sorry about Mike. How are Buzzy and Laura?"

"Numb." Betsy sat down again. Her eyes were red and she looked haggard. "As soon as I finish here, I'm going to join them and Jake at the rectory to talk to Father Den. After that, we'll go to Driggers Funeral Home. The faster we can make arrangements, the better."

I sat cautiously on a couple of soup cartons. The O'Toole office was as cramped as my own. "I'd hoped Mike was improving. What happened?"

Betsy took off her half-glasses and laid them on the desk. "Mike never got out of the ICU. For some reason, they couldn't control his pain no matter how many meds they gave him. He was in utter agony." She stopped, pressing her palms against her eyes. After sniffing a couple of times she put her hands in her lap and shook her head. "I couldn't stand watching him. None of us could. This afternoon he went into cardiac arrest. They tried to save him, but . . ." She made a helpless gesture. "I'm trying not to blame the doctors. In hindsight, I wonder why they didn't send Mike into Seattle where there are more sophisticated facilities. They could've used one of those medevac copters."

I had no answer for Betsy. "Maybe," I said after a long pause, "it wouldn't have made any difference. His injuries must've been more serious than we first heard."

"They were, I guess." Betsy grimaced. "I can't even remember all of the bad things the doctors told us. I don't want to remember."

"I don't blame you." I slid off the soup cartons. "I'll let you get back to work so you can meet up with the rest of your family. Truly, if there's anything I can do, let me know. You were such a help to my brother when he was filling in while Father Den was on sabbatical."

Betsy nodded halfheartedly. "Easy to do. Ben's a great guy."

"I know." I went around the desk and put my hand on Betsy's arm. "Please tell the family I'm thinking of them. Praying, too."

"I will," she said, standing up again and hugging me. "Thanks. By the way," she went on, releasing me and checking her watch, "if you see Kenny, tell him we leave here at four-fifteen. We can meet up at my car."

After exiting the office, I stopped, wondering if I should pick up something quick and easy for dinner. It seemed strange to be in the Grocery Basket and not tossing items in a cart. But I couldn't act as if nothing had happened to the people who worked at the store. I began walking faster, trying to ignore the dozen or more customers I saw who were talking softly to one another or staring blankly ahead as they moved in solitude down the aisles.

When I got to the entrance, Kenny was about to enter the store, apparently having finished his sad task with the reader board. I waited for him to get inside before I delivered the message from his aunt.

He nodded but didn't speak.

"You shouldn't have to be doing this," I said quietly. "None of your family should. I've heard you're smart, so you've probably already figured out that life is often cruel and we're all mortal."

Kenny nodded again. He looked at me with soft brown eyes. "I remember when the man you were going to marry was killed. I was there, at the summer solstice parade. I didn't see what happened because we were all down the street by the post office. But I heard the gunshot. We thought it was a firecracker."

I tried to fend off the ghastly image when Tom fell dead at my feet. Five years had passed, yet the memory still could send devastating chills down my spine. I did my best to curb my emotions. "That's what I mean," I said, my voice steady while shoving the horrific scene back into the darkest corner of my mind. "You and Mike must have been close."

"We were," Kenny replied. "Well . . . the last couple of years it was different. I was going to college here and then to the U. He was into cars and trucks. I suppose we'd both changed." His tone turned wistful. "I guess that's part of growing up. We went in different directions."

"That's natural," I conceded and tried to smile. "You did a good job with the reader board. I know it was a hard thing to do."

Kenny's expression was wry. "Not as hard as saying good-bye."

"No," I agreed. "No, it isn't. Letting go is even harder."

"You can't change what's already happened," he murmured and turned to glance at the reader board's message. "I put that sign up, but I won't take it down. I want to make sure everybody remembers."

THIRTEEN

WHEN I GOT BACK IN THE CAR, I CALLED GINNY. RICK AN-swered. He told me that both mother and baby were asleep. I suggested dropping the present off and seeing the new addition at another time. "Do you have a name?" I asked.

"Brandon," Rick replied. "It goes with our older two, Brad and Brett. I suppose he'll end up being Bran. I told Ginny that Brandon Erlandson was kind of a mouthful, but she insisted. I gave in. If we'd had a girl, we planned to call her Brianna."

"Brandon's a nice name," I said. "I'll put the present on the porch."

After I rang off, I removed the small gift card and wrote a short message: "For Brandon—wishing you and your family much happiness in the years to come."

As I tucked the card in with the present, I glanced again at the reader board. The irony of welcoming a new baby boy into the world and saying good-bye to a young man who had left us wasn't lost on me. The weather's mood was changing to gloomy. Gray clouds were settling in over Alpine, promising rain before evening. Feeling sad, I started the car and headed for the Erlandson house.

Their neat frame bungalow on Pine between Seventh and Eighth streets looked soothingly quiet. I left the present by the front door, got back into my Honda, and followed Seventh up to Tyee. Taking a right, I drove to Vida's house. Her Buick was in the driveway, so I assumed she was home.

"Well now!" she exclaimed as she ushered me into the living room. "I've been trying to call you. I should've dialed your cell phone."

"I take it you've heard about Mike?"

"Yes," she replied as I sat on the sofa and she stood by the hearth. "Marje Blatt called me. Doc had phoned her. He'd contacted the hospital in Monroe and was given the terrible news." She glanced at a framed photo of her loathsome grandson on the mantel. "Just think—Mike was only a year or so older than Roger." She squeezed her eyes shut and shuddered. "Shall I make tea?"

I declined the offer. Vida sat down in an easy chair while I told her about my visits to the sheriff's office and the Grocery Basket.

She nodded when I finished. "I tried to call the O'Tooles a few minutes ago, but Betsy had just left. Tell me more about Julie Canby. I scarcely know her. What did she say about the tragedy?"

"She was cooking when the mayhem started. Julie mentioned that she felt sorry for De Muth because he always seemed unhappy. No family, at least not close by. In fact, we don't know much about him."

Vida drummed her short nails on the padded chair arm. "True. I'm trying to recall when he came to Alpine. The repair shop's previous owner was Milt Weiss. He and his wife, Ema-

line, sold it to De Muth when they—foolishly, in my opinion—
moved to Arizona. That would be about six years ago."

"We must've done a story on it," I said. "Sky Service and
Towing has always run a small ad in the paper."

"Yes. I believe Leo passed on the details about the new
owner and Scott Chamoud wrote a short piece." She paused
again. I was certain that she was diving into her deep well of
memory. "There wasn't much to write about. Alvin De Muth
was from east of the mountains. He preferred small towns."
Vida grimaced. "Scott said he was a man of few words."

I nodded. "So I'm told. Milo did a background check. If
he'd found anything about Al, he might've mentioned it."

"He might not." Vida grimaced. "Milo can be very unforth-
coming."

"Maybe," I said, "I should see if Milo wants to eat the other
crab tonight. Marisa and I only demolished one between us. I
froze the torte." I stood up. "How was your evening with
Buck?"

She got out of the easy chair but didn't look at me. "Fine." I
waited while she arranged some of the family photos on the
mantel. Fondly, she fingered Roger's picture and moved it closer
to the front. "You'd think," she said, finally coming toward me,
"that Mike O'Toole's youth and general good health would
have seen him through this, wouldn't you?"

"I'd hoped as much," I said, "but they didn't. He's not the
first young person around here to die in a vehicular accident."

"Still," she added, glancing back at her grandson's smarmy
smile, "I get the shivers when I think of something like that
happening to Roger. Young people shouldn't die before their
time."

"I know."

We walked to the front door. "It's very different raising children these days," she murmured when we got to the porch. "So many more temptations. Not that it's ever easy, but I don't recall sending our three girls out the door and constantly fretting over what might happen to them before they came home again. Or even," she added, more softly, "if they'd come home at all."

I shot her a curious glance as she walked down the front steps with me. "Adam is several years younger than your daughters. I have to admit I worried quite a bit about what could happen when he was out of my sight. Being a single working mom and living in a big city made it even harder."

Vida stopped at the bottom of the steps. "Of course," she remarked in a vague tone. "It feels like rain." Her gaze moved south to Tonga Ridge, which was virtually obscured by gray clouds.

"It's not cold enough for frost, though," I said. "I think I'll call Milo to see if he's free for dinner."

Vida nodded absently. "The park by Redmond has a windmill."

I glanced at her. "What's that got to do with . . . anything?"

"Milo's future son-in-law is half Dutch," Vida replied in her usual brisk voice. "That's why Tanya and her fiancé are being married there. The nearest windmill is in Marymoor Park on Seattle's Eastside."

We walked on to the curb. "Will everyone wear wooden shoes?"

"Perhaps." Vida shrugged. "They can't do anything more unconventional than some of the marriage ceremonies I wrote up this summer. The Roberson-Corey wedding on horseback at the Evergreen State Fairgrounds was the worst. So disgusting having the bridesmaids and groomsmen carry those satin-trimmed shovels."

"And because Britney Roberson's dad owns Platters in the

Sky and takes out a weekly ad, we were forced to run pictures to prove it," I murmured, opening the door on the driver's side.

As Vida waved me off, I decided to call Milo from my car. A whole crab and most of the garlic bread was left over, but Marisa and I had eaten most of the Caesar and potato salads. I dialed the sheriff's cell in case he'd left the office.

"Last call for crab," I said. "Are you interested?"

"Yeah. Six?"

For some reason I thought the single-word query was *Sex?* It took me a second to realize I was mistaken. "That's fine. See you." I rang off. The Grocery Basket was closer to my house than Safeway, but I didn't feel up to coping with the gloomy atmosphere pervading the O'Tooles' store. I turned right on Sixth, followed Cedar to Alpine Way, and continued to Safeway, which anchored the northwest corner of the mall. It was starting to drizzle when I pulled into the parking lot.

The deli section was toward the front end. As I waited for the clerk to fill a medium-size carton with potato salad, I heard a commotion coming from farther down the aisle. Holly Gross had grabbed a little girl, who was kicking and yelling. A toddler in the cart's kiddy seat was screaming his head off, and a third youngster was trying to climb into the sweet potato bin. I turned away, trying to ignore the unruly Gross tribe. Memories of Adam having a tantrum at a Fred Meyer store in Portland came back to me—a frightening and embarrassing occasion when he'd tried to swallow a miniature soldier I'd refused to buy for him. After much choking and turning my son upside down, the tiny GI had been dislodged. Luckily, Adam got over public displays of temper at an early age. I finally got it through his ornery little head that if he ever pulled any more stunts like that, I would *never, ever* buy him anything he didn't need. I'd pointed out that there was a difference between *needs* and

wants. On my way to the checkout stand, I realized I'd forgotten to take care of Adam's most recent requests. Although they
were *needs,* the outlay of money would shrink my meager sav-
ings. I'd go online, compare prices, and have the *needs* shipped
directly to St. Mary's Igloo.

In the express line, I heard a familiar voice. "Are you diet-
ing?"

I turned to see Mitch Laskey, who had placed a brick of
cheddar cheese, a pint of whipping cream, and a can of pumpkin on the conveyor belt. "I don't need to do diets. Neither do
you," I added, gesturing at Mitch's lanky form.

He nodded. "Brenda tries every fad diet that comes along. I
don't know why. She's tall, and an extra ten pounds looks good
on her. I can't eat the pumpkin pie she's going to make all by
myself."

I paid cash for my purchases and waited for Mitch. "I suppose," he said after collecting his items from the courtesy clerk,
"you'd like to know about our visit with Jica Weaver in Snohomish yesterday."

We stopped just short of the exit. "You found out something?"

"Yes and no," he said. "Jica assured us that Clive is a peace-
ful type and insisted that even provocation wouldn't drive him
to violence. She didn't see the fight, and she dismissed Clive
taking responsibility as some kind of noble or gallant gesture."

"To what purpose?"

Mitch looked bemused. "It translated as protecting a lady's
honor."

The concept sounded unlikely. "Any lady in particular?" I
asked.

"No. Frankly, I thought she was kind of nuts, but Brenda
didn't agree. The word my wife used was *fanciful.*"

I grappled with the distinction. "She means Jica is . . . delusional?"

"Not exactly." Mitch stepped aside for a young couple who'd just entered the store. "Brenda thinks Jica's created an emotional haven, possibly to keep some very ugly experiences at bay."

"That could be," I said. "She seems fragile in every way."

"Not a local?"

"No." I frowned. "I shouldn't say that. I honestly don't know."

"Brenda thinks Jica's in love with Clive." He shrugged. "Women are better at gauging that sort of thing than men. Why else would Jica pay for his attorney?"

I nodded. "I gathered she's very fond of him."

"So it seems." Mitch glanced outside where the rain was now pelting the parking lot. "By the way, I heard about the O'Toole kid. That's damned rough." He looked grim. "You know the family pretty well, I gather."

"Yes. I've already talked to Betsy and Mike's brother, Ken."

"Nothing worse for parents." Mitch paused, slowly shaking his head. "Hey," he said suddenly, "I'd better go. Brenda won't have time to make the pie for dessert if I'm not home before five."

After exiting, we walked in opposite directions to our cars. Puddles were already accumulating on the concrete and the sky had turned very dark, with the wind blowing down off the invisible mountains and through the river valley. I all but ran to my Honda. Behind the wheel, I brushed water off my face and turned on the engine and the headlights. I reversed cautiously out of the diagonal space, then crept along to turn off onto Park Street and Alpine Way. My windshield wipers did their highest-setting best to let me see at least ten feet in front of me.

But I wasn't prepared for the sudden crash of metal on metal that sent me forward so sharply that the seat belt seemed to squeeze the air from my lungs. I braked, but the Honda still skidded slightly before coming to a full stop. I sat for a moment to make sure I had all my faculties and that my appendages were in working order. I turned off the ignition and looked to see where the car had been hit. A battered red beater had backed into the rear door on the driver's side. I could hear screams but couldn't tell where they were coming from. I took off my jacket, put it on over my head, and got out of the car.

Holly Gross was leaning into the beater, yelling at her children. Obviously, she had reversed out of her parking place too fast and hadn't seen my car. To my further dismay, the rear fender had been damaged, jamming it into the tire on that side. I couldn't drive my Honda home.

Holly had finally managed to quiet her trio of kids. She whirled around to look at me. "Move your damned car, bitch!" she shouted. "I can't get out of here."

Shock wore off quickly and anger took over. "I can't," I said, waving in the direction of my rear left tire. "Are you insured?"

Holly stopped by the rear end of her beater. "Shit, you can get somebody to yank that piece of metal out of the tire. Where's that tall, skinny guy I saw you yakking with?"

"Gone," I snapped.

"So?" Her sharp chin jutted. "Get him back here. He works for you, doesn't he?"

"I'm calling the cops," I said, starting back to the Honda to retrieve my purse.

"Hey! No way!" Holly yelled. "I'll get a guy from the store to do it."

I kept going. Holly followed me. Her flimsy cotton jacket

was already soaked, her blond hair was dripping wet, and her eye makeup was streaming down her cheeks. As I fumbled for my cell, she leaned into the car through the open door.

"Don't even think about it," she said, her tone menacing.

"Get the hell out of my face!" I shouted over the honking of a horn. "We're both blocking traffic."

I'd found the cell and was dialing 911 when Holly grabbed my left wrist and gave it a painful twist. "That's my kids honking!" Her eyes glittered with wrath. "Hang up!"

I swung my right arm and hit her in the head with the cell phone. She let go, reeling slightly. The call went through as I heard Beth Rafferty's calm voice on the other end.

"Safeway parking lot car wreck and catfight," I said quickly.

"Emma?" Beth said, recognizing my voice. "Got it. Injuries?"

"Not yet, but likely." Holly was coming at me again, but I'd moved enough so I could swing a leg and catch her at the knees. She fell forward into my lap. Beth had ended the call. Holly didn't get up. She was crying and blubbering. I shoved her off my lap. She sank to the ground with a dull thud.

I was able to close the car door and lock myself in. Feeling a trace of pity, I watched Holly stagger to her feet. The horn-honking continued. I couldn't be sure if it was her kids or an outraged shopper trying to get past our cars. As Holly finally stood up, I saw Dane Pearson, the Safeway manager, hurrying toward us with a couple of other employees and several customers. I rolled my window down halfway.

"What the hell . . . ?" Dane put an arm around the sobbing Holly before looking at me. "Ms. Lord?" he said, incredulous.

"I called the cops," I said. "Medics, too."

"Okay." Dane passed Holly on to a slim young man who

guided her back to the beater. "What happened?" the store manager asked, leaning down next to my car.

"See for yourself." I gestured behind me at the wreckage.

Dane and the third employee, a middle-aged woman, inspected the damage. Meanwhile, Holly had gotten back into her car with the young man's help. The gawking customers had sought cover from the downpour in their own vehicles or inside the store. I could hear sirens in the distance.

Dane walked over to me. "Did Holly back into you?"

"Yes." I took a couple of deep breaths. "She must've been going too fast for these conditions. I was barely doing ten miles an hour when she crashed into me."

"Okay." He moved to get in front of my Honda, where he waved and shouted to the patrol car that was pulling in. A moment later Dustin Fong headed my way. He spoke briefly to Dane before reaching my Honda. "Are you hurt?" the deputy asked, polite and calm as usual.

"I don't think so," I replied. "I'm kind of shaky, though."

Dustin looked apologetic. "You'll have to fill out an accident report. What happened?"

I explained how Holly had backed out too fast and too blindly. "You should make sure her three kids are okay," I added. "I think she lacks proper maternal instincts."

He turned to look around. "How many? Holly and two kids are headed this way."

"Oh, crap!" I cried. "Now what?"

Dustin was up to the challenge. His sturdy six-foot frame blocked the Gross onslaught. Holly had stopped crying, but was shrieking invective over the deputy's shoulder. Most of it, I gathered, was aimed at me. Glancing at my watch, I saw it was almost five. I decided to call Milo and ask him to pick me up. The Honda would have to be towed.

"Slow down," the sheriff ordered in that laconic tone I knew so well. "You're a wreck but you're safe in a park?"

I kept an eye on the Gross gang as Dustin led them to his patrol car. "Hang on," I said to Milo before leaning out the window. "Get the toddler, Dustin!" I yelled. "There's one more kid still in the car."

Apparently Holly wasn't counting heads, Dustin hadn't remembered there were three kids, and Dane was dealing with more gawkers. The medics were just pulling in.

"Okay," I said into the phone as I slumped in my seat, "if you want to eat crab, you'll have to collect the cook from Safeway's parking lot. Holly Gross backed into me and my car's not drivable."

"Shit." Milo groaned. "Some weekend. Okay, I'll be there in fifteen minutes. Have you called Cal Vickers to tow your car away?"

"No. I'll do that now." I rolled up my window. "I also have to fill out an accident report."

"Skip that," Milo said. "I'll bring one with me. I should stop by the office anyway. Doe's going off duty at five and I want to make sure that Bill Blatt is up to speed on everything."

"I'll wait inside the store. Dustin's got all of the Grosses rounded up and they're getting into his . . . hold it, he's coming this way. I'm hanging up."

"Ms. Lord," he said as I rolled my window back down. "There's room in the patrol car for you, too. Do you want to come with us?"

I gaped at the deputy. "Are you kidding? The only way I'd ride with that bunch is if you gave me a weapon. Your boss is picking me up. He's also bringing along an accident report form."

Dustin looked as if he was trying not to smile. "That's good.

We'll need your side of the story. Ms. Gross insists it was your fault."

"She would." I shook my head. "Those poor kids. Are they okay?"

"I think so." Dustin looked uneasy. "They've got a ton of energy. But the medics will check them out. Are you sure you're all right?"

"I'd better be," I said, "or else your boss is going to go hungry. If I suddenly collapse, the sheriff can haul me off to the ER."

Del Amundson had gotten out of the medic van. Dustin excused himself to meet the medic in front of the patrol car, which, I noticed, was rocking a bit. I could only guess what mayhem the Gross clan would commit before Dustin finished with them.

Dane had disappeared briefly, but I saw him coming over to my Honda. He was carrying four grocery bags, presumably containing Holly's purchases. "I suppose this will be in the *Advocate*," he said.

I nodded. "We report all accidents. It's not your fault, Dane."

His round, rain-spattered face looked bleak. "I know that, you know that, but Holly says she's going to sue me for not providing decent lighting in the parking lot. Not to mention," he went on, juggling the sacks, "it looks to me as if her kids shoplifted a bunch of candy. The bill was on top and I noticed that there weren't any M&M's or Reese's Peanut Butter Cups. They've done it before." He sighed. "Glad you're all right, Ms. Lord. I guess I'll write off the candy as a business expense." Trying to avoid the ever-growing puddles, he headed for the patrol car, where the Gross children were getting out and being herded to the medic van.

I dialed Cal Vickers's number. The Texaco service station was by the mall, just a couple of minutes away from Safeway. His son, Chuck, answered and told me he'd come right over.

The patrol car pulled out as soon as the medic van moved out of the way. Dane waved a weary arm at me as he walked by my car and headed back toward the store. The slim young employee returned. He was wearing a rain poncho and carrying a big flashlight. I guessed that he'd been sent to guide traffic around the parking lot's blocked aisle.

Chuck Vickers and Cal's towing truck entered and stopped at the far end of the row. I flashed my headlights. He reversed, coming slowly in my direction. A moment later, he approached me.

"Hi," he said bending down. "Do you want me to take your groceries out first?"

"I've only got a couple of items," I said. "Go ahead, I'll walk to the store and wait inside for my ride." I didn't mention who was picking me up. Tales of Sheriff Dodge coming to the rescue of Publisher Emma are the stuff that rumors are made of.

"No way!" Chuck grinned, looking like a younger, more animated version of his dad. "I'll take you there before I tow your car. Deal?"

I smiled back. "Sure." Grabbing my purse and the salads, I checked to make sure I wasn't leaving anything vital behind. "Let's go."

We hurried to the tow truck's cab. Chuck stayed right behind me, making sure I didn't break a leg climbing into the passenger seat. "What," he asked after he got behind the wheel, "about the other car?"

"It belongs to Holly Gross," I said. "She's gone off with one of the deputies to fill out an accident report."

"Holly!" He snickered. "My dad swears she hit on him the last time she got gas at our place. She didn't have enough money to pay, so she . . . well, you know. I guess she usually goes to Gas 'n Go at Icicle Creek. Maybe she works off the bill with Mickey Borg." He grimaced. "Sorry, Ms. Lord. I shouldn't say stuff like that."

"It's fine," I said as Chuck shifted out of neutral into drive. "I'm no fan of Holly. If she doesn't get her car towed, Dane will have to do it."

"Right." Chuck turned the truck toward the store entrance. "That's a real bummer about Mike O'Toole. It rocked my world. We went through high school together and you never think somebody your own age is going to die. And then . . . blam!" He shook his head in disbelief.

"You were friends?"

"We hung out in high school," Chuck replied. "We were both on the football and basketball teams." Pulling up in front of the store, he gave me a rueful look. "He was a starter in both. I kept the bench warm. Remember that game five, six years ago against Sultan? We were underdogs, but with seconds to go, Mike intercepted a pass and scored a touchdown. Big upset for the Turks, big win for us Buckers."

I vaguely recalled the game. A win against any team in any sport was unusual for Alpine High's athletes. But I hadn't remembered Mike's key role in the victory. "He must've relished being a hero," I said.

"Oh, yeah." Chuck had turned somber as he gazed through rivulets of rain on the windshield. "Before I started at Washington State, I asked him if he'd ever thought about going on to college and playing football. Mike told me he didn't want to. He was tired of school. He'd always been into cars." Chuck shrugged. "I figured he'd take those mechanic courses the community college offers, but he never did. I guess he thought on-the-job training was better."

"As in being taught by Alvin De Muth?"

"Right. I guess Al was a good mechanic. Nobody in our family ever had him work on a car or truck, because Pop can do it." Chuck paused and frowned. "Now both Mike and Al are dead. Weird, isn't it?"

"Yes," I said, and wondered if *weird* was the right word.

FOURTEEN

Five minutes after Chuck Vickers dropped me off, Milo showed up at the store. "Jeez," he said, after I got settled into the Grand Cherokee, "I never should've stopped by the office. Holly's a real piece of work. My ears are still ringing from listening to her yell at me. And those kids! It was like a freaking zoo."

"You don't need to tell me," I said. "Did she claim that I was the one who caused the accident?"

"You bet. Then you beat her up." Milo snickered. "I'll admit she looked in bad shape. I guess I won't take you on in a barroom brawl."

"Don't worry," I said. "I'm very tame if I don't get riled up."

"Right." He glanced at me and chuckled. "You're pretty good at wrestling."

I took a deep breath. "Milo—I know where you're going. Stop now. I am not in the mood for any more physical exertion this evening."

He kept his eyes on the road as he turned onto Alpine Way. "Okay."

I was surprised, having expected him to argue, turn sullen, or be dejected. I quickly changed the subject. "Do you remember Mike O'Toole playing football for the Buckers?"

"Sure. He was pretty good. Rip Ridley told me once that if Mike really worked hard he could make all-conference." The sheriff made a left onto Fir. "Coach said the kid had good hands when it came to basketball, but he wasn't very tall and his outside shooting was erratic." Milo pulled into my driveway. "Is Cal going to fix your car?"

"I hope so," I replied, collecting my purse and the Safeway bag. "I *think* he can."

"You may have to take it to Bert Anderson," Milo said.

I didn't speak again until we'd gotten out of the Cherokee and were going into my log house. "Maybe I should," I said.

Taking off his all-weather jacket, Milo looked puzzled. "Should . . . what?"

"Take the Honda to Bert. I could talk to him about the brawl."

"Why? Hasn't Mitch gotten his side of the story? If you want, you can look over the statement he gave us," the sheriff went on, following me out to the kitchen.

"Oh—I don't know," I said, putting the salads in the fridge. "When it comes to a homicide, I always like to get my own slant on things."

"Oh, God!" Milo laughed, shook his head, and opened the cupboard where I kept the liquor. "Emma Lord, Girl Detective. This one's a slam dunk. Forget about it."

"I can't." I bit my lip. "I know you're right, but I'm responsible for every word that goes into the paper. I don't want to find out after we've gone to press that we could be sued because one of us screwed up. Furthermore," I continued, while Milo got ice cubes out of the freezer compartment, "now that we're going online, I don't have the luxury of waiting six days before I make a fool of myself on the Internet."

Milo dropped the ice into glasses. "You're going online?"

"I think I just said that."

The sheriff poured Scotch into his glass and Canadian into mine. "Will that bring in money?"

"It better," I said, picking up my drink from the counter. "That's why we're . . . oops!" The glass slipped from my hand and fell to the floor. It didn't break, but the liquor and the ice were all over the place.

"I'll get it," Milo volunteered.

"No." The sheriff was a haphazard housekeeper. I wanted to make sure the floor was completely dried. When it came to walking, I was clumsy.

"I'll fix you another drink and take it out to the living room," he said. "I think you're still kind of shaky from the accident."

"Thanks." I took some rags out of a drawer, bent down to retrieve the ice, and began wiping up the mess. Milo got out another glass for me and went through the drink-making process a second time. Somehow he managed to keep out of the way. A couple of minutes later, he loped off to the living room. I sat back on my haunches, making sure I hadn't left any wet spots. The floor looked pristine. As I tried to stand, a shock of pain zigzagged through my lower back. Dropping back to my knees, I let out a piercing yelp and leaned against the sink.

"What the hell . . . ?" Milo said, coming to my aid. "What's wrong?"

"My back!" I cried. "I did something stupid. It hurts like hell."

"Can you stand all the way up? Here," he said, holding out a big hand. "Take it real slow."

I had no choice. Every small movement was agonizing. Leaning on the sheriff, I struggled to get to my feet. "Oh, God," I gasped, "I don't think I can walk."

"I can carry you," Milo said. "Or should I? Maybe you ought to stay put."

I winced from pain. "No. Park me on the sofa." He scooped me up. I squeezed my eyes shut, trying not to moan and groan. For such a big guy, the sheriff could be surprisingly gentle. He kicked a couple of throw pillows out of the way before setting me down.

"Here," he said, picking up the pillows. "You want these behind your head?"

I nodded. Milo put the pillows in place and glanced at my Canadian whiskey on the end table. "How in hell are you going to drink this without spilling it all over the place?"

"I don't know," I admitted. "I think there are some straws in the cupboard where I keep glassware."

Milo rubbed at his chin. "Maybe you need another pillow." He frowned. "Didn't the medics check you out?"

"No." I tried to lift my head but the pain intensified. "Damn! I was fine, really. The medics had their hands full with the Gross bunch."

"*Gross* is right for that wrecking crew." The sheriff took his cell phone out of his flannel shirt. "I'm calling Doc Dewey."

"Oh, don't!" But it was too late to stop him, and he was probably right. I wasn't going to cure myself by lying helplessly on the sofa. Eyeing the drink that Milo had set on the end table, I made a couple of futile efforts to shift my body into a more comfortable position.

"Doc's coming," the sheriff said after a brief exchange. "Thank God he still makes the occasional house call."

"He was trained by the best," I said. "His father."

"True." Milo studied my miserable form. "You need a blanket?"

"No. Hand me the drink. Maybe I can throw it in my mouth."

The sheriff took another pillow from the opposite end of the sofa and put it behind my head. "There," he said, handing me my drink. "See if you can keep from dumping it all over your . . . chest."

I managed to take a couple of sips. Milo had made a very strong drink. I took two more sips. Satisfied that I wasn't going to spill the rest of the cocktail, he sat down in the easy chair. I swallowed more whiskey. The sheriff scanned the TV listings in the morning edition of the *Times*.

I'd relaxed a bit, easing the pain. Maybe I'd survive after all. "Do you think Holly has car insurance?" I asked.

"She'd better," Milo said, lighting a cigarette. "It's a state law."

"And you're running out of room in the jail." I took another sip, actually more like a big gulp—and giggled. "Hey, how 'bout tossin' me one of your Mar'bros?"

He reached again into his shirt pocket, but hesitated. "Maybe not. You might set yourself on fire."

I'd downed more whiskey. "No, I won't," I asserted, dangling a hand in the direction of the carpet. "Jus' pu' 'nashtay on the floor."

"No." He settled back into the easy chair. "Doc'll give you hell if he catches you smoking. I ought to know. Besides, you're kind of . . . giddy."

"Giddy?" For some reason, the word made me giggle again. "Never hear' you say 'giddy' before."

"Never had to use it," Milo said, sounding vaguely amused.

"Giddy, kiddy, widdy, Bo Diddly," I muttered before finishing my drink. "Tha's *funny*." I hiccuped. And hiccuped again.

The phone rang. The sheriff gestured at the end table. "Do you want me to answer it?"

I shook my head. The phone rang two more times. I changed my mind. "Sure."

Milo got up as the fourth ring sounded. He was halfway across the room when the call trunked over. "It's three AM, and do I know where my Emma is? I can't sleep without her," the voice on my machine said. "I'm heading for the Loire Valley tomorrow. Are you coming with me or shall I jump off the balcony at Chenonceau and drown myself in the River Cher?"

Milo glared at me. "Is that the asshole from the AP?"

I nodded—and hiccuped.

The sheriff retrieved his cigarette and drink from the side table by the easy chair. He loomed over me. "I thought you dumped him."

I nodded again—and hiccuped.

"Where the hell *is* this bozo?" Milo demanded. "If you dumped him, why are you supposed to be wherever he is?"

I waved an impatient hand. A fresh twinge of pain consumed me. I winced and hiccuped at the same time. The sheriff turned away sharply, going to the front window. "Here's Doc. Try not to make a complete fool of yourself, okay?"

I couldn't respond. I was still hiccuping. Milo opened the front door. Doc Dewey, who was wearing a rain hat, came into the living room. I thought the rain hat was absolutely hilarious. I giggled and hiccuped and dropped the almost empty glass onto the carpet.

Suddenly I felt utterly debilitated. The hiccups stopped as soon as Doc took off his hat. He and Milo were both a blur. Their voices seemed to be coming from far away, echoing as if they were talking through a drainpipe.

" . . . in the kitchen . . . couldn't get up . . ."

" . . . broken? Then probably a muscle . . . take a look . . ."

While Doc opened his medical case, Milo scooped up my glass and took it out to the kitchen. When Doc started asking me questions, I tried to focus on him. Everything was still fuzzy. I thought I heard him tell Milo that at least the liquor had relaxed me, which, I gathered, was good. Doc did some poking and probing before requesting me to make several movements that ordinarily would've been simple. I had difficulty understanding what he wanted, and when I finally got the gist of his instructions I discovered that bending, stretching, and whatever other requests he made caused me to hurt.

"It's not serious," he said, "though I want to take some X rays tomorrow or Monday if you're not better." Doc paused and wagged a finger at me. "No more booze for you tonight. It might give you temporary relief, but liquor masks the pain." He paused, apparently waiting to see if his words had sunk in. I nodded, probably looking sheepish. Doc turned to Milo. "Did you hear that?" Milo, who had refilled his glass while he was in the kitchen, answered that he understood and asked Doc if he'd like a drink.

"No thanks," Doc replied, taking a medicine bottle out of his case. "If you mixed the one Emma drank, I'd never be able to drive home. I'm going to give her some Demerol and write a prescription for more along with methocarbamol to relax the muscles. You can get them filled at Parker's before they close at seven."

"Will do," Milo said, looking faintly chastened.

"Do it now," Doc ordered the sheriff. "If you drink the rest of whatever you've got in your glass you'll have to arrest yourself for a DUI. Now go get Emma a glass of water." As Milo loped back to the kitchen, Doc called after him: "Just water," he repeated loudly before looking at me again. "How bad is it right now?"

"Not so bad," I said, wondering where my euphoria had gone.

"Try not to do much for the rest of today and tomorrow. If," he went on as Milo returned with the water, "it gets worse, call me. Day or night. Got it?"

"Yes." I took the water from Milo and the pills from Doc.

"They work pretty fast," Doc said.

"Good." I swallowed them both at the same time and managed not to choke. Or hiccup. For the first time since Doc walked through the door I studied his face. He looked tired and drawn. "You better take the night off," I said.

"I can't. The last week or so Elvis and I've been working long days and almost as long nights. This is a bad time of year for flu and colds and every other bug that comes along. Not," Doc added, "to mention people getting themselves killed or injured in highway accidents." He stared at Milo. "Well? Why are you standing there? It's almost six-thirty. I'll stay with Emma while you're gone."

"Okay, okay," Milo said, taking his jacket from the small coatrack by the front door. "I'm on my way."

If I hadn't been in such a mess, I would've smiled. Doc—and occasionally Vida—were the only two people I knew who could give the sheriff orders. Gerald Dewey was a few years younger than Milo, but somehow Young Doc, as he had been known in his father's time, had managed to channel Old Doc's command along with his compassion. A minute later Milo was gone and Doc sat down in the other easy chair.

"Is he going to stay with you tonight?" Doc asked bluntly.

I made a face. "Are there *any* secrets in this town?"

"Not many," he said. "I'm asking the question from a medical standpoint. It's not a good idea for you to be by yourself."

I sighed. "I hadn't planned on an overnight. I invited Milo for dinner—just dinner—last night, but his ex-wife came to town."

"Oh—yes, Tricia." Doc smiled and shook his head. "Tanya Dodge. I delivered her. It seems like it was only a few years ago. My dad delivered their other two kids. Where have all those decades gone?"

"You've saved several lives in those years," I said.

He frowned. "And lost some, too."

"But you've also delivered a lot of babies."

"True." Doc turned melancholy. "Mike O'Toole was one of them."

"Oh." No wonder Doc looked sad. "Do you know what happened? I mean, the medical reason he didn't pull through?"

"Cardiac arrest," Doc replied, his usually kind face hardening.

"But," I persisted, realizing that as the Demerol began to ease the pain, the fuzzy feeling was coming back, "he was so young and apparently fit. What triggered cardiac arrest?"

Doc took off his glasses and leaned forward in the easy chair. "Why are you asking me that?"

I shrugged, causing the pain to intensify. "I don't know. It just . . . bothers me. I thought maybe you talked to the doctors in Monroe."

"I did." He stood up, walked over to the side table by the other chair, and took a big gulp of Milo's Scotch. "Damned fool thing to do," he muttered, setting the glass back down. "Let's say I'm not the only fool in town." He went back to his chair. "How do you feel?"

"Better. Sleepy." I tried to smile. "I don't get it. About being a fool, I mean. Am I being dense?"

Doc shook his head. "No. I'll be quiet and let you drift off."

"Th-th-thanks . . . for . . . c-c-coming." The words stumbled out of my mouth.

"Not a problem."

A few minutes later, I heard Milo return. He and Doc talked

for what seemed a long time, but probably wasn't. I couldn't hear what they were saying. The words were disjointed and immediately floated out of my brain. My log cabin grew silent. I assumed Doc had left. The sheriff was in the kitchen, probably trying to find his dinner. I didn't remember anything else until I woke up almost three hours later.

Milo had the TV on, but the sound was very low. He was watching ESPN's baseball experts rehash an American League divisional play-off game between the Yankees and the Twins.

He clicked off the TV. "You're awake?"

"Uh-huh. Who won?"

"Yankees in the eleventh, end of series, and on to the ALCS against the Red Sox. How are you doing?"

"I'm stiff," I said, making an effort to move around a bit. "I hurt, but not like I did earlier."

The sheriff checked his watch. "It's after ten. You're almost due to take that pain stuff I got at Parker's."

I nodded as I got into a semi-sitting position and studied the directions on the methocarbamol. "I'll take this muscle relaxant now. I'm hungry. What's left of the crab?"

"Not much." Milo came to rearrange the pillows behind my head. "A couple of legs and part of the stomach. There's some of both salads. You want to eat now? I can bring the food out here."

"Please," I said after swallowing a methocarbamol.

He started for the kitchen but stopped. "Cal Vickers called. He can't do that job on your car and he doesn't have your kind of tires in stock. The Honda dealership might have some on hand."

"So what do I do? Have the car towed to Bert Anderson's place?"

"That's what Cal suggested. Bert doesn't work Sundays, though."

"Damn." I considered my options, which were few. I couldn't drive to Sunday Mass. I couldn't drive to work Monday. Maybe I couldn't even walk. I had to use the bathroom, so I'd find out if I could stand up.

"Oh," Milo said leaning through the kitchen doorway, "you've got to fill out that accident report. I want it dated today."

"Great," I muttered. Heaving a sigh, I threw off the afghan Milo had put over me while I slept. Taking my time, I managed to get into a sitting position, set both feet firmly on the floor, and steadied myself on the sofa arm. I hurt, but the pain was bearable. It took me a couple of minutes to walk the short distance from the sofa, past the end table, into the hall, and on to the bathroom. I refused to look at myself in the mirror. It was one thing to feel miserable. There was no point in confirming what I already knew: I must have looked frightful.

When I emerged a few minutes later, Milo was in the easy chair and my dinner sat on a serving tray I kept in the dining alcove's breakfront.

"Thanks," I said, flopping onto the sofa.

"You must feel better," he said. "You look pissed."

"I'm not," I responded. "Well . . ." I squirmed a bit, trying to get into a reasonably comfortable position. "I *am* pissed, at myself and that half-witted tart Holly. Of course she has to be poor or I could sue her." I studied the items on the tray. "I need some melted butter for the crab."

Wordlessly, Milo went back to the kitchen. When he returned, he handed over not only a cup of melted butter but also the accident report form. "You can do that while you eat," he said, settling back into the easy chair. "Try not to mess it up with your food."

I shot him a dark glance. "Why can't it wait a few minutes?"

"Because you're going to take more of that pain stuff and you might get goofy. I've had enough witness statements this past week from drunks and nutcases. I'd like to get one that makes sense for a change."

"Fine." Cautiously, I leaned to my right to pick up a pen from the end table. After putting in my name, address, the date, and where the collision occurred, I slathered a chunk of crab in the melted butter. "I'm not sure about the time the accident happened," I admitted.

Milo, who was using the remote to switch channels, looked up and scowled. "You're off to a bad start. You called me about a quarter to five. Put down four-thirty or maybe a little later."

I wrote in "4:40 PM" as I chewed on romaine lettuce. "Sorry," I said a moment later, "I don't know what kind of car Holly was driving."

"Jesus!" Milo was exasperated. "Dustin told me it's a 1982 Plymouth Caravelle. For a reporter, you don't seem to notice much."

The sheriff was right. "True," I said. "I must've been more shaken up than I realized."

"Are you sure you can do the damned diagram?"

"Back off, will you?" I snapped. "I'm starting to hurt like hell."

Milo ignored me and continued to change channels until he got to *The Searchers*. I stopped filling out the form and ate the rest of my dinner. By eleven o'clock, John Wayne had decided to let Natalie Wood live, though not necessarily happily ever after for either of them. *Like real life,* I thought. *No guarantees.* I finished my dinner but was still debating with myself about strangling the greedy, selfish Milo Dodge for eating almost an entire crab all by himself.

"Want to watch the news?" he asked.

"I want my pills," I retorted. "I won't finish this damned report until I get them."

The sheriff clicked off the TV and hoisted himself out of the easy chair. "I'll bring some water." He stopped halfway to the kitchen. "After I left Parker's, I stopped by my place and grabbed some stuff so I could spend the night. I'm getting up at first light to hit the river where the Tye meets the South Fork. If you have any problems, call Doc."

"Fine." I didn't bother to look up, but focused on the report, showing the position of my car and Holly's in the Safeway parking lot. Ten minutes later, I'd downed the Demerol and finished the paperwork.

"Here," I said, waving the report at Milo. "I'm still lucid. Don't lose this while you're fishing."

Milo ambled over to the sofa. "Can you get into bed by yourself?"

"I think so," I replied, handing over the accident form. "I'm not going to try it until the painkillers kick in."

"How long?"

"I don't know. Ten, fifteen minutes?"

"Okay." Milo crossed the room to reach behind the easy chair. "I'll do my thing in the can now. Is Adam's room made up?"

"Yes."

The sheriff had picked up a worn black gym bag and was heading for the hall. Guilt was seeping into my brain. It was remarkably generous of him to play nursemaid. I shouldn't have been annoyed because he'd eaten so much crab. I shouldn't have griped about the accident report. I shouldn't have stomped all over his attempt at flirtation. I should make sure he knew I appreciated not only his help but his friendship. Milo, more than anyone including Vida and Adam, knew my little log house so intimately.

I closed my eyes, wondering how to repay him. When I opened them, it was daylight and the sheriff was gone.

SHORTLY BEFORE NOON ON SUNDAY VIDA SHOWED UP ON MY doorstep. I still hurt, but the pain was bearable. It took me a long time to fix some breakfast and get dressed. Even as Vida charged through the front door, she was chastising me.

"I cannot imagine," she said, taking off her black swing coat and hanging it on a peg by the door, "why you didn't call me last night. I had to hear about your disaster from my nephew Billy at church. Surely you could have let me know. However did you manage on your own?" She paused, gazing down at me from under the brim of a brown velvet pillbox with a pheasant feather band. "Or did you?"

"Did I . . . what?"

"Manage alone."

"Milo stayed here. He was coming to dinner, remember?" I shifted around on the sofa. "He left early to go fishing."

Vida didn't respond at once. "I see," she said at last, and sat in the sheriff's favorite easy chair. "You should've called Doc."

"We did," I replied. "He came over right away."

"Oh." Vida's sharp gaze roamed around the living room. Maybe she was looking for signs of debauchery. "Very kind of Doc."

"Yes." I couldn't quite sit up straight. "He seemed . . . a bit odd."

"Odd?" Vida scowled. "That's unusual. Like his father, Gerald Dewey is very sound and has good sense. What do you mean by 'odd'?"

"I'm not sure," I admitted. "I was kind of out of it last night."

Vida fingered her chin. "Doc and Dr. Sung have both been very busy. I'll ask my niece Marje if she thinks Doc's working too hard."

Knowing how quickly rumors spread, I downplayed my comments. "Maybe I misunderstood Doc. I was fuzzy while he was here."

Vida looked affronted. "I won't suggest to Marje that Doc is behaving oddly. He may be working too hard. He's no spring chicken."

"True," I agreed. "We need a third doctor in SkyCo. Maybe I'll write an editorial about it for this week's paper."

Vida stood up. "And how will you get to work tomorrow?"

"I don't know. Cal's having my car towed to Bert Anderson's shop."

"I'll pick you up at ten to eight." She patted her velvet hat and tucked a couple of errant gray curls under the small brim. "Leo has the bakery task tomorrow, but you should remind Amanda that it's her turn Tuesday. Is there anything I can do for you before I leave?" She saw me shake my head. "Very well. I'm on my way to see my sister-in-law, Ella. She's not herself since she had that stroke last summer," Vida went on as she reached for her coat. "Of course she wasn't that sharp to begin with."

I started to get up, but Vida raised a hand. "Don't. Sit. Rest. I can see myself out."

"See you tomorrow," I called after her.

I spent the rest of the afternoon dozing and reading. Another postseason baseball game, Houston versus St. Louis, started at five. Shortly before the pregame show, the phone rang. I fumbled with the receiver but finally got it in the vicinity of my ear.

"Do you see what I see?" Rolf Fisher asked.

"I see a bottle of Demerol and a cane," I retorted. "What now?"

"I'm twenty yards away from the Loire in a delightful French cottage for two. The autumn leaves are turning gold and amber, the river is flowing gently, the ducks and geese are . . . Did you say Demerol?"

"Yes. I hurt my back. I was in a car wreck yesterday. If you must talk, talk fast. I'm due for my next pain pills in ten minutes."

"Well. That's not very promising when it comes to travel, is it?"

"No travel of any kind. My car has to be fixed."

"You need a cane?"

"I lied about the cane. Why not? You lie to me all the time. For all I know you could be lying right now and instead of the Loire Valley, you're standing on the banks of the Dosewallips River over on the Olympic Peninsula and contemplating a hike to Mystery Mountain."

"I'm not," Rolf said, sounding self-righteous. "In fact, a quaint native from Orleans is reversing his BMW out of the driveway after we shared a fine meal at a fine restaurant in Blois."

"Good for you. Look," I said, not in the mood to play any more games, "stop needling me. I couldn't come to France if I wanted to. Which I don't. When and if you ever come back to this part of the world, give me a call—if you feel like it. If I feel like it, I'll answer. Okay?"

A long pause ensued. "I think you've made yourself clear." Rolf's usually flippant tone was so formal that it might have belonged to the quaint native from Orleans. "I have nothing to say except *adieu*."

The phone went dead. I set the receiver down and held my head. Rolf had so many qualities I really liked. He was smart, open-minded, funny, charming, and attractive. At least *I* thought he was attractive. It wasn't easy in middle age to find a man—*any* man—with so much going for him. And he was single, having been a widower for several years. Maybe it was a good thing I hadn't fallen in love with him. But now, in my typically perverse fashion, I suddenly missed him. Maybe he was never moving back to Seattle. Maybe he'd spend the rest of his life in Europe. Maybe I'd never see him again. Maybe I was nuts.

"Demerol," I murmured, reaching for the bottle on the end table. Before I could remove the lid, the phone rang again. I pounced on the receiver. "Yes?" I said breathlessly.

"I simply don't believe it!" Vida exclaimed. "Milo and Tricia are getting back together! Doesn't that beat all?"

FIFTEEN

I WAS STUNNED. HUMAN BEHAVIOR IS OFTEN PREDICTABLE: A teenager rebels against authority; a seemingly happy couple splits up; a husband has an affair; a wife drinks too much; and the New York Yankees don't make it to the postseason every year. But Milo and Mulehide getting back together was never in my crystal ball.

I must've looked stricken. It was just as well that Vida couldn't see my face, although she undoubtedly realized the news would distress me. For a long moment I was too stunned to speak. "How did you find out?" I finally asked.

"From Thelma Petersen, Milo's aunt," Vida replied, sounding even more brisk than usual. "While I was at the retirement home for lunch with Maud Dodd, I called on the Petersens to personally apologize for the cornucopia typo. Tricia had stopped to see Aunt Thelma and Uncle Elmer before leaving town yesterday morning." A brief pause could've been intentional to let Tricia's departure time sink in to my addled brain. "This second marriage has been in trouble for the past two or three years," she continued. "I always wonder why a woman would marry a man who cheats on his wife when she knows from personal experience he has a roving eye. She sets herself up for betrayal. I'm not including Tommy as that sort of man," Vida added quickly. "His situation was much different with an emotional disaster for a wife."

"Very . . . true." I knew I sounded vague, though it wasn't because of the reference to "Tommy," as Vida always called the love of my life. Tricia's Saturday morning departure spoke volumes. Milo's ex had probably spent the night with him. No wonder he hadn't been annoyed by my refusal to have sex with him. Maybe he was all worn out. Or perhaps I'd overreacted to what might have been a lighthearted response. "Is Tricia getting a divorce?" I asked.

"She's seeing an attorney tomorrow," Vida said. "Peter—her second husband—moved out shortly after Labor Day. Tricia's selling the house. I suppose the sale will be divided between her and Peter. Frankly, Thelma doesn't seem too happy about this reconciliation. She never cared much for Tricia. Elmer didn't have much to say, but of course he never does. He was busy making Christmas gnomes out of papier-mâché." She paused. "Or were they elves?"

I didn't give a damn if they were hippopotamuses. "So," I said, still trying to conceal my shock, "you figure Tricia's moving back to Alpine?"

"It's the sensible thing for her to do," Vida responded. "I can't imagine why she'd want to stay on Seattle's Eastside. My goodness, it strikes me as being much like California. Not that I've been to Bellevue more than twice."

I didn't bother to point out that Vida had never been to California at all. "I hope Milo and Tricia know what they're doing," I said without enthusiasm. "I have to take my medicine now. I'll see you tomorrow."

"Of course." A brief silence ensued at her end of the line. "You're doing well, I take it?" she asked in a more solemn tone.

"I'm improving," I said. "Doc may take an X-ray tomorrow just in case."

"You should have it done before you go to the office," Vida said. "Marje will be there at eight even though the clinic doesn't officially open until eight-thirty. I'll call now and let her know we're coming. It'll provide an excellent excuse for me to ask her if Doc is worn out."

I was in no mood to argue. "Okay."

We said good-bye and hung up. I sat on the sofa, staring into space. My brain told me I should be happy for Milo and Tricia. But I wasn't. Instead, I felt a deep sense of loss. A wife usually doesn't take well to a husband whose closest friend is another woman. It was Milo's companionship that I would miss most.

Or was it? I didn't know what I thought. Maybe I just needed time to think through this jarring development. I opened the pill bottle, took two Demerol, and wondered if I should call Milo. But I refrained, assuming he'd call me to find out how I was doing.

I was wrong. He never phoned. I thought that was odd. If he'd gone fishing at first light, he should've come off the river by noon. As the hours passed, I grew irked, annoyed, and downright angry. By the time I went to bed, I'd made up my mind not to call him at all.

Monday morning, Doc Dewey appeared more like himself when Vida and I met him in the waiting room just after eight o'clock.

Doc did the X-ray while Vida stayed in the reception room to grill Marje Blatt. The medical news was good. "Just one of those crazy things," Doc said. "You probably got jarred up when Holly hit your car. Then, after you got home, you moved too fast or the wrong way, and—bingo! You're in trouble. How's the pain?"

"Better," I said. "I'm cutting back to one Demerol."

He nodded. "That's fine. But if it starts to hurt more, go back to two pills. If you keep improving, by tomorrow I'll switch you to ibuprofen, but stay on the methocarbamol. Take it easy today, okay?"

I promised that I would. Five minutes later, Vida and I entered the office. Amanda Hanson was behind the desk. She gave us a frosty smile. "I was wondering if I got the starting time wrong," she said. "Kip is the only one here besides me."

I explained that Leo was on the bakery run and after a weekend, Mitch often made his visits to the sheriff and the courthouse before coming to the *Advocate*. "I had to see Doc Dewey," I went on, noting that Vida was looking daggers at Amanda. "I was in a collision Saturday. I hurt my back and my car has to be fixed before I can drive it."

"That's a shame." Amanda didn't sound sincere.

The phone rang. Vida had stomped into the newsroom. I followed her. "Did Marje have anything of interest to say?" I inquired.

"I had no chance to ask," she admitted, taking off her raincoat. "The phone rang three times while I waited for you. Monday mornings at the clinic are always hectic." She gestured toward the reception area and lowered her voice. "Far too cheeky. How long must we put up with her?"

I was about to reply when Amanda appeared in the newsroom doorway. "Cal Vickers had your car towed to Bert Anderson's place. Call him around nine after he's checked out the damage." She didn't wait for my acknowledgment before going back to her desk.

"You see?" Vida said. "Cheeky, lacking in respect."

"You know we're stuck with her for five to six weeks," I murmured. "Ginny's going to take all of her maternity leave. The only reason Amanda would quit is if she was needed sooner at the post office."

"Or," Vida retorted in a low tone, "you fired her."

"She's doing the job as far as I can tell. Let's be patient. Amanda's whole personality seems to have changed. I've always thought of her as kind of flighty."

Vida looked thoughtful. "A personal crisis of some kind?"

"Maybe." I glanced over my shoulder. Amanda couldn't be seen from my vantage point by Vida's desk. "She's probably close to forty. Midlife, ticking biological clock, menopause, who knows?"

"True." Vida sighed and sat down just as Leo entered.

"Cinnamon rolls, three kinds of Danish, and some of the Upper Crust's new shortbread cookies." He set the lavender box on the table by the coffee urn and looked at me. "I heard you ran into somebody over the weekend."

"It was the other way around," I said.

"So I figured." Leo began placing the baked goods on the tray. "Holly Gross, right? Are you okay?"

"My back hurts, but it's improving." I paused to greet Kip, who was coming from the back shop.

"You're on the job," he said and smiled. "I heard you wouldn't be able to come to work."

"Did you plan to stage a coup?" I asked, smiling back at him.

Kip laughed. "No. Until about a year or so ago, I always thought coup was pronounced *coop*."

I took a raspberry Danish out of the box. "Who told you I was incapacitated?"

"Chili," he replied, reaching for a cinnamon roll. "She saw Cammy Anderson at the mall yesterday. They go way back. I guess Cammy's dad, Bert, told her about the wreck. Is your car really totaled?"

"No." I shook my head. "Honestly, I don't know how people get their facts so mangled. It's a good thing we have to verify . . ." I stopped as Mitch breezed through the door. "Don't you dare," I said, pointing a finger at him. "What fanciful tale have you picked up about my fender bender at Safeway?"

Mitch looked puzzled. "What fender bender?"

"You didn't check the sheriff's log this morning?"

He shook his head. "Not yet. We had a minor debacle at home. Sorry I'm late. What happened?"

I explained as briefly as I could. The saga was starting to bore me. "That's it," I concluded. "What was your debacle, Mitch?"

He chuckled. "Nothing serious. Brenda burned her hand on the stove. Very minor, but she can't use her loom for a couple of days."

I went into my cubbyhole. A few minutes later, I saw Vida march over to Mitch's desk. In what seemed like a furtive manner, she spoke to him for several minutes. The conversation ended when Mitch got up from his chair, put his jacket back on, and went off on his daily rounds. Leo had already left. Just before nine, I accosted Vida.

"Is there a problem here that I don't know about?" I inquired.

Vida met my gaze head-on. "Yes and no." Again, she lowered her voice. "It occurred to me that Brenda might want to fill in for Ginny if Amanda becomes intolerable. But Mitch says that although his wife has worked as a legal secretary, she isn't interested in a job that would tie her down to a regular schedule. He also felt that it wasn't a good idea for them to be employed in the same place. He thought they might get on each other's nerves."

"Well . . . I suppose that could happen," I allowed. "She does have her weaving business. It must be something she loves to do."

"Perhaps." Vida looked uncertain. "Mitch mentioned that with Christmas coming up, Brenda will be busier than usual."

"True," I agreed. "As for Amanda, let's give her a little more time. Her attitude may be caused by a lack of self-esteem or not being convinced she can handle the job."

"Piffle." Vida scowled at me. "Self-esteem indeed! Whoever invented that term? Maybe I *should* write an advice column. Far too many people are wrongheaded these days. They're filled with nonsense, putting labels on every possible human trait. No matter how destructive or silly a person may be, there's no need to take responsibility for even the most deplorable behavior. I find it all very tiresome."

"You're serious?"

"Yes." Vida waved an impatient hand. "I know what you're thinking. We might get sued, there could be repercussions, readers may be afraid to air their problems in print, I'd be taking on too much—and so forth. But I feel as if a voice of reason—along with common sense—is needed in this community. I'm willing to take the risk. Are you?"

I honestly didn't know. "I can ask Marisa Foxx about our liability."

"Do that." Vida rested her chin on her hands. "Most daily papers carry advice columns. It's not as if I'm inventing the concept."

"True," I agreed. "Let me mull a bit."

"Of course."

I refilled my coffee mug and went back to my office. Like Vida's "Scene Around Town" items, I knew that if she wrote an

advice column, it'd be well read. It'd also get tongues to wag-
ging as subscribers tried to figure out what wife was having an
affair with what husband, whose teenage daughter wanted a
tattoo, which neighbor was throwing debris into another
neighbor's yard, what family had feuding members who refused to be under the same roof for holidays, and which business owner had asked how to handle a light-fingered employee.
I got so caught up in Vida's proposal that I forgot to call Bert
Anderson about my car. At nine-thirty, he called me.

"It's not too bad," Bert said in his raspy voice. "I can get
your new tire from the Honda dealership, but it won't be here
until tomorrow. The whole job, including the tire, should cost
around four fifty."

I winced. But I had to be realistic. "Okay. I still have to find
out if Holly Gross has insurance."

"Good luck with that," Bert said.

After hanging up, I pondered my next move. If I'd been
dealing with someone more reasonable than Holly, I'd have exchanged insurance and other pertinent information at the accident site. But Holly wasn't reasonable. For all I knew, she
could've been drunk or on drugs. I dialed Marisa Foxx's number. The phone was answered by Judi Hinshaw, another one of
Vida's swarm of relatives. Judi told me her boss was with a
client, but would call back in an hour or so. I told her about the
collision and my need to know if the other party was insured.

"The sheriff should be able to tell you that," Judi said.
"Like so many Alpiners, Mrs. Freeman's agent is Mr. Shaw."

"Uh . . . I'm not talking about Molly Freeman," I said.

"You're not?" Judi sounded puzzled.

"No. It was Holly Gross."

"Oh!" Judi exclaimed. "I heard Molly Freeman was the one
who hit you in the Grocery Basket parking lot. Somebody said

Mike O'Toole's death had really upset her. It's understandable, since she and Principal Freeman take a continuing interest in Alpine High grads."

Holly, Molly, Polly Wolly Doodle all the day. I sighed in frustration. How could such a simple incident get so screwed up in the telling? "I wish it had been Molly Freeman," I said. "She's far more responsible than Holly Gross. Furthermore, it was at Safeway."

"Oh! Holly's such a ho—oops! I spilled coffee on my desk," Judi said. "I'd better hang up. Try the sheriff."

I felt like saying the sheriff was already trying me—or at least trying my patience and good nature.

Grow up, I lectured myself. I dialed the main number for SkyCo's law enforcement office instead of the direct line to Milo. Still behaving like an adolescent, I hoped he wouldn't take the call.

My wish was granted. Lori Cobb asked me how she could help. "Mr. Laskey just left," she said. "Did you want to tell him something?"

"No," I said. "I want to know if Holly Gross has car insurance."

"She doesn't," Lori replied. "Furthermore, her driver's license was pulled a month ago. That's twice in the past two years, both times for DUIs. You'll see the details when Mr. Laskey gets back to your office. Holly's going to have to get a bicycle."

Washington State laws were tough on drunken drivers—when they got nailed. "Had she been drinking when she ran into me?"

"No," Lori said. "Holly only drinks at night and she doesn't like to pay for her booze."

"Define *pay*," I murmured. "Is she facing jail time?"

"I doubt it." Lori sounded grudging. "She's got kids, and the first time she had to pay a fine and do the electronic home monitoring thing. I figure that's what will happen again, though the fine will be stiffer and the driver's license won't be reissued for two years." ·

"That's tough," I said, feeling sorry for her kids, if not for Holly.

"Got to hang up," Lori said. "Fred Engelman's leaving for work, and I have to give him his personal belongings."

After Lori rang off I called Bernie Shaw, who commiserated before reminding me that my car insurance had a five-hundred-dollar deductible. "Sorry, Emma, but it's just as well you aren't putting in a claim. Insurance companies are getting even stricter about canceling policies. There's nothing an independent agent like me can do about it, either. Just be thankful you've got personal liability."

"Right. When I pay the premium every . . ." I stopped as it suddenly dawned on me that I didn't know what Bernie meant. "I'm sorry. Why should I be thankful?"

"You don't know?" He sounded surprised.

"Know what?"

"That Holly wants to sue you," Bernie replied.

"That's absurd!" I shouted. "She hit me!"

"Now, Emma, don't attack the messenger," Bernie said, reverting to his genial insurance agent's tone. "Holly claims one of her kids has whiplash and that when you attacked her she hurt her arm and her shoulder. I suppose there's nothing official yet. It's Monday morning."

"It sure as hell is," I huffed, glancing out into the empty newsroom. Vida must have left while I was talking to Lori Cobb. "Holly can't possibly be serious," I went on, trying to regain my composure. "She can't afford a lawyer, and she's in deep trouble with the law for driving without a valid license.

We'll be running an item in the police log column, including the citations she got. Furthermore, *she* attacked *me*."

"That may be true," Bernie said, and paused. "But I understand she has a witness who was in the Safeway lot Saturday."

"A witness? Who?"

"Mickey Borg, from Icicle Creek Gas 'n Go."

DESPITE MY VOW TO IGNORE MILO, TEN MINUTES LATER I stormed into his office. "Tell me what you know about Holly and this mess she's making for me," I demanded, standing in front of the sheriff's desk.

"Oh, crap!" Milo dropped the cigarette lighter he'd been holding. It fell to the floor and apparently bounced out of reach. He grunted as he bent down to retrieve the lighter. "You seem to have improved," the sheriff remarked wryly. "What got you into a freaking tizzy now?"

"Bernie Shaw says Holly is suing me. Do you know about it?"

Milo lighted his cigarette. "She yelled and screamed and made all kinds of threats when she was here. I didn't pay much attention. Holly can count herself lucky if she doesn't end up in the slammer."

"You don't have room," I said, simmering down a bit. "She claims to have a witness—Mickey Borg."

"Mickey?" Milo shook his head. "That figures."

I finally sat down. "What do you mean?"

"You don't know?" The sheriff was faintly incredulous. "Mickey's been one of Holly's best . . . let's say 'customers' for a long time."

"You mean even now that he's married to Janie, Fred's ex?"

"Hell, yes." He brushed some ash from his shirt. "According to Fred, Janie knows about it. She's not a happy camper these days."

"I guess she wouldn't be," I murmured. "No wonder she told Mickey to go home without her. Fred never played around as far as I know. I suppose he was too drunk most of the time."

"That sounds right," Milo agreed. "Hey, stop tying yourself into knots. You know damned well Holly won't carry through."

"Maybe I should talk to Mickey."

"Bad idea. I'll do that."

"You will? When?"

Milo shrugged. "Probably on my way home. I usually get gas at Cal's, but Mickey's place is practically next door to my house."

"You'll let me know what he says?"

"*If* he says anything."

"Right." Of course I wanted to ask Milo about Tricia, but I couldn't bring myself to broach the subject. He'd probably intended to tell me about their plans Saturday night, but my disaster had interfered. Maybe he hadn't phoned me yesterday because he knew I'd still be dealing with a painful back. The sheriff was fiddling with his lighter, standing it up on end and then putting it aside. *Speak, Emma,* I ordered myself. *Milo's waiting for you to say something.* I spoke—but uttered only innocuous words. "Any luck on the river yesterday?"

He shook his head. "No real action. But I saw a deer." He puffed on his cigarette and exhaled. "I should've had a rifle instead of a rod."

I grimaced. "How can you do that? I couldn't."

The sheriff shrugged. "What's the difference between a fish and a deer? You'd eat both of them."

"Yes, but deer have such wonderful eyes. Fish are . . . fishy-eyed."

"Cows have nice eyes," Milo pointed out.

"But I don't get up close to a cow very often." I stood up. "I have to go back to work. Let me know what Mickey says."

"Will do."

I hurried through the reception area. By the time I got outside, I was furious with myself—and with Milo. We were a pair of middle-aged gutless wonders. I started along Front Street, stalking as if I were hunting some kind of prey. A cow, maybe. I'd wrestle it to the ground. I'd turn it into ground round. I'd . . .

I stopped at the intersection of Front and Fourth. The early fog had lifted. The morning air was fresh and crisp. A freight train whistled as it rumbled slowly through town. Instead of going back to the *Advocate,* I turned the corner and headed for Railroad Avenue. The BNSF Railway freight was long, maybe close to a hundred cars, and some of them were double-decker containers. I waited quietly, fascinated as always by the variety of old and new, multicolored, graffiti and tag art decor, contents that were concealed and open cars full of gravel, all heading east up through the eight-mile Cascade Tunnel. The sight was soothing, reminding me there was always a sense of mystery and discovery to what was around the bend or over the hill.

The last car passed by. It wasn't a caboose or, as we sometimes called it, a crummy. Twenty-odd years ago, FREDs—flashing rear-end devices to detect hot boxes and other potential problems—had made the caboose obsolete. Somehow, freight trains didn't seem complete without their colorful punctuation marks at the end. Vida loved to tell about standing by the tracks when she was young. She'd wait with her chums for the caboose and shout, "Throw me a fusie!" Sometimes one of the train workers would comply, especially if it was close to the Fourth of July—or Independence Day, as Vida always called it.

I crossed the tracks and headed for Bert Anderson's auto repair and chop shop, figuring that as long as I was going to have to pay for the Honda's damage, I might as well get the project under way. I went by Alvin De Muth's truck stop and repair area, noting that someone had put a CLOSED sign on the front door. The used-car lot next door was quiet, with only a young couple strolling among the dozen or more vehicles. I walked faster, hoping that the activity would loosen up my back muscles. Beyond the Nissan dealership and the DMV office, I turned into Bert Anderson's shop, which was located in a refurbished building that had once been part of a shingle mill.

Bert's wife, Norene, was at the desk in the small front office. She looked up and smiled. "Hi, Ms. Lord. Sorry about your accident. Bert's over on the other side of the tracks in the wrecking yard. Should I let him know you're here? He can't see much from there since he put up that big fence."

"No," I said. "Just tell him I'll be paying for the repair. And the tire, of course. I'll put it on my Visa."

Norene made a note on a green pad. "Okey-dokey. I heard you had back troubles after the accident. How're you doing?"

"Much better," I said. "I walked here from the sheriff's office."

"Good for you." She smiled again and rubbed her upper arm. "Would you believe this bee sting still itches from over a week ago? I was lucky I could work at all after that happened. I took last Saturday off to get my strength back."

"I heard you had a severe allergic reaction," I said. "Bees should go away by this time of year."

She nodded, her mass of auburn ringlets jiggling and bobbing from the top of her head to her sloping shoulders. "It wasn't as if I'd disturbed them. I went outside for a smoke. Somebody once told me cigarette smoke kept the bugs away, but that's not so. I had to give that nest a good whack after I got stung. I ran like the dickens back to the tavern."

"Maybe the bee that got you was the last of the season," I said. "Is there anything else I need to do now, like see an estimate?"

She rubbed her arm again. "Did Bert give you a ballpark figure?"

"Yes."

"He'll stick to it," Norene promised. "That's how he keeps his customers." She peered out from under her curly bangs and pointed to the entrance behind me. "Here's Bert. Now I can go home and do laundry. I only come in to check the books once a week. Nice seeing you." She waited for her husband to enter the office, told him she was off, and left via the back way.

"Hiya," Bert greeted me. "You don't look too miserable." He chuckled. "So Holly's playing the fender bender for all it's worth."

"It's not worth anything to her," I retorted. "She may go to jail."

Bert rubbed his slightly bulbous nose. "Nah. She'll lose her license and have to wear one of those monitor things for a while, but they won't put her in a cell. Hell's bells, she's a mommy. They get special treatment. Especially *her* type of mommy." He winked. "Holly knows how to please little boys and big boys, too."

I didn't pretend to be amused, but I remained civil. It's never a good idea to displease someone who's going to make out an invoice that's payable upon receipt. "How soon will my car be ready?"

Bert gazed up at the ceiling. "Oh—I can do the actual repair this afternoon. Then it depends on when the tire gets here. With any luck, maybe around noon tomorrow."

"Any chance you've got a loaner?"

Bert shook his head. "Not really. Just about every car or truck here has a problem or is ready to be junked."

"If the tire isn't here until tomorrow, why can't I use my spare?"

Bert made a face. "I wouldn't advise it. It's kind of flimsy. You couldn't take it out on the highway. Even around town, we've got our share of bumps and lumps and potholes. You'd think Mayor Baugh would get that stuff fixed. Fuzzy might as well have stayed in Louisiana. After all these years in Alpine, he still has that Big Easy mentality."

"It's funding," I said. "The voters turned down the last street project." An idea occurred to me. "Would any of your vehicles awaiting demolition have a tire that'd work on the Honda?"

Bert shifted his burly body from one foot to the other. "Oh . . . I doubt it. You're not desperate to go someplace, are you?"

"I don't like being dependent on other people," I said. "I feel at a disadvantage in terms of my job. If I need to chase down breaking news, I can't call a cab because we don't have any around here."

"Emma." Bert put out a hand. I took a step backward, assuming he was about to touch me with his greasy fingers. "Look," he went on, dropping his hand to his side, "I'll do my dangedest to get the car to you by lunchtime. But it's up to the Honda folks to send the tire. Forget about your spare or a used one. It'd take a search party to find anything usable around here."

"I can look," I said. "I saw a blue Toyota parked alongside the building. Who does it belong to?"

"Norene," Bert replied. "She just drove off in it."

"That's the only one you've got on the premises? What about the wrecking yard?"

"Forget it." Bert's smile seemed forced. "Hey, Emma— I mean, *Ms. Lord*—it's going to be okay. Relax. I'll call you as soon as they roll that tire in here tomorrow."

I felt as if Bert and I were having a war of wills. Maybe it was my fault. I was being unreasonable, no doubt as a result of the rotten weekend I'd just endured. I'd already jumped all over Bernie Shaw; now I was taking out my frustrations on Bert Anderson.

"You're right," I said, managing some sort of smile. "I'd better get back to the office. For all I know, there *is* breaking news. Thanks," I added, speaking over my shoulder as I walked past Bert and headed out the front door.

Crossing the railroad tracks, I walked along Seventh to Front. By the time I reached the corner at Sixth, I wasn't feeling so vigorous. My watch told me it was a quarter to eleven, time for more meds.

Amanda, who was on the phone, barely acknowledged my return. Kip, however, looked glad to see me. "I wondered where you were," he said. "Nobody seemed to know."

I gazed around the otherwise empty newsroom. "You mean Amanda didn't know?"

"She just said you'd been gone for an hour or so."

"Maybe I didn't tell her," I admitted. "Maybe she was on the phone. I don't remember." There was no need to tell Kip that Holly's threat of a lawsuit had sent me rushing off to see the sheriff. "I just came back from Bert Anderson's shop. I *may* get my car back tomorrow."

"Bert's okay," Kip said. "He's a decent mechanic, but not in De Muth's class. I don't know why Bert needs those Dobermans. All he's got behind that fence is a bunch of junk."

"Dobermans?" I frowned. "When did he get them?"

"He hasn't yet," Kip said. "He's getting them from a kennel in Minnesota. Chili heard about it from Cammy, Bert's daughter. Is that an item for Vida's 'Scene'?"

"Maybe when the guard dogs get here," I said. "Give her

a note or send her an email. Her computer expertise is improving."

"Which," Kip said, gesturing toward the back shop, "is why I was looking for you. We haven't put any updates on the online version except for some classified ads and a couple of promos Leo got in the mail. Is there something we can use before we actually go to press?"

I considered the question. "Not really. Nothing newsworthy has happened since Clive was charged. Mitch would let me know if Clive's attorney was going to ask for bail." I paused. "Do you know if we got a funeral notice for De Muth?"

Kip shook his head. "It'd come to Vida, but she hasn't given me anything."

"Okay." I started for my cubbyhole. "I'll see if the sheriff knows anything about that."

Jack Mullins took my call. "We don't have the stiff back yet," he said. "SnoCo won't have the tox screen completed until the end of this week. Hey, you want to claim the body?"

"Huh?"

"Nobody else has, and it turns out De Muth was one of our own."

"What do you mean?"

"A Catholic," Jack replied. "Father Den told me yesterday after Mass that he knew De Muth. I told Father Den I'd never seen him in church. Have you?"

"No. I couldn't make it yesterday because of my back. If De Muth didn't attend Mass, how did Father Den know him?"

"He came to the rectory a couple of times," Jack replied. "You know Den—he's closemouthed, and not just when it comes to the confessional. He sort of blew me off by saying that De Muth had a troubled conscience. Hell, who doesn't?"

"My brother, Ben, would call that PriestSpeakeasy," I said.

"It's designed to do what Father Den did—blow you off." It wouldn't do any good for Jack or me to probe further, so I took a conversational detour. "No De Muth relatives, ex-wives, kids, or close friends, I gather. What about those young guys that Alvin was mentoring as mechanics? Somebody told me he was rather close to a couple of them."

"As in pervert?"

"No, as in avuncular."

"Wow. That sounds worse than pervert." Jack clucked his tongue. "You writer types, with all your two-dollar words."

Jack was no dummy. He went on, "Okay, so I admit I never heard any weirdo stuff about De Muth. That kind of weirdo, anyway. In fact, it was always the opposite—he was a real loner."

"Do you know who he mentored?"

"Not offhand, but Mike . . . oh, crap! I keep forgetting the poor kid's dead. Maybe his brother, Ken, would know. I'll ask around," Jack said.

"Talk to Harvey Adcock," I suggested. "He's seen De Muth come into the hardware store with a young man a few times."

"Sam Heppner already asked Harvey," Jack replied. "Harvey admitted he only *assumed* that De Muth and the kid were related. He didn't recognize the kid, but he thought there was a resemblance between the two of them. You know Sam—he's like Dodge, wanting facts, not guesswork. Sam insisted the only resemblance Harvey could offer was that De Muth and the younger guy were both dark-haired, about the same height, and had two arms and two legs."

"The son angle is probably a dead end," I said, "but the kid could be local. Let me know if you hear anything important."

"Are you thinking De Muth had a yen for younger guys?"

The question surprised me. "No. But there's a possibility."

"He wouldn't be a first," Jack said without his usual flippancy. "I doubt Norm Carlson would run one of those 'Have You Seen Him?' pictures on Blue Sky Dairy's milk cartons."

"Why not?" I said.

"Norm guards his wholesome image like Elsie the Borden Cow."

I didn't argue, but after we rang off, I considered running a description or even a sketch in the *Advocate*. "The Kid," as I was calling him, could be a crucial factor in the investigation.

Abruptly, I stopped thinking along those lines. There was no investigation. Alvin De Muth's death was an open-and-shut case. Clive Berentsen had confessed, a bunch of witnesses had been on the scene, and charges had been filed. End of story.

So why did I feel that we'd only read the preface?

SIXTEEN

JUST BEFORE NOON, VIDA RETURNED TO THE OFFICE. "WHAT," she demanded, "is this scribbling about Doublemint Punchers?"

I was momentarily stumped. "Oh—Doberman pinschers," I said, pouring my cold coffee back into the urn. *Waste not, want not.* Emma, the Frugal Editor. "Kip's handwriting isn't very legible. He says Bert Anderson's getting a pair to guard his junkyard."

"Oh, for heaven's sake!" Vida tossed the note aside. "Who'd steal anything out of that place? Bert's canny. He salvages any usable parts."

"Maybe the yard is where he stores valuable bits and pieces he can use or sell."

"Perhaps," Vida allowed, "but those dogs can be quite vicious. And so noisy! My daughter Beth had a neighbor who owned a Doberman. She was scared to death to let the children play in the yard because she was sure the dog could leap the fence. Fortunately, the neighbors moved a few months later."

"A dog's behavior depends on how it was trained," I said, recalling an incident that had figured in a homicide several years ago.

Vida sniffed disdainfully. "If these Dobermans are supposed to guard Bert's junk, he'll train them to attack."

"They may be trained already," I said. "He's getting them from Minnesota."

"Minnesota," Vida murmured, sitting down. "I can't imagine living where the land is so flat. I don't care very much for eastern Washington, but at least it's got some parts that aren't like a pancake."

I didn't comment further. To my knowledge, Vida had never been out of the Pacific Northwest. She'd lived her entire life in Alpine and rarely strayed far from the I-5 corridor between the Canadian border and Oregon. A few years ago, we'd spent some time in Cannon Beach on the Oregon coast. Although Vida thought the town's seaside architecture had a certain charm, she'd gone on to say that life on the beach must get tiresome. "The tide comes in and the tide goes out," she'd told me. "So predictable, with exact times just like a bus schedule. I much prefer living in a place that's nestled in the mountains." Like Alpine, of course. Valhalla would have suffered by comparison with Vida's hometown. "Are you eating in?"

I confessed that I hadn't thought about it. "Are you?"

Vida made a face. "I planned to, but the celery and carrot sticks and the hard-boiled egg I brought to the office suddenly don't appeal to me. I certainly don't want to go off my diet, yet I feel the need for something a bit more hearty."

Vida's so-called diets were a joke among the rest of us. She had a large frame and she was tall. Ten, even twenty pounds either way were scarcely noticeable. "The Venison Inn?" I said.

She hesitated. "Yes, I believe they have some low-calorie items on their menu." She checked her watch. "It's ten to twelve. Shall we go?"

"Sure." I stood up as Vida went back to her desk to retrieve her purse and coat. Before I could get farther than the middle of the newsroom, Amanda entered.

"Here," she said, handing me a WHILE YOU WERE UNAVAILABLE note. She turned around and left.

Marisa Foxx had returned my phone call at ten-forty. Annoyed, I considered chewing out Amanda, but I conquered the urge, mouthed the word *Wait* to Vida, and went into the front office.

"I wish," I said, trying to remain pleasant, "you'd given me this when I got back here an hour or so ago. Ms. Foxx is probably at lunch."

Amanda was gathering up her own belongings. "Yes," she replied. "She probably is. I'm meeting her at the ski lodge coffee shop. I may be a few minutes late getting back." With another frosty smile, she slung her hobo bag over her shoulder and went out the door.

Vida had edged her way closer to the front office. "Well now! What was that all about?"

"I've no idea," I admitted. "I don't think Marisa and Amanda are friends. Marisa has never mentioned her." I paused. "On the other hand, Marisa is rather cagey about personal matters. Maybe that's why she and I get along. Neither of us is willing to open up to other people."

Vida, who is also reticent about her private life, yet ferrets out every detail and nuance of anyone who crosses her path, nodded. "That's possible. I'll have to ask my niece Judi about it."

Going out the door, we almost collided with Mitch Laskey.

He made a bow. "Off to lunch? I may be late getting back. Brenda has to have that burn checked out at the clinic. It's worse than we thought."

"Dear me," Vida murmured, glancing at me. "I suppose she can't drive, either."

Mitch smiled at his colleague. "We seem to be the designated drivers. See you soon."

Vida and I continued down the street to the Venison Inn. "I'm beginning to wonder about Brenda," she said. "She seems to have a great many problems."

"Don't we all?"

"Well . . . yes, of course." Vida let me go inside first. It wasn't a sign of deference to The Boss, but because she inevitably stopped along the way to the booth, interrogating each person she knew and thus holding up her companion and occasionally a few other customers as well.

For once, the restaurant was less than half full. It wasn't quite noon and the rush would be on in the next five to ten minutes. Vida found slim pickings for her gossip basket. By the time she joined me in a booth—with a window view, of course—the only snippet she'd gleaned was that Francine and Warren Wells were thinking about spending Christmas in Bavaria.

"They call it their third honeymoon," Vida said in disgust as she slid into the opposite side of the booth. "Married, divorced, married again." She shook her head. "That's all very well and good, but how many honeymoons do people really need? And Bavaria! Why not save money and just drive over to Leavenworth?"

Vida referred to the town on the other side of Stevens Pass that had become a destination not only for winter sports but for tourists year-round. Within Leavenworth's city limits, most of the buildings along Highway 2 were built in the Bavarian style. Shops and restaurants featured German goods and food. During the Christmas season, special passenger trains were put on for day trips so that visitors could enjoy the sights, sounds, and smells of an ersatz Bavaria. On one of Tom's visits to Alpine, we had driven there to spend the night. It was a magical time. The memory was still as vivid as it was bittersweet.

"Of course," Vida continued after briefly studying the menu, "Francine must make good money with her women's apparel store. I only go there when she has a clearance sale. Since they got back together, Warren may nominally manage the shop, but I doubt he does much in the way of work." She paused. "I'll have the steak sandwich special."

I looked at the menu's description: rib-eye steak on a French roll with fries, onion rings, and a salad. "That's definitely hearty," I said.

To my surprise, Liz, the Burger Barn's surly waitress, suddenly appeared bearing two glasses of ice water. "You decided yet?" she asked. Before either Vida or I could respond, Liz scowled at my House & Home editor. "What's with that piece in the paper about me moving here from Idaho?"

Vida stared unblinkingly at Liz. "I interviewed you, or don't you remember? Frankly, I didn't learn anything to justify a feature story, so I put a brief mention in my 'Scene' column. Had I known you were working two jobs, that would've provided more human interest."

"I'm not working two jobs," Liz snapped. "I quit the Burger Barn last Friday. Now I'm here. Are you going to put that in the paper, too, or are you finished prying into my private life?"

Vida wore her Cheshire Cat expression. "Your job is *not*

part of your private life. And, I might add, I certainly will mention your change of employment. If I don't, readers will think we made a mistake. That simply won't do."

Liz's face grew tighter with Vida's every word. "Mistake? You've already made enough," she declared. "If everybody in this burg knows everybody else, then they've already figured out where I work."

"Well . . ." Vida appeared to ponder Liz's words. "Given your career path in Alpine, will you be at the diner or the ski lodge next week?"

Liz, who looked as if she wanted to throttle Vida, took a deep breath. "Just give me your order. I've got other customers waiting."

Vida pretended to study the menu. "The special, medium well done, with Roquefort dressing on the salad, and please don't skimp. It's very annoying when the dressing runs out before the greens do." With an emphatic gesture, she slapped the menu closed.

Liz turned to me. "What about you?"

"The same," I said, avoiding the waitress's sour expression, "but I want my steak rare."

"All the steak sandwiches are medium," Liz said in triumph.

"Okay. In that case, I'll have the beef dip rare."

Liz smirked. "All the beef is well done."

"I see. How about a bowl of gruel?"

"We don't serve gruel," Liz said.

"Gee, that's a shame." I gave up. "Let's do the steak sandwich."

Without another word, Liz stalked away.

Vida's eyes could have drilled holes in the disagreeable waitress's back. "She won't last long here, either. I'm sure she was fired from the Burger Barn." Vida rested her chin on her hands. "Why is Liz so unpleasant? Why, having an obvious dislike of other human beings, does she work as a waitress? There are many kinds of jobs for unskilled people in which you don't have to interact with the public."

"Why Alpine?" I mused. "Did you ask her?"

"Of course. She mumbled about wanting a change of scenery. Ah!" Vida was leaning halfway out of the booth. "Here comes Betsy O'Toole with Roseanna Bayard." She paused and frowned. "They're being seated toward the front. We must stop to chat on the way out."

Liz served us without comment. Vida asked for a refill of her water. Her request was granted with a frown. The rest of the lunch hour was spent in speculation about what might happen to Clive Berentsen, Holly Gross's threatened lawsuit, how Buzzy and Laura O'Toole would cope in the wake of Mike's death, and the need for another doctor in Alpine.

"Which reminds me," Vida said as we got out of the booth, "I should try again to talk to Marje and ask if Doc is doing too much. Maybe I'll go to the clinic now. Marje usually eats in."

I was surprised. "You're passing up a chance to talk to Betsy?"

Vida grimaced. "I can't be everywhere at once—though I'd like to."

I sensed that Marje and Doc weren't the only people on her inquisition list. The Laskeys might still be at the clinic. Even if they'd come and gone, Vida could still quiz her niece about Brenda. "Here," I said, handing over two fives and my lunch bill. "Pay this for me. I may spend a few minutes with Betsy and Roseanna. No tip."

Vida nodded. "Certainly not."

She paused at Betsy and Roseanna's booth just long enough

to be polite. Roseanna offered to scoot over so I could sit next to her. Betsy, who hadn't yet shed her air of grief, still made an effort to lighten the mood. "I hope you learned your lesson about shopping at Safeway, Emma. How do you feel?"

"Better." I tried to smile. "The truth is, I couldn't bear to see the reader board again."

"Understood." Betsy passed a hand across her forehead. "I was going to see you after lunch. The funeral will be Thursday at ten. We'd have preferred to hold it sooner, but we wanted to get it in the paper and have Vida mention it on her program Wednesday night. In fact, I wish we could've held the services today. Jake suggested putting the funeral information on the reader board, but Buzzy and Laura couldn't deal with that. The message up there now is heartbreaking enough."

"It is," I agreed, noting that Betsy had eaten only a small portion of her Reuben sandwich.

Roseanna, however, had demolished most of her Cobb salad. "I thought they'd have an autopsy," she said. "There was one for Buddy's mother a few years ago. Of course," she added with a slight shudder, "that was different. Genevieve had been poisoned."

My mind went back to those disturbing days that followed Genevieve's death. It had occurred at the parish rectory on my brother's watch. Ben had been filling in for Father Den while our pastor was on sabbatical. The tragedy had far-reaching consequences beyond the Bayard family. I felt like shuddering, too.

"An autopsy on Mike wasn't necessary," Betsy said, bringing me back to the present. "The surgeon in Monroe asked if we wanted one, but Doc Dewey advised Jake that the family should refuse to consent. We knew the cause of Mike's death. Why put us through more misery?"

"I agree," I said. "How are Buzzy and Laura doing?"

Betsy crumpled her napkin and put it next to her plate. "Not very well. How could they be otherwise? Buzzy's beating himself up for not making the trip to Monroe and Laura is inconsolable."

Roseanna shook her head. "It all falls on you and Jake. I marvel at how well you're coping."

"It's an act," Betsy replied. "Somebody has to prop up the rest of the family, and I'm it. Jake is channeling his grief by fixating on the truck. It may have been old, but he kept it up. It was totaled, of course. But my husband considered it as . . . well, part of the family, an heirloom from his father and a symbol of . . . what? The store's longtime presence, I guess. Maybe Jake's the wise one. It's easier to mourn a thing instead of a person." Her expression turned droll. "I don't mean to sound disrespectful, but I almost think Jake would like to hold a memorial service for the truck and have Bert Anderson bury it instead of demolishing the darned thing."

Roseanna finally put her fork aside. "Betsy, you're awful. Keep it up, it'll help you and everybody else get through this. Life's no picnic."

I smiled at Betsy. "Roseanna's right. Haven't we all had some horrible bumps in the road?"

All three of us were quiet for a few moments. It was only the approach of Liz that made me slip out of the booth. "I don't know about you two, but I've had enough lip from that waitress for one day."

"She's a pill, all right," Roseanna said softly. "Maybe she's had a few horrible bumps, too."

"Maybe," I said. "I'll see you both . . . later." I didn't want to say *at the funeral*. I suppose it was because none of us should have to attend a funeral for a young man. Or maybe we three middle-aged women didn't want to acknowledge our own mortality.

It was after one when I got back to the office. It was almost two when Amanda showed up. I wasn't in a mood to coddle her. "Lunch here is an hour unless it involves business."

Amanda seemed unfazed. "Okay." She turned to her computer in an obvious gesture of dismissal.

I stalled for a few moments, pretending to study the posted ad rates. It was very difficult to keep from asking Amanda why she'd had lunch with Marisa. But that would switch the boss–employee relationship to girl talk. I kept my mouth shut and retreated to my cubbyhole. If I wanted to know what the long lunch session was about, I'd have to take my turn at telephone tag and call Marisa.

I told her I had a couple of questions, adding that she could bill me since they were lawyer–client queries. "First, is it likely that Holly Gross can sue me for allegedly running into her car and then beating her up?"

As was customary, Marisa didn't answer immediately. "Those *are* two questions. Were there witnesses?"

"Holly claims Mickey Borg saw the incident. She must be lying."

"I'd have to depose him," Marisa said. "Has Dodge talked to him?"

"I don't know. He told me he would."

"Good." Marisa paused. "As for the alleged attack on Holly, that's another matter. Once again, witnesses would be crucial. Are you aware of anyone who saw how the fracas began?"

"No, but Dane Pearson, the Safeway manager, showed up

with a couple of employees about the time Holly finally surrendered."

"Bad choice of words," Marisa murmured. "It makes you sound like the aggressor, going for the jugular. Better to say 'hostilities ended.' "

"Right. I suppose it's a 'she-said, she-said' situation."

"It is without witnesses," Marisa agreed. "As for Holly actually carrying out her threat, you'll have to wait and see what happens. There might be some reckless attorney out there who'd take note of the fact that you're a newspaper owner and think big bucks are involved."

"Gee, I could disprove that in about thirty seconds."

"I know," Marisa said, "but the shyster lawyer might not. I'd better hang up. I've got a client coming in at two-thirty."

"One last thing," I said, lowering my voice. "Amanda Hanson mentioned having lunch with you. I didn't realize you were pals."

"We're not," Marisa said. "It was business."

"Ah. And you can't tell me because of attorney–client privilege."

"Right. Talk to you later, Emma."

"Sure."

Business. I wondered what kind of business. The way my last few days had gone, maybe Amanda wanted to sue me, too. I glanced at my watch. It was two-twenty-three. Not yet time for more pain pills.

Unfortunately.

LEO GAVE ME A RIDE HOME. HE WAS ON HIS WAY TO THE SKI lodge for the annual fall chamber of commerce dinner. Vida had also volunteered to be my chauffeur, but she was going in the opposite direction to the country club for a fiftieth-wedding-anniversary party honoring old friends who had lived in Alpine for years, but retired to Palm Springs.

The mail was prosaic; there were no calls on my answering machine. Rolf apparently had given up. After I poured some Pepsi over ice and opened my laptop, I saw an e-mail from Adam. "What," he had written, "has two arms, two legs, and could offer up a Mass for his mother if his teeth weren't ch-ch-chattering?"

I grimaced at the monitor. How could I have forgotten my son's *needs*? I couldn't claim that I'd been out of commission and unable to buy the required items. Not only had I intended to shop online for him in the comfort of my living room, but I'd gone to a real store to buy a baby gift for Ginny's newborn. Where were my priorities? I looked at the time on Adam's message. He'd sent it only ten minutes ago. Since it was midafternoon at St. Mary's Igloo, he might still be at the computer.

"Your mother is an idiot," I began. "Never mind that some doofus hit my car in the grocery store parking lot or that I screwed up my back in the kitchen (no ambulances or sirens involved—I'll heal, so will the Honda). I'm going to order your gear right now and have it sent via express mail. Meanwhile, please offer Masses for two recently deceased Alpiners, Alvin De Muth and Mike O'Toole. If you have any Masses left over, say one to give me the grace so I don't flatten the above-mentioned doofus the next time I run into her—or vice versa."

I was on a site that sold thermal wear when another message from Adam popped up. "I should've given you more notice re the warm stuff. Suddenly it's below freezing at night and I should know better by now, but . . . well, maybe you've noticed that getting ordained doesn't guarantee personality changes. Skip the express because if it snows too much that doesn't mean the stuff will get here any faster than by standard delivery. Are you sure you're okay? Who's the doofus? Maybe I shouldn't ask, since it might cause you to have Bad Thoughts. On the other hand, being a priest's mother doesn't change your personality, either, so you're probably wishing that the doofus would drive over a cliff. Meanwhile, who are the dead people? I don't think I ever heard of the first guy but is the O'Toole one of the Grocery Basket family?"

I wrote back, assuring Adam that I was doing fine. I also told him he wouldn't know De Muth, but that Mike was Jake and Betsy's nephew, though I doubted that he and Adam had ever crossed paths. After I saw the steep increases for express shipping to Alaska, I followed my son's advice and opted for the cheaper rate. By six-thirty, I'd filled his requests and hoped the items would arrive before he was buried under four feet of new snow. I was heading for the kitchen when the phone rang.

"Ms. Lord?" a male voice said in an uncertain voice.

"Yes?"

"This is Walt Hanson. Is my wife working late tonight? She hasn't come home and nobody answers at the newspaper office."

I thought back to my leave-taking with Leo. It had been a little after five. Vida had already offered to take me home, but that was when my ad manager spoke up and said he was headed for the ski lodge. At that point, Vida bade us good night and went on her way. I recalled glancing out into the front office but couldn't see Amanda from that angle. Vida hadn't paused in her exit, but that didn't mean Amanda wasn't still there. My House & Home editor might have simply snubbed our temporary receptionist. It had taken a few minutes for Leo and me to gather our own belongings. I couldn't remember seeing any sign of Amanda when we left around five-ten.

"No," I finally answered. "I think she quit around five. You might call Kip MacDuff. He usually stays on a bit later than the rest of us, especially when we're this close to deadline. He'd be home by now."

"Okay," Walt said. "I'll do that."

Five minutes later the phone rang again. "Kip told me that Amanda was gone when he left around five-thirty," Walt said. "He was sure there was no sign of her and he closed up." A slight pause followed. "Did Amanda mention anything about what she was doing after work?"

"No." I hadn't spoken to her after the reminder about taking only an hour for lunch.

"Would she have said anything to anybody else?"

Obviously, she hadn't given Kip any information; nor did I think she and Vida had spoken during the course of the afternoon. If Leo had talked to her, he hadn't brought up her name on the short ride home. "I honestly don't know where she might have gone. Shopping, maybe?"

"I don't think so," Walt said, sounding worried. "We were supposed to have dinner with Derek and Blythe Norman and some other people from the hatchery. We planned to arrive at the Normans' house around six. I called them before I called you just in case Amanda was running late and had gone there first. They hadn't seen or heard from her."

"Do you know if her Miata is still parked by the office?"

"I asked Kip about that," Walt replied. "He didn't think it was. She'd been pulled in next to his pickup after she got back from lunch."

Kip was the type who noticed such things. "I don't know what to tell you, Mr. Hanson. I'm sorry. Let me know when she shows up."

"Um . . . yes, I will. I . . . sure."

Walt definitely sounded upset. I almost suggested that he call the sheriff's office, but being an hour and a half late wasn't enough to qualify as a missing person.

"Please do call me," I repeated. "Maybe she ran into a friend. I'm sure she must be fine."

"I hope so," Walt said. "Thanks." He hung up.

I sat on the sofa for a long moment, knowing that neither of us believed the last few words we'd spoken.

SEVENTEEN

B Y TEN O'CLOCK, WALT HANSON HADN'T CALLED BACK. MY anxiety grew, though I told myself that if Amanda had shown up, the couple had probably scurried off to Derek and Blythe Norman's house. Walt could have been in a rush and forgotten he'd promised to keep me informed.

I finished an e-mail to my brother, Ben, who was again coming off the bench to sub for another priest. Father Jimbo, as Ben called him, was doing research on St. Leo the Great, the fifth-century pope who had guided the church through some rugged years of chaos. During a six-month leave of absence, Jimbo planned to study the Vatican archives for evidence of St. Leo's influence in Gaul. Ben, however, figured he was actually studying menus, wine, art, and really crazy Italian drivers on the Via Veneto. My brother's current assignment was in Boston where he was doing some studying of his own, mainly of American history, the Boston Red Sox, and the MTA.

My next dose of pain medication was due at eleven, so I had almost an hour to go. Restless, I wandered over to the front window and looked out into the October night. All was quiet, with only the amber glow of house and streetlights blurred by the thickening fog. A car slowly passed by and turned into Val and Viv Marsden's driveway. My brain went into overdrive as I suddenly remembered that Val worked with Walt Hanson at the fish hatchery. Maybe the Demerol had addled my mind. Feeling like a moron, I hurried through the front door.

The Marsdens had parked in their garage, but had to come back outside to enter the house. I called to them as I ran across the yard.

"What's wrong?" Viv shouted in alarm.

"Nothing," I assured her, reaching the fence between our properties. "That is, nothing with me. Were you at Blythe and Derek's house for dinner tonight?"

"Yeah," Val replied, laughing and shaking his head. "That was more fun than bunions."

I cut to the chase. "Were the Hansons there?"

"Not exactly," Viv said. "They came, they saw, they tried to kill each other. And that was before they ever got inside the house."

I was relieved that apparently Amanda was alive and well, but curious about the behavior of both Hansons. I posed a question that might've been considered bad manners for anyone who didn't live in a small town or work on a newspaper. "What were they fighting about?"

Val shrugged. "No clue. They came in separate cars, arriving at the same time." He glanced at Viv. "When was that? Around seven-fifteen?" His wife nodded. "Anyway," Val went on, "they started to fight. Yelling, screaming, the whole nine yards. Amanda finally got back in her Miata and took off. Walt came inside but wouldn't talk about it. He had one drink and left."

"Walt didn't even finish his drink," Viv put in. "He just

stood around, fuming and looking as if he'd punch out any-body who spoke to him. But he did mutter some kind of apology before leaving."

I noticed that Viv, who was wearing a bejeweled angora cardigan, had begun to shiver. "You're cold," I said, also feeling a damp chill setting in. "Go warm up. We can talk later."

Val didn't require further persuasion, but Viv hung back. "How's Amanda working out for you?"

"Okay." I wouldn't criticize Ginny's sub. Viv enjoyed gossip-peddling as much as most Alpiners. "Walt called to ask me if she was working late. She wasn't." I was shivering, too. "We'd better warm up before we get pneumonia."

Viv didn't argue. I went back to my snug log cabin, wishing I'd built a fire. The reason for Amanda's tardiness wasn't as important as the ruckus that had followed. Val and Viv had already told me the marriage was in trouble. Maybe the Hansons had reached the end of their rocky road. Selfishly, I wished that if they were having a marital war, it wasn't on my watch. Very few people—except perhaps Vida—could close the door on serious problems before going to the job.

The following morning, Vida picked me up at ten to eight. "Why," she demanded after I told her about Amanda and Walt, "didn't you call me? I got home from the anniversary party before nine. Those Palm Springs retirees have no stamina. Far too much sun."

"I didn't know anything until I talked to the Marsdens. At that point, all I wanted to do was take my pills and go to bed."

Vida harrumphed—but mildly. "Oh, yes, I realize you're not quite yourself." She paused to look around before backing into a parking slot in front of the office. "Did we get that new photo of Mike O'Toole? I must write his obituary today. I dread . . ." She paused again, even though she'd negotiated the parking task. "Here comes Amanda. That red Miata certainly stands out."

"Great." My tone was dour. "Let's avoid her by hightailing it into the office first."

Vida looked surprised. "You don't *want* to talk to her?"

"Not right now. I need to fuel myself first."

We got out of the Buick before Amanda had finished parking. "I forgot," I said as we hurried through the front door. "She's on the bakery run today. If she remembers."

Kip had plugged in the coffeemaker while Leo and Mitch, armed with their mugs, waited patiently and tossed around ideas with Kip for making good use of our online site.

Vida, of course, wanted only water. After filling her glass, she turned to me. "Did you ask Marisa about my advice column?"

I blanched. "I forgot. I'm so sorry. I'll call her again today."

Leo stared at Vida. "Advice column? Oh, Duchess, that's great! When do you start dishing?"

"Dishing?" Vida wrinkled her nose. "Oh—you mean offering sound advice. Actually, I thought I might mention the possibility on my radio program tomorrow night."

Mitch held up his empty mug as if he were toasting Vida. "You go, girl. It'll be the best-read part of the paper."

Vida all but simpered. "Except for 'Scene,' of course. Which reminds me, who has an item for this week's edition?"

I couldn't think of anything off the top of my head. I avoided Vida's request and scurried into my cubbyhole to call Bert Anderson about when my car would be ready. Unfortunately, he wasn't sure. The tire hadn't yet arrived although he was about to start the bodywork. Bert told me to check back around noon.

A glimpse into the newsroom indicated that the coffee was made. As I was about to get out of my chair, I saw Amanda enter with two bakery bags from the Upper Crust. "Doughnuts, bear claws, and a new kind of Italian slipper with peaches instead of apples," she announced in a voice that had all the warmth of a recorded message. I held back, watching her arrange the goodies on the tray. I still wasn't prepared to face the unpleasant Ms. Hanson. Nor did it appear that she wanted to communicate with her fellow employees. Amanda moved efficiently, dismissing a comment or two from Mitch with brief responses I couldn't hear. Ignoring Leo, Kip, and Vida, she finished her task and marched off to the front office.

I went out to pour my coffee and snatch one of the Italian slippers before they all disappeared. Mitch was making chattering-teeth noises and holding on to himself as if to keep warm. "There's a cold front around here this morning," he said quietly.

Kip grabbed a doughnut and shook his head. "Weird."

"Unacceptable," Vida murmured.

"Maybe she needs a friend," Leo said softly. "I'll volunteer."

I gave him a quizzical look. "You sure?"

He shrugged. "It can't hurt."

I nodded. "Then do it. I thought anything would be an improvement over Ginny's constant complaints, but the current atmosphere around here is throwing me off-balance."

"You're not alone," Mitch said in a low voice. "Ginny's gripes were legit and we could laugh about them." He gestured toward the front office. "That one's getting disruptive."

"Agreed," I said before taking my mug and pastry into the cubbyhole.

I dialed Marisa's number. Judi Hinshaw put me through. Compared with my still-befogged state, Marisa sounded aggravatingly fresh and alert. "An advice column." She laughed. "Frankly, I marvel that Vida didn't do one years ago. I've never known anyone to hand out advice so freely, even when it's unasked for. Of course I haven't experienced it much firsthand, but Judi has talked about her aunt's . . . readiness to counsel anyone, solicited or otherwise."

"So how do we keep from getting sued?"

"That's not a problem," she assured me. "If people write in asking for advice, they accept responsibility for getting it. As long as Vida doesn't overstep the bounds of anonymity or suggest something illegal, you're off the hook. Of course people will talk, guess, surmise, and wonder, but that can't be helped. The person seeking help must realize that in a sense, they're already violating their own privacy, whether or not they sign their real names. I'm anxious to see how this turns out."

"I'm just anxious," I admitted. "Okay, I can green-light her, right?"

Marisa laughed again. "How can you stop her? I mean, you *could,* but you'd probably need some counseling yourself after Vida reacted."

"Too true." I paused, forcing myself to keep from mentioning the Hansons' row. Marisa was too sharp not to realize that I was trying to get her to unload on me about Amanda, her alleged client. I thanked her and rang off. A moment later I got a call from Marje Blatt.

"Doc wants to know how you're feeling," she said in her brisk tone.

"Better," I replied, "though I didn't sleep well. I'm still hurting."

"Do you need to continue the Demerol for another day?"

"Yes. It's our deadline, so I have to muster all my strength."

"I'll let Doc know," Marje said. "His first patient just arrived."

"He's off to an early start," I remarked.

"This visit isn't on the regular schedule. I'll call you later."

Two minutes after I'd disconnected the call, Vida stomped into my cubbyhole. "We still don't have a more recent picture of Mike O'Toole. I just called Betsy at the Grocery Basket— I didn't want to bother Buzzy and Laura—and I talked to Jake. Naturally, being a man, he had no idea where to find a photo of Mike. I'll have to wait until Betsy gets back from her doctor's appointment."

"Betsy?" I stared at Vida, trying not to become distracted by her big black hat with its cluster of white and gray pigeons circling the crown. "That's odd. I wonder if she's Doc's unscheduled patient."

Vida leaned on my desk. I half expected the pigeons to fly off her hat and attack me. "What do you mean?"

I explained about Marje's call. "Of all the O'Tooles, Betsy is the last one I'd expect to fall apart."

"You don't know that she did," Vida pointed out. "She may have hurt herself or she's coming down with something and doesn't want it to get out of hand before the funeral Thursday."

"That could be," I allowed grudgingly.

Vida sensed I was troubled. "Well?"

I shook my head. "I don't know. Something's not right about . . . I'm not even sure *what* it's about. I don't suppose Marje would know why Betsy showed up on the clinic doorstep this morning?"

Vida put a finger to her cheek. "She would if it was strictly a medical problem. Marje isn't supposed to divulge information, but . . ."

"But her aunt is so gracious about visiting hospitalized friends and sending get-well cards and mentioning their names in 'Scene.' "

"Alpiners' health is a concern for everyone." Vida looked

almost as if she believed what she was saying. To be fair, she
was right. "I suppose," she added in a musing tone, "I could
ask Marje about Betsy so that I'd be able to allude to the
O'Toole tragedy in 'Scene' in a tasteful way that would rally
support for their loss. It'd actually be doing the family a favor,
wouldn't it? Such a sad time for the O'Tooles."

"That's very kind," I said with a straight face. I wondered if
the pigeons might start to weep. "By the way, Marisa says you
can go ahead and do an advice column. If you want to mention
it tomorrow on your program that's fine, but let's get something in the *Advocate* first. Have you talked to Spencer Fleetwood about it?"

"No," Vida replied, her face brightening. "I won't until just
before airtime. The paper will have been out for several hours
by then."

"Good."

Vida returned to her desk. I leaned to one side, wondering if
she'd picked up the phone to quiz Marje. Instead, she was facing her computer and pounding away on the keys. She'd probably wait until after Betsy left to make the call.

I took a last look at my editorial on the perils of Highway 2
and the state's wishy-washy efforts to stop the carnage. While
I rarely concerned myself with how much space my copy took
up, the piece was only two columns by five inches. I had room
for a second, though related, two hundred words on why we
needed more doctors in SkyCo.

An hour later, I'd finished proofing Mitch's copy on De
Muth's murder, Mike's fatal crash with quotes from Milo
about Highway 2's lethal record, and a summary of issues facing the next county commissioners' meeting Thursday night.
Mitch's articles didn't need much editing. It was a relief to have
a pro as our general reporter. He had tried and failed to get a

description of the young man Harvey Adcock had seen with De Muth at the hardware store. Harvey might know all about nuts and bolts, but when it came to people, he was vague. The sketch I'd considered running wasn't doable.

A little after ten, Vida came back into my office. "I haven't heard back from Betsy yet, and I have to see Donna Wickstrom to take pictures of her art gallery renovation. She's having an open house Friday night. If Betsy calls, would you ask her if someone could drop Mike's photo off here or call the gallery so I can pick it up on my way back to the office?"

I promised I would. "Can you," I inquired, bracing myself for what I presumed would be a small outrage from Vida, "let Amanda know that if Betsy phones, she should let me take the call?"

Vida pursed her lips. "Oh . . . very well," she murmured, "if I must, I must." She and her pigeons flew out of my cubbyhole.

When my phone rang twenty minutes later, it was Betsy. Apparently Amanda had acquiesced to Vida's request. "Emma," Betsy said, sounding frazzled, "I'm so sorry it took so long to get back to you and Vida. I forgot to bring Mike's photo to work. It's been just an awful morning, between funeral arrangements, trying to get Buzzy to focus on the job, comforting Laura, and . . . never mind. If I get it to you this afternoon, is that soon enough? Kenny can drop it off."

"That sounds fine," I assured her. "As long as we have it no later than three or four o'clock. How recent is it?"

"It was taken last Christmas," Betsy replied. "Mike was our Erica's date for the high school winter ball. Her boyfriend got mumps and had to cancel, so Mike filled in." She laughed softly. "He told Erica that if she weren't his cousin, he'd be glad to be her escort anytime. We all thought that was . . . so . . . sweet." Her voice caught on the last few words.

I grimaced. "Hang in there, Betsy. You're tough. You're strong. The rest of the family really needs you."

"Ohh . . ." I heard her take a deep breath. "You're right. I'm the one who holds up the tent pole. Today started out on a horrific . . . skip it, here's the fish guy. He can't find Jake." She rang off.

Wishing I could help Betsy, I put the phone down. I was taking my coffee mug out into the newsroom to get a refill when Ginny cruised in pushing a baby stroller. "Where is everybody?" she asked as I came out to greet her. "I wanted to show off Brandon, but my fill-in didn't seem interested. Isn't that Amanda Hanson?"

"It is." I bent down to look at the sleeping infant. "Oh, he's cute!" Vida's unflattering description had led me to believe otherwise, but of course she'd seen the baby only hours after he was born.

"You think so?" Ginny smiled faintly. "I never think they're all that cute at first. Maybe girl babies are cuter. I wouldn't know."

"You're keeping him anyway?" I said, admiring the little pink face, the swath of fair hair under the yellow knit cap, and the tiny fingers.

"Oh, yes!" Her smile widened. "He's actually a good baby. Is Kip in the back shop?"

"He usually is. Everybody else is out just now. They'll be sorry to have missed you. Especially Vida."

"She's offered to bring us a casserole for dinner tonight, but I told her to wait until later in the week," Ginny said. "Her cooking isn't very appealing." She grimaced. "It was kind of her though. I'd better catch Kip before he disappears, too." She pushed the stroller toward the back shop. "Thanks so much for the outfits. They're really nice."

"You're more than welcome." I moved closer and lowered my voice. "We'll be glad to have you back on the job."

"Really?" She seemed genuinely surprised. "I was kind of awful before Brandon came along."

"Understandable," I said, and gave her a quick hug.

I was about to pour more coffee when I heard someone yelling in the front office. The shrill sound came from a woman and sounded familiar, but it wasn't Vida or Amanda. I set the mug down on Mitch's desk and hurried to the reception area.

Patti Marsh leaned over the counter, screaming at Amanda, who was cowering behind her chair. Patti's fingers were curled into claws as if she intended to go for the other woman's throat.

"Hey!" I shouted, stretching out an arm to prevent Patti from trying to get at Amanda. "What's all this?"

Patti stepped back a few paces, switching her angry eyes from Amanda to me. "I didn't know you hired whores," she screeched. "Look at her! She thinks she's such a hottie, but she's just another tramp."

"You ought to know," Amanda snarled, keeping her voice down. "You're not just a tart, but an *old* tart. You're pathetic." With one last withering look, she came out from behind the counter and walked purposefully down the hall to the back shop.

"Go ahead," Patti yelled, "you can run, but you can't hide!"

I took a deep breath. "Okay, Patti, what's going on with you two?"

Patti slumped against the counter. "Amanda's a real nasty piece of work." Her lower lip trembled as she struggled for composure. "I'm no angel, but . . ." Tears welled up in her eyes. "Oh, what the hell—maybe she's right. Maybe I'm not just an old tart, but an old fool."

Despite my prickly relationship with Patti over the years, this wasn't the first time I'd felt sorry for her. She'd had plenty of bumps in the road, too. Subtlety was pointless. "Is she carrying on with Jack?"

Taking a Kleenex out of her corduroy jacket, Patti nodded. "She wants to marry him. Can you beat that?"

"Ah—no." I paused while Patti used the tissue to dab at her eyes. "Jack's a bit . . ." I stopped, trying to be tactful. "He's several years older," I finally said, unable to come up with a more flattering word.

Patti nodded. "He's sixty, she's not yet forty. Or so she claims." Her face looked unusually haggard. Maybe, I realized, it was because Patti's only makeup was a haphazard smear of pink lipstick. "Why Jack? Why not some other woman's man?"

It was a valid question, though I could understand his attraction for women. Age hadn't erased all of his appeal. Jack was good looking in a dark, saturnine kind of way; he was shrewd, even smart, having steered his mill through precarious times; he had money; and he was single. With two failed marriages behind him, I figured Jack wouldn't want to strike out with a third try. He preferred to go down swinging—and had found a patsy in Patti. The live-in arrangement suited him fine.

I asked the obvious, if touchy, question. "How does Jack feel about Amanda?"

Patti made a disgusted noise. "She's fairly young, fairly good looking, and more than fairly easy. Last night I caught him with her at the house. Jack thought I wouldn't get back from Snohomish until later in the evening, but I didn't feel so good. Oh, shit!" She slammed her fist on the counter. "You can tell Amanda that if she wants Jack, she can have him. I'm outta here."

I watched Patti stalk out through the front door. The phone on Amanda's desk rang, so I took the call.

"Emma?"

"Janet?"

"Yes. Why are you answering the phone?" Janet Driggers asked.

"Our receptionist has stepped away. What's up?"

"I was calling Vida," Janet replied. "I'm working at the funeral home today instead of at the travel agency. Is Vida around?"

"No. Can I take a message?"

"Sure. Alvin De Muth has left the building. The SnoCo ME sent the final autopsy results late yesterday, and the body was claimed last night. De Muth's on his way to . . . someplace. Where'd I put that form?"

"Whoa! Who claimed him?"

"Just a sec . . . Here it is." Janet cleared her throat. "His wife. You know, it's one thing to want a guy's body while he's still alive, but why bother when he's dead? Unless, of course, you're into that sort of—"

"Janet," I all but shouted, "stop! Are you telling me that De Muth was married?"

She laughed in her throaty manner. "I guess I am. Apparently, they were estranged. Or maybe just strange. Her name is Lorna Irene De Muth and she's from the Denver area. Al did the paperwork. *My* Al, that is. The other Al's handwriting is worse. He's a bit stiff these days."

"Mrs. De Muth came all the way here to collect the body?"

"No. She sent us a signed affidavit and a copy of their marriage certificate," Janet explained. "We shipped De Muth out this morning. If you know anybody ready for the Grim Reaper, we have a vacancy. Two, in fact, after poor Mike O'Toole's service."

I was accustomed to Janet's gallows humor and uninhibited

sexual comments that kept her sane while earning a living off the dead. "We could use a respite from tragedy around here," I remarked.

"Speak for yourself," Janet shot back. "Al and I have bills to pay. Shall I e-mail this info to Vida?"

"Go ahead. She'll be back before lunchtime. I don't suppose Mrs. De Muth sent a photo of her husband?"

"No. Don't you have one on file?"

"We might," I said as Amanda entered the hallway from the back shop. "Scott Chamoud did a short article on De Muth a few years ago. Got to dash. Thanks, Janet."

Amanda peered out into the front office. "Is that bitch gone?"

"Yes," I replied. "There's not much room here for hiding. Did you expect her to jump out of the broom closet and pounce on you?"

"It wouldn't surprise me." She uttered a truncated laugh. "Sorry about that. Is Patti a head case or what?"

I made eye contact with Amanda. "Why do you ask?"

"Why do you think?" She shrugged. "Patti walks in here and starts screaming and looks as if she's going to physically attack me. Is that normal around this place?"

"Of course not." I could've added that upon occasion, an irate reader would make threats, but that was an on-the-job hazard. "Look," I went on, deliberately blocking Amanda's path to her chair, "I'm not sure you're suited for this job. I realize this is only your third—"

"Hey!" Amanda cried. "I'm doing the work, right? What more do you want?"

"No disruptions," I said. "No face-offs in the front office. No disappearing acts. No having to wonder what the hell is going to happen next. No phone calls at home from worried husbands. In short, I don't want any more muss and fuss. Your attitude and your disruptions aren't professional. In other words, I want you gone."

"Fine." Amanda reached over the counter to snatch up her handbag and jacket. "Fine. I'm gone."

She got as far as the door, dropped her purse, and burst into tears.

My shoulders sagged. "For God's sake, what now?"

"Jimmy," Amanda blubbered, or at least that's what it sounded like. She was leaning against the door, shaking and sobbing. Maybe Amanda and Patti would meet outside and have a cry-off. Or kill each other. Either way would work for me.

I'd misheard. "*Ginny!*" she yelled. "Ginny and her damned baby!"

I gaped at Amanda. "Ginny's baby? What're you talking about?"

"It's . . ." She squeezed her eyes shut, wildly waved a hand, and uttered a few agonized, meaningless sounds.

"Hey!" I exclaimed. "Sit. Please. You're hysterical."

I'd shoved the chair out from behind the counter, rolling it closer to Amanda. She covered her face with her hands and sobbed some more. It was obvious that she couldn't focus on anything, let alone get control of her emotions. I took her by the arm and led her to the chair a mere couple of feet away from where she'd been standing. As an afterthought, I locked the front door. This kind of drama was bad for business. I almost wished I kept a bottle of booze in my desk drawer, just like an old-fashioned hard-drinking journalist.

Amanda was still crying, but at least she didn't seem to be going into convulsions. "Please," I said, crouching next to her and feeling some peculiar twinges in my back. "I don't understand what you're trying to tell me. About Ginny and the baby,

I mean. Is it because they're the reason you've come to work here?"

Several seconds passed before she responded, and when she did, it was only a wobbly, negative shake of the head.

"Then what is it?"

She shook her head again, but the sobbing had abated.

"Do you want some water?" I asked.

"No," Amanda answered in a barely audible whisper. "I should go."

I hesitated. The last thing I wanted was for Ginny to come from the back shop and have a run-in with Amanda. "Let's take some time to cool off," I suggested. "You think about what I said, and I'll see if I can reconsider. Come back after lunch, okay?"

"Well . . ." She picked up her handbag and stood up. "Maybe."

While Amanda put her jacket on, I unlocked the door. She walked out without another word or backward glance. Shoving the chair behind the counter, I tried to gather my strength, calm my tattered nerves, and stretch my back to make sure I hadn't incurred any further damage. I couldn't remember such an unsettling start to a day. As Ginny and the baby reappeared, I tried to take comfort from the sight of mother and child placidly coming my way.

"Kip thinks Brandon looks like me," Ginny said. "I think he looks like Rick. What do you think?"

The baby had opened his eyes and was yawning. "I can't tell," I admitted. "Did Amanda say anything to you when you arrived?"

Ginny looked puzzled. "She said hi and that Brandon was a nice baby and . . . well, that was it. Why?"

"Because she just had a fit and left. What are you doing for the rest of the morning?"

"I'm going to the grocery store to get . . ." She stopped and stared at me. "What do you mean? Amanda quit?"

"Not exactly." I grimaced. "It's all kind of weird. I thought if you could fill in until lunchtime . . . Oh, never mind. We'll manage."

Ginny gazed down at Brandon. "I'm nursing him, but he won't be hungry again until one o'clock. I suppose I could stay for an hour or so. I did it before when the other boys were small."

"I remember." The baby-on-board venture had worked well enough until the boys had started walking. Chaos had ensued, forcing Ginny to leave them at Donna Erlandson Wickstrom's day care. As Ginny's sister-in-law, she'd charged only half the usual rate. "I'd really be grateful for your help," I said. "I'll pay, of course."

"You don't need to," Ginny said.

"But I will. Or give you a gift certificate. Whatever." I smiled. "Believe me, I appreciate you now more than ever."

I was helping Ginny and the baby get settled in when the phone rang. I was closest, so I answered. "Ms. Lord?" Bert Anderson said. "Your car's ready to roll."

"Great," I said. "I'll come by in an hour."

"You need a ride?" he asked.

"I can probably get somebody here to bring me," I replied. "At least one of them should be around before lunchtime."

"If not," Bert said, "Ginny Erlandson is coming by later when Rick drops off their SUV. I'll ask if she'd mind collecting you on her way."

I glanced at Ginny, who was taking off Brandon's cap and jacket. "Ginny's right here. I'll ask her myself." I hung up. "What are you driving, Ginny? Bert Anderson's expecting Rick to bring in your SUV."

Ginny nodded. "Bert's going to fix that damage from hitting

the planter. I borrowed my mom's car this morning. It's that dark green Subaru parked next to Kip's pickup."

"This has been a terrible week for vehicle damage around here," I remarked. "Especially since Al De Muth and his expertise aren't with us anymore. Of course it was a worse week for him."

"Yes," Ginny said, moving the stroller into various positions. "Getting killed, I mean."

I nodded. Ginny not only lacked a sense of humor, but seldom recognized irony. "Here comes Vida," I said. "I'll let you two chat it up."

"Okay." Ginny pushed the stroller a few inches to the right. "Do you think Brandon's in a draft?"

"The counter shields him from the doorway," I said. "He's fine." I hurried back through the newsroom, pausing only to pour some hot coffee. I could hear Vida ooh-ing and aah-ing in the front office. My phone rang again.

"Is this a wrong number?" Rolf Fisher inquired in a bemused tone.

"Probably," I said. "You're wrong if you think I'll come to France."

"Too late," he said. "I've met *une femme très enchantée.* We are about to open a dry white Pouilly-Fumé, not to be confused with the Burgundy wine of the same name. This heavenly gift of Bacchus is almost as bewitching as my lovely guest."

"You're not casting any spells in this direction," I said. "In fact, the sheriff just rode in."

"*Mon Dieu!* I'm forced to offer my attentions to Mimi." Rolf cut me off. *In more ways than one,* I thought as Milo ambled into my office.

"You already look pissed," the sheriff said, taking off his regulation hat, which just barely cleared the door frame. "I've got bad news."

"Is there any other kind?"

As he sat down, his big frame dwarfed my visitor's chair. "I can't break Mickey Borg's story without breaking his arm. He says he saw the incident and will testify in court that it was your fault. You hit Holly's car and beat her up. She's hired a lawyer. Have you got a Plan B?"

EIGHTEEN

"That's ridiculous," I said. "Where the hell was Mickey? Hiding in a grocery cart? Did you talk to Dane Pearson at Safeway?"

"The manager?" Milo turned in the chair and stretched his legs. "Dwight asked him about it. Pearson didn't see Mickey, but he admitted that it was raining so hard he couldn't see much of anything."

"Swell." I picked up my coffee mug, but realized that my hand was shaking. "Oh, crap!" I pushed the mug away. "You drink it. I don't need more caffeine to make me jumpy. It's been a really rotten morning."

"Is that why Ginny and the kid are out front jawing with Vida?"

"Yes."

The sheriff shoved the mug back in my direction. "Well?"

"Well what?" I snapped.

"Aren't you going to go into one of your usual long and drawn-out explanations of why you look like bird crap?"

"Oh." I made a sour face. "So now I even look bad. It's not enough that I feel bad, right?"

Milo shook his head. "Don't pick a fight, Emma. I'm not in a very good mood, either. I'm damned sick of babysitting so-called prisoners. Why doesn't that hotshot attorney of Clive's get him out on bail? Why can't Fred just lock himself in the john over the weekends instead of bugging the hell out of me and the rest of my staff? Why won't . . ." He stopped as his cell rang. "What now?" he muttered, checking the phone's tiny screen. "Dodge," the sheriff said in a weary voice and glumly listened. "So? Give it back to Spike Canby. Hey, I don't give a damn what he said. He can shove it up his ass for all I care."

"What was that about?" I asked as Milo closed his cell phone.

"Just in case, we sent that pool cue those kids found to the lab in SnoCo. They didn't find zip. I knew they wouldn't. The damned thing had been in the water too long. I told Dwight to give it to Spike whether or not it belonged to him. He doesn't know his ass from a hole in the ground anyway, and Julie Canby told Sam Heppner that they *were* short a pool cue. Spike can replace it with . . ." The sheriff frowned. "Why would any-body take a pool cue?"

"I thought Spike told you they sometimes disappear."

"So he did." The sheriff was still looking thoughtful. "Maybe somebody dropped something into the river or the creek and used a pool cue to get it back. Clothes, maybe."

It wasn't like Milo to speculate. "You mean anywhere along the river? Or at the tavern?"

"How many people who live on the Sky or Burl Creek have a pool table? Even if they did, why take a cue outside?"

I was impressed. "Good point. So you think the one the kids found in the underbrush on the river is from the ICT?"

"Maybe." Milo shook his head. "Hell, even if that's right, what does it mean?"

We both sat in silence for a few moments. "I heard from Janet Driggers," I finally said. "De Muth was married. Did you know that?"

"No, not until Al Driggers told me." Milo sighed. "The final autopsy on the vic didn't show anything new or different."

"So I gathered from Janet." I resisted needling the sheriff about not giving me the information earlier. "Are you going to contact Mrs. De Muth?"

"Doe got a call from her last night. Nothing she could add except that they'd been separated for several years, but not divorced."

"That's odd," I remarked.

"Is it? Saves money on lawyers if you don't intend to get married again," the sheriff said. "I've known some people like that, including two or three couples here in Alpine who separated, but still lived in the same house. The Skylstads did that for years until Cap fell for one of the Gustavsons and Bessie wanted to marry a guy from Index. The Skylstads finally got a divorce but couldn't agree which one of them should move. They had a big house on First Hill and their kids had moved away so they divided the place and kept right on living there with their new spouses."

"That must've happened before my time." I watched Milo's face closely, half expecting him to make a reference to his own changed marital situation. As far as I could tell, there was no reaction.

"I was in high school back then." Milo took out his cigarettes. "The only one of that foursome who's still alive is Bessie, and she's in the nursing home with Alzheimer's. The poor old gal probably doesn't remember which husband was which—or if she ever had a husband." He lighted his cigarette and took a deep puff.

"I suppose," I said after I'd gotten my ashtray out of the drawer, "I'll have to talk to Marisa Foxx about Holly."

"She's sharp. If Mickey's lying, Marisa will nail him to the courtroom wall."

"Why would he lie?"

Milo snickered. "I can think of one reason. Can't you?"

"Holly's charms are worth a perjury charge? Get real."

The sheriff's hazel eyes locked on my face. "You don't know?"

I scowled at him. "Know what? I'm not up to playing games."

"Let's say it beats child support," Milo said in his laconic voice.

My jaw dropped. "You mean Holly's kids?"

"One of them, anyway." He took another puff and exhaled. "Hell, Emma, don't you listen to the grapevine? Hasn't Vida told you?"

"Apparently not." I leaned to one side, trying to see around Milo. Mitch was talking to Leo, but Vida wasn't at her desk. "Are you saying that the paternity of Holly's kids is common knowledge?"

"No. But Vida knows all, and sometimes she knows when to keep her mouth shut." The sheriff lowered his voice. "We got a domestic violence call back in . . . March? April? Your ex-reporter, Scott Chamoud, got it off the log and put it in the paper, but as usual we withheld names and didn't give a specific address, just that the incident occurred at Spruce and Second streets."

"The trailer park," I said, vaguely recalling the item.

Milo nodded. "You got it. Anyway, Bill Blatt and Doe Jamison responded. The disturbance was between Holly and Mickey. She was pregnant with her third kid and demanding that Mickey pay her off. As so often happens with those domestic battles, they'd both calmed down by the time the deputies got there. Luckily, they didn't turn on Bill and Doe. That's why we hate to get involved in domestic brawls."

"I know. Jack Mullins got a broken arm once and Sam Heppner got hit in the head with a fireplace poker."

"Concussion," Milo recalled. "Sam spent three days in the hospital. I suppose you've already figured out that Vida squeezed the names and details out of her nephew Bill."

I was puzzled. "I don't recall her mentioning it. That's odd."

Milo chuckled. "She can keep some things under those weird hats of hers. Hey, what's Ginny doing up front?"

"Amanda needed some personal time," I replied, not wanting to go into the details. It was almost eleven-thirty. I still had to proof Vida's copy and go over Leo's ads.

"Cute baby," Milo said, taking a big sip of my coffee. "Brendan?"

"Brandon." I realized that the sheriff was making uncharacteristic chitchat. Stalling for time, maybe. "Hey, big guy," I said, "it's Tuesday. Do you remember what that means?"

Milo's innocent expression was also unlike him. "That tomorrow is Wednesday?"

I sighed. "You know damned well it's our deadline. And if you don't then you haven't paid much attention for the last fourteen years."

He shrugged, pushed back in the chair, and stood up. "I know when I'm not wanted. See you."

I watched him stop in the newsroom to talk to Mitch and Leo. The three of them seemed to be yukking it up. Ten minutes later, Vida reappeared and came into my office. "Have you read the Lofgren-Sanford engagement copy yet?" she asked.

"No. Why?"

MARY DAHEIM

"I must make a change. The would-be groom's first name is Ronald, not Donald." She grimaced. "That's the trouble with handwritten announcements these days. The younger generation has horrid penmanship. Imagine! Not teaching cursive or penmanship in the schools. What's to become of this country?"

"They can't tell time on a clock with hands," I said. "It's all digital."

Vida agreed. "Oh, yes! As for spelling, they don't use actual words. When I was at my daughter's house for dinner the other night, I happened to see Roger's cell phone. Goodness, do you realize what can be done with those devices? I knew that some of them could take pictures and play music, but Roger's is the latest model, and I can't even begin to recall all of its functions. I glanced at the screen and saw what is called a text message." She picked up one of my memo pads and wrote, 'u r : (me 2 c u 2' followed by what looked a backward C.

I shook my head. "What's that last thing you put down?"

"It's supposed to be a crescent moon," Vida replied. "As you know, I'm not an artist."

"I can make this out," I said a bit sheepishly. "It's shorthand for texting. Some of these symbols show up in e-mails. You must've seen them in the ones you get for the paper."

"Rarely," Vida snapped. "The people who send me e-mails are usually older and wiser."

That was probably true. "Okay, I think the message says 'You are sad. I am, too. See you tonight.' The moon—I think— means night, and it makes sense in context."

"Oh, heavens!" Vida scowled at the notepad. "I upbraided Roger for this sort of thing, but he laughed and insisted everybody does it. Maybe they do, in which case I should apologize to him. He's merely communicating in a more up-to-date manner. I seldom reproach him, and now I feel mortified."

"You shouldn't," I said. "Frankly, I find this sort of thing an abuse of the English language."

"Yes," Vida allowed, "that's why I was upset. He's been to college and I felt he should know better. Now I realize he's ahead of the curve when it comes to technology."

I couldn't look Vida in the eye. If her grandson took an AK-47 to the mall and shot down six innocent shoppers, she'd make excuses for him. I tossed the used page in the wastebasket. "Why was Roger sad?" I asked, hoping that it was because he'd been hired for a full-time job.

Vida looked embarrassed. "I've no idea, because I didn't realize what the letters and numbers meant. Maybe it was the other person who was sad. One of his chums, no doubt. He left not long afterward, and I haven't seen him since. I must call and apologize." Her usually purposeful walk slowed as she exited my cubbyhole.

It didn't take long to go over Vida's weekly contribution to the *Advocate*. Her style was folksy and would never win any journalism awards. She wrote her features as if they were letters, not newspaper stories. That was fine with her readers, who apparently felt she was taking them into her confidence.

It wasn't quite noon, so I called Marisa, hoping to catch her before she went to lunch. She was eating in according to Judi Hinshaw, who transferred my call.

I kept my account of Holly's purported lawsuit short. "And no, I've no idea who Holly has hired to represent her."

"At this point," Marisa said, "I don't care if she's hired Clarence Darrow. If Mickey Borg is lying to the sheriff, his eyewitness story has to be exposed before we ever get inside a courtroom. If Holly formally charges you with assault, it's a criminal case."

"Oh for . . ." I stopped. "I hadn't thought of that."

"Dodge should've," Marisa said. "Didn't he mention it?"

"No." Resentment welled up. Was Milo so wrapped up reconciling with Tricia that he didn't give a damn what happened to me? Or wasn't he taking Holly seriously? "No," I repeated. "Except for the hiring of a lawyer, the sheriff didn't have much else to say. Although," I added lamely, "he thought that you could handle Mickey Borg on the witness stand."

"We don't want to get that far," Marisa said. "Talk to Dodge. I won't bill you for something that should go away."

"Okay." I remembered something Marisa had told me when she was at my house for dinner. "I hate taking up your time, but the other night you mentioned that awhile back Holly wanted to see you about doing pro bono work for her. Judi told her your services weren't free. Was Holly trying to get child support from her kids' deadbeat dads?"

"Yes. I never spoke to Holly, though."

"So how does she get by? I don't recall her ever working."

"That depends on your definition of work."

"Supporting three kids as a hooker in Alpine?"

"She lives in a trailer and she's probably on welfare. For all I know, she got another attorney to handle the child support issue. He or she may be the same one she claims to have taken on her lawsuit," Marisa said, speaking faster than usual.

I realized that Marisa was growing impatient. She wouldn't be lunching at her desk unless she was busy. "I'll let you go," I said, "but I heard Mickey Borg is supposed to be one of kids' father."

"That might explain why he'd lie for her," Marisa said.

"Thanks, Marisa," I said as Vida stomped into my cubbyhole. "I'll let you know what happens next." I hung up.

"I've rarely seen the likes of this!" Vida declared, waving a computer printout at me. "It's an e-mail from Janet Driggers about Alvin De Muth. He had a wife. Why didn't that ever come to light?"

"Probably because his wife—or widow, I should say—lives in Colorado," I replied. "Is there any mention of children? I forgot to ask."

Vida was still annoyed. "No. Mrs. De Muth is the only survivor." She scrutinized Janet's message. "She wants the body shipped to a funeral home in Denver. I'll write this up now. I'm eating in today."

As she left my office, Ginny came in. "Rick's taking the SUV to Bert Anderson's place. Is it okay if I leave now so I can pick him up?"

"Sure," I said, noting that it was twelve-fifteen. "Can I hitch a ride? My car's supposed to be ready, but I'll check with Bert to make sure."

"Okay," Ginny said. "I'll get Brandon ready to go."

Bert, however, had bad news. "Sorry, but I got sidetracked. One of Blue Sky Dairy's trucks had an electrical problem. Can't let the town go without milk. I'm finishing that job now, so I'll get back to your Honda as soon as I grab a sandwich. Your car will be ready by five."

"I hope so," I said.

I went to the front office to tell Ginny I wouldn't be tagging along. She offered to fill in again if we had any more problems. I said thanks, hugged her a second time, touched Brandon's soft cheek, and watched mother and son exit. I got my jacket and purse, planning to run across the street to the Burger Barn. Before I could get to the door, Betsy O'Toole practically bowled me over as she tried to come inside.

"Emma!" she cried. "I'm so glad you're here!"

"Why?"

"We have to talk," Betsy said, her eyes red and her skin so

pale that the freckles had all but disappeared. We were both on the threshold. I was leaning against the door to keep it open. If Betsy came in, we'd have no privacy from Vida. Fortunately, she couldn't see us from where she was sitting at her desk.

"Let's go to the Venison Inn," I said, taking Betsy's arm and moving away so the door could shut.

She tried to hold back. "But I can't let anyone see me like . . ."

"You want Vida to see you?"

"Oh. I thought she'd be at lunch."

"Not today." I let go of Betsy's arm. "We can eat in the bar. It's never too full at lunchtime."

"I can't eat."

"You look like you could use a drink."

"I could, but I won't. What would our customers think if they saw me . . ." She stopped just short of the restaurant's entrance, using the reflection on the door's plate glass for a mirror. "Oh, God, I look ghastly. I should've put a grocery bag over my head."

"Let's go to the bar," I said. "We won't have to wait to be seated."

Inside, I hustled Betsy down the row of booths, talking her ear off about something-or-other to give the impression we were wrapped up in our conversation and couldn't pause to exchange greetings. The Reverend Poole was sitting with an elderly woman, Scooter Hutchins studied flooring samples under the watchful eye of a well-dressed younger man, four members of the community college faculty including the dean of students were engrossed in the menus, and Stella Magruder's husband, Richie, was chatting with Harvey Adcock. If any of them noticed our quick passage down the aisle between the booths, they didn't try to detain us.

"Corner table," I murmured, nodding as far away from the bar activity as we could get. If Betsy changed her mind about a drink, I'd have one, too. My back still hurt but I hadn't taken a Demerol since breakfast.

Betsy half fell into the chair, glanced at the array of bottles behind the bar, and opted for a drink after all. "A screwdriver," she said. "I can pass that off as orange juice." She started to pick up a menu but let it fall from her hand and expelled a huge sigh. "Emma, I don't know what to do. Maybe I should talk to Father Den instead of you, but I'm too ashamed. What would your brother or your son say?"

"About what?" I asked, wondering if Betsy had cracked under the relentless stress of the past few days.

The faintest hint of a smile played at her mouth. "I forgot. You're not a mind reader." She looked past me toward the bar. "Oh, no—here comes Sunny Rhodes. Can you head her off? She'll talk me to death."

I got up and managed to meet the bartender's wife halfway. "Two screwdrivers," I said in a low voice. "Betsy's very upset, so don't let anybody pester her, okay? I can get the drinks when I see they're ready."

"Then come now," Sunny said. "It won't take Oren long. Poor Betsy. Poor family." She shook her head before beckoning to her husband and giving him our cocktail order. "You never know with kids these days, do you? It's a wonder my hair hasn't turned white worrying over Davin all these years. Thank goodness he's out of his teens now."

"He's got his AA degree," I said as Oren Rhodes offered me a sympathetic smile. "That's great."

Sunny nodded. "Now if he could just get a decent job. At least he's stopped hanging out with Roger. That was always a dead-end trail." She gasped and her blue eyes widened in horror. "Oh, no! I shouldn't have said that. Please, please don't tell Vida."

I promised I wouldn't. "I'm not a big fan of Roger's, either. He hasn't done anything really stupid, has he?"

Sunny turned away to hand me our drinks. "No. No, of course not. He's just . . . Roger. Let me know when you're ready to eat. We're shorthanded, so I'm filling in. Good help's hard to find."

"I'll second that," I muttered, thinking of Amanda.

By the time I sat down, Betsy had regained some of her composure. She raised her glass. "To Mike."

"To Mike." Our glasses clicked. "Have you slept recently?"

"Some," she replied after taking a big sip. "Jake's so restless. He keeps waking me up." She sipped again. "You've got a deadline. I don't want to keep you away from work too long."

"We're on schedule," I assured her. "So far."

Betsy's gaze roamed around the bar. The usual workmen in their flannel shirts, parkas, and hooded jackets lined the bar stools, knocking back enough beer to get through the rest of the day. I avoided eye contact with any of the customers. I didn't want to be accused of snobbery for not offering so much as a friendly smile. My gaze fixed on the wall behind Betsy where an old framed photograph showed a logger sitting in front of a donkey engine, the steam-powered hoist used to haul logs out of the woods. His shoulders slumped, his hands rested slackly between his knees, and his clothes were grimy. Maybe he was the donkey puncher, taking a blow while waiting for more timber headed down a steep hill to the yard, the mill, or the holding pond. I wondered what, other than an honest day's work, was on his mind. Life was said to be simpler a hundred years ago. I didn't believe it. It was only slower.

"Doc called me this morning at six-thirty," Betsy said, startling me out of my reverie. "He had a problem and asked if I could come to the clinic before their patients showed up. So I did." She hung her head, hands wrapped around her glass.

I waited.

Betsy looked up and cleared her throat. "I'm going to tell you what he told me and I'm going to do it as fast as I can because it upsets me so much." She took a deep breath. "The surgeon in Monroe told Doc they couldn't get the pain meds to kick in because Mike was so full of cocaine and speed and God-knows-what that there was no way to deal with his suffering or prevent cardiac arrest, so he died."

Betsy's face hardened. She took another drink from her glass and ran a finger under each eye, maybe to make sure she wasn't crying. There were no tears. Maybe she had none left.

I didn't know what to say. "Is that why Doc told the family not to consent to an autopsy?"

"Yes. He didn't want us to know." She shook her head. "But Doc's conscience bothered him. He got to thinking about the other kids in the family and their friends. He asked if any of our four had done drugs. I told him I thought they'd probably tried pot, but nothing else. You don't know, though, do you?"

"You don't want to know," I said. "That's stupid, but I felt that way about Adam, especially after he went away to college. To this day, I've never asked him what he tried or didn't try. He'd tell me, though. I suppose that's why I never asked." It was my turn to take a big drink.

"So what do I do now?" Betsy said, as much to herself as to me. "Ask Father Den's advice? Have Doc talk to the kids? I haven't even told Jake. I just want all of us to get through the funeral. I guess," she went on ruefully, "I had to talk to somebody and it turned out to be you. Maybe I thought that since you raised a child on your own and he became a priest, you had some special gift."

"Oh, God, no." I laughed in an odd sort of way. "I had nothing to do with it. I was stunned when Adam told me about his decision. In fact, I was upset. But one of my few virtues is that I know how to keep a confidence. You have to in the newspaper business. I think you're right when it comes to waiting until after the funeral to tell the others, including Jake. I gather he's been hit hard by this whole thing."

Betsy nodded. "He's always felt responsible for Buzzy, and that carries over to Buzzy and Laura's kids. Doc raised a good point, though. Somehow we've got to open up about Mike."

"Honesty is the best policy," I said, and immediately wished I could retrieve the cliché. "I mean . . ."

Betsy held up a hand. "Stop. It's not that simple. What Doc means is that somebody around here is dealing. That's why we have to get the word out. Whoever it is should be charged not just with dealing or possession, but with murder."

NINETEEN

B ETSY REFUSED TO ORDER ANY FOOD, BUT I GOADED HER into sharing my shrimp Louie and some of the sourdough bread that went with it. She had to keep up her strength, and she couldn't get through the day on one screwdriver. I'd asked her if she intended to go to the sheriff before confiding in the rest of the family about Mike's apparent drug use.

"It wouldn't be right until we've all had time to recover from the shock," she'd told me. "Then we can discuss what to do. Maybe Doc should talk to Dodge. The sheriff likes facts, and Doc can get accurate information from the Monroe hospital. Besides, I think Doc's conscience would rest easier if he's involved in what I hope leads to nailing whoever's dealing that wretched stuff around here."

I agreed that was probably the best route to take. We parted just after one o'clock. To my surprise, Amanda was back on the job.

"Well?" she said as I arrived. "Am I fired?"

"No." I braced myself on the counter. "But I can't have scenes like the one with Patti. And don't bother to remind me she probably started it. You could've defused the confrontation by walking away and letting one of us know. We're all well versed in deflecting angry readers."

"I don't think Patti knows how to read," Amanda retorted.

"That's not the attitude to take around here," I said. "We may be a small staff in a small town with a small newspaper, but we try to be professional. Personal relationships should be left outside the front door. I doubt you'd get away with that sort of thing at the post office."

"It's never happened there."

"Lucky postal workers," I murmured. Amanda bristled. "Hold on," I urged, trying to sound more sympathetic. "Even though I don't get it, I won't ask about your reaction to Ginny and her baby. Okay?"

Amanda's face tightened. "Fine."

"Good." I forced a smile and started into the newsroom.

"How old are you?"

I turned around. "Why do you ask?"

Amanda opened her mouth to speak, and then clamped it shut. She shook her head and focused on her monitor.

Vida was heading for the back shop, and Mitch was looking at photos on his screen. "Did you see these?" he asked when I stopped by his desk. "They're the ones I shot at the O'Toole kid's vigil. Leo took some, too. He's not that bad with a camera." Mitch moved the monitor so I could see the screen.

I leaned on his desk. "That's a good one of the younger set."

"I've got IDs for this bunch," Mitch said. "I didn't find out who some of the others were. I figure there were a couple hundred people at the park that night."

I recognized Davin Rhodes, Melissa and Erica O'Toole, Mike Corson, Carrie Amundson, and two of Ed and Shirley Bronsky's kids, Rick and Molly. "That's a good shot, nice angle. Their faces capture the sadness of the moment. You must've been kneeling."

"I took it lying on a picnic table bench." Mitch switched to a different shot. "This is the only decent one I got of the older O'Tooles, but it's almost too heart-tugging."

I agreed. "Laura looks ghastly and Buzzy's a blank, as if he doesn't know where he is or what he's doing. Jake's eyes are closed. Betsy seems detached. She's almost literally out of the frame."

"It's as if she's trying to disappear to avoid the anguish," Mitch said. "The O'Toole story was tough to write, especially the sidebar that goes with these," he went on, clicking through several more crowd shots. "I talked to both Jake and Betsy that night but not to the kid's parents. Somehow, I couldn't." His lean face was grim.

I nodded. "The worst of it is that they still had hope that night. If Mike had lived, the photos would be an answer to a prayer. But . . ." I stopped and shook my head. "Maybe we shouldn't run them."

"Your call," Mitch said.

I thought for a long moment. "No. We have to. They show community and caring. The pictures capture one of those special moments when people put aside their own agendas for a common cause. You must've had to deal with lots of grieving families and friends in your time with the *Detroit Free Press*."

Mitch sighed. "Too many."

Leaning on the desk had become painful. I straightened up. "Are we missing something?"

Mitch hit a couple of keys, apparently sending one of the photos to Kip in the back shop. "Such as?"

"I don't know. I feel as if . . . well, there's something about what's happened in the past week or two that's odd, even for

Alpine." I caught Mitch's skeptical expression. "Trust me," I said. "It's not woman's intuition."

"Reporter's intuition?" Mitch suggested. "You have a sense of small-town vagaries. To me, coming from Detroit, Alpine seems like the calm *after* the storm."

"It's not the tavern brawl or the truck going off the highway or even the loss of two lives in a very short time," I said, feeling frustrated as I began pacing the newsroom. "Is there some elusive common thread?"

"Bad karma." Mitch pushed his chair away from his desk. "It happens. You're not expecting a third death, are you?"

"I'm not superstitious," I said. "Oh, I know things often come in threes, but that's because people expect them to and start counting."

Mitch stood up to get a coffee refill. "An old Hollywood and showbiz myth, usually about three celebrities croaking within a few days."

"Yes." I paused by Leo's desk, torn between loyalty to Betsy and professional responsibility. Mitch had written the news article about Mike's fatal accident, and he'd also done the accompanying story on the vigil. I'd never dream of going public, but as the primary reporter, Mitch had to understand the background to avoid getting blindsided if the news leaked out from another source. I was still pondering when Vida made her entrance. If I confided in Mitch and not in Vida, she'd never forgive me. I decided to keep my mouth shut for now.

Vida, however, sniffed in the way she had of alerting people that There Was Something She Needed to Know. "You," she said, confronting me, "look like the cat that ate the canary."

It struck me that Vida was the cat and although I wasn't a canary, I was definitely catnip. But I did my best to put her off. "I had lunch with Betsy. She's fraying around the edges. Take a look at Mitch's photos from the vigil for Mike."

Vida was sidetracked, but I knew it wouldn't take her long to return to the mainline. While she studied the pictures, I retreated to my cubbyhole. She didn't resume her quest until a few minutes after two.

"I hope you had more luck with Betsy than I did with Marje," she declared, settling into one of my visitors' chairs. "My niece insists she has no idea what's bothering Doc Dewey. Unfortunately, I believe her. Marje admitted that Betsy had an unscheduled appointment, though she didn't know why. Did Betsy tell you anything we should know?"

I shook my head. Technically, my denial wasn't a lie. Betsy didn't want Mike's drug habit made public. "She's worn out," I said, "from having the family lean on her. Did you see Mitch's vigil pictures?"

"Very effective," Vida responded. "I should've gone, but I . . ." Uncharacteristically, her voice trailed off.

I assumed she didn't want to discuss Amy's need for maternal comfort. "I didn't see Roger with the younger set. Who did he go with?"

Vida's quick, sharp glance jarred me. "I'm not sure."

"Oh." I kept my tone casual. "I saw some of his buddies, like Davin Rhodes and a couple of other kids, but he wasn't with them."

"Young people change," Vida said, her gaze fixed not on me but on the topographic map of Skykomish County above my filing cabinet. "They have different interests, they grow apart." She suddenly stood up. "Goodness, I must prepare for my program tomorrow night. Dr. Medved is my guest so I plan to ask him about special problems with pets this time of year. As a veterinarian, he's probably heard some horrific Halloween tales about nasty children tormenting dogs and cats." She hustled out of my office. To my surprise, Vida hadn't pressed me further about my lunch with Betsy.

My phone rang; I picked it up on the second ring. "We need to talk," Milo said.

I was startled. "Isn't that a woman's line?"

"Don't be a wiseass. Have you got a few minutes to spare?"

"It's deadline day," I reminded the sheriff, "but we're on schedule. So far. Unless, of course, you have breaking news."

"I'll break something if you don't give me a straight answer," he retorted. "Meet me by the river in back of the ICT."

"I don't have a car."

"It's not back yet?" Milo sounded irritated.

"Not until five. Is five-fifteen soon enough?"

He didn't answer immediately. "It'll have to be."

"Why can't you pick me up?"

"Because I can't." He hung up as raised voices erupted in the newsroom. *Now what?* I wondered, getting up and recognizing Leo's voice. He was coming toward me with a small, dark-haired woman right behind him. She was yapping away, apparently reproaching my ad manager. I didn't recognize her at first. Vida had half risen out of her chair; Mitch stood by his desk.

"Emma," Leo said, "you've met Janie Borg?"

I put out my hand. "It's been a long time," I said, smiling.

Janie took my hand and shook it in a tentative manner. I thought she looked relieved. "I'm upset," she said, glancing at Leo. "Sorry, Mr. Walsh. Seeing Amanda out front upset me even more."

"Forget it," Leo said with his crooked grin. "You girls have a heart-to-heart, okay?" He patted Janie's shoulder and winked at me before going to his desk. Mitch continued on his way to the back shop. Vida was scowling but reluctantly sat back down at her desk.

I closed my door. "Coffee or tea?" I asked before I sat down again.

"No. I'm fine." She offered me the hint of a smile. Up close I could see that there was some gray in her short black hair, but she still retained the gamine-like air I recalled from the few times I'd seen her.

"What made you think Leo wouldn't let you talk to me?" I inquired.

Janie's dark eyes looked misty. "Because of Mickey."

"Mickey?" I feigned ignorance. "What do you mean?"

"The lawsuit. The parking lot collision. Holly." She toyed with the silver chains of her necklace. "Mickey's such a bastard. I shouldn't have married him. I was on the rebound. From Fred. Poor Fred."

"You're not happy?"

She shook her head. "I'm miserable. I want out."

"I understand you and Fred still have feelings for each other."

"Oh, yes." Janie smiled wistfully. "But I'm scared. It might be the same-old, same-old. With Fred."

"Not if he spends his weekends in jail," I pointed out, and wondered why Janie was telling me her troubles.

"True. But difficult. Weekends should be fun. Together."

I was beginning to think that Janie's staccato manner of speaking would be enough to drive anybody to drink. "I certainly don't hold Mickey's alleged witnessing of my car accident with Holly against you."

"Good." Her smile was more genuine, but she still kept fidgeting with the silver chains. "Will it be in the paper?"

"At this point," I replied, "we'll run only a brief mention of the incident in the weekly report from the sheriff's log."

Janie seemed relieved. "Good," she repeated, letting go of the necklace and standing up. "I won't say anything. For now. Thanks."

"Wait," I said sharply. "Say anything about what?"

Apparently I'd startled her. Janie had that deer-caught-in-the-headlights look. "Mickey." Suddenly she burst out laughing and clapped her hands. "Yes," she said. "Much better. Fred out, Mickey in. 'Bye." Still amused, she opened the door and hurried through the newsroom.

"Well?" I said as Leo entered my cubbyhole. "Is Janie Borg nuts?"

"It could go either way," Leo replied. "I tried to keep her from bothering you. Frankly, I couldn't figure out *why* she came here. I knew we were in trouble when she took one look at Amanda and started to spout a bunch of crap about the town sluts."

"Meaning Amanda and Holly?"

Leo grinned. "I don't think she meant Vida."

"Or me, I trust."

"Let's assume that. Mitch told me about the pool cue that wasn't used to kill De Muth. I stopped in this afternoon to double-check the new ad for the ICT. Spike Canby got the cue back while I was there."

"And still didn't recognize it?"

"He didn't—or so he said—but Norene Anderson did." Leo sat on the edge of my desk. "She was sure it came from the tavern's rack because she used it to bust up a bees' nest outside."

"What did she do with it after bopping the bees?"

Leo's expression was wry. "She didn't know. Norene claims she doesn't remember what happened after she got stung except for coming inside, taking a couple of allergy pills, and putting a mixture of baking soda and water on her arm. She was miserable for the rest of the evening, but toughed it out. It wasn't until the next day that she saw Doc Dewey on an emergency basis. Her arm had swollen up so much that she hardly slept that night."

Leo's version of Norene's account matched what I already knew. "Maybe she couldn't sleep because one of the customers got killed." A salient omission dawned on me. "Do you know when she got stung?"

"I gathered it was an hour or so before the brawl started," Leo said after a pause. "She mentioned still being groggy when Berentsen and De Muth went at it."

I nodded. "It sounds as if she left the cue outside. If I'd taken some whacks at a bees' nest, I would've run away as fast as I could. The pool cue would be excess baggage."

"So you're thinking . . ." Leo stopped as Vida entered my office.

"You two seem very involved in a discussion," she said. "Would I be wrong in suspecting that it pertains to the ICT tragedy?"

"How did you guess, Duchess?" Leo's manner was droll.

"It's deadline, so we have to make sure there are no loose ends," Vida replied. "Shouldn't Mitch be involved?"

I shrugged. "His coverage is fine. We can only deal in facts."

"So," Vida asked, "are the facts consistent with hearsay and unsubstantiated quotes from witnesses?"

Leo and I exchanged glances. "That depends," I finally said. "Is Mitch still in the back shop?"

Vida looked into the newsroom. "He just came out. Do you want him in here?"

I told her I did. Leo smiled. "Is this an impromptu staff meeting?"

"More like brainstorming," I said. "Kip's got a full plate putting the paper together, and I certainly don't want Amanda in here."

I paused as Mitch sauntered in. "Is this somebody's birthday," my reporter asked, "or are we all fired?"

Vida sat down in one of the spare chairs. Leo deferred to Mitch for possession of the other visitor's spot. "I'm not a newshound," he said to Mitch. "In fact," he went on, turning to me, "am I needed?"

"Yes," I assured him. "You know a lot about this story, not to mention the people involved."

Leo nodded. "I'm Mr. Glad Hand, sucking up to possible revenue providers, no matter how irrational and impossible they may be." He slid off the desk and moved over by one of my filing cabinets.

"Mitch," I began, "do you have hard copy on all the statements that the sheriff and his deputies took?"

"Yes," he replied. "Mullins let me make copies. Shall I get them?"

I pondered the question. "Later, maybe, to compare notes with the official statements. It won't be easy since so much of what the rest of us heard wasn't taken down in writing."

Vida lifted her chin. "I recall everything that was told to me."

I smiled. "I know. You don't need notes or a tape recorder. But the rest of us do, and much of what we heard was off the cuff."

My three staff members looked at one another and then at me. Leo was the first to speak. "What's the point?"

"Omissions and contradictions." I turned to Mitch. "You must've covered courtrooms in your time."

"Oh, yes. My first beat included circuit court cases, mostly of a criminal nature. I thought it'd be interesting, even exciting. I fell asleep twice before noon on the second day of my first case, an armed robbery involving fatalities. Voir dire is a good cure for insomniacs."

I nodded. "I had the same experience at *The Oregonian*." I noticed that Vida and Leo looked as if they were growing impatient. "I'm not satisfied with this homicide being so cut and dried. First, the weapon was never found, and yet everybody agrees it was a pool cue. Second, none of the cues showed any signs of being used on De Muth. Third, the cue found by those college kids had been in the river—or the creek—too long to offer any forensic evidence. Do you follow me?"

"In other words," Vida said, "that was the lethal cue."

Mitch seemed skeptical. "Why do you say that?"

Vida bridled at the question. "Isn't it obvious? If De Muth was actually killed with a pool cue, it had to be the one that showed up later. Somehow it was removed from the tavern and thrown in the river."

Mitch started to respond, but Leo spoke first. "Nobody could've walked out of the ICT with a pool cue and not be noticed. They're hard to hide up your sleeve."

"That's my point," I said. "Norene was stung before the brawl."

Vida looked pensive. "Why would a pool cue be outside?"

"At the ICT?" Mitch laughed. "Why not? Or maybe it wasn't. Somebody could've used it earlier and left it by the rear door. That's only a few feet from the pool table."

"There's another thing," I said. "Did anybody at any time say they actually saw Clive hit De Muth with a cue?"

A long pause ensued.

Mitch spoke first. "Clive confessed." He leaned forward, pointing at my monitor. "Pull up the story I did last week. Check the wording. It's an indirect quote, but it's from Clive's official statement."

I get flustered when anyone watches me use my computer. Fortunately, my staffers kept quiet while I first highlighted Maud Dodd's senior citizen column with its MAUD file name instead of MUTH for the tavern death. Then I almost hit Delete instead of Save. Finally, I managed to get Mitch's story on the screen.

"Here's your indirect quote from Clive Berentsen," I said, moving the monitor so that we could all see it.

Leo leaned over Mitch's shoulder and read aloud: " 'Berentsen admitted that he got into an argument with De Muth and tempers flared. During the brief exchange of blows, Berentsen stated that he swung a pool cue in self-defense, and that was when the victim fell to the floor. Stunned witnesses didn't immediately realize that De Muth was dead. When he became unresponsive, tavern owner Spike Canby called 911 to summon the sheriff and medics.' "

Mitch was grimacing. "I should've caught that," he murmured. "That's slipshod reporting."

I offered him a commiserating look. "So should I."

"And," Leo put in, "so should Dodge and his deputies."

Vida disagreed. "Slipshod, no, careful, yes," she told Mitch. "You wrote that as you understood it. Unless Clive or one of the witnesses swore up and down that he actually hit De Muth, you couldn't do otherwise. Did you talk to Clive in person or is this information taken from the statement?"

"From the statement," Mitch replied, "which was given to Dodge. I wanted to see Berentsen, but he refused to see me. Once he was arrested, he didn't want any visitors."

I appreciated Clive's feelings at the time. "I talked to him later," I said. "I think Jica Weaver did, too. When I saw him he was still blaming himself for killing De Muth. But," I continued, aware that deadline was approaching, "the question is, What do we do now? We have to find out if anybody actually saw Clive hit De Muth with the pool cue."

Leo stepped back from my desk. "Is he covering for somebody?"

"Maybe," I said, "but I don't know who. The only one I can think of that he'd want to protect is Jica, and she was outside when the brawl started. Everybody agrees to that."

"A simple yes or no from Clive would do it," Mitch said, still looking chagrined. "I can talk to him right now and ask if he remembers the cue hitting De Muth's head. If Clive didn't land that blow, somebody else did. Doc Dewey's preliminary findings suggested that the lethal whack could've been with a pool cue. The SnoCo ME didn't say otherwise."

"Do it," I said. "In fact," I went on, standing up, "I'll go with you."

Mitch looked wary. "You don't trust me?"

"Of course I do. But I want to hear Dodge's version of his interview with Clive." I put on my jacket and grabbed my purse. "Let's go."

Vida looked miffed. "I suppose," she said to me in a voice that bordered on sarcasm, "you don't believe that I should talk to my nephew Billy to make sure he hasn't omitted something that might be helpful."

I didn't dare hesitate. "Sure. Come along." I glanced at Leo.

"I'm out," he said, his eyes twinkling. "I've never tried to get Dodge to advertise for perps. He's got limited vacancies, the food stinks, and I understand his coffee is barely drinkable."

I patted Leo's shoulder as I went out the door. "It's improved since Lori Cobb took the receptionist's job. Hold down the fort. And make sure Kip's not having a nervous breakdown."

"Aye, aye, Commander." Leo stood at attention as we left.

Amanda didn't bother to look up when we went through the front office. Just outside, I stopped. "Don't wait for me," I said to Vida and Mitch. "Amanda never really told us what she saw."

Mitch paused in his step but Vida kept going, charging along Front Street like a water buffalo gone berserk. A light rain was beginning to fall as dark clouds settled in over the town. I went back inside and confronted my temporary hire.

"Okay," I said. "Tell me exactly what you saw of the tavern fight."

Amanda eyed me with suspicion. "Why? I already did."

"No," I replied, "you passed it off as if someone hadn't died before your very eyes. That's not a very credible response."

"Sorry, but that's the truth. Neither Walt nor I saw the actual blow. Any of the blows, for that matter. We just heard raised voices and some noise. Those two big hulks—the Peabody guys?—blocked our view."

I had to take Amanda at her word. "Okay," I said, noting her hostile stare. "We're going to press so we have to make sure we've got everything right. Mitch and Vida have gone to see the sheriff. I'm going, too. This is the kind of story that has to be absolutely accurate."

"Good luck." Amanda turned back to her computer.

When I reached the sheriff's office, Vida was talking to Lori Cobb. Bill Blatt was nowhere in sight; nor was Mitch. Vida saw me step through the door. "Billy's on patrol," she announced. "Milo isn't here, either. We've come on a fool's errand."

"Where's Mitch?" I asked.

"Talking to Clive," she replied. "I'll join him to make the trip here worth my while." Since Vida's back was turned on Lori, I assumed she couldn't see the younger woman shake her head and roll her eyes.

But nothing escapes my House & Home editor. Whirling around so fast that I thought the pigeons would fly off of her hat, Vida wagged a finger at Lori. "That attitude shows very poor manners, young lady. Your grandparents wouldn't be proud of you."

Lori's eyes widened in astonishment. "I'm sorry, Mrs. Runkel. I goof off sometimes because . . . well, because working in law enforcement can be a total downer."

"Living can be, as you put it, a downer as well." Vida's expression didn't soften. "Acting silly and poking fun at others never solves problems, it only creates more."

Lori hung her head. "Yes, ma'am."

"Very well," Vida murmured. "When will the sheriff be back?"

"I'm not sure," Lori admitted. "He didn't say."

Vida harrumphed. "Milo shouldn't do that. Was he called out?"

Lori shook her head. "No. He took off about twenty minutes ago in his Grand Cherokee. He did mention a donkey."

"A donkey?" Vida scowled. "The Overholts' donkey, perhaps. Unless the Dithers sisters have added a donkey to their stable of horses. How very odd. We must check this out." She paused. "I'll join Mr. Laskey and Mr. Berentsen."

Lori meekly returned to her desk. "How," she asked after Vida was out of earshot, "did Mrs. Runkel see me when I was behind her?"

"She has eyes in the back of her head," I responded, only half joking. "Maybe she caught your reflection in the window glass. Mrs. Runkel seems to be off her feed lately. Something's bothering her. I was surprised when she reprimanded you. Or maybe I should say I was surprised at the way she did it. She's usually more subtle."

"Flu, maybe," Lori said.

"Maybe." But I didn't think so. In fact, I couldn't remember the last time that Vida had been sick. I often wondered if she scared the germs away by sheer force of will. "If Milo's gone, I've wasted my time."

"Did he know you were coming?" Lori asked.

"No. I'm supposed to meet with him later, though." I rested my elbow on the counter. "Is Clive the only prisoner?"

Lori nodded. "It's been a quiet week. Of course it's only Tuesday."

"Nothing new in the log since this morning?"

"No."

Dustin Fong entered from the hallway. As usual, he greeted me with a polite, almost deferential smile. "I see Clive has company. Or," he went on, lowering his voice and moving to the work area inside the counter, "is Mrs. Runkel here about her grandson?"

I stared at Dustin. "Her grandson? Roger?"

Dustin looked embarrassed. "It hasn't been logged yet."

" 'It'?" I said, noticing that Lori also seemed surprised.

The deputy moved close. "Dwight Gould charged him with a DUI about an hour ago. He was driving erratically along River Road."

All my favorite fantasies about Roger in handcuffs and leg irons deserted me. "He's not in jail, is he?"

"Oh, no," Dustin replied. "It's his first real ticket. He got off with warnings the other times."

I realized warnings were never officially logged, but the DUI would be made public. "How many other times?"

Dustin grimaced. "I'd have to check."

"Don't," I said. "I wonder if his grandmother knows."

Dustin thought not. "Unless Roger or his parents told Mrs. Runkel, she'd have no way of finding out so fast. Bill Blatt issued one of the warnings. I guess he really lectured Roger, but it didn't do much good. Being a family matter, Bill kept it to himself."

"Bad idea," I murmured. If Vida was already suffering from some sort of stress, Roger's escapade would only make things worse. "When will Bill get back?"

"A little after four unless there's a problem," Dustin said. "He's patrolling Highway 2. Dwight's got in-town duty this afternoon."

It was a little after three, an hour before Vida's nephew would return to headquarters. "It might be best if Billy—I mean, *Bill*—tells Mrs. Runkel about Roger. She's going to have a fit."

"I'm afraid so," Dustin said, looking sympathetic. "She dotes on that guy. My grandmother is like that." He smiled. "As far as she's concerned, I'm perfect. She's very traditional when it comes to Chinese ideas and attitudes, so all of us grandchildren respect her as an elder. I hope Roger appreciates—and respects—his grandma."

"Me, too," I mumbled, and realized that both Dustin and Lori were eyeing me with curiosity. "Sorry. I was wondering if Bill gets back after Vida leaves, could you ask him to stop by the office before five?"

"Sure," Lori said. "I shouldn't say so, but this serves Roger right."

I stared at Lori. "Why is that?"

She looked toward the hallway, no doubt to make sure Vida wasn't there. "I'm older than Roger, but when we were in grade school he was a troublemaker from the start. He was always big for his age, so he'd bully and pick fights with the other kids. Roger always insisted it wasn't his fault, the other kids started it. My mom told me Mrs. Hibbert was in the principal's office so often that the school board should hire her."

"That must've been just before or after I moved here," I said. "Did Amy Hibbert's meetings with the principal do any good?"

"I don't know," Lori said. "I went on to high school, but I heard when Roger was in fifth grade, some older kids beat him up. Roger had been especially mean to one of the little girls in his class. Her big brother and his pals wanted to teach him a lesson."

"Whose sister was it?"

"I don't remember." Lori smiled sheepishly. "When you're in high school, it's your whole world. You don't pay attention to grade school kids anymore."

"True." I glanced at my watch. "I'd better dash. Vida and Mitch must be having quite a talk with Clive Berentsen."

Lori nodded. "His girlfriend, too. She's kind of strange, but nice."

I was surprised. "Jica Weaver's here?"

Dustin was smiling. "She's been here for over an hour. It's a good thing we don't enforce the visitation rules."

"What are they doing in there," I asked, "having a picnic?"

"In a way," Lori said. "Ms. Weaver brought a gift basket from Port Chatham in Everett. It's crammed with really good seafood and a bunch of other yummy stuff."

"Gee," I said, "set up a buffet. Clive may be willing to share."

"He probably is," Lori said. "Should I ask him?"

"No thanks," I said. "Tell the sheriff I'll meet him after five."

The rain was coming down much heavier, but at least there was no wind. I'd considered walking to the chop shop to collect my car, but maybe I'd have to hitch a ride. Back at the office, Amanda glanced up to actually acknowledge my entrance. "A Mr. Fisher called," she informed me. "He says if he doesn't hear from you by midnight in his time zone, he'll commit suicide."

"It's after midnight where he is," I said, "so he's dead by now."

Amanda looked surprised, possibly even shocked. "He's not local?"

"Not exactly," I said.

"He sounds . . . interesting." Amanda sounded as if she were purring. "He must've really pissed you off."

"He often does," I snarled, and fled the front office.

Leo and Kip were coming out of the back shop. "Are we set," Kip asked, "or are we waiting on whatever Leo told me you were trying to find out about the ICT story?"

"We're waiting." I turned to Leo. "The ads are ready?"

"We just finished," he replied. "We picked up an extra twenty inches from out-of-town advertisers who want to be on our Internet site and in this week's paper."

I beamed at both Leo and Kip. "Excellent! Nice job, guys."

"Give the credit to Kip," Leo said. "Anything new on Berentsen?"

"Only if you like smoked salmon and Dungeness crab," I snapped.

Leo looked bemused. "Just another day at the jail?"

"Jica Weaver brought Clive a Port Chatham gift basket," I said, trying to find my better nature. "I didn't see her or Clive, but we've got another problem. Vida doesn't know it, but Roger got a DUI this afternoon. It hasn't been logged yet, so we don't have to put it in this week's edition. When Vida finds out, you can guess her reaction."

Kip was taken aback. "Wow! If she's at the sheriff's office, how come she doesn't know?"

"Because she was in Clive's cell with Mitch and Jica enjoying smoked oysters and kippered salmon and God-knows-what-else. Vida wouldn't dream of asking us *not* to run the item," I went on, collecting my wits, if not my less fractious persona. "But she's going to be horribly embarrassed. I don't feel sorry for Roger, but I sympathize with Vida."

"Hey," Leo said, patting my arm. "It serves the kid right.

What the hell was he doing in the middle of the day under the influence?"

"Driving along River Road," I said, noting the gleam in Leo's eye. "Are you thinking what I'm thinking?"

"I'm thinking a couple of things," Leo replied. "He got sauced at the ICT or he bought beer at the Icicle Creek mini-mart. He's drinking age, but his mental age is about six."

Kip shook his head. "Dumb. If he bought a six-pack, what did he do? Sit by the river and drink the whole thing? Not," he added quickly, "that I haven't done some crazy stuff in my time, but Roger's a little old for that, at least during the day. Was he alone?"

I admitted I didn't know. "Dustin told me about the incident, but it was Dwight who nailed Roger and he wasn't at the office."

Leo went to his desk. "Thank God I wasn't around that much before my kids achieved real adulthood. It's a wonder they ever did. I set a crappy example."

"Being a parent is scary stuff," Kip said as he started for the back shop. "Let me know if we've got . . ."

He stopped as Mitch entered the newsroom. "For what it's worth," my reporter said, looking thwarted, "Clive isn't sure he connected with De Muth's skull. He says he must have or De Muth wouldn't have dropped like a load of bricks. Your call, Ms. Publisher."

"So it is." My aching back was more painful. I realized that I hadn't taken a pain pill since breakfast. That was a sign that I was healing, but I didn't need any more distractions so close to deadline. "Okay," I finally said as I burrowed for the small pill box in my purse, "nothing has changed. Clive's sticking to his statement. Unless we hear anything new or different between now and actual press time, it's status quo for this week's edition."

"Got it," Kip said.

Mitch nodded. "Hard news, straight facts."

"Right," I said, pouring water from the dispenser. "Accident, self-defense, whatever it was, we don't speculate."

"It may never go to trial," Mitch said. "Clive's attorney will plea-bargain. Believe me, I've covered enough homicides in Detroit to know that you'd be surprised—and incredulous—at how little punishment is meted out for crime involving a fatality."

I swallowed a Demerol and a methocarbamol. Kip had returned to the back shop, and Leo was on his cell phone. "I can imagine," I said. "The jails there must be filled to capacity. I'm not singling out Detroit. Most big cities and states have a problem with . . ." I stopped. "Where's Vida?"

Mitch sat down at his desk. "She was still gabbing with Jica Weaver. Clive's girlfriend was about to take off for Snohomish."

"Oh." I realized that this was the first encounter between the two women. It might take awhile for Vida to learn Jica's life story. "By the way," I said, "did you hear anything about the sheriff and a jackass?"

Mitch chuckled. "Is this a joke or do I say 'which jackass'?"

"That's why Milo wasn't at the office," I explained. "You'll get used to stories around here involving wild and not-so-wild life."

"I hope I can tell the difference," Mitch remarked. "If there is one."

"A fine line sometimes," I said before going into my cubbyhole.

I spent the next few minutes checking for late news that might have a connection or an impact on Alpine and Skykomish County. Nothing in the past three hours was newsworthy, but I always made sure we weren't overlooking a local angle to a regional or even national story.

By four-thirty, Vida still hadn't returned. She had submitted all of her copy, so there was no pressing need for her presence. I assumed that Bill Blatt had showed up before she'd finished interrogating Jica Weaver. Maybe it was just as well that Vida didn't come back to the office. She'd be in a very bad mood.

At five o'clock there was still no sign of her. I became anxious. I was to meet Milo in a few minutes, but reluctant to leave until I'd heard from my House & Home editor. I dialed the sheriff office's number. A breathless Lori Cobb answered.

"I was just leaving," she said. "Are you calling for the sheriff?"

"Not really," I said. "I wondered if Mrs. Runkel had left yet."

"Oh, yes," Lori replied. "She's been gone for over an hour."

I was surprised. "She has? Is Dodge there?"

"He never came back from wherever he went," Lori said. "Sam Heppner's in charge right now. Do you want to talk to him?"

"No, that's okay. Thanks, Lori." I hung up.

Leo poked his head in the doorway. "Closing time, boss. Another day, another dime."

"Hooray." I made an attempt to smile, but couldn't quite manage it. "You didn't hear from Vida, did you?"

"No." Leo frowned. "That's odd. Even if she found out about Roger, she'd call to let us know she wasn't coming back here today. Maybe she's at his house talking to him and his parents."

I considered the idea. "It makes sense. Vida would never desert Roger in his time of need."

"You got that right." Leo raised a hand and said good night.

I glanced out into the newsroom. Mitch was also leaving, calling to Leo to wait up. I drew back, not wanting to interfere with male bonding. It wasn't until they were gone that I realized I didn't have a ride to Bert's chop shop. Hurrying into the front office, I caught Amanda just as she was leaving.

"Any chance you could give me a lift so I can collect my car?" I asked, wishing like hell that I didn't have to beg a favor from the not-so-friendly hired help.

"Sorry," Amanda said. "I'm meeting someone on the other side of town. I'm already late." She opened the door but didn't move. "I forgot—there's a message for you from Mrs. Runkel. It's there by the computer." She continued on her way.

I leaned over the counter and snatched up the phone memo. "Mrs. R." it read. "Won't be back this afternoon. Crisis has arisen."

The call had come in at three-forty. I silently cursed Amanda and headed for the back shop. Kip was my last hope.

"I know you're up to your ears," I said, "but I'm marooned. My car's supposed to be ready, it's raining really hard, and I have to meet the sheriff at five-fifteen."

"Hang on," Kip said, focused on the screen that showed the editorial page layout. Surreptitiously, I checked my watch. It was five after five. Maybe, I thought, I should call Milo and tell him I'd be late.

"Got it." Kip grinned at me. "I wanted to make sure Mrs. Dodd's senior citizen column didn't have any R-rated typos. Sure, I can run you over to Bert's. Maybe I'll stop on the way back and pick up my dinner at the Burger Barn."

Kip was putting on his jacket when my cell phone rang. As usual, it took a few seconds to dig the thing out of my big purse. The voice on the other end sounded upset. "Emma? This is Amy Hibbert. Do you know where my mother is? She's not picking up her cell or her home phone. I can't find her. Is she okay?"

TWENTY

I WAS ALARMED. "NO. I THOUGHT MAYBE SHE WAS AT YOUR house."

"I haven't heard from Mama since this morning," Amy said. "We've had a . . . well, sort of a problem, and I really need to get hold of her. What time did she leave work?"

"Vida," I said for the benefit of Kip who was giving me a curious look, "was at the sheriff's office the last time I saw her." I managed to keep my voice calm, even casual. "She was sitting in on an interview with Clive Berentsen. I left before she did. I haven't seen her since, though she called around a quarter to four to say she wouldn't be back at work today." I phrased my response to give Amy the impression I didn't know anything about Roger's problem. The whole mess must be humiliating for the family.

"It's not like Mama," Amy said. "I'm worried."

So was I, but I didn't want to exacerbate Amy's distress. "You could call Lori Cobb," I said. "She might know where your mother went after she left the sheriff's office. Lori should be home soon. She was just leaving at five when I spoke to her."

Amy thanked me and hung up. Kip was standing by the door. "Vida's *missing?*"

"Not exactly," I said, "but her daughter can't locate her and I've no idea where she is. Her cell's batteries may have gone out. Amy's calling Lori Cobb to find out when Vida left the sheriff's office and if she said where she was heading from there. Let's go. I'll check in with Milo on our way. I'm already late."

As soon as we pulled out in Kip's pickup, I dialed Milo's cell. He didn't answer, so I left a message saying I was on the way to get my car.

At the first left turn, Kip braked to wait for oncoming traffic. "You're meeting Dodge by the river? Is this late news or . . . ah . . ."

I interrupted to spare him embarrassment. "A romantic rendezvous in a downpour? No. I haven't a clue."

"Does he realize we're up against deadline?" Kip asked, making the turn onto Fifth Street.

"Probably not," I said. "He never does. We got lucky when he arrested Clive Berentsen on a Tuesday night."

Approaching Railroad Avenue, we heard the train whistle and the clanging of bells. "Shoot," Kip said as the guardrails on the semaphore went down three cars ahead of us. "We're stuck. This westbound freight's twenty minutes late. I usually hear it from the back shop about a quarter to five."

A small town's routine, I thought. No need for clocks and calendars, just look and listen to the river's flow, the snow line in the mountains, the leaves changing color, the rhythm of the rails. No need to hurry, never far to go. After so many years, I was beginning to feel that I was no longer a stranger in Alpine.

"Hey," Kip said, breaking into my idle musings, "would you mind calling the Burger Barn to put in a pickup order for me?"

"Sure," I said. "What's their number?"

Kip grimaced. "I forget. Call the Venison Inn. I can remember that one. They'll do take-out for me. Double bacon-and-cheese burger, fries, coleslaw, and a strawberry shake. Thanks."

The freight's lead engine shone through the rain. To block out the rumble of the boxcars, I put my finger in the ear I wasn't using for the phone. I gave Kip's order to Sunny Rhodes. "It should be ready soon," she said. "Tell him to come around to the back. He knows the pickup drill."

"Thanks. You're putting in long hours," I remarked.

"That new waitress wasn't just a no-show," Sunny said, sounding not so sunny. "She quit. Good riddance, I told Oren. Liz was a lizard-breath, breathing bad attitude on the customers. Got to run. 'Bye."

The train clattered on to the west. Kip tapped his fingers on the steering wheel, as if to keep time with the rumbling of the rails. "Thanks, Emma," he said after I turned off my cell. "The inn's fries are better than the Burger Barn's."

"Right," I said in a vague voice. "Have you run into that new waitress, Liz?"

"You mean the one Vida did the thing about in 'Scene'?" Kip saw me nod. "A couple of times at the Burger Barn. She acted like she was pissed off. Or maybe it was just me."

"No," I said as the last train car passed by. "She quit the Burger Barn and moved on to the Venison Inn. Now she's quit there, too."

Kip eased his foot off the brake pedal as the semaphore arms went up. "Quit or got fired?"

"Quit. Maybe I'll call Sunny after the dinner rush is over."

"Why," Kip asked as we crossed the tracks, "do you want to know?"

"It seems odd," I replied. "Liz moves here from Idaho, gets a job, leaves, and then does the same thing a couple of weeks later."

"Some kind of drifter, maybe." Kip turned onto Railroad Avenue. "It could be she has relatives here. She wasn't a bad waitress, she just had some real negative 'tude."

"Human interest," I murmured.

"Huh?"

I shook my head. "I'm justifying my curiosity with reporter lingo. What makes somebody move like a vagabond? Rootless, restless, maybe even reckless?"

Kip pulled up in front of Bert's chop shop. "The Three R's of drifters? Maybe you do have a story there."

"Doubtful," I said, picking up my purse. "Liz isn't the type to unload on a stranger who'll put her in the spotlight. That'd be the last thing a drifter would want. Thanks, Kip."

"Do you want me to stick around in case your car's not ready?"

"No," I said, opening the passenger door. "Bert would've phoned if it wasn't fixed. Call me tonight when the paper's locked up."

"Got it."

I put my jacket's hood up over my head and squinted into the driving rain. Luckily, the area in front of Bert's shop was paved. Getting mired in mud wasn't uncommon in Alpine during the fall and winter. We had too little pavement and too much dirt. Living so close to nature has its drawbacks. Even concrete gets covered with dead leaves in October. There was no doormat, so I did a little dance to scrape off the cedar cone clusters and the maple seedpods from my shoes. My Honda was parked next to the building. I hoped that was a good sign.

Norene Anderson jumped when I opened the door. "Ms. Lord!" she gasped. "You scared me. I thought you were . . . someone else."

"Sorry." I smiled as I approached the desk. "Is my car ready?"

"Uh . . . yes." She moved away from a steel bookcase jammed with ledgers and manuals. "Let me see . . . the invoice must be someplace . . ." Her hands shook as she rearranged various items on the cluttered desk.

"Are you okay?" I asked. "You seem upset."

"Well . . ." Keeping her eyes on the desk, she raked her fingers through the auburn ringlets that straggled down to her eyes. "It's been busy. I can't . . ." Norene knocked over a ceramic pen and pencil holder. A few pens rolled off the desk onto the floor. "Oh, no!" She ducked under the desk. "Your invoice," Norene said after awkwardly reappearing with two pens and a sheet of paper. "Bert's no good at cleaning." She brushed cobwebs, dust, a couple of feathers, several dried leaves, a gum wrapper, and what looked like cookie crumbs from her clothes. "You want to check this out before you sign off?"

I scanned the invoice. It looked accurate to me. The total came to $515 plus some small change. I signed all three copies before handing my credit card to Norene. "Where's Bert?" I inquired as she ran my Visa through the machine.

"He's . . . here somewhere," she said. "Maybe at the yard." Returning the credit card, she again avoided looking at me.

"Kind of sloppy weather for him to be in the yard," I remarked. "Did you pave it when the fence was put up?"

"No." She handed me the pink sheet marked CUSTOMER COPY. "We don't need anything fancy there. Bert keeps the good stuff locked up out back."

"Thank him for me," I said, noting that it was almost five-thirty. "I have to dash. I'm late for an appointment."

Norene nodded in a distracted manner.

I stopped short of the door. "Oh!" I exclaimed, turning around. "I forgot my keys."

Norene gave another start. "Keys? Yes, yes. Let me get them. They're on the board over here." She went into the narrow hallway. I waited . . . and waited. Finally she came back with the keys in her hand and an anxious expression on her doughy face. "There you go. G'night."

Outside, I hurried around to my car, pausing to turn on the small flashlight that was attached to my keychain. I wanted to make sure the dent had been fixed properly. Visibility was poor and my light was feeble, but I couldn't see any telltale sign of where Holly's beater had hit my Honda. The new tire seemed fine, too. Bert had done a good job.

I got behind the wheel, checking out the interior. It was clean. While I might have a cluttered and haphazard office, I refrain from trashing my car. Maybe it's because years ago in Portland some idiot had broken into my Chev. The only items in the car had been a six-pack of Pepsi, my ten-dollar sunglasses—and Adam's cherished Speed Racer action figure. The thief had taken it all, and my five-year-old son had been devastated until I bought him a replacement. If a crook would smash a window to steal less than thirty dollars of loot, any removable items could be a temptation.

Satisfied that everything was in order, I buckled my seat belt and was about to turn the ignition key when I glanced at the rearview mirror. Something or somebody was moving thirty or so yards away by the end of the building. I hesitated, trying to see who or what was going on behind me. Through the heavy rain, the blurred shapes of two people looked as if they were grappling with each other. Or maybe it was horseplay. Natives on the west side of the Cascades rarely let a downpour interfere with their fun.

But suddenly the pair didn't seem to be enjoying themselves. They'd moved a few yards closer. One was a man, the other a woman. He was dragging her by the arm, struggling to a parked car at the edge of Bert's property. I hadn't yet turned on my headlights, but a car passing on Railroad Avenue gave just enough illumination that I recognized Bert and Norene. Apparently they had come outside through a rear entrance. Norene had either been mistaken or had lied when she told me her husband was across the street in the wrecking yard.

I rolled my window down a scant inch, trying to hear what they were saying. Their sparse, disjointed words sounded like protests from Norene and growls from Bert. He was forcing her into the car's passenger seat. After slamming the door, he scrambled around to the other side and got in. I watched as Bert started the engine, made a screeching U-turn on the slick pavement, and gunned the engine as soon as he reached the street. He was driving the blue Toyota I'd seen parked outside the chop shop on my previous visit.

It took me a few moments to gather my wits. I was about to turn on the ignition when my cell phone rang. "Where the hell are you?" Milo demanded. "I've been sitting on my dead ass for twenty minutes."

"I'll be there in two," I promised. "Exactly where are you? I can only see about six feet ahead of me in this deluge."

"I've been waiting by Mickey Borg's minimart. We had a little chat. I'm done here. Meet me in the parking lot at Gus Swanson's Toyota dealership." The sheriff clicked off.

The car lot was a block and a half away on Railroad Avenue, but the parking area and main entrance faced Front Street. I took a right on Seventh and a left on Front. I pulled in as close as I could to the showroom's double doors. Milo was only a couple of minutes away, so I stayed in the car. Through the plate glass windows I could see Gus with a female potential customer. He moved slowly around a silver Celica, apparently pointing out its merits. The woman, who had her back to me, was wearing a yellow rain slicker with the hood up. Gus was doing all the talking; his would-be buyer nodded a couple of times.

The Grand Cherokee pulled in next to me. I rolled down the passenger window and called to Milo. "Why are we here?" I asked.

"Unlock the damned door, okay?" he ordered, looking exasperated.

"Okay." I waited until he slid into the passenger seat and tried to get his long legs into a comfortable position.

"Damned midsize sedans," he grumbled. "Can't you at least move the seat back for somebody who's not a damned midget?"

"Move it back yourself," I retorted. "What's with all this meet-me-by-the-river crap?"

"Long story." He took off his tall regulation hat and winced as he finally got settled into the seat. "I went to see Mickey Borg at the Gas 'n Go about his eyewitness account of your ruckus with Holly. He wasn't in the Safeway parking lot that evening. He was at the Venison Inn, getting tanked with Gus Swanson."

I was surprised. "How'd you find that out?"

Milo looked bemused as he nodded toward the showroom. "Didn't you see her?"

" 'Her'? What are you talking about?"

"Look," said the sheriff. "She's turning this way."

As the woman studied the Celica, she slipped off the slicker's hood. I gasped. "It's Liz, the bitchy waitress!" Stunned, I watched Gus lead her into the cubicle that served as his office. "I don't get it," I admitted, turning back to Milo. "What does Liz have to do with any of this?"

Milo looked downright smug. "Liz is De Muth's widow."

"What?" I shrieked.

The sheriff was obviously enjoying himself. "Her full name is Lorna Irene Zobrist De Muth. Liz is a nickname. She and Al separated several years ago, but never divorced. Liz came up here for one last try at reconciling. She stayed at the Alpine Falls Motel, and it didn't take her long to figure out that De Muth wasn't interested in getting back together. She was almost broke, so she worked as a waitress to pay her way back home."

"Hold it," I said. "Liz is from Idaho."

Milo chuckled. "Idaho Falls, Colorado, thirty miles west of Denver. Anyway, when De Muth got killed, she was upset but realized she was still his legal wife and would inherit whatever money or property he owned. She couldn't have kids, and that was one of their big hang-ups. De Muth wanted a family, so did she, but she refused to adopt."

"Maybe that's why De Muth mentored those kids who wanted to be mechanics. They were his surrogate sons." I tried to sort through this latest discovery. Milo rarely dug into people's private lives unless they were involved in a criminal investigation. "How did you find out? Is Liz a witness or . . . what?" I avoided saying *suspect*. It didn't seem possible.

Milo's self-satisfied air fled. "By chance. I had to check out cars this afternoon." He stopped to light a cigarette. I rolled the windows down just enough to keep from getting asphyxiated. "I ended up here."

"Cars? What for?"

"Never mind. Bottom line is Mickey can't support Holly's innocent-party status." The sheriff flicked ash out through the open window instead of into the ashtray. "You're off the hook. I wanted him to tell you in person that he lied. But things got complicated."

"No kidding," I murmured. "Does it matter that we're sitting here in a downpour watching the Widow De Muth buy a car? Do you care that my back is killing me? Would it interest you that Bert and Norene Anderson may be killing each other at this very moment? And how about Vida being missing in action?"

The last query caught Milo's attention. "Vida? What happened?"

I explained, including, of course, Roger's DUI. "She's not answering her cell or home phones," I said. "Naturally, her daughter Amy is worried. So am I. It's not like her."

The sheriff tapped his fingers on his knee. "It wouldn't be," he muttered. "Unless . . . skip it for now. As soon as Gus closes this deal, we're going to take a formal statement from him."

"Gus? Why? Didn't you do that already?"

"He lied."

"About what?"

"The ICT brawl." Milo inhaled, exhaled, and tapped more ash out the window. "He didn't want to get any deeper than he already is with Delphine and his wife. The poor bastard's between a rock and a hard place with those women. When it comes to his private life, Gus is one mixed-up dude."

And you're not? I didn't say it out loud, but it crossed my mind. I looked inside the showroom. Gus and Liz were still in the cubicle. "So we sit here for how long?"

"As long as it takes." The sheriff tossed his cigarette out the window, an unlawful act in SkyCo. At least there was no danger of starting a forest fire in the middle of a drenching rain.

"Isn't it too soon for Liz to have her inheritance? How's she paying for the car?"

Milo shrugged. "That's up to her and Gus. If he figures she's good for it down the line, something can be worked out." He reached inside his jacket. "Want a Cert?"

"Why not?" I said, taking a mint from the roll. "I may

starve to death at this rate. Aren't you concerned about the Andersons? They were really going at it."

He shook his head. "Not unless they kill each other."

"What about Vida?"

The sheriff sighed. "Sounds like Roger's got himself into a real jam this time. I figure his grandma is trying to sort things out."

"How? Bribing you or one of your deputies?"

Milo didn't answer, but stared straight ahead where Gus and Liz were still wheeling and dealing in the office.

"If," I said after a long pause, "Vida's giving aid and comfort to the grandson, why doesn't Amy know where her mother is?"

"Maybe Amy doesn't know where Roger is," Milo said and gestured toward the dealership. "Here they come. Let's hope Liz doesn't want to take Gus on a joyride."

I watched as the two people inside exchanged a few words and shook hands. Liz pulled the slicker's hood over her head before going outside. Without so much as a glance in our direction, she walked briskly to a VW Beetle in the customer parking area.

"Must've borrowed that," Milo murmured. "I think it belongs to that jerk who runs the Alpine Falls Motel." He reached for the door handle. "Wait here. I won't be long."

"Hey!" I shouted. "I'm coming with you."

"No, you're not. This is business."

I hit the power lock button on the driver's side. The sheriff yanked at the handle a couple of times, but knew he couldn't open the door on his side. "Goddamnit, Emma, I'm not fooling around. Open this sucker before I blow my stack."

"Go ahead. I didn't drive over here to sit around and watch puddles form in Mayor Baugh's crumbling streets. This little excursion has made me even crankier than when I started out.

Why can't I be on hand when you take down Gus's formal statement? It's a public document and if I need to, I'll put it in this week's edition. Or, as usual, have you forgotten about our Tuesday deadline?"

"You can't come because . . ." Milo had started off shouting, but paused and lowered his voice to a rumble. "Because I've got something else to do in there."

"What? Take a whiz on that Celica?"

The sheriff leaned toward me, his hazel eyes narrowed in a glower that would intimidate the most hardened criminal. For a moment, I thought he was going to use strong-arm tactics to make me unlock the doors. I froze in place and held my breath.

"Screw it." He sighed wearily and sat up. "Go ahead. I don't give a rat's ass anymore."

I hit the button again. We got out of the car and without another word walked into Swanson Toyota.

"It's The Man," Gus Swanson said with a wide, if not genuine, grin. "And he's got a pretty girl with him. Is this the daughter who's getting married?" He laughed heartily at his own humor.

Milo looked down at me. "No. This is my mother. They let her out of the asylum for the evening. Let's do it, Gus. Have you finished the revised statement?"

Gus shot me a puzzled glance. No doubt he was wondering why the *Advocate*'s editor was tagging along. "I thought," Gus said to Milo, "you had to witness it."

The sheriff shrugged. "I trust you. You stepped up to the plate and admitted the first statement wasn't the whole truth. I understand why you tried to keep a low profile. Pleasing a woman," he went on as if I weren't standing two feet away, "is tough enough, but having to put up with two of them is a real pain in the ass. The big thing is you came forward. If you hadn't, and we found out later that you left out crucial information, you could be charged with obstruction of justice."

Gus nodded. "The statement's in my office. So's the other paperwork. It's all set. I'll sign mine, you sign yours." He led the way. I trailed the sheriff and wondered what the two men were talking about. Maybe the Demerol and methocarbamol had addled my wits. After we were seated, Gus turned to me. "Will this be in the paper?"

"That depends," I replied, pretending I knew what was happening.

Gus looked worried. "Does it have to?"

"I'll be the judge of that," I said. "That's why I'm here." I gave Milo a sideways glance. "We're up against deadline and the sheriff is always so considerate when it comes to the *Advocate*."

Gus picked up a pen and signed the form on his desk. "Is that okay?" he asked handing the statement to the sheriff.

Milo read what looked like a half-dozen lines of handwritten information. "Sounds good." He folded the sheet of paper and tucked it inside his jacket. "My turn," he said to Gus.

"Right." The car dealer handed a folder to Milo. "Everything's been worked out. This is one terrific car. Grace Grundle drove her Camry less than ten thousand miles in the past six years."

Milo warily eyed Gus. "Are you sure you got out all the cat hair and dander? Grace took those damned animals for a drive around town every Sunday. We're talking serious allergies here for one of the drivers."

"You bet. It's good to go," Gus assured the sheriff. "When will your daughter pick it up?"

"Probably over the weekend." Milo dashed off his name and handed the folder to Gus. "Tricia's bringing her up here, then they'll drive home separately."

"Sounds great," Gus said, the phony grin back in place. "You're a stand-up dad. I hope your little girl appreciates you."

"Right." Milo stood up. "Thanks again, Gus. See you." The sheriff loped out of the cubicle. I followed him outside.

"What was that all about?" I asked before we reached our cars.

"My wedding present to Tanya and Buster or whatever his name is," the sheriff replied. "They need a car, so I bought a secondhand one. It's cheaper up here than in the Seattle or Bellevue area. You want to get some dinner?"

"No," I said, brushing raindrops off my face. "I want to know how Gus amended his statement about the ICT brawl."

Milo didn't answer right away. He squinted through the rain and adjusted his hat. "Gus neglected to mention not what he saw but what he didn't see. He's absolutely certain that Clive swung the pool cue at De Muth but missed. Now what will I do if I arrested the wrong guy?"

I hesitated. "Find the right one?"

The sheriff grimaced. "How?" He shook his head, walked over to the Grand Cherokee, and left me standing in the rain.

TWENTY-ONE

A T LEAST I HAD ENOUGH SENSE TO GET OUT OF THE RAIN. Worried, confused, angry, and in pain, I sat in the Honda pondering my options. Inside the dealership Gus Swanson was talking to one of his employees, Brant Hutchins, son of Scooter and Lois Dewey Hutchins as well as Doc Dewey's nephew. It was a typical example of Alpine's verdant family tree. As I watched them with cursory interest, it suddenly dawned on me that Brant had worked at Cal Vickers's gas station for a while as a mechanic.

Following my not-always-infallible instincts, I got out of the car and went back into the dealership. Gus looked at me with a smile.

"Don't tell me you want to trade in that Honda for a Toyota," he said. "It's a smart move, though."

"I know they're both good cars," I said, "but that's not why I came back." I turned to Brant. "May I talk to you for a few minutes?"

Brant looked surprised. He also didn't seem to know who I was. "Okay. But why? Is it about your car?"

"No." I smiled apologetically at Gus. "I've interrupted. Go ahead, finish whatever you're doing and I'll browse."

Gus had stopped smiling. Maybe after a long day on the floor the false cheer began to wear thin as seven o'clock closing time approached. "I think we're done here," he said. "This fine lad has agreed to try his hand as a salesman." Gus nudged the younger man. "Let's see if you can coax Ms. Lord into a Prius. She's a big booster with her outstanding environment editorials. Someone's pulling up. I'll handle it."

I followed Brant into the cubicle, letting him practice the make-yourself-comfortable ritual. He seemed uneasy about settling into Gus's chair, but managed eye contact with me. "How can I help you, Ms. Lord?" he asked after I'd turned down his offer of coffee or springwater.

I offered him a friendly smile. "I'm not here to buy a car, so relax. You started working for Gus as a mechanic, right?"

Brant nodded. "After I graduated from high school, I got some experience at Cal Vickers's gas station, but he doesn't take on complicated jobs. He recommended me to Gus. Then last summer, I screwed up my right arm in a river-rafting accident." His fair skin flushed slightly. "It was a dumb stunt, kind of . . . well, showing off."

I recalled the brief story we'd run in the paper. "You recovered?"

"Mostly," Brant said ruefully. "But after Uncle Gerry operated, he told me my hard-wrenching days were over. If I went on working as a mechanic I'd seriously screw up my arm. That's why I'm training as a salesman." He made a face. "I love cars, but I'm not into the selling part. It's not me."

By chance, Brant had touched upon the topic I wanted to discuss. "Did you go through the college program or did someone teach you?"

"Al De Muth took me on." He paused, looking at his hands. I wondered if he wished they were smeared with grease. "He did it for free. Al was a really cool teacher. Honest, too." Brant glanced out into the showroom, probably checking to see if Gus was within hearing range. From where I sat, the owner was out of sight, probably cozying up to whomever had just come in. Brant lowered his voice anyway. "Al was always up-front with people. He'd tell them the truth, good or bad. That's one reason why I don't want to sell cars. It's like you have to . . . not *lie* exactly, but always talk and act positive. It doesn't seem right to . . . not exactly cheat people, but you aren't straightforward with them. Like Al would've said, in the long run honesty pays bigger dividends, not just for the customer but for yourself." Brant made a face. "Sorry to go on and on like this. Gus isn't a crook or anything even close, but it's a relief not to have to be giving you a lot of hoo-ha to make a sale."

"I understand," I said. "Al sounds as if he had integrity."

"Oh, for sure." Brant's tone was emphatic. "I was totally bummed when he got killed. It's weird. Clive isn't a mean kind of guy."

"Was Al feisty?"

Brant thought for a moment. "Not really. He had a temper, but you had to get to know him. He was kind of standoffish, but he liked teaching young guys like me. Mentoring, isn't that what they call it?"

I nodded. "Didn't Al mentor Mike O'Toole?"

"Yes." Brant's unlined, almost beardless face suddenly looked older. "Poor Mike! Omigod—what's to say about the bad stuff around here lately?" Again he paused, shaking his head. "Mike was two years behind me in high school. He was okay, though sometimes he pissed people off. Dumb stuff, like getting other kids to jump off the high diving board at the pool

or race mountain bikes on the ice. He'd do it first and then dare
the other kids to try it. Talk about showing off—that was Mike.
He wasn't a bad guy, he just made some bad choices. When
you're young you've got to prove stuff to yourself. Nobody can
tell you what's good or bad. I ought to know." Brant looked at
his hands again.

"Taking chances," I remarked. "Often you learn the hard
way."

"Oh, man," Brant said, shaking his head, "that's the truth.
Look at poor Mike. He won't have another chance to figure it
all out."

"No," I said quietly, "he won't." I waited for Brant to speak,
but he seemed to be lost in some kind of dream. Or nightmare.
I changed the subject. "Getting back to Al, I wonder if being
hard to know irked some people." Noting Brant's curious expression, I tried to clarify what I meant. "You're a native. You
know how Alpiners take things more personally than big-city
people. A newcomer who keeps to himself might cause hard
feelings."

Brant still didn't seem to understand what I meant. "You
mean they'd give him a bad time somehow?"

"Kind of. I'm thinking more about grudges and resentment."

"Wow," Brant said softly. "That's harsh. Like maybe there
was a feud between him and Clive Berentsen?"

I shrugged. "No. In fact," I went on, lowering my voice,
"your boss insists Clive never made contact with the pool cue."

Brant looked shocked. "Gus?" He stood up halfway out of
the chair and searched the showroom again. "Gosh!" he exclaimed softly, sitting down again. "I thought he didn't see anything. He worked late that night so he stopped by the ICT to
have a beer and get a sandwich."

The sanitized version, I thought. Maybe Gus really wanted to patch up things with his wife. Or was he trying to keep a low profile for Delphine's sake? "That's why Dodge came here," I explained. "Gus wanted to set the record straight."

Brant frowned. "I don't get it. Does that mean it was just an accident and not Clive's fault?"

I didn't respond immediately because I wasn't sure what it meant. "The only certainty is that Al died from a blow to the head," I finally said.

"Wow." Brant still seemed to be digesting my words. "This is all sort of . . . what's the word they use nowadays? Surreal?"

I kept from cringing at the overworked and often inapt adjective. "Some might say so." With a smile, I stood up. "Thanks, Brant. I appreciate your time. If," I went on as he came around the side of the desk to join me, "you really don't want to be a salesman, but you know what makes a good mechanic, why don't you think about teaching?"

The young man stared at me. "Teaching? Wouldn't I have to go to college for years and years like Uncle Gerry did to be a doctor?"

"Not with vocational programs," I said. "Experience is key. You admired Al's teaching skills, so you know what makes a good teacher."

Brant was silent for a moment. "I never thought about it. It's always been working with cars or listening to my dad try to get me to work for him at the home interiors store, but that's salesman stuff, too."

"Young people should chart their own futures," I said. "My son went off in about ten different directions before he became a priest."

Brant seemed overwhelmed at the thought. "Awesome. I could never do that. But I'm not a Catholic."

I laughed. "I wasn't trying to convert you, just making a point. It often takes time to figure out the right niche."

He walked me to the door. Gus was at the far end of the showroom, pointing out the features of a new Toyota Tundra pickup to an older man I didn't recognize. I thanked Brant and made my exit into the still-heavy rain.

Inside my car, I took out my cell and dialed Amy Hibbert's number. She answered before the first ring stopped. "Yes?" she said, breathless.

"It's Emma," I said. "Did you track down your mother?"

"No." Amy sounded crestfallen. "I hoped she might be the caller."

"I'm sorry," I said, in apology for dashing Amy's hopes. "Have you called Buck Bardeen?"

There was a brief silence. "Should I?" she finally asked.

Given Amy's concern, her response seemed odd. "Why not?"

"Um . . . I'm not sure if . . . yes, maybe I will."

"Good," I responded. "Keep me posted, okay?"

Amy promised she would. Growing more concerned, I focused on mundane matters. I phoned Kip, telling him that Gus had changed his statement. "Read me how Mitch handled those statements in his follow-up story on De Muth," I said. "I don't want to screw this one up."

The reference to witnesses was, as I recalled, only a paragraph long. It didn't name the customers, except for Clive Berentsen and Alvin De Muth. I'd written the first of the news stories under deadline pressure the night that Clive was arrested. Spike and Julie Canby were mentioned as the tavern owners, noting that they'd been at the scene.

"Discretion is good," I told Kip. "If there's a trial, then we can quote witnesses. By the way, you haven't heard or seen Vida, have you?"

"No. Is she still AWOL?"

"Yes, unfortunately."

"Have you told the sheriff?" Kip's usual calm sounded shaken. "Officially, I mean."

"That's up to Amy," I said. "If it's a false alarm and we put it in the paper, Vida would be horribly embarrassed. Amy may have talked to her cousin, Bill Blatt. Even if he's off-duty, it wouldn't stop him from trying to find his aunt."

Kip agreed. After we signed off, I sat behind the wheel, pondering my next move. It was after six o'clock, but I'd lost my appetite. Realizing that I'd tensed up during the past few minutes and was almost due for another pain pill, I reached into my purse. Maybe I could cut back on the Demerol and take only a methocarbamol. Using the small flashlight on my key ring, I found the muscle relaxer pill, took it out of the compartment—and dropped it on the car floor. Swearing like a logger, I fumbled around the brake and gas pedals but couldn't see or feel the damned thing. I'd tracked in a few leaves on my shoes. The pill was under a couple of dead alder leaves. So were some feathers that must have also stuck to my shoes. I was about to follow the sheriff's bad example and toss the debris out the window when it dawned on me that the feathers looked unusual. Not a jay, a crow, a cedar waxwing, a sparrow, or a robin. These feathers were gray, white, and black.

Pigeons. We didn't see them often in Alpine. Leo joked it was because we have only one statue in town, the life-size bronze of mill owner and town founder Carl Clemans. I couldn't recall the last time I'd seen a pigeon.

Except on Vida's hat.

I was overreacting. *I'm no ornithologist,* I told myself. Even if I was right about the feathers having adorned Vida's hat, I could have stepped on them at the office, on the sidewalk, or while Vida and I were both at the sheriff's headquarters.

But I hadn't been near Vida since midafternoon. I'd checked

my car for cleanliness at Bert Anderson's shop. Nothing was
out of place. Wouldn't I have spotted the debris if someone else
had left it in the car? If the stuff had stuck to the soles of my
shoes, I'd missed seeing it. That meant I'd tramped on the
leaves and feathers in the past half-hour, either at Swanson
Toyota—or Bert's body shop. The matter should've been triv-
ial, even comical, if Vida hadn't dropped out of sight.

I thought back to the fracas I'd witnessed between the Andersons. Norene had been upset, scared, too, when I entered
the shop. She'd said something about . . . what? Expecting
someone else instead of me? Who? Not Vida. I couldn't think
of any reason for her to call on Bert. Maybe I was obsessing
needlessly. Tracking dead leaves, faded petals, or anything else
in Alpine's wet weather was common. But not knowing Vida's
whereabouts was as unusual as it was alarming.

I was stumped. Through the rain-streaked windshield, I saw
Gus and his customer yukking it up by a sleek black Toyota
Avalon. Brant had disappeared. I still held the white pill in my
hand, realizing I didn't have any water or soda to wash it
down. I might as well go home. After putting the methocarbamol back in the pill box, I pulled out of the lot and drove
onto Front Street. I'd gone only a block when I heard sirens
and saw flashing red lights racing in my direction.

At a few minutes after six with the rain still pouring down,
there were only a half-dozen vehicles on Alpine's main drag. Just
to be on the safe side, I pulled over to the curb in front of the
PUD office. Straining to see through the windshield where the
wipers couldn't work as fast as the falling rain, I saw that
the first set of flashing lights was on a patrol car. The medic van
followed and just before I was about to pull back out onto the
street, a fire engine turned off Sixth and onto Front. Looking in
the rearview mirror, I saw the patrol car and then the medic van

take a left onto the Icicle Creek Road. I set the emergency brake, got out my cell phone, and called the sheriff's office.

Sam Heppner answered. "What's going on?" I asked.

"We've got a situation," Sam replied.

"No kidding. Come on, Sam, I'm up against deadline."

"Not my problem," he responded in his usual taciturn manner. "Hang up, Emma. We need to keep the lines clear."

Badgering Sam wouldn't do any good. I knew that from past experiences with the tight-lipped, sometimes surly deputy. I disconnected the call before he could do the same at his end.

The fire engine had also turned onto the Icicle Creek Road. Even in light traffic I didn't dare make a U-turn on the slippery street. Instead, I went right at Sixth and again at Railroad Avenue. With any luck I could catch up with the emergency vehicles by following the sirens.

I was retracing the route Kip and I'd taken to get to Bert's chop shop, but that wasn't the site of the "situation." Neither was Swanson Toyota. I'd reached the Icicle Creek Road, pausing at the arterial sign and trying to determine where the sirens were coming from. To my dismay, they'd stopped. I considered my options. The Icicle Creek Road dead-ended north of town. Wherever the crisis was, it had to be either across the bridge to River Road or straight ahead. I was still mulling as an SUV rushed past me, made a sharp turn onto the other side of the railroad tracks, and sped east. Despite the vehicle's speed, I recognized Milo's Grand Cherokee. I followed him as he passed Gas 'n Go and the ICT and crossed Icicle Creek.

I fought back a rising sense of panic. All I could think of was that Vida might somehow be involved. But Milo was slowing down as he went past the small older homes huddled close together on the other side of the railroad tracks. Although the sirens had gone mute, I could see the cluster of flashing red lights off to the left. Milo's Grand Cherokee stopped on the muddy verge that separated patchy stands of grass from the asphalt road. By the time I drove up behind his SUV, he was already striding up the short driveway of a frame bungalow.

"Milo!" I called as I got out of the car, "wait!"

The sheriff stopped, turning to look in my direction. "Oh, for . . . Emma, get your ass back in that Honda and move on out!"

I ignored his order. By the time I reached him, he was on his cell. "Okay," he said, turning his back on me. "Then I'm coming in."

Milo's long legs covered the short distance to the front porch before I could argue with him. I was too worried to care what he wanted or didn't want me to do. The flashers from the three emergency vehicles blinded me momentarily, but I caught up with the sheriff just as he went inside the house.

Jack Mullins was in the living room along with Del Amundson and another medic. The firefighters were either still outside or in another part of the small house. Under a striped afghan, a shivering figure on the sofa made strange little mewing noises. It took me a few seconds before I realized it was Norene Anderson.

I hung back near the open door. My initial reaction was relief that Vida wasn't the one in apparent distress. I remembered that the Andersons lived in this part of town, but I'd never been inside their house. Del and the other medic were trying to talk to Norene. Jack's eyes slid in my direction, but he didn't say a word. Milo's back was still turned, seemingly unaware that I was on the premises.

"How bad is it?" he asked the medics.

"We won't know until we get her to the hospital," Del replied, lowering his voice. "Fractured cheekbone maybe, multiple bruises, cut lip. We don't need the firefighters. Tony and I can handle it. This room's not very big. We need some maneuvering space with the gurney."

Milo looked at Jack. "Tell the firemen they can go. Where's Julie?"

"In the kitchen," Jack said, starting for the door. "Should we put out an APB for Bert?"

"Hold off on that," the sheriff replied and turned around. "Oh, for chrissakes!" he shouted as he finally spotted me. "Didn't you hear me?"

"The whole neighborhood can hear you now," I said quietly as Jack hurried outside. I gestured at Norene. "Is this what it looks like?"

"Work it out." The sheriff turned on his heel and left the room.

I followed him. The kitchen was separated from the living room by an Inglenook. Julie Canby was closing the refrigerator. "Coffee coming up," she said, seemingly unruffled. "How's Norene?"

Milo shrugged. "Pretty banged up, but at least she's alive. They're taking her to the hospital."

"Good," Julie said. "That's the best place for her. Thank God she was able to call us. Spike couldn't understand a word she said. Just as well." She checked the coffeemaker. "I can cope better with a crisis than he can. Anyway, Spike has to hold down the fort at the tavern. Thank goodness we're so close to Bert and Norene's house."

I finally spoke up. "What was Norene able to tell you?"

"That she got beat up," Julie replied. Given the circumstances, I found her aplomb admirable. Being a nurse, she was accustomed to crises. "Or so I pieced together," she added. "Poor Norene."

I ignored the dark glare the sheriff was giving me. "By Bert?"

Julie shrugged. "I guess. He wasn't around when I got here. For all I know, it was a burglar. Norene's car is gone. I suppose Bert took it—or the burglar stole it." She looked again at the coffeemaker. "Who wants java?"

I said no; Milo said yes. While Julie poured coffee into two mugs, the sheriff was still glowering at me. "Have you got some kind of death wish? You could've been killed, you moron."

"So could you," I retorted. "I didn't see you pull a gun before you came into the house."

Milo sighed. "I suppose you'll put this in the damned paper."

"I will if it goes in the log," I said. "Where's Vida?"

"How the hell do I know?" the sheriff shot back. "I'm surprised she didn't get here before I did."

"She's still missing." I paused as Jack entered the kitchen.

"Coffee," he said after giving Milo and me a curious glance. "Good idea, Julie. I'll have some. Bit of sugar, no cream."

Just another day with law enforcement, I thought, and got to my feet. "Okay," I said to Milo, "I'm leaving. If you don't care what's happened to Vida, I do. Meanwhile, you'll be hearing from me again before eleven. Whatever went on here has to be in the *Advocate.*"

"Knock yourself out," Milo muttered before turning to Jack. "We'll stay on the job until we find Bert. I'm going to let the other deputies know what's going on and make sure we're all up to speed."

"Overtime," Jack said. "That's . . ."

Not wanting to get in the way of the medics, I decided to leave via the back door. It wasn't easy to see through the heavy rain, but the Andersons' backyard looked neglected. There was nothing but overgrown grass, untended berry vines, and weeds. As I started down the unpaved driveway, I heard a sudden loud rumble that made me jump. *Calm down,* I lectured myself, realizing the noise signaled the fire engine's departure. Still unsteady, I stumbled on a rock, but awkwardly regained my balance. The twisting movement caused sharp pains in my back. "Damn," I said under my breath. I'd forgotten to ask Julie for water so I could wash down my pill. Taking a few tentative steps, I headed back inside. Climbing the four wooden stairs leading to the door made me wince. I rapped twice; within a few seconds Julie let me in.

My return didn't seem to surprise her. "Forget something?" she asked. No doubt it was a frequent query for ICT patrons who left all sorts of belongings at the tavern—including their spouses.

I explained about needing some water. Milo was standing up, looking out the window on the west side of the house and talking on his cell phone. "No," he was saying, "let's not drag in the state patrol yet. Bert's got to be around here someplace."

Julie poured me a glass of water. I thanked her before taking both a methocarbamol and a Demerol. If the pain didn't ease quickly, I wasn't sure I could drive home.

"What happened?" she asked.

"I reinjured my back," I said after gulping down the first pill. "I pulled something a few days ago." I couldn't stop my eyes from veering in Milo's direction. He'd just rung off and had turned around.

"Want to ride with the medics?" he said in a dour tone. "They haven't left yet."

"I'm fine," I snapped.

"Hmmph." Studying me from head to foot, he scratched his head. "You don't look it. I've seen drowned rats in better shape."

He was right, of course. My hair was bedraggled, my makeup was long gone, and my jacket had gotten dirty somewhere along the way. But his remark riled me. A snicker from Jack Mullins annoyed me even more. "It hasn't been a good day." I said grimly.

"No shit." Milo turned away to stare out the window again.

Just as I was swallowing the second pill, Del Amundson called out from the living room. "All clear. We're out of here."

Julie was observing me with a slight frown. "You don't seem like yourself, Emma. Can you drive?"

It was another question she'd probably asked hundreds of times at the tavern. "I'll be okay," I assured her. "Maybe I should sit for a few minutes until the meds kick in. I'll go into the living room."

I avoided the sofa where Norene had been lying. Instead, I sat in a well-worn recliner that I assumed was Bert's usual place. I'd just gotten into what felt like the least uncomfortable position when the medics turned on the siren as they drove off. My irritation with Milo hadn't ebbed. It struck me that ever since I'd heard about his plans to reconcile with Tricia he'd been treating me like cat dirt. Maybe he'd never really cared for me. I was a convenience, an occasional substitute for the real thing, a bench player who got into the game when the star athlete went down with an injury.

Jack Mullins snapped me back into reality. "Hey," he said, standing next to the recliner, "I'm sorry for laughing about Boss Man's big, bad mouth. He's probably sorry, too. It's just that he . . ."

Boss Man lurched into the room. "Saddle up," he said to Jack. "I'll take my car. We've got a hostage situation at First and Spruce."

Jack looked dazed. "Hostage? Who? What?"

Milo had already reached the front door. "I'll alert the rest of the troops. Get going. It's at the trailer park, Space Fourteen. It belongs to Holly Gross and she's got Vida Runkel."

TWENTY-TWO

"**H**OLY CRAP!" JACK CRIED, GRABBING HIS JACKET OFF OF A hat rack by the door. "What the hell is that all about?"

He hadn't posed the question to me, and even if he had, I was too stunned to say anything. As Jack hurried off, Julie came into the living room. "What's happening?" she asked, her composure finally wavering.

"I wish I knew," I murmured. "I'm going to find out. Are you staying here or going back to the tavern?"

Julie made a face. "I'm not sure. Are you okay?"

"Not really," I said, struggling to get out of the recliner.

"Wait." Julie pulled a lever on the chair's side. "I'll get this thing more upright. Then I can help you stand."

"Thanks." I let her take both of my hands and carefully put me on my feet. "Ah," I said, trying to judge the level of pain. "Thanks again."

She shrugged. "No problem."

"I've got to call the office," I said. "Could you hand me my cell? It's in my purse, but I'm afraid to bend down to reach it."

It took Julie only a moment to find the phone. My fingers

were shaking along with the rest of me. After three abortive attempts, Kip answered. "What's going on?" he asked. "I keep hearing sirens."

"I'll give you details later. Put the paper on hold. This sounds insane, but Vida's being held hostage by Holly Gross at the trailer park, Bert Anderson's missing, and his wife is in the ER."

Kip didn't respond for so long that I thought we'd been cut off—or he'd passed out. When he finally spoke, his voice was almost unrecognizable. "I can't wrap my head around this. *Vida's a hostage?*"

"So it seems. I've got to go. Stand by."

Julie was staring at me as if she thought I'd lost my mind. "Emma! What did you say about Mrs. Runkel?"

I shook my head. "Don't ask," I said, dialing Mitch's number. His phone rang six times before switching over to voice mail. "Damnit," I said, moving toward the door while trying to ignore the pain that hadn't begun to ease yet. "I'm sorry, I have to go. Thanks for your help."

But Julie wasn't put off easily. "Wait!" she called after me as I limped down the front steps. "I'll go with you."

My first reaction was an emphatic *no*. But Julie was a nurse. Maybe it wasn't a bad idea. "Okay," I shouted back at her.

By the time I got settled behind the wheel, Julie had gathered up her jacket and purse, shut the front door, and slid into the passenger seat. "How's Holly involved in all this?" she asked.

"I don't know," I replied. "None of this makes sense." *It's a wonder I'm making sense,* I told myself. *I can't get rattled, I have to stay focused, I can't think about Vida being in danger.* Realizing I was driving too fast, I eased off on the gas pedal. *Keep talking, Emma. Change the subject.* "Tell me more about Bert and Norene. Did they fight a lot?"

"I don't think so," Julie answered after a pause. "Norene

complained about various health problems, but they were minor. I'd listen and give advice she probably didn't follow." She glanced at the ICT as we drove by. "Poor Spike. He's on his own tonight unless he can find subs for Norene and me." Julie sighed before continuing. "Norene isn't a happy person, but she puts on a cheerful face for the customers."

I winced as I made a sharp turn onto Icicle Creek Road. "Not happy? How come?"

"You know how some people enjoy their misery?"

"Oh, yes."

"Norene is like that. I almost feel sorry for Bert."

"Almost?" I gritted my teeth before making the turn onto Spruce.

"Bert's a peculiar guy," Julie said. "Their house is a dump. Yet he often tosses money around as if he were printing it in the backyard. He claims it's from his rich aunt in Canada."

"Maybe it is," I said as we passed by the high school's football and baseball fields. "Did you know Al De Muth was married?"

"You're kidding." Julie sounded incredulous. "Al always seemed so lonely. Or at least *alone*. Where is Mrs. De Muth?"

"Heading back to Colorado to bury the body," I replied. "Did you ever run into a waitress named Liz who . . ."

I lost my train of thought as we crossed Fourth Street. My log cabin was a block and a half away on Fir. Ten minutes ago, I would've gladly gone home to collapse. But the shocking news about Vida had triggered an adrenaline rush. Surely she wasn't really being held hostage. It was too outrageous, too inexplicable, too preposterous. There was no reason for her to get involved with Holly Gross. Despite my incredulity, I felt my heart pounding faster as we approached the trailer park.

Two patrol cars barred the way to the thirty-odd mobile

homes behind the tall wood fence. The third patrol car and
Milo's Grand Cherokee were pulled up in the driveway. Jack
Mullins and Doe Jamison were putting up yellow crime scene
tape. I pulled onto the verge, avoiding the ditch next to the
property. The medic van arrived, stopping under the streetlight
on the other side of Spruce. Rain was pelting the emergency vehicle's roof like so many transparent pebbles.

"Sleet," Julie said. "I can hear it on the roof of your car.
What now?" she asked, leaning forward to peer through the
curtain of rain.

I turned off the engine. "I'm calling my reporter," I said, dialing his number. "If he doesn't answer this time I'll leave a
message." After six rings followed by voice mail, I told Mitch
that his lead story about De Muth's death might have slipped
into second place. "This is no joke," I emphasized. "And bring
a camera." I disconnected before turning to Julie. "Stay put.
I'm going to see what's happening."

"I'll come, too," she said, unbuckling her seat belt.

"No. Please don't." I saw Del Amundson and the younger
man he'd referred to as Tony get out of the van. "Maybe you'll
be needed by those two. Just wait."

If Julie resented my officious attitude, it didn't show. It fleetingly crossed my mind that she was enjoying herself. I, however, wasn't. Jack and Doe had been joined by the medics. My
walk was a bit unsteady, but the Demerol was finally working
to ease the pain.

"Hey!" Jack called to me, "shouldn't you be in the ER?"

"It's probably filling up," I responded, my beat-up shoes
getting sucked into the mud by the ditch. "What's going on?"

"We're not sure," Doe replied. "Somebody in the trailer
next to Holly's reported a commotion. Dwight went to check it
out and saw Bert's car parked outside. When he knocked, there

was no response except for Vida, shrieking her head off. Dwight phoned Holly, who told him to buzz off. She insisted everything was just fine. Dwight didn't believe her. He could hear Vida in the background yelling 'hostage.' "

"Incredible." At least Vida was able to yell. "Is Bert in there, too?"

"We don't know," Jack answered. "Dodge is trying to find out."

Del Amundson was huddled inside his red-and-white raingear. "All we need is a big wreck out on Highway 2. What a crappy night."

"How's Norene?" I asked.

"She'll live," Del said. "Dr. Sung's seeing to her."

"Did she say Bert beat her up?"

Del shrugged. "She's incoherent, kept jabbering about barbecues or some damned thing." He shook his head. "Poor Tony," he said, gesturing at the other medic who was still standing near the van. "It's his first week on the job. He's from Sultan, got home a couple of months ago from medevac duty in Iraq. Maybe he figures it was quieter over there. Hey, Tony— meet the folks before the bullets start flying."

There was no time for introductions. Although I couldn't see Milo, I could hear him through a bullhorn. "You've got three minutes to come out of there, Holly. Otherwise we're coming in. You decide."

I edged away from the others, trying to get closer to the trailer park entrance. Jack grabbed my arm. "Don't even think about it, Emma."

"Where are they?" I asked, wiping rain out of my eyes. "I haven't been here in ages."

"Space Fourteen's on the right, third down from the middle," Jack replied. "You can only see the front end from here."

"What about Vida? And Holly's kids?"

"They're all crammed in there like sardines as far as we can tell. Bert, too." He apparently caught my agitated expression. "I don't know what to tell you. It's a mess. Oh, hell!" He looked beyond me to the street. I turned to see what had caught his attention. The headlights of at least two other vehicles shone through the rain. "Is that Fleetwood with his remote gear?"

"Yes," I said, though I couldn't resent Mr. Radio rushing to the scene. "The fire engine, too, but no sirens."

"And the state patrol," Doe announced. "It's the snoopy citizens we don't need. I'll tell the troopers to get them out of here."

Looking around, I realized that a handful of people were braving the rain to satisfy their curiosity. "Jeez," Jack muttered, "why don't those morons stay home and watch cop shows on TV? They'll get more action and stay dry. This is . . ." His shoulders slumped. "I don't know what the hell it is. A farce? Or . . . what?"

"You tell me," Spencer Fleetwood said, somehow managing to look suave and sound mellow even with rain dancing off his expensive parka. "Hello, Emma. Mind if I talk to Jack?"

"Go ahead. I'm just here for the excitement." I turned away. To my surprise, a state trooper was escorting someone who seemed to be in handcuffs. As the pair approached, I didn't recognize the officer, but to my horror I realized that the other person was Vida's grandson, Roger.

I hurried to reach them. "What's going on?" I demanded.

The tall, craggy-faced trooper, whose name tag IDed him as Morrison, frowned at me. "Sorry, ma'am. You have to move along."

I didn't budge. "I know this young man," I said. "I'm Emma

Lord, from the *Advocate*." I paused to study Roger. He had his head down and seemed to be crying. "His grandmother works for me and she's—"

"We know," Morrison broke in. "Please step aside."

I obeyed. Jack was being interviewed by Fleetwood, Doe and the other state patrolman were trying to disperse the growing numbers of spectators, and Julie had gotten out of my car to talk to the medics. No one was watching me. I crept along a good ten feet behind Morrison and Roger. The big beefy pain-in-the-butt was definitely handcuffed. I should've felt pity for Roger, but I didn't. I was too worried about Vida.

"That's it!" Milo shouted through the bullhorn. "Send the kids out. Now!"

"Damn," I said under my breath. How could Holly allow her children to be part of such a volatile situation? I stopped as Morrison and Roger turned into what I assumed was Space Fourteen. I skulked on, keeping to the shadows. I could see the sheriff, Dwight Gould, Sam Heppner, Dustin Fong, and Bill Blatt. Only Milo turned to look at the newcomers.

"What's this?" He paused. "Roger. I think I get it."

The trailer door opened. Two small figures—one of them holding the toddler—scurried out. Bill and Dustin rushed to snatch up the trio. When Bill spotted his cousin, he stopped in his tracks. "You asshole!" he yelled at Roger. "I *knew* you were mixed up in this!"

Roger gave a muffled response but didn't lift his head. I leaned back against the nearest trailer, hoping to stay undetected. As Bill and Dustin hurried away with Holly's kids, I noticed that a few of the trailer residents were watching the drama from their doorways.

Milo was back on the bullhorn. "One of your customers is here." He glanced at Roger. "Let Mrs. Runkel out."

The door remained closed. The only sound I could hear was the rain, slapping away at the trailers and pummeling the ground. I shivered, not from cold so much as from nerves. Milo moved restlessly, but never seemed to take his eyes off the trailer door. I saw him tense, then raise the bullhorn again. "Stop fooling around! Come on. Do it!"

Nothing, just the rain and the dark and the tawdriness of it all. I wondered if Julie had taken charge of the children. I wondered what Vida was doing inside the trailer. I wondered when this nightmare would end and we could all go home and someday laugh about what had happened on this miserable October night.

A shot made me jump. A second shot sent me reeling against the trailer's cold, wet side. I think I prayed. I know I felt sick. But I had to get closer. Throwing aside caution, I slogged my way to Space Fourteen.

I stopped just short of the trailer, propping myself up next to an old rusting barbecue. Milo hadn't seen me. He was yanking at the trailer's door while the other deputies pulled out their weapons. Del Amundson and Tony were hurrying toward us.

"Get away, Emma," Del called to me. "Go!"

I refused, my gaze fixed on Milo. The door suddenly opened, almost knocking him over. I gaped in astonishment as Vida emerged. *She isn't wearing her hat.* It was the only thing I could think of before I started to laugh hysterically.

Nobody noticed me. That was good. I heard Vida say there was probably a dead body inside. As I got myself under control, I saw her look at Roger, shake her head, and walk away in the opposite direction.

Milo, Dwight, and the medics went inside. Morrison hauled Roger off, probably to the patrol car. Sam Heppner stared at me. "Where did you come from?" he asked in his typically sour tone.

"Hell and back," I said weakly. "Who's dead?"

"I don't know," he answered.

From inside the trailer I could hear hysterics not unlike my own. Milo stood in the doorway. "Bert Anderson's a goner. Holly shot him. Cuff her and get her out of here. It's a crime scene."

"No kidding," Sam muttered. "Beat it, Emma. You could've gotten killed." He looked beyond me. "Oh, shit, here comes Fleetwood. Why don't you people stop getting in the way?"

I didn't bother to answer him and he didn't bother to wait. For once, Spencer Fleetwood looked unsure of himself. "Where's Vida?" he asked. "She isn't the one who . . ." He couldn't finish the question. It suddenly occurred to me that he, too, was worried about her safety, if only because of her ratings for KSKY.

"She's fine," I said. "I think. The victim is Bert Anderson."

Spence looked puzzled. "Body shop Bert? How does he fit in this?"

Moving away from the barbecue, I was finally able to stand on my own two feet. "I don't know." I took a deep breath. *The barbecue,* I thought suddenly. Del had mentioned Norene jabbering about barbecues. It dawned on me that she wasn't incoherent, she was trying to say something important. "Um . . . ," I said, hoping I didn't look sly, "I'll get back to you on that, Spence."

"Where are you going?" he called after me.

I kept moving. "I've got a deadline, remember?"

TWENTY-THREE

VIDA WAS NOWHERE TO BE SEEN WHEN I GOT BACK TO THE street. "Bill Blatt took her to her car," Dustin explained. "She was parked just around the corner. I think she was going home."

I felt a hand on my arm. "I'm going in the medic van with the kids," Julie said. "They seem fine, but I don't know who can care for them. They can stay with Spike and me, at least for a while."

"You're very kind," I said, patting her hand. "Thanks."

"Thank *you*." Her smile was bittersweet. "My own kids by my first marriage are grown, so I have to wait for grandchildren. I haven't felt this needed in a long time. Making onion rings isn't very fulfilling."

As soon as I got back in the car, I called Kip. "Turn on the radio," I said. "Vida's safe, but we've got huge breaking news from the trailer park. Holly shot Bert Anderson and Roger's under arrest."

"Oh, God! I don't know whether to cheer or boo."

"I'll tell you all as soon as I see Vida. Hang in there."

Vida's Buick was in her driveway. As I pulled up, the living room lights went on. Suddenly I had qualms about facing her. But it was necessary. I girded myself for what could be an awkward confrontation.

"Don't say a word," she said as she opened the front door. "I know exactly what you're thinking."

I was sure she did. "Can I say I'm sorry for you?"

"No." Her gray curls were a mess and her face was drawn. "Come to the kitchen. I'll make tea and put Cupcake to bed. It's very late for him." She led the way, as purposeful as ever despite her ordeal.

I didn't speak until after the canary was covered for the night and the teakettle was on the stove. "Look," I said as she sat down opposite me at the kitchen table, "I don't want to talk about Roger as much as I want to tell you who actually killed Alvin De Muth."

"You don't have to tell me," Vida said. "I know."

I couldn't help but smile. "Yes, I imagine you do. Did you know it before you ended up in Holly's trailer?"

She shook her head. "Not for certain. But I began to realize the truth when I saw Roger at Bert's body shop. Drugs!" She threw her hands up in the air. "How foolish of people. We turn a blind eye on what we don't want to know. Poor Amy and Ted—they suspected, of course, but they simply wouldn't deal with the problem. In denial, as I was. They're with Roger now at the sheriff's office. I couldn't go with them. This is something the three of them must sort out together."

I was surprised. "You're right. Still, I thought you might . . ."

"No." She removed her glasses and started rubbing her eyes. "Ooooh! I did the right thing—and don't remind me I've been blind."

In less tragic circumstances, I'd have mentioned she *would* be blind if she kept grinding her eyes. But this was no time for flippancy. "Does Milo know Bert was dealing?"

"If he doesn't, Roger will tell him." She dabbed at her eyes with a paper napkin before putting her glasses back on. "Bert got his start with gypsy truckers. So many of them are on some kind of drugs to stay awake at the wheel. Cooperating should gain Roger some mercy."

"People do such self-destructive things," I said. "Mike O'Toole might be alive today if he hadn't been on drugs."

Vida gave me a sharp glance as the teakettle sang. "I suspected as much. How did you know?"

"Betsy." I grimaced. "I wasn't supposed to let on. The rest of the family won't find out until the funeral's over."

"They know," Vida said, standing up and going to the stove. "They just won't say it out loud. Bert's drugs, I assume."

"I'm sure of it. I'm also sure that Norene guessed what her husband was up to, and that's why they had such a row earlier this evening. She finally pieced it together—the sudden flurries of money, the young people who came to the shop, and of course the night Al De Muth died. Del mentioned that Norene kept jabbering about 'barbecues.' That made no sense to him, but it finally dawned on me what she meant."

"Oh, indeed." Vida nodded emphatically before taking two tea bags out of a canister. "The bar, the bees, and the pool cue. Men often have no imagination."

"Del had other priorities," I said, cutting the medic some slack. "I assume Norene left the pool cue by the back door after whacking the bees' nest. I'll bet it was gone when she looked again. A few minutes earlier, De Muth went outside to relieve himself. Bert arrived about then and before the two men went inside, there must've been a confrontation. From what

I've heard about De Muth, he not only had great integrity but took a paternal interest in the young men he'd trained as mechanics. If he'd discovered that Bert was dealing drugs, he probably intended to turn him in. Maybe he'd already told Bert what he planned to do."

Vida grimaced. "That wasn't very prudent of De Muth."

"No, but he was a moody guy with a hair-trigger temper. They started to fight. I figure Bert grabbed the cue and struck the fatal blow. Maybe Al went down. Or maybe Bert thought he'd intimidated Al."

"That," Vida declared, "would've been foolish on Bert's part. Then again, Bert was a foolish sort of person."

I agreed. "But what is more convincing when it comes to Bert being the one who delivered the fatal blow is what happened when Al and Clive went after each other. The severity of head or brain damage doesn't always show up immediately. Al had mentioned having a headache, but the others took it as a joke. No one saw Clive actually hit Al with a cue. Clive didn't think he made contact, and the onlookers didn't react at once when Al went down. Consciously or subconsciously, they may have realized that Clive's pool cue didn't make contact. Only Julie, who hadn't witnessed the fight but is a trained nurse, realized that Al was dead."

Vida was still at the stove, waiting for the tea to steep. "It makes sense. Bert must've tossed the cue into the river before he came back to the tavern. I wonder if Norene went back outside at some point to retrieve the pool cue and couldn't find it. She may have suspected what had happened between her husband and De Muth. Holly might have had some inkling about what had really happened, too. It seems she was the—what do you call it? The 'mule'? She'd go up to Canada and bring back the drugs." Vida sighed. "It's all so very sordid."

I nodded. "Bert's rich Canadian aunt, or so Julie said he'd tell people when he had a windfall. I assume Bert fathered one of Holly's kids and Mickey Borg was another of the dads. I don't know who or if there was another man involved. Maybe one of them did double duty."

Vida had her back turned as she poured our tea into English bone china cups. "I know who the third father was."

"You do?"

"Yes." She moved slowly to the table, balancing a cup and saucer in each hand. "It was Roger."

"Oh, no!" I was aghast. "Is that how you ended up in the trailer?"

"It was." She showed no expression as she sat down and passed me the sugar bowl. "Billy told me about Roger's driving violation. Naturally, I was upset. I called Roger on his cell. He asked . . . *begged* me to meet him at Bert's to give him some money. For the ticket, I assumed, though I found it odd that he wanted me to come to the body shop. I couldn't refuse, but when I arrived, he said he needed four hundred dollars. That sounded too high for a DUI. He also seemed very unlike himself—nervous, jumpy, incoherent. I looked at his eyes. He wasn't drunk—he was on drugs." She heaved a big sigh and sat back in her chair. "I realized Roger wanted the money for more drugs. I told him no. It was hard to say that. But I did. I should have done it long ago." Vida began to weep.

I reached out to touch her arm. "Oh, please don't beat yourself up over this. It's called 'tough love' and it's supposed to . . ." I withdrew my hand. "Oh, Vida, I don't know what it does. But you did the right thing."

She sniffed a couple of times. "Yes, yes, so I did," she murmured, sitting up straight. "Roger became angry, got in his car, and drove off. I felt terrible so I followed him to the trailer

park." She sniffed again but was regaining control. "I've had
suspicions for some time. Amy and Ted have had money woes,
but never explained why. Last summer I ran into Amy at kId's-
cOrNEr. She was buying baby clothes. I asked who they were
for, and she seemed evasive, but finally said a niece of Ted's had
recently given birth. Both of Ted's nieces are single, though that
doesn't mean much nowadays. But I do know when my daughter is lying. Something was amiss."

"Holly was the miss," I remarked.

Vida took a sip of tea. "The *mistake* is more apt. Twice in
the past few months I've seen his car going into the trailer park.
To my knowledge, no one from his peer group lives there. I put
two and two together—and they added up to Holly. I parked a
half block away and walked to her trailer. It was easy to find
because there were some battered toys and a deflated plastic
kiddy pool near the door. Roger was already there, trying to
get money or drugs from Holly. I started to rebuke them, and
they both became angry. I was about to leave, but Bert showed
up. He saw me with Roger and assumed I knew about the drug
connection with Holly. Bert became very menacing. Then
Roger took my billfold and ran off. I figured he intended to use
my ATM card to get money. I suspect that after Roger went to
a cash machine, he realized he didn't know my PIN number, so
he lost his nerve and fled."

"That," I said, "must be when the state patrol picked him
up." I considered the article we'd have to run in the *Advocate*
and how mortified Vida would be. "I don't know what to say."

Vida looked resigned. "Nor do I."

"Why did Holly shoot Bert?"

"After Holly had sense enough to let her children leave the
trailer, she and Bert argued. I think," she went on with an ap-
palled expression, "Bert wanted to use me as a hostage to get
away, but he wasn't willing to take Holly with him. Really, it

was all such a mess, and with the police outside, they were both panicking. Bert got out his gun, and then there was a tussle and Holly ended up with it and . . ." Vida looked up at the ceiling. "She shot him. Twice. And then she sort of collapsed."

I was in awe of Vida's courage and stamina. "Unbelievable."

"No. Very believable. Unfortunately." Vida stood up. "More tea?"

"No thanks." I glanced at the coffeepot-shaped clock. It was after eight. Somehow it seemed as if it should be much later. "I have to help Kip with the paper." I also stood up, trying to ignore the lingering pain in my back. "In fact, I'd better go." On impulse, I put my arms around Vida. "I'd never, ever want to upset you. How am I going to handle this?"

Vida felt rigid in my embrace, so I let go of her. "Well now," she said, "you can't do it by yourself."

"Mitch may be able to help."

She shook her head. "I don't think so."

"Why not?"

"You really don't know, do you?"

"Know what?" I was starting to feel as if I were in a heavy fog.

"That Mitch and Brenda went to see their son tonight."

"Their son? Where is he?"

"At the Monroe Correctional Facility. He's serving a sentence for selling drugs. Leo found out and told me after he went to dinner with his old friend from out of town who was visiting his own son. It's a plague, I fear. But that's one reason the Laskeys moved here."

I held my head. "Oh, for . . . I knew there must be something."

"Yes." Vida was clear-eyed now. "I'll help put the paper to bed. I should ride with you since I don't have my wallet back yet. Or my hat . . . it must be in the trailer. Oh, well. I won't

take time to put on another. It'll only get soaked in this heavy
rain." She checked the stove to make sure it was turned off and
put on her coat. "Let's go."

OF COURSE KSKY BROKE THE STORY BEFORE WE DID, BUT IN
deference to Vida, Spence treated Roger's role with kid gloves.
Her show would air in its usual time slot Wednesday evening.
She postponed Jim Medved's appearance and expanded the
program to a half-hour. Vida wanted to discuss drug addiction
with Doc Dewey, Dr. Sung, Milo, and—to my surprise—Roger.
Her *Cupboard* would garner the all-time biggest audience in
SkyCo's radio history. Leo told me that new advertisers were
beating down Fleetwood's door to help sponsor the show.

Meanwhile, Kip had not only gone to press but helped me
do a breaking news story for the online edition. I didn't get
home that night until almost two AM. I was still so keyed up
that I hardly slept. When I got to the office just after eight,
Amanda gave me a big smile.

"You've had a big adventure," she said. "I thought you
might take the day off."

"Can't," I said, puzzled at her sudden change in attitude.
"You seem very chipper."

She laughed. "Maybe life looks a bit brighter to me today."

I looked back out into the street. "It is. The rain's stopped."

"Not that." She was still smiling. "Holly's going to jail, isn't
she?"

"Yes, I suppose she is." I leaned on the counter. "I didn't realize how much you disliked her."

"It isn't that," Amanda said. "It's her kids. They're going
to need a home. After we heard on the radio what happened
last night, Walt and I finally had a heart-to-heart talk." She

leaned her head back and briefly closed her eyes. "It was way overdue. But," she went on, looking at me again, "we've had problems with starting a family. It seems that neither of us can have children." She bit her lip. "I shouldn't be talking about this. Sorry."

"Go ahead," I said. "I've heard every other horror story in the past twenty-four hours."

"Well." She rested her elbows on the desk and held her face in her hands. "We kept blaming each other instead of being rational. I used to be sort of laid-back. Walt has always been fairly even-tempered. But this problem gnawed away at both of us. Every day it was a war zone when we were together. I was so sure it wasn't my fault as much as it was Walt's that I got to the point where I was willing to let some other guy try to get me pregnant before my biological clock ran down."

"A guy like Jack Blackwell?"

She gaped at me. "How did you guess? Oh!" She clapped both hands to her head. "Patti! She must've told you something."

I nodded. "She did—sort of."

"Talk about desperation." Amanda shook her head. "Anyway, Walt and I've agreed to take in those poor kids that Holly will have to give up when she goes to jail. We can be foster parents or down the road even adopt them. I've been checking out agencies online, but it's hard to tell which ones would be right for us."

A light dawned in my brain. "Such as Journeys of the Heart?"

Amanda looked surprised. "How did you know that?" Before I could answer, she clapped a hand to her cheek. "Oh! You saw me looking at that adoption agency on the computer here. Did you already guess what I was thinking?"

"No," I admitted. "I thought it was an Internet dating service."

"Oh, no!" Amanda laughed. The sound evoked the bubbly woman I recalled from previous encounters. "I wasn't *that* desperate. I talked to Marisa Foxx the other day about our options. We have an appointment with her this afternoon. Is it okay if I leave for about an hour at three?"

I grinned. "You go, girl. And good luck."

I was both dazed and relieved as I went into the newsroom. The rest of the staff was already engaged in deep conversation about the previous evening's activities. I managed to slip away into my cubbyhole and collapse in my chair. It was going to take me some time to sift through the recent deluge of events. Still, I felt some sense of satisfaction. The people most important to me had all survived. Scarred, maybe, but in one piece. Life would go on as it always does, not smoothly, not without shocks and surprises, and not always with happy endings. I knew that better than anyone. When it came to fairy tales, my own story had ended in gunfire.

It was almost noon by the time I went to see the sheriff. He was in and Clive Berentsen was out. "Craziest case I ever had," Milo said after I sat down in his office. "Jica or whatever her name is came to pick Clive up. She's taking him to New Mexico or Arizona or both for a sun break."

"Say," I said, "did you know about Bert's drug dealing?"

"I had to wonder. Truckers do drugs, Bert sometimes dealt with trucks." Milo offered me a mint, which I accepted. "But so did De Muth and Berentsen."

"Oh." I rolled the mint around in my mouth. "I recall somebody saying you'd gone off yesterday to do something about a donkey. I just realized it might have been a mule, as in Holly's part of the operation."

The sheriff looked puzzled. "No. I don't remember what I said, unless it was about Mulehide and going to buy that damned car for Tanya. This wedding thing is going to keep me broke."

"You'd better stop calling your ex Mulehide now that you're getting back together," I said.

"What?"

"The reconciliation." I saw Milo's obvious lack of comprehension. "Aren't you two giving yourselves a second chance?"

"Hell, no. Are you nuts?"

To my astonishment, a wave of relief washed over me. I almost swallowed the mint. "You're not?"

Milo was scowling at me. "Who told you that?"

I blanked out. "I'm not sure. Vida, maybe, but she must've heard it from somebody else."

"Oh, for chrissakes! I mentioned to Jack or Lori something about how Tanya wants Mulehide and me to act like we're on good terms for the wedding, but even that's a pain in the ass. Or at least in the checkbook. 'Think about appearances,' is how she put it. 'We're still family.' Bullshit. It's not my fault she and that creep she ran off with are splitting up. Hell, she even stayed over with Linda Grant from the high school so she could visit my aunt and uncle at the retirement home. She probably wanted to make sure they'd pony up with a big wedding gift. Fat chance. Look up 'tightwad' in the dictionary and you'll see pictures of Aunt Thelma and Uncle Elmer." He shook his head in apparent disbelief before peering more closely at me. "What's with you? You look kind of strange. Are you still slugging down that Demerol?"

"No. Yes. Uh . . . I'd better dash." Clumsily, I got out of the chair. "Good luck with Vida's show tonight."

"I canceled," Milo said as he stood up. "I decided to let Bill

Blatt take my place. Make it a family affair with Vida, Roger, and Bill."

"That's nice," I said.

Milo shrugged. "I don't like doing media stuff. Why don't I listen to the show at your place? I'll pick up a couple of steaks."

"That sounds . . . good," I said. "See you at six?"

Milo had moved next to me. "Did you say 'sex'?"

I smiled up at him. "Maybe I did."

He smiled back.

ABOUT THE AUTHOR

Mary Daheim is a Seattle native who started spinning stories before she could spell. Daheim has been a journalist, an editor, a public relations consultant, and a freelance writer, but fiction was always her medium of choice. In 1982, she launched a career that is now distinguished by more than fifty novels. In 2000, she won the Literary Achievement Award from the Pacific Northwest Writers Association. In October 2008, she was inducted into the University of Washington's Communications Hall of Fame. Daheim lives in Seattle with her husband, David, a retired professor of cinema, English, journalism, and literature. The Daheims have three daughters: Barbara, Katherine, and Magdalen.

ABOUT THE TYPE

This book was set in Sabon, a typeface designed by the well-known German typographer Jan Tschichold (1902–74). Sabon's design is based upon the original letter forms of Claude Garamond and was created specifically to be used for three sources: foundry type for hand composition, Linotype, and Monotype. Tschichold named his typeface for the famous Frankfurt typefounder Jacques Sabon, who died in 1580.

Chetco Community Public Library
405 Alder Street
Brookings, OR 97415

WITHDRAWN